Alan McCluskey

The Keeper's Daughter

The Storyteller's Quest - Book Two

Secret Paths Editions

First published in November 2011
Secret Paths Editions, Mureta 2, 2072 Saint-Blaise, Switzerland.

ISBN 978-2-9700756-3-9

2

Already published

The Reaches - The Storyteller's Quest Book One
ISBN: 978-2-9700756-0-8 (ebook)
ISBN: 978-2-9700756-1-5 (print)

Coming soon

The Starless Square - The Storyteller's Quest Book Three
The World o'Tales- The Storyteller's Quest Book Four

Table of Contents

Prologue 7

Chapter 1 - Open Questions 9

Chapter 2 - The Healing Song 26

Chapter 3 - Lucie 45

Chapter 4 - Class begins 70

Chapter 5 - The Watchers' Dance 92

Chapter 6 - The Necklace 113

Chapter 7 - The Company of Watchers 136

Chapter 8 - Sparing Partners 157

Chapter 9 - The Dawn of Chaos 180

Chapter 10 - Women's business 203

Chapter 11 - Preparations 225

Chapter 12 - The rebellion 251

Chapter 13 - Calm before the storm 275

Chapter 14 - The Trial 301

Chapter 15 - The Exodus 325

About the author 347

More information 349

Prologue

A narrow metal construction descended the immense glass face of the west wing of the hothouse, its surface sculptured with intricate folds and delicate engravings. The proud work of art of one of the city's most well known artists. It supported a spiral stairway that wound in ordered metallic curves between the twisted branches and the heavy hanging leaves to the dense jungle below. Jake moved out cautiously onto the stair head, its glass surface slick with condensation. Hot up-draughts rose to meet him bringing with them the sweet, sickly smell of exotic flowers. Gripping the handrail tight, he took a hesitant step downwards, his feet uncertain on the slippery surface. Brilliant coloured birds squawked from amongst the fleshy leaves below, the most adventurous of them flitting up to peek at him then diving back into the cover of the leaves. As he took a further faltering step, his bare feet slipped on the dripping glass and he lurched forward. Loosing his balance, he tumbled over the low railing and fell headlong towards the steaming jungle below. After a moment's terror, he instinctively stretched his wings breaking his fall, and then glided in tight circles around the spiral stairway admiring the rainbow-coloured reflections from the tiny water droplets that hung from the leaves and branches. He penetrated the steamy jungle and came to rest on a narrow shingle path next to a small pond on which floated a family of water lilies. He folded his wings and shifted nervously from one foot to another to get his balance. All his senses were on alert. Instinct told him there was danger nearby. Swivelling his head left and right he could see nothing of concern. Then he glanced up in front of him only to find himself looking into the piercing eyes of a giant eagle towering over him.

Chapter 1 - Open Questions

Carnage

"Mass suicide in Castle: thirty-four bodies unearthed", the headlines were splashed in bold, dramatic characters across the whole width of the page above a picture of the Sollarini Castle perched sinister and forlorn on a hilltop against the backdrop of the Black Forest with himself prominent in the foreground. The Daily Pick, of course, which other newspaper would have the flair to sniff out such a sordid affair so quickly, despite all the precautions the Police had taken.

Dieter tossed the newspaper on the table where it landed between an unfinished letter and a just-as-unfinished glass of schnapps. The forensic experts, who had been hard at work all morning, had finished now. So less caution was required. Whatever had happened there, it had been sudden and totally unexpected.

He hadn't been able to prevent the press getting hold of the story. Too many people in the area had relatives or acquaintances working in the Castle. The news had spread like a shockwave. Shock was the right word. People were devastated. The area thrived thanks to the castle and its rich inhabitants. Count Sollarini had a reputation throughout Europe for his eccentric behaviour, his lavish banquets and his deep pockets.

Dieter's superiors wouldn't like the press getting involved; that was for sure. They'd be down his neck as soon as they caught sight of the tabloid. This was his first major case. Nobody else had wanted it.

Too weird! He couldn't blame them really, who'd want to take on thirty-four deaths in one go? A lot of people at headquarters would be delighted to see him make a mess of it. It wasn't that he was ambitious, he was just good at his job and worked hard.

The phone rang in his pocket. "What did I tell you?" he said to himself pulling it out and opening it. "Inspector Dieter Dram," he announced, turning to look round the large sitting room in which he was standing. "Yes Sir. I've seen it." He gave a half-hearted poke with his foot at a chewed bone abandoned by a large dog now sprawled dead on the rug near the table. "No. I did not speak to the press." He stepped around the body of the Count, covered with a white sheet, lying next to the dog and strode to the mantle piece. "Yes Sir. The whole area is cordoned off."

Thank heavens the place was so cold. The bodies didn't smell too much. "OK. When will you arrive?" He studied a business card abandoned on the mantle piece: Dr. Jakob Leuchtli, Energos. "OK. I'll meet you at the station." And he hung up, slipping the card and the phone into his jacket pocket. A cough behind him brought his attention back to the present. Turning round, he saw a small, thin man with greying hair and a mild, red face, one of the local constables. The man hesitated in the doorway.

"We've found another body," the man said almost apologetically. "You wanna see it?"

"I think I've seen enough for now," Dieter replied.

"But this one's different."

The man seemed determined he go and look. OK. He'd go and see what made the thirty-fifth one special.

"How come we didn't find it earlier?"

"The door was locked. We only just located the key."

"Where was it?"

"In the Count's bedroom, by his bed."

The long corridor on the third floor housed the most spacious and luxurious bedrooms. It was lined with family portraits, aging men and women fixed with their stern, reproachful looks and their best clothes. The disapproving look in their eyes made Dieter feel uncomfortable as he hurried after the policeman. The man stopped in front of the last door along the corridor, unlocked it and indicated that Dieter should go in. Dieter took a deep breath, expecting the worst.

Compared with other rooms on that floor, this bedroom was quite modest. Must have been reserved for less important visitors, he noted. On the single bed lay the body of a young man, fully dressed. In his early twenties, he was slim and pale and had odd black stains on his hands. The most striking thing about him was his face that was contorted with extreme pain.

As Dieter moved closer, the flickering of a monitor on the floor by the bed caught his attention. Flat horizontal lines traversed the screen, seemingly unmoving. Wires led from the monitor and disappeared under the bed. Pulling gently on the wires, he recovered a small leather skullcap to which the wires were attached. Electrodes, he noticed. He guessed it was for measuring brainwaves as the cap could easily fit on the young man's head. Why did he constantly have the impression that someone was trying to confuse him if not annoy him with seemingly irrelevant but pointedly significant clues?

Returning to the bed, Dieter realised that the youth was clutching something in his hand. With the help of the policeman he was able to prize a small necklace from his grasp. It was made of a tiny stone on a leather thong. Examining it closely he discovered that the stone had an eye engraved on it. An inexplicable shiver ran down his spine. Taking a small plastic bag from the stock in his pocket, he slipped the necklace inside and sealed it before putting it into his pocket.

"You said the door was locked?"

"Yes, Sir."

Dieter went over to the door and tried the handle. The door couldn't be unlocked from the inside without a key. "So this young man was locked in," he said more to himself than the other.

"Maybe he had a key," the policeman ventured, looking around the room for signs of one.

Back at the bed, Dieter slipped his hand cautiously into the jacket pockets of the dead man. He found no key, but he did find a folded piece of paper, a passport and a library card. Carrying the paper closer to the window where the light was better, he unfolded it and read: Sorry Sally. I couldn't contact you all. The Count left me no time. Don't blame yourself for what is about to happen. It is the only way. Think of me. Tyrell.

Dieter re-read the message several times before folding the paper again and sliding it into one of his little plastic bags. Turning to the passport, its owner was called Tyrell Merz Sollarini and had just arrived from a stay in England. So the young man was a relative of the Count. The library card confirmed the name and indicated that Tyrell used it at Avan University where he was a member of the Department of Theosophy. This last piece of news surprised Dieter. He'd read about Theosophy, the subject had intrigued him, but he hadn't imagined there could be a university that offered a degree in the subject.

Hanging loose

Dieter sat alone in the Count's study in one of the thickly padded leather armchairs. The man certainly had taste. A set of elaborate crystal glasses lined the shelves of a glass-fronted cabinet alongside an excellent selection of spirits, Schnapps in particular. Several oil paintings by well-known German artists of the last century adorned the walls. They were a bit old-fashioned for Dieter's taste. The stuffed head of a deer hung over the fireplace, its glassy eyes gloating over the demise of its owner. No books though, no computer or television either.

Dieter needed to think this through and thread the threads together to complete the picture. Parts of it were hanging loose, disconnected from the rest, like the Sally girl or the Swiss Doctor. He refused to believe that such things were devoid of sense and was convinced they wouldn't resist him much longer.

There were thirty-five bodies all cut down in mid-action without the slightest sign of attack or violence, all except the young man, that is. The young man, with that look of extreme pain frozen on his face, struck Dieter as the crux of the affair. He had the strange impression that the pain came from elsewhere, beyond that room, beyond the castle, but he couldn't say why.

The Count had locked him in a room where there was equipment to monitor brain waves. But whoever had removed the equipment from the young man's head had left the monitor switched on. What unfinished business lay there? The same young man knew in advance that something terrible was going to happen and saw it as inevitable. So at least one person knew a catastrophe was likely.

What's more, the young man was to contact a girl called Sally, who would have understood what had happened to the extent that she might blame herself for it. And she was not alone. Why else would Tyrell have written: "...contact you all..." And then there was... what was his name. He fished the visiting card from his pocket. Dr. Jakob Leuchtli in Switzerland. The Count wasn't the type to leave things lying about. The Castle was impeccably tidy. Anything found on a table was necessarily part of a current activity. So Leuchtli must also have been "current" too.

On an impulse he took out his phone and dialled Leuchtli's number. To his surprise he got the Swiss police instead.

"I'm trying to reach Dr. Leuchtli," he explained.

When challenged to say who he was and what his relationship was with the Doctor, he silenced his annoyance and explained: "I'm Inspector Dram of the German special investigation squad. I'm investigating a serious crime in Germany. Do you think I could speak to your superior?"

The woman at the other end apologised with her strange accent and said she would put him through. Police inspector Jurg Meider was the man's name.

"Good afternoon, inspector Meider," he said once they were connected. He decided to divulge part of the case to Meider, calculating that it might provoke a similar frankness on the part of his Swiss counterpart.

The inspector seemed shocked and asked several questions.

"Yes. We are checking for poison. An autopsy is underway. But it seems unlikely."

Dieter flipped over Leuchtli's business card and read two names written in pencil: Rafter and Sally. How clumsy of him not to have noticed them before.

"So why do I get redirected to the Swiss police when I phone Dr. Leuchtli?" he asked.

Apparently the Doctor was suspected of murder. Several bodies had been found in the basement of Leuchtli's company Energos in the Jura Mountains. The hypothesis was that they were victims of an experiment. The staff weren't very forthcoming, Meider told him, as if they were afraid to talk. A warrant was out for Leuchtli's arrest, but he was nowhere to be found. The last place he'd been seen was at Avan University where he was working on a top-secret project with Professor Rafter, Head of the Theosophy Department.

Jackpot! Dieter thought, as a number of threads of the story suddenly fitted snugly together where no connections had existed before, bridging hitherto impossibilities with alarming ease. He decided not to share that advantage with his Swiss colleague so, asking Meider if he planned to visit Avan, Dieter took his leave and hung up.

The Minster

Rain was falling heavily as Sally and Professor Rafter approached the Minster that lay in a large square amongst the narrow winding streets of the Old Town. On all sides a black-clad host converged on the West Front, filed through the heavy wooden doors beneath the rose window and dispersed into the shadows of the nave beyond. Shuffling forward with the silent crowd, Sally and Rafter finally gained access to the Minster and found a couple of free seats close to the left aisle. The Minster was packed.

Sally had been dreading this moment. Tyrell had been a frequent visitor in her dreams these last days. For many years they had been sworn enemies. Tyrell had used every occasion to torment Sally, who was one of Rafter's best students before she also became his assistant. As they were in the throes of countering Leuchtli's diabolical plans for a sinister technology he called The Machine, they had discovered that Tyrell had sided with the Doctor and was working against them. However, thanks to the Professor, Sally and Tyrell had reconciled their differences in a most startling fashion. In the end, Tyrell had sacrificed himself to save her. The thought of his last words to her, as he relieved her of the deadly onslaught of energy that would surely have killed her had she born it a moment longer, were like a deep wound that would not heal.

Rafter too was subdued, his head bowed, as he towed over most of those who surrounded them. The loss of his assistant had hit him hard. He had manoeuvred Tyrell into changing allegiances causing the assistant to take the risk that had resulted in the catastrophe that brought them all together in the Minster. Sally knew the Professor could not and would not forgive himself. She regretted it. She knew it was not his fault but he was inconsolable and she sorely missed Rafter's usual sparkling humour. It would have been so comforting in the circumstances.

Both of them were dressed in black. Rafter, elegant as always, had donned his best suit over a white shirt with a black tie and shiny black shoes. His hair, still wet from the rain, was greying at the edges. His nose was strong, his chin decisive and his eyes were a penetrating blue. In normal times, a constant hint of a smile softened what might otherwise have been a stern face. Now, in the dimmed lights of the Minster he looked stricken. Sally wore a knee length black velvet dress she'd borrowed from her close friend Keira's wardrobe. She had chosen it because it went so well with the green of her eyes and the auburn of her hair. Now she wished she'd chosen something warmer. She was wet from the rain and it was bitterly cold in the Minster. Keira was another cause for concern. Neither she nor their new friend Brent had returned from the Reaches, a parallel world where Sally had left them.

Sitting near the back she was able to watch the mourners as they continued to file in. People of all ages made their slow way down the central aisle, many stricken with grief, a lot in tears. A tall young man in an elegant dark grey suit caught her eye. He was clearly not one of the mourners. There was something about him that didn't fit. Everybody was crushed with grief, whereas he was very much alive as his sharp grey eyes roved the congregation. He had a thin moustache and carefully groomed black hair. She reckoned he was in his early thirties. He stopped to question one of the vergers at the entrance who peered around the nave and then nodded in her direction. The man turned to look directly at her, a piercing gaze that scrutinised her for a long moment making her feel extremely uncomfortable before he thanked the verger and moved away down the aisle.

Leaning over to the woman next to her she asked in her best German who the man was. The woman seemed surprised she didn't know.

"That's the inspector who's investigating up at the Castle to find out who murdered all those people," the woman said, a sob in her voice.

Sally thanked her, trying to keep any trace of panic from her words. As many people probably knew some English she couldn't risk talking openly to Rafter about her fears so she pulled a notebook out of her pocket. It had been a present from Brent who always carried such a notebook with him for dreams and stories. While she had crossed the Reaches, Brent had made a long voyage through the Dream Realm till he finally found his way to join her in the Reaches and helped her repair the damage done by Leuchtli and the Count. Withdrawing the pen from the spiral spine of the book, she jotted down: POLICE INSPECTOR GOT HIS EYE ON ME, and handed it to Rafter. He shot her a worried look and then wrote: I'LL HANDLE HIM.

They had to interrupt their written conversation because the congregation had all risen and the organ had begun a funeral march. Sally turned to watch what was happening as the main doors of the Minster were thrown open to let the coffin bearers enter. Hardly had the first coffin crossed the threshold, when a violent gust of wind drove a wall of rain into the Minster in the wake of the bearers drenching all that stood around the porch. One by one the soaked coffins bedecked with flowers glistening from the rain were borne down the central aisle in an interminable procession that underscored the horror of so much death. Here and there amongst the coffins walked men and women, drenched by the downpour, carrying the different banners of the Sollarini Clan hanging limp and lifeless.

No consolation was to be had from telling herself that if they hadn't died it would be her and many others that would be lying dead now. It was then that Sally noticed that the first rows of benches before the choir stalls had been removed to make way for the thirty-five coffins. When all the coffins had finally come to rest, the men, women and boys of the choir filed down the aisle and took their places in their raised seats on either side of the unending rows of coffins. The organ ceased its playing and for a moment only sniffs and sobs filled the air. Then the choir burst into song. It was a hymn she knew well and although she didn't know the German words, she sang along as best she could, tears streaming down her cheeks.

Out manoeuvred

Once the ceremony was over, the congregation began to shuffle its slow way out into the downpour. As Rafter turned to step out into the aisle, a thickset man in a dark grey suit stopped him and presented his police ID card.

"Please accompany me, Professor Rafter. I am from the police investigating this tragedy and I have some questions I'd like to ask you."

Rafter politely agreed and turned to indicate that Sally should follow him.

"I need to speak to you alone, Professor. My colleague will look after the young lady till you get back."

Rafter obviously didn't agree but he couldn't make a scene there during the funeral. The moment had been cleverly chosen. So he accompanied the policeman who led him to a small side door. Bewildered, Sally looked round to see who it was who would 'deal' with her. The tall man with the black moustache was standing right next to her.

"Miss Sally," he said in impeccable English, "I have to apologise for not knowing your family name. I am Police Inspector Dieter

Dram in charge of investigations into these tragic deaths. Would you mind if we talked for a while?"

The man unsettled her. She was sure he had orchestrated the removal of Rafter to get her alone.

"Do I have any choice?" she asked.

He smiled. It did wonders for his face, making him almost attractive. "Well, maybe not."

"OK. Let's go then", she replied, taking the initiative.

He slipped his arm in hers in an easy-going gesture making it clear who was in control and accompanied her out of the Minster and into his waiting chauffer-driven Mercedes.

Doing Battle

A tearoom! It didn't make sense. She'd expected to be interrogated at the police station, but he'd taken her to a tearoom. The place was unbearably quaint. Pink dominated all: pink china dolls sat on shelves along the walls, pink lace covered the tables and pink curtains hung at the windows. There were even imitation pinks in tiny vases on the tables. It was the sort of place you'd expect old ladies to meet and gossip in. It was certainly not the haunt for a young dynamic police inspector. Maybe he saw it as a personal joke at her expense.

He'd chosen a small alcove where they could talk without being disturbed by the other customers. She suspected he'd had the place reserved in advance. What other surprises had he planned for her? Caution, she thought, he's a dangerous man.

"What would you like to drink?" he asked amiably once she was seated.

"A tea, please, with milk."

"We also have some very good cakes if you'd like to go and look at the selection over there."

Seizing the occasion to get away from him, if only for a moment, she went to admire the wide selection of cakes. Not that she was in the slightest bit hungry, on the contrary. He made her anxious.

What should I do? she asked in her head, addressing Vee her faithful companion. She'd become acquainted with Vee on her journey through the Reaches. It was a long story. Intensely disliking him at first, she'd come to appreciate and finally love him. For a long time she'd seen him as a separate person, although nobody else could see him. Then in the dramatic moments that had led to the death of

Tyrell and the destruction of his uncle's castle in the Reaches as well as the whole valley in which Sally was staying, Vee had become a part of her, a male voice in her head. Sally now realised that Vee must have always been a part of her, but in the Reaches, which was not like her world, Vee had manifested himself as a separate person who could cook food and fetch water and save her life and even make love to her.

Careful, Vee said, he's talking to you.

" ... so what have you chosen?"

"It's very kind of you," she replied, deciding it was better to stay polite and distant, "but I don't feel so hungry after all."

Once the drinks had been served, Sally took the lead. "You said you wanted to talk to me. I'm sure it wasn't about cakes that you intended to talk."

He smiled again. This was like a sophisticated game in which she suspected the stakes were high. She had made the first move but that might turn out to be to his advantage.

"Were you and Tyrell lovers?" he asked in a bold opening move.

Sally almost choked on her mouthful of tea but concealed the fact by wiping her mouth delicately with her fingers.

"Are you jealous already, inspector?" It was a silly if not dangerous gambit that she might well pay dearly for.

"Don't play with me, Miss. This is a serious business."

He'd changed his angle of attack, trying officialdom and authority. She chose not to respond, at least it gave her time to think but it gave him a net advantage. Changing her mind, she admitted: "No. We were never lovers."

"Do you know why all these people died?" he asked changing once again to a seemingly frontal attack.

Tricky one, she thought.

Careful, Vee said. He knows something he hasn't revealed yet. Try part of the truth, he suggested.

"I imagine they were carried away by a massive catastrophe, maybe on another plain."

It was his turn to remain silent but this time it was clearly to his advantage as he waited for her to go on. Sally let the silence last, hoping to push him to question her further, but he made no move.

"Do you believe in Black Magic?" she asked him.

She must have hit a sensitive spot because the skin below his eye twitched involuntarily.

He's going to play his trump card, Vee said.

"Tyrell left a letter for you Sally," the Inspector announced.

Better not show too much interest. "Ah. So that is why you thought we were lovers?"

Play at detective with the detective, she thought, and see if he rises to the bait.

"When a man writes a beautiful woman a letter knowing he is about to die, that sounds like love to me."

Mixing flattery and innuendo while hinting that there was more to come – a very sophisticated move. He'd also managed to re-centre the discussion on the letter, reminding her that she wanted to read it. Clever indeed. If she continued to show no interest, it might look suspicious.

"Presumably you are going to show me Tyrell's letter sooner or later. Do you enjoy tormenting girls who've just lost a dear friend?"

Sally doubted he'd react to such a challenge, but it was worth a try.

"You are right. I was forgetting how this must seem to you," and he took the folded paper out of his jacket pocket and handed it to her.

He'd given in too quickly, she thought. Was he playing the good guy before he struck again? She unfolded the paper and read Tyrell's last message. Think of me, he'd written, echoing what he'd said in the Reaches on that fateful morning. She couldn't help herself as tears sprang to her eyes and rolled down her cheeks.

"Excuse me," she said to him, trying to take advantage of her own unbidden emotions. She needed to respond about the question of guilt. That had to be her next move, but emotions had blurred her thinking.

Say he'd come to you wishing to discuss something vital about his family but you had not had time to listen to him, suggested Vee.

She looked up and stared directly into the Inspector's eyes. "Before he left with the Count for Germany he came to me. He wanted to talk. He said something was amiss. Something about occult forces."

There's that twitch again, Vee commented.

"But I didn't have time to listen to him. Maybe if I had been able to hear him out, we might have avoided whatever it was that happened." Ouf! That exhausted her. There she was battling her way forward while he relaxed listening.

Attack! Vee said.

"You know there is something occult going on here, don't you inspector? I'm right in my guess, aren't I?"

It was his turn to be cornered. He shifted slightly in his seat as if he were uncomfortable. There was much more to this than the death of Tyrell and his clan, Sally calculated. The ringing of his telephone interrupted their battle. Excusing himself, he moved away to answer.

Shall I listen in? Vee asked.

Can you do that?

Yes. Useful, she thought. She calmed her thoughts so as not to distract Vee whom she imagined following the inspector across the tearoom to the door. It was a long wait. Vee returned just before the inspector.

He's promised someone to keep you here as long as possible, Vee said. There are plans to kidnap you later today, I think.

What? she said, almost forgetting herself and speaking out loud.

"I think I've drunk too much tea, inspector. Can you tell me where the ladies' room is?" she asked, trying her best to put on a coy expression.

The inspector pointed to stairs that descended into the basement and went to sit down toying with his phone.

Keep an eye on him, Vee, while I try to find a way out.

The stairs wound steeply down to the basement where toilets, storerooms and kitchens were kept. Someone had carelessly left an old raincoat and a sou'wester on a peg. She quickly donned the coat that hung almost to her feet. She folded up her hair under the hat and pulled it down around her ears concealing part of her face.

Most of the doors went nowhere, but one led to a narrow corridor that ended in a metal door. It was locked, but the key was hanging conveniently on a nail above it. She unlocked the door and stepped outside.

It was then that Vee spoke urgently in her head: He's on to you. Lock the door behind you.

The courtyard was full of rubbish and boxes and stank unpleasantly of sauerkraut and beer. She hurried towards the main exit.

No, Vee said. That leads out right next to his car. Take that narrow exit over there.

She didn't have time to ask him how he knew such things. She just obeyed. Stepping out onto a busy street she slowed her pace so as not to attract too much attention.

Take that alley over there on the right, he instructed.

There was barely room to move forward as houses on both sides seemed to lean towards each other. Emerging in a large cobblestoned square, she made her way around the outside in front of the colourfully painted buildings. There were fewer people here and she felt conspicuous.

We need to get away fast, she said to him. He'll be setting the whole police force on us.

The train would be too obvious, Vee said. The river might work but I don't know if we can navigate on it. Turn here! he said, interrupting their conversation.

At least she had the right clothes on for such rainy weather.

How about the national park? Maybe we could borrow a bicycle, she suggested.

Too conspicuous, was his answer. We need to get far away as fast as possible, he added.

They were nearing the edge of the park. Sally flared her nostrils. Horses, she thought.

It might work, he replied, but we mustn't be seen.

Her half sister An, who lived in the Reaches, had taught her how to handle horses during her stay there. Sally wasn't exactly a horse whisperer, but she was quite good.

A number of ponies were grazing in a paddock at the edge of the park. Nobody was around. Sally leaned up against the barrier and sent out welcome messages to one of the largest ponies. It tossed its head and looked in her direction. Trying again, Sally was rewarded by the pony taking several steps in her direction. On her third attempt the pony came right up to her and nuzzled Sally's shoulder. Stroking its head, she whispered in its ear of riding free through the forest, of fresh grass and good oats. The animal whinnied softly. Sally climb cautiously onto the barrier and slid one leg over the horse's back. Holding on to its mane she made a brief tour of the paddock and headed for the gate. It opened easily as she let herself and the pony out. Closing it after her, they trotted off in the direction of the park and the forest beyond.

Once they had galloped a way into the park, leaving the houses behind, she pulled out her phone and dialled Jenny. Jenny was a

Swiss friend who was staying at Sally's place in Avan. Sally was to give her and some friends lessons in dream travelling in what they'd affectionately called the Dream Class.

"Hi Jenny. I've gotta be quick. I'm in a mess."

She briefly explained what had happened. Jenny immediately agreed to come and fetch her.

"It'll take us two days. Can you hide out that long?"

They agreed on a meeting point thanks to a suggestion from Vee.

"What about Rafter?" Jenny asked.

"I don't know. He was being questioned by the police too." Sally added: "I must go. We won't be able to talk on this phone, he'll have it traced."

Jenny sent love from all of them and Sally hung up.

Gentle persuasion

Rafter sat in an armchair, his eyes closed, his hands clasped in his lap, breathing gently. They'd parked him in an unused office in the local police station saying that they were awaiting the arrival of Inspector Dram. A casual observer, like the policeman on post outside the glass door of the office, might have thought Rafter was asleep. Such was not the case, however. He'd spent the hour and half that they kept him waiting in meditation. He'd sent a dream message to his good friend Alo who was a shaman in Avan. Alo knew all about the adventure in the Reaches and the destruction of the Cellerini Clan as they were called in the Reaches and had helped train Sally, Brent and Keira for that mission.

Rafter wasn't concerned for himself, but he was concerned for Sally. He cast out his mind in search of her and found her not so far away. He could not read her thoughts but he was reassured to sense that she was all right. He suspected she was on the move, possibly quite quickly. He sent her a dream message too, although he was less sure it would reach her. Neither he nor Alo had had time to train her in such things. That was something he planned to remedy with the Dream Class. A smile flitted across his face at the idea, what he saw as an exciting new approach to learning. Sally's friend Jenny had suggested it and he'd accepted immediately. With the funeral they'd had no time to begin.

The feeling that someone was about to arrive brought an end to his meditation. Whoever it was gave off a scent of both decisiveness and anxiety. Something must have gone wrong, Rafter thought, but he had no more time to pursue the idea as the door opened and a tall young man entered. "Good afternoon Professor Rafter. I am inspector Dieter Dram of the Special Investigation Squad. May I apologise for your long wait. My talk with Sally was much longer than I expected." Rafter was amused by this clumsy attempt at intimidation. At the mention of Sally, he noticed a nervous twitch around one of the Inspector's eyes. Something must have upset the man's plans.

"I trust it was as interesting as it was long," he said noncommittally.

"It was indeed," the man said with a broad smile.

Bluff on my friend, Rafter thought, finding the exchange comical. Enough, he thought, let's get down to serious business.

Rafter stood, aware that he was taller than the young man, and took the inspector's hand in his saying in an almost fatherly tone: "Take a seat inspector. Why don't you tell me what it is that is bothering you?"

A bemused look crossed the man's face as he struggled to understand what was happening to him. Rafter gave him no time to recover. Guiding him to a chair, he helped him sit down and then sat squarely opposite.

"What was it you were saying?"

The inspector was still struggling to regain control as Rafter patted him on the hand.

"It is Sally," the man said unwillingly.

"Ah yes." Rafter replied understandingly. "I thought it was."

"She's run away."

The man was beginning to sweat in his mental struggle to resist Rafter's hold on him.

"Where do you think she's gone?" Rafter asked.

"I've no idea. We can't find her anywhere. Though we've discovered a horse was stolen from the stables so we think she might be in the park." Clearly his efforts to fight against Rafter's domination were flagging.

"That seems very unlikely," Rafter suggested. "Sally doesn't like horses at all," he added firmly. Rafter decided to push the man a little further. "And why do you want to find to Sally?" he asked.

"I have to … I must keep her …"

Rafter was witness to a ferocious battle as the man fought with all his force to break free of the mental hold that gripped him. Clearly there was something the inspector had been told not to say at any price.

Rafter relinquished his hold a little. "So I think we've sorted that out," he told the Inspector. The man looked immensely relieved and thanked Rafter. "You don't need to see me out. I can find the way." Rafter bent forward, shook the man's hand and made for the door. He stepped out into the corridor and nodded to the policeman who was on guard. Glancing back, he noticed that inspector Dram was still seated, a confused look on his face.

He hailed a passing taxi and asked to go to his hotel and then on to the airport. In the car he called Alo and learnt that Sally had been in contact with Jenny and that the whole Class were en route for the Black Forest to fetch her. He smiled at the thought of the four or five friends charging across Europe to the rescue. Relieved that Sally was OK, he set out for home as fast as he could.

Out of the mists

Mists swirled around the base of the castle as Dieter climbed the stairs to the battlements. Stepping out onto the parapet that encircled the castle roof, he took a deep breath of fresh air. The upper floors of the castle emerged from a spectacular sea of clouds that floated in brilliant sunshine. In the distance he could see the crests of neighbouring wooded hills that peeked out of the mist.

What exactly had happened, he wondered. Both Sally and Rafter had slipped so easily through his fingers. The girl had disappeared just after the call from the Grand Master. She couldn't possibly have known what had been talked about. Yet the moment he'd returned she'd fled. As soon as he realised she'd gone, he sent out an alert. How could she possibly have eluded the local police in a town she was quite unfamiliar with? Had she had an accomplice, he wondered. They'd found no clues apart from a missing horse and even that had proved to be a dead end as the girl was afraid of horses apparently. Then there was the Professor, a charming, gentle man. They'd had a long conversation about this and that but nothing interesting had come of it. A slight uneasiness flickered across his mind, but he dismissed it as the result of fatigue. He badly needed a rest.

He was about to return to the stairs and make his way down when his thoughts were disturbed by his phone ringing. It was the Grand Master.

"So you've lost them both! Even though I told you they had something I urgently need." was all the voice had to say.

"The girl escaped just after our call," Dieter replied. "We haven't yet caught up with her."

"And the Professor?" the Grand Master asked.

"We talked, but I learnt nothing from him," Dieter admitted.

"You really are a soft-brained idiot," the voice on the phone said. "He wound you in a spell and bent you to his will. I trust you said nothing about me." The voice had taken on a threatening tone.

"Of ... cccourse ... nnnot," Dieter stuttered.

"You would have if I hadn't taken precautions," the voice said scornfully. "I'm not sure I can trust you any more inspector."

Dieter had begun to tremble as fear coursed through his body.

"Can I trust you?" the Grand Master asked.

"Of course," Dieter replied in a strangled voice, grasping his own neck. He sank to his knees, he could hardly breathe.

"We shall see. Meet me tomorrow evening at the Lodge. And make sure you catch that girl. She's got something I need." And the man hung up.

Chapter 2 - The Healing Song

A state of confusion

Jake sat perched on a low branch of a tree preening his feathers after a well-earned mouse. Apprehensive, he swivelled his head to peer left and right, but no danger was in sight. Flying alone for the first time, he searched for Mia who'd been carried off by a band of thugs. When he first discovered that he'd turned into an owl, a fellow owl had accompanied him on his quest. That owl was no more an owl than he. In reality, it had been a shaman, like Jake. Except that Jake was a novice. Confusing? Well yes, he had to admit it. Now there was an appropriate word, he thought: 'confusing'. Originally it had meant to bring to ruin; when everything got mingled together just like him now.

Once his shaman friend had left, he'd spent the rest of the journey balanced on El'na's shoulder, when she wasn't off in a huff irritated by his behaviour. One of the Littl' People who lived nearby, the girl - well she looked like a girl, but really she was a woman - had befriended Cian'la – that was her full name in the Reaches although most people called her Nala, and those who knew her in the Real world called her Sally, which was her name there. Where was he? Ah yes. El'na had befriended Cian'la some time earlier and so was able to lead him to her. Yes.

The threads of the story really were in a muddle, he remarked to himself, and the more he tried to sort them out, the more muddled they became. In the Real world Jake wasn't his name either. He was called Brent. And then there was Mia whose name was really Keira. She'd been his lover in the Dream world, but in the Real world she was Sally's friend and lover. Jake gave up. It was hopeless. And to think that he had once prided himself on being a storyteller, Brent grumbled to himself, feeling more and more like a testy old literary critic that had retired after shooting down his thousandth book, well, not his, other people's.

If he'd been paying attention, and owls were generally quite good at that and so was he normally, he'd have noticed that people were sneaking up on him. Instead, he muttered to himself about the complexity of the literary worlds. He did hear the whoosh as the net flew through the air in his direction, but it was already too late. He had been caught napping - although he hadn't actually been asleep unless of course he was dreaming, which might have been the case, but he doubted it. Hm. He'd lost the thread again.

Ah yes! He was on his way to be put into a cage and there was nothing he could do about it. Why didn't stories just move forward in straight lines from a beginning to a predictable end instead of stopping and starting and jumping from here to there without warning. He was still grumbling to himself about the uneven quality of stories when he was carried in his cage into a rough camp that stank of burning flesh: 'meat' men called it. His cage was dumped unceremoniously on a pile of dirty clothes and his captors went off to stuff themselves with scorched meat.

Next to him, tied to a bed, lay a girl in a pitiful state. Her hair was matted with mud and her arms and legs were blue and green in places with bruises. Well he thought, at least I've found Mia, if that was any consolation. Not that he could do much to help her, being captive himself. If anybody needed soothing now, it was surely him. And he continued twittering grumpily to himself. Anyway, Mia didn't know he was an owl and he certainly wasn't going to tell his former lover that he'd been transformed into a feathery uselessness. Hopeless, worthless, futile, you name it. Ha ha! Futile. Leaky it'd once meant. Sure, he was seeping out all over the place, mixing every metaphor he met.

Hell

A noise brought her back to the surface. Surely not the nightmare starting over again! She had lost count of the number of times. She would have groaned if she could, but no sound escaped her mouth.

Her tongue hurt. Maybe she had bitten it, or maybe someone else had bitten it. She couldn't remember. A sickly slime oozed from her mouth and dribbled down her chin. There seemed to be no end to it and there was nothing she could do about it. Her hands and feet were attached to the bed where she lay, splayed out, open to all comers. The leather thongs cut deep into her skin every time she tried to move.

Water. If only she'd had some water; to wash herself clean. Deep, deep inside her she hurt. All the rest was nothing in comparison. Pain and disgust and filth filled her till it brimmed over, flowing out where ever it could. No amount of water could wash that away. No amount of scouring would make her clean again. It clung to her, it ate into her flesh, it penetrated deep into her mind. Not even fire could put an end to it. And she wanted to put an end to it, to be finished, to wipe the slate clean, to uncoil and slip away, to expire and move beyond this world, first into darkness, maybe always in darkness but then maybe into whiteness, bright white, ... If only she could see that light.

She struggled to open her eyes and finally managed to open them slit-wise and stared in front of her. Two giant eyes stared unblinking back at her. Pitch black, brimming over with sadness and pity and helplessness. The bird was held captive like her. She closed her eyes and gave in, letting the pain roll unhindered over her in ever increasing waves till it finally burst from her mouth in an unending scream that wrenched asunder the tent in which she was enclosed, scattered all those who stood nearby and set fire to the surrounding trees. Well at least now they would let her die in peace...

"Who is responsible for this?" a male voice roared in fury. "How dare you treat the girl like this? I will have you all flayed alive!"

Only silence answered his challenge.

"Even this bedraggled bird is worth more than all of you together," he continued to roar.

"Grandson, please stop shouting," an old woman's voice rang incongruous in the silence that followed. "You are scaring her even more. Help me undo these thongs and get someone to fetch warm water," she said. "If you want to kill those who did it, go do it somewhere else. This girl has seen enough horrors."

Mia felt her arms and legs being released. She felt a little hand stroke her forehead. A sponge with warm water was gently applied to

28

her face removing the filth that was caked around her mouth and nose and neck.

"You poor thing," the old woman was saying.

And then she quietly hummed a lullaby as she rinsed Mia's breasts and smeared ointment on the gashes left by nails and teeth. Working her way down, she reached Mia's pubis and examined the wounds. Warm water flowed between her legs as the woman squeezed the sponge. It stung terribly but it was also a relief.

"I'm going to feel inside you to check that no serious damage has been done."

It was agony, but the old woman was extremely skilled in her ministrations.

"I'll squirt a liquid inside you to prevent you from getting with child from any of these brutes. But first I'll help you drink some of this tea. It'll make it easier for you to forget and get to sleep for a while. Don't worry. I will remain with you. And my grandson will protect us."

Mia swallowed the sweet tea with difficulty. Despite the little she was able to take, its effect was rapid and she felt herself relaxing and slipping into sleep.

When Mia awoke, the old woman had finished cleaning her and tending her wounds. Even her hair had been washed. She was still sore, especially between her legs, but she felt better. She had been dressed in a clean white nightdress and now lay on a comfortable bed under a soft blanket with several large pillows propping up her head.

Turning to look to the bedside, Mia saw that someone had set the owl in its metal cage on the bedside table where it slept, oblivious to what was going on around it. The little old woman sat next to the owl's cage, watching her closely, long silvery hair hanging down over her shoulders reaching almost to her waist. Mia wanted to thank her, but she found it impossible to speak. The old woman straightened the shawl she wore around her shoulders over her cotton blouse and leaned closer.

"Don't worry. I understand," the old woman said. "The bird has lost its voice too. So you go well together," she said with a smile. "As soon as you are ready to travel - we'll use a cart for you - we will be riding north into the Black County. My grandson is taking us home to the town of Granwich. In the mean time, maybe you could try eating a little soup."

At the thought of food, Mia felt a wave of disgust rise in her throat. Unable to control herself she vomited onto the bedside carpet. Wracked with continuing spasms in her stomach although nothing was left to throw up, she felt herself sink back into despair.

"I'm sorry," the old woman said, wiping Mia's mouth clean with a moist cloth. "I was too quick for you. Have a little more of my tea instead and then get some rest." She helped Mia sip a few mouthfuls of tea and then laid her back on the bed. "My name is Marie Regina, by the way. But most people call me Ma'gina." she said with a smile.

Mia opened her mouth and whispered "Mia."

"Welcome Mia," she said taking Mia's hand in hers. "You see, you can already say your name." And she planted a little kiss on Mia's hand. "Now, off to sleep with you."

The Black Country

"Look over there," Ma'gina said pointing at the distant town, pride in her voice. "That's Granwich. We'll be there before sunset. It's the largest town in the area and it's been our home for generations."

Mia turned her head to look. Riding in the cart was none too comfortable despite all Ma'gina's endeavours. Mia still couldn't walk unassisted. Turning her head to look required a considerable effort.

"I see why they call this the Black Country," she remarked, surprised at the inky cast of both the countryside and town alike.

"It's traces of black obsidian in the soil and in the rocks," Ma'gina explained. "The town is built of the same rocks. When there's been a summer storm and the rocks shine in the new found sun, the colour is most beautiful."

Mia sat back on her cushion between the many sacks of merchandise piled on the cart, pulling the cloak Ma'gina had given her tightly around her shoulders. Whatever she did, she couldn't shake off the cold. Then she looked at the woman. Despite her age, Ma'gina was remarkably alert and agile. Mia found it impossible to guess how old she was. Mia had spent most of the waking time since her nightmare with Ma'gina. Her grandson wisely kept his distance, presumably judging that Mia might not welcome the presence of men.

"What will become of me when we reach Granwich?" The question had been on Mia's mind for a while but only now did she have the strength and the courage to ask.

"I have spoken to my grandson about you. He is deeply pained about what happened. He feels responsible for what the men did. He says we owe you a great debt. I have suggested you stay a while with me. If you wish, you can be my apprentice. I have extensive knowledge about simples; maybe you can learn something from me. You could help me gather plants and learn how to prepare all manner of remedies."

Mia thought for a moment. Yes the idea pleased her. She who deeply needed to heal herself might well recover best by helping to cure others. Such learning might also prove very useful in the world she came from. The knowledge of plants there had largely shifted into the hands of men who rode rough shod over traditions and whose only interest was profit.

"Yes. I'd like that," she replied with a rare smile.

"Good. Then it is settled," Ma'gina concluded.

"And what about the bird?" Mia asked.

On those occasions during the last days when she had been alone, she'd taken to talking to the bird. She told him stories of the world she came from. Although the dialogue was only one way, she had the impression he was interested in what she had to tell. He'd cock his head on one side and stare at her. The thought that he might go away made her sad.

"The owl has been promised to the Keeper of Granwich."

When Mia looked perplexed, not understanding what a keeper could be, Ma'gina added: "In other towns they'd call him the mayor."

Mia shifted on her cushions again, trying to find a comfortable position.

"The Keeper wants the bird for his aviary. On the outskirts of town there is a large garden full of all manner of exotic plants and birds. It is one of the jewels the town prides itself in. The current mayor is head of the gardens. He is a kind, intelligent man and his niece is very good with birds. The owl will be in the very best hands there." Seeing the sadness on Mia's face, she added: "When you can walk better I will take you there to visit him."

The Apotheka

The Apotheka, as Ma'gina called the place where she worked, took up the entire ground floor of her house in the centre of Granwich. It was made up of a small reception room where visiting customers and patients were received, a treatment room for those who needed more physical manipulations like massage, palpation, bone-setting, stitching, abortion, a laboratory for preparing salves, balms, unguents as well as potions, concoctions, enemas, elixirs and philtres, and a large store room out back where all the raw materials could be stocked or laid out on shelves to dry or to mature hanging from the ceiling. There was also a library full of old parchments and leather-bound books. It was here that Mia spent most of her afternoons.

When Ma'gina had learnt that Mia could read and write, she had been set to begin a new book detailing those simples that were most commonly used, illustrating each with drawings and schemas. It was Mia that chose the simples to work on from the many Ma'gina showed her.

"First you must sit in front of the simple and meditate," Ma'gina had told her. "Listen to the silent message it sends you. Hold it in your hand and sense its vibration."

Mia could spend up to a week on one simple, studying the ingredients it was made of, the places where they were to be found. She felt its texture, smelt its odour, made drawings of it. She also went through the process of preparing the simple with guidance from Ma'gina.

In the mornings Mia assisted Ma'gina when she received calls from people in need of her skills. The old woman explained many things to her during the consultations. "Feel this bone," she would typically say, laying Mia's hand on the place in question. "Feel how it pulls against the muscles around. It's the result of your fall," she would add for the benefit of the person she was treating. And Ma'gina would show her how to dispel the tension with gentle massage. Mia was surprised that she was able to touch other people after what had happened to her. At first she had been more than reticent, but Ma'gina had insisted and the thought of reducing the suffering of others made it easier for her.

Sometimes Ma'gina was called to visit a person who was unable to come to the Apotheka. On those occasions, Mia stayed at home using the time to continue her studies. In the months she'd been there she had not yet been out. She had seen very little of Granwich for it had been night when she had first arrived. One evening at dinner, Ma'gina announced that she had to visit a young girl in a nearby quarter the next morning and asked if Mia would like to accompany her. Mia had mixed feelings about the idea. She was content to stay at home. The outside world had become a source of apprehension for her. Sometimes she had nightmares about the town and its dark corners. But at the same time, she was intrigued by the town whose life bustled outside, beyond her reach.

"I would like that," she told Ma'gina. "Should I prepare anything for the visit?"

Ma'gina indicate that it wouldn't be necessary this time; she would just take her usual bag of simples. Ma'gina then changed the subject and they did as they often did of an evening, they sang together local songs that the old woman had been teaching her. The common people of Granwich had their own local dialect that they called Gran and most of the songs were in dialect. Mia loved the songs, even those that were sad. They made her happy. They reminded her of life in the world she came from. There she used to sing a lot.

A visit

Mia ate little at breakfast. These days she ate little anyway, but this morning she ate even less than usual, as she felt uneasy about going out for the first time. Ma'gina had had new clothes made for her. Nothing too fancy, but they were comfortable and practical: a couple of sturdy skirts that reached to her ankles, some long-sleeved cotton blouses, long woollen socks and a pair of boots. Mia was glad she also had a thick shawl that morning, as the air was fresh.

Walking beside Ma'gina, it was the smells she noticed first. A bouquet of odours surrounded each shop, singling it out from all the others. The smell of the people was much less pleasant. Had that always been so? She couldn't remember. The men, in particular smelt revolting. Bile rose threateningly in her throat. She instinctively moved closer to Ma'gina.

"This is the merchant quarter," Ma'gina explained. "Unlike the richer quarters, houses here are not built with black stone, but with brick made from black sand."

Mia turned to look at the houses around her. Many had three or four stories with steps up to the main door. There were also often narrow stairs leading down to a basement. Many people greeted Ma'gina. She was clearly well known around town.

"The girl we are going to visit belongs to a richer family. They are one of the Patriciat, the noble families who rule the city. The Patriciat are not like us. They alone have the ability to change form. Each of them has a number of forms they can adopt."

It reminded Mia of her friend Cian'la. "I have a friend whose family can also shapeshift although I don't think she could do so herself." Mia realised she had told Ma'gina nothing of her adventures in the Reaches with Cian'la and Jake. She had said nothing either about coming from another world. It seemed safer not to.

"You must tell me more about her later," Ma'gina suggested.

Their conversation stopped there as they had arrived at their destination. The house was much grander than those she'd seen in the merchant quarter. Wide stairs led up to a large oak door, flanked by generous windows delicately veiled in thin lace curtains. Ma'gina did not use the main steps though. She led Mia via a side gate and down a shingle path to a small door at the back of the house for visitors like herself. Knocking, she announced their arrival to the servant. They were ushered inside and led down a long corridor to a small sitting room that smelt faintly of flowers. The two women remained standing, waiting for the girl's mother to arrive.

A tall woman swept into the room and greeted Ma'gina. She was much more richly dressed than Ma'gina. Her gown was made of deep green silk and her hair was tied up elegantly on the top of her head. She looked as if she were ready to go out to pay a visit to someone important. Mia wondered if she was always dressed like that when she was at home. Ma'gina curtsied, Mia tried to imitate her.

"Who's this?" the woman asked pointing at Mia as if she weren't there.

"This is my assistant, Mia."

Mia shrank away from the woman's disdainful stare.

"Are you sure it is a good idea, given the circumstances?"

Ma'gina nodded, smiling at Mia. "I am absolutely sure, Madam."

The woman seemed satisfied, albeit unwillingly so, because she moved to the door and said curtly: "Follow me."

As they entered the girl's room, a young girl staggered up from her bed and lurched across the room, trying to escape by a side door. Seeing that she was about to fall, Mia stepped forward and caught her. Instead of the thanks Mia expected, the girl pummelled her with angry fists. Lack of strength and utter despair caused her to cease almost immediately as she broke down in sobs laying her head on Mia's shoulder. Mia stroked her short hair and guided her back to the bed. Laying the girl on the bed, Mia sat next to her, holding her hand.

The girl was barely thirteen, a frail slip not yet really out of childhood. She was dressed in a flimsy nightdress and clung tightly to a blanket she'd slung around her shoulders. Her eyes were red, her face blotched. She'd clearly been crying. The girl's anger and despair was so familiar to Mia. Had she not been fighting against such feelings for months? How could men do such a thing to someone so young? It wasn't human. And to think that she herself had once loved and been loved by men.

"What would you prescribe?" Ma'gina asked, bringing Mia back from her thoughts.

"The same thing you gave me when this happened to me."

The mother gave Ma'gina a startled look and then turned back to Mia. "My daughter's name is Gwen. I would be very glad if you could stay a while with her while I talk to Ma'gina."

Indicating that she agreed, she turned back to Gwen. "I'm going to give you some tea, Gwen," she said, sitting on the bed next to the girl. "It will help you sleep for a while. I will stay with you. Nobody will hurt you now."

Between girls

Mia must have dosed off because the return of the two women almost made her jump. Gwen slept on.

"I have asked Ma'gina to let you stay a few days to tend to Gwen, but she insists you decide yourself if you accept."

The idea of being away from Ma'gina was upsetting ... and in a house with people she didn't know. Mia hesitated. At that moment Gwen awoke. Opening her eyes, she stared at Mia, a frightened look in her eyes.

"You see," Mia said. "I told you I would stay with you. And I'm still here." Mia turned to the mother and nodded in answer to her question. "I will stay."

"Good," the mother said. "Ma'gina tells me you know nothing of our customs. We have no time to tell you what to do and what not to do. I'll have a bed added to the room and all the meals for both of you will be brought here. There is a toilet for commoners just down the corridor. Should you need anything else, ask a servant to let me know."

Mia nodded that she had understood. "There's just one thing," she said surprising the woman who clearly wasn't used to commoners setting conditions for Patriciat. "Please make sure that no men enter this chamber."

Her surprise changing to approval, the woman replied: "A wise suggestion."

And as an afterthought, Mia added: "Can a Patriciat man take on the form of a woman?"

The directness of the question startled the mother. "Normally not."

"Better keep all animals out, too." Mia added, thinking out loud.

Beginning to get irritated with Mia's behaviour, the woman headed for the door. "I will make sure no men, in whatever form, get access to my daughter." And she left.

She can't be easy to live with, Mia thought. Glad she isn't my mother. But then again, this situation is not easy for her either. She must surely blame herself for what happened. Mia wondered how the man had managed to gain access to such a young girl.

"I'll leave you my bag of simples," Ma'gina said. "And I'll be back tomorrow afternoon." Ma'gina took Mia in her arms and then turned to go but hesitated for a moment. "A word of advice, Mia. The Patriciat are not used to people like us giving them orders. Be careful how you say things." And, with a wave of her hand, she left too.

Turning back to Gwen, she saw the girl was still looking at her. "My name is Mia," she began. "Would you like me to sing you a song? Ma'gina has been teaching me songs in Gran."

The girl looked worried. "We Patriciat are not allowed to use Gran," she explained.

"But as I am not Patriciat, I should be able to use the dialect, should I not?"

That was all very well, Mia thought, but most of the songs were about love and certainly not appropriate in the circumstances. She did at least know one lullaby. She made a mental note to ask Ma'gina to teach her others. "Make yourself comfortable, Gwen, and I will sing you a lullaby."

After the first three verses Gwen was already asleep. Mia sang on. She loved these old songs. The pulse of the Gran beat in her veins as she sang. When she reached the final cadence and took a shuddering breath, such was her emotion at singing, soft clapping came from the door.

"That was most beautiful," a servant girl said in a hushed voice. "You have a wonderful voice."

"Thank you." You know what it means to be Gran, young girl, Mia thought. "Do you think I can get something to eat? I haven't eaten since this morning."

The girl curtsied and disappeared only to reappear shortly after carrying a small tray with bread rolls, slithers of goats' milk cheese and watered red wine. Placing the tray on the table, she was about to leave when Mia called her back.

"Can you sit with me for a moment. I am new in Granwich and I know nothing about your ways and customs. Maybe you can tell me about life in the house."

The girl seemed uncomfortable. Mia wondered if she was just shy or if there was some other problem. "My name is Mia. I am Ma'gina's assistant," she said hoping the introduction would help.

"And I am Susie," the girl said with a curtsy. "I work in the kitchen and run errands."

"Why don't you take a seat, Susie?"

"We are not allowed to sit when a Patriciat is in the room."

Realising that she herself was contravening the code, Mia hastily rose and moved closer to Susie. The girl was younger than her. At most she must be sixteen. She was dressed simply in a long dark skirt and a white blouse. Her feet were bare. She would have been pretty if it hadn't been for the nasty rash at the corners of her mouth.

"How long have you had that rash?" Mia asked, not bothering about how uncomfortable asking such a question might make the girl feel.

"It comes and goes," Susie replied, clearly embarrassed.

Mia fetched an ointment from the bag of simples and spread a little on Susie's finger. "Rub that into the rash," she instructed. "It might sting at first, but the rash will be gone in the morning."

The girl looked delighted as she smeared the substance on her face.

"Why don't you go to someone like Ma'gina for help?"

"The likes of me haven't the coins for such things."

Mia heard Gwen stirring behind her so she thanked Susie for the food and added: "We'll talk more later."

"You have the most beautiful voice I have ever heard," Gwen told Mia, her own voice full of enthusiasm.

Amazing, Mia thought, how quickly young people forget. At that moment the door opened and Gwen's mother strode in. She had changed clothes in the mean time and now sported a tweed jacket over a dark blue gown with a hat perched on her head. "I see you two are getting along well and Gwen has got some of her colour back."

Mia wondered why the woman didn't take her daughter in her arms. Maybe she didn't want to crease her gown or maybe the Patriciat were not accustomed to showing affection in front of commoners.

"You must hear Mia sing, Mam," Gwen said with enthusiasm. "She has such a beautiful voice."

The mother glanced at Mia sizing her up before turning back to her daughter. "I don't have the time now, Gwen. I have an important meeting. Maybe tomorrow." And she left as abruptly as she had come.

It crossed Mia's mind that she had remained seated throughout, completely forgetting that she was supposed to stand. Too late now.

Gwen must have noticed Mia's troubled look, because she said: "Don't bother about my Mam. She's not always like that. This business with me has given her a lot of bother."

Gwen started crying again so Mia took her in her arms and sang the lullaby softly. The song calmed the girl, but once it was ended her distress reappeared.

"That meeting, the one my Mam talked about, it's a meeting with the Patriciat to decide what to do with my uncle. And it's all my fault."

The girl began crying again. Using lullabies and trying to get her to forget wasn't going to work. The girl needed to talk.

"It's your fault?" Mia asked, hoping she wouldn't make things worse by asking.

"Mam says I encouraged uncle."

"Encouraged?"

"He liked to wrestle with me. It was fun, until ..."

Here we go, Mia thought. It took Gwen an hour to tell the whole story, in fits and starts, with tears and anger and laughter. Yes, laughter. The girl poked fun at the shortcomings of the man who had proved incapable of carrying through with his acts.

"It's late, Gwen," Mia said, "I think we should both get some sleep."

"But I'm hungry," the girl protested, standing up and stretching.

Mia looked round for the tray with bread and cheese, but Susie had tidied it away. "Can we call someone?" Mia asked.

"No need. Let's go to the kitchens."

"Is that wise? Someone might see us."

"Who cares? This is my house," she said pouting.

"But I will get into trouble," Mia insisted.

Gwen opened a clothes cupboard and rummaged around in the boxes piled up at the bottom of it. Pulling out a rough pair of working trousers, a shirt and a simple tweed waistcoat.

"Then I'll dress as a boy and no one will recognise me."

It was true that with her slim figure and short brown hair she could be mistaken for a boy. Gwen tossed the blanket she had wrapped around her shoulders onto the floor, pulled the nightdress over her head and let it fall next to the blanket then she began pulling on the trousers. There were dark bruise marks on her ribs and around her arms just above the girl's wrists. Mia cursed herself for not checking the girl's body more thoroughly. She hurried to fetch an ointment and smeared it on the bruises then helped Gwen don the shirt and waistcoat.

"OK. Let's go."

The kitchen was still busy when the two of them arrived. Women, who were dressed in the same uniform as Susie, were tidying away the evening's dishes and cutlery and cleaning the working surfaces. All of them stopped to stare at Mia and the boy when they entered. It was Susie that got them out of a difficult situation.

"Good evening Miss. Can I help you?" she asked, winking discreetly at Mia.

"Yes. The boy is hungry. Have you got some more bread and cheese?"

Susie didn't reply but went immediately to fetch food that she placed in front of the boy.

"This is my friend Mia," Susie told the women. "She's the singer I told you about."

"Give us a song," an older woman said as she leaned on her broom.

"I can't. We are not supposed to be here." Mia said, worry in her voice.

"Don't bother about the Patriciat," Susie said, glancing at the boy. "They've all gone out to a meeting."

"Come on Miss," the older woman pursued. "Give us a love song to warm our hearts."

Mia looked questioningly at Gwen.

"It's all right," the disguised girl said.

So taking a deep breath, Mia launched into a song about a boy and girl who loved each other despite the refusal of their parents to let them meet. When she finished there was a moment's silence before all the women burst into applause. The old woman, tears in her eyes, thanked Mia with a generous hug.

"You should sing at our Meet. It's tomorrow evening," the woman said.

Seeing that Gwen had finished eating, Mia wanted to hurry back to their room but she was curious about the Meet.

"What's that?"

"We commoners get together from time to time to sing and dance and talk. We call it a Meet."

"It's a nice idea, but I don't think I will be able to come as I have to look after Gwen."

"That'll be no problem. Gwen can come too." And turning to the boy she added: "You'd like that Gwen, wouldn't you?"

So much for the disguise, Mia thought. "That would be far too dangerous," Mia insisted.

"Maybe you should return to your room, Mia," Susie suggested. "The Patriciat will be back soon. We can talk about this later."

So saying goodnight to the women, Mia and Gwen made their way back to their room, closing the door firmly behind them.

Good news!

"I hear you are to sing at the Meet this evening," Ma'gina commented. She'd just arrived for the visit she'd promised. "You don't waste time," she said laughing.

Mia was embarrassed and could find nothing to say.

"Don't be embarrassed, girl. This is good news."

"It would be if Gwen didn't want to come with me."

"Why can't I come?" Gwen butted in. "No one will recognise me with my disguise."

Mia explained the disguise to Ma'gina who offered to give Gwen a salve that would change the look of her face for a short while.

Gwen was delighted. "I told you it would be all right, Mia."

Ma'gina laughed again. "I see you are much better, Gwen."

"It's Mia's singing," Gwen said triumphantly, doing an improvised dance around the room.

"Well. I don't think I'm needed here. I'll leave you two girls to get on with your business," Ma'gina said, heading for the door. "See you this evening."

The Meet

When Mia, Susie and Gwen arrived at the Meet the event was already in full swing. A group of musicians were playing a popular air on flutes, violins and drums and the audience were tapping the rhythm with their hands. Susie had led them in through a small side door that brought them into the large hall next to the small stage. Mia could see that the place was packed; over three hundred people, she thought.

"You're next," Susie told her.

Gwen, disguised as a boy again, was holding Susie's hand. The two were to stay together until Mia had finished. That was the arrangement.

The audience applauded enthusiastically as the music came to an end. A tall man dressed in the bright red jacket of the master of ceremonies jumped up on stage, held up his hands for quiet and called out to the audience: "Our next act is something very special, something you may only hear once in your life time. I'm talking about Mia the Singer. Let's give her a warm welcome."

People applauded, many of them craning their necks to try to catch a sight of her. In her world, Mia had often sung on stage, but that didn't stop her having stage fright. And, as the man said, this was a very special occasion. The musicians who'd played before her had laid down their instruments and sat on the edge of the stage leaving the way open for her. As she climbed the few steps onto the stage, she looked out over the audience who all looked back, expectant.

"Good evening," she said in Gran.

The audience appreciated her making the effort to speak their language and they all called out "Good evening". Taking a deep breath she launched into the first song. She'd chosen a funny story in Gran about a man who lost his pig and found a wife instead. The people obviously knew the song by heart because they sang along with the chorus. When the last verse was finished, people broke into thunderous applause. Mia bowed deeply and smiled at Gwen who was waving wildly at her.

Her second song in Gran was a ballade about a woman who set out to travel around the world. It told of her marvellous adventures in the strangest of places. Once again the audience was delighted. Her next song was the sad tale of a man who fell in love with a bird. It turned out to be a princess but unfortunately she only liked women.

As the audience applauded she notice that Gwen seemed tired and was leaning rather heavily on Susie. "This will be my last song," she said, calling for quiet when some people grumbled that it was already over. "I've chosen this one specially to thank you all for your wonderful welcome." It was the song of the proud history of the building of Granwich. By the time she reached the second verse the musicians had crept back on stage behind her and began accompanying her. By the fourth verse the whole audience was standing, swaying from side to side in time with the music, many people singing along with the song. The song ended with a thunderous round of applause and people stomping their feet in appreciation.

But something was wrong! A fight had broken out close to Gwen and Susie. Two men were trying to drag Gwen towards the little door by the stage.

Mia screamed: "Stop them!"

The audience suddenly ceased applauding. Shock rippled through the audience as people tried to understand what was happening. Spotting Ma'gina in the audience, Mia called out: "Ma'gina, they're trying to take Gwen!"

What happened then was difficult to understand. Mia had never seen anything like it before. A woman jumped into the air and changed shape into a majestic eagle that flew low across the room, people scattering to get out of her way. The thugs were still struggling to get a hold on Gwen who was being defended by all the people around her. The eagle made short work of the men, attacking with its claws and beak. And then, just as suddenly as it had begun, the fight was over. Mia jumped down from the stage and flung her arms around Gwen, hugging her tight.

"Are you all right, my little love?" she said.

"Susie was so brave," Gwen said.

Mia hugged Susie too.

Ma'gina had made her way through the crowd that continued to mill in the hall. No one had left yet.

"I think you should sing one more song," Ma'gina suggested.

Mia stared at her for a moment, not immediately grasping what she meant. Then she turned back to the stage, climbed the steps and began singing the lullaby she'd sung to Gwen when they first met. The hall was absolutely still. No one moved. Not a sound could be heard but her voice. The fight had left her tense, but as she sang she felt herself relaxing as she gave more and more of herself to the song. She had never known her voice so expressive before. Tears began running down her cheeks as she reached the last verse. When the song was over there was a long silence as if people wanted to live on in the song. Mia wiped her eyes and bowed deeply. Little by little the audience began to applaud until they were all applauding heartily; many of them calling out her name.

When the applause had died down and Mia had finished her bows, she left the stage to join Gwen, Susie and Ma'gina. The thugs apparently had been escorted away by some of the men. She wasn't immediately able to reach her friends though because many people came to congratulate her and shake her hand. Some of the older people even gave her a hug. It was Ma'gina that finally extricated her from the overjoyed Gran people.

"I'd like you to meet Lucie," Ma'gina said.

Lucie must have been about the same age as Mia but she was a little taller and her brown hair was much longer than Mia's. Unlike the other Patriciat women Mia had met, Lucie was not dressed in silks. Instead she wore sturdy trousers, pulled up and knotted just below the knee, leaving room for calf-length leather boots. Like many women in Granwich she wore a white blouse and over it she sported an elegant tweed jacket. Her shoulder-length hair hung loose, framing a broad smile. The girl shook her hand and said in a self-assured voice: "You sing wonderfully, Mia. Congratulations."

Thanking her for the compliment, Mia looked around wondering where the bird had gone. "Where's the eagle?" Mia asked.

"She's standing right in front of you," Lucie said with a broad smile. Seeing Mia's astonished look, she went on to explain: "The Patriciat generally have several forms and one of mine is the eagle. It turns out quite practical as I am a bird keeper in my uncle's botanical gardens."

"And it was the eagle we have to thank for saving Gwen," Mia said.

"And Susie!" Gwen added.

"And Susie," both Mia and Lucie echoed, laughing together.

"I will accompany you back to Gwen's house, just in case you have any problems with her parents," Lucie said. "I'd like to make you a proposition," Lucie continued. "Every year we have a concert in the Botanical Gardens and I'd like you to sing for us then."

Glancing at Ma'gina, Mia said: "When is it? I don't know how much longer I will stay here."

"In about a month's time," was Lucie's reply.

"You can stay as long as you like, Mia," Ma'gina added.

"Please stay!" Susie and Gwen said in chorus.

Those two have become really good friends, Mia thought. If ever she were to leave they'd have each other for company and support. As they stepped outside, they got another round of applause from a small crowd of people who didn't want the evening to end. They were invited to go for a drink and something to eat by one of the women who owned a restaurant.

"I'd love to come," Mia replied in Gran. "But I really must take my little friend here back home. I will willingly come another time. Thanks."

Lucie linked arms with Mia who in turn linked arms with Ma'gina. Susie and Gwen walked a little bit ahead, holding hands and chattering quietly together.

"I would like to visit the Botanical Gardens," Mia told Lucie. "Ma'gina said she would take me there. Apparently you have a bird that is a friend of mine."

Lucie looked surprised. "Which bird is that?"

"An owl that Ma'gina's grandson gave to the Keeper."

"Ah!" Lucie said, finally understanding. "The only problem is that I haven't received it yet."

"That's odd," Ma'gina said, surprised. "We gave it to some men to deliver to the Keeper ages ago. I'll check up and find out what happened."

"You do that. I wouldn't like one of my birds to go astray."

Ma'gina turned to Mia: "Lucie is one of the finest bird keepers in the country. I swear she could make even a silent bird talk."

Lucie bowed in response and all three laughed.

Chapter 3 - Lucie

A new acquisition

Lucie had just turned twenty. As a member of the Patriciat she would soon have to marry, but her uncle was a considerate and understanding man who preferred to let her continue helping him with the birds in the aviary knowing that was what she loved best. She had quite a reputation for her skill with birds. Rumour had it that she could talk with them. Being able to adopt the form of a bird helped her a lot.

Her uncle was both Keeper of Granwich and Head of the Granwich Botanical Gardens. The gardens were famed across the whole country for their rich collection of exotic plants and birds. The hot houses stretched across a large area of the gardens. Lucie loved to wander amongst the steamy plants once the visitors had left.

Not that she wasn't interested in men, her thoughts returning to the question of marriage, she'd already had a number of flirts and people had told her that she was quite attractive, but she was never as happy as when she cared for her birds. She was concerned that if she were to marry she'd have to move away and would no longer be able to be with the birds anymore.

"Excuse me, Miss."

It was Thomas the garden help, wearing the long green apron most of the commoner staff wore about the gardens. He was well passed the age for working and walked with some difficulty, but he'd worked so well for her uncle and his father before him, they couldn't bring themselves to turn him away.

"A new bird has arrived for you."

Good news, indeed, she thought. It must be the owl Ma'gina had promised her.

"Thank you, Thomas. Why don't you go and have lunch? Go get something at the canteen before all the visitors arrive. I'll deal with the bird."

"Thank you Miss."

He limped off across the lawn shooing away the peacocks that came in the mistaken belief he'd brought them something to eat. She liked Thomas. They often made the slow rounds of the gardens together talking about flowers and birds and nature in general. In his long life he'd learnt a lot and he was quite willing to share it with her. She liked him too because he was neither condescending like most of the older Patriciat men she met, nor was he obsequious like most men from the commoners that she had to deal with.

The owl had arrived by cart.

"Good morning, Miss," the carter greeted her. "I'm to apologise for the delay in delivering this bird. We had some problems getting it to you."

Lowering the side of the cart he pulled over a cage.

"Would you like me to carry it anywhere for you?"

She knew that look in men, especially commoners. He'd willingly take a turn in the hay with her; that was clear.

"No. That won't be necessary. Should you wish, you can go and get a drink at the canteen. Tell them Mistress Lucie sent you."

She took the cage from him and headed for the aviary that lay amongst some trees on the far side of an expansive lawn. Sometimes she was grateful that commoners were intimidated by the Patriciat, it saved her all sorts of bother. As she approached the aviary, the birds must have seen her coming because they began calling out to her in their different languages. But instead of entering the aviary she turned aside and entered a smaller building that she fondly called her 'reception room'. It was here that she got to know new birds when they arrived.

She set the cage on a table and sat down nearby to watch him. An owl, indeed. A tawny owl. He hadn't been well tended for she noticed. Few people knew how to look after birds properly, especially not those poachers who occasionally brought her special goods.

"You must be hungry," she said.

Such an owl shouldn't be so thin, she thought.

"Let me hunt something down for you." It was a figure of speech she often used. She wasn't really going to hunt, although as an eagle she could hunt whenever she liked. In fact, she had a stock of mice and other little creatures for such occasions. Grabbing a mouse by its tail, she tossed it into the cage through the bars where the owl made short work of it.

She sat back in her chair and continued to observe the bird. No wing feathers seemed to be missing but she had the feeling they drooped, as if the bird were carrying a heavy load. She could have sworn it was depressed. What's more, it was strange that it made no noise. Most owls were quite talkative. She'd known several that hooted at her for hours, especially when she was trying to concentrate on something else.

"What have they done to you to make you loose your voice?" she asked him.

He stopped preening himself and stared unblinkingly at her for a moment, his head cocked on one side. Then he resumed preening.

"OK. That's a good start. It looks like we're going to need some time to get to know each other better. I have things to do now, but I will come back for you later in the afternoon."

She hung the cage from a hook fixed in the ceiling, just in case a stray cat got into the place.

"You'll be safe up there," she told him. "By the way, my name is Lucie," she said smiling at him. Then she turned and left.

A proposition

It was her habit to have lunch with her uncle in the canteen at least once a week before the rush of visitors arrived at the Gardens. Both Patriciat and commoners visited the Botanical Gardens. It was one of those rare places in Granwich where they mixed, although there were two separate restaurants to cater for the two groups. The restaurants were not the best part of the Gardens, Lucie had to admit, but the food was OK … from time to time. There was no law that sanctioned the separation between the groups; it was just a convenient habit. Tastes were different as were the means the people had available. Commoners tended to be louder and more exuberant, laughing and joking and singing sometimes as well. Whereas the

Patriciat were more sophisticated, more elegant in their dress and more refined in their conversations and tastes.

Her uncle was already seated at their table by the window. She saw that he was deep in conversation with a tall, stocky man with untidy, short brown hair and a sharp angular nose. She didn't recognise him. Lucie guessed he was a foreigner, because of the strange cut of his clothes, a badly made jacket and trousers in flimsy grey striped material, the likes of which she had never seen before. To give her uncle time to finish, Lucie first greeted the girls behind the counter in the commoners' part of the restaurant. Unlike many of her fellow Patriciat, she did not shun the contact of commoners. Having enquired about them and their families, she wished them a good day and went to join her uncle.

"Who was that, uncle? I didn't recognise him," she asked as she sat down and unfolded her napkin.

"A foreigner, although he speaks our language well. He's professor in a university across the waters. I didn't quite catch his name, something like Lewschtly."

Lucie broke open a bread roll and spread herb butter on both pieces. Handing one piece to her uncle, she asked: "So he's interested in the Botanical Gardens?"

Her uncle looked uncomfortable. She rarely saw him apprehensive but now he surprised her with his anxiety.

"What's the matter, uncle?"

"The man, who is apparently very influential, enquired about the possibility of your getting married."

"What!" Lucie exclaimed, incredulous. "He must be joking. He doesn't even know me."

"I am afraid he's deadly serious. He talked of asking permission of the Patriciat at their next gathering in a month's time. I can't see how I can stop him."

Lucie put down the bread she was about to eat and stared out of the window. She could see the aviary quite clearly from where she sat. This was worse than anything she could have imagined. A foreigner. He must have seen her when she arrived but had not waited to greet her. What was the man playing at?

"Tell him that I want a formal meeting with him in a week's time. Then I will reach my decision in three week's time. There is to be a big concert here in the Gardens. I will announce my decision then."

Her uncle stared at her, astonished at her reaction. "Are you all right?" he asked, his voice full of concern.

"Yes, uncle. I am fine. But should I decide to refuse this offer I will fight him in a duel in front of the Patriciat, as is my right."

Her uncle had gone white with fear. "You can't do that," he said with a strangled voice.

"I can, and I will," she said.

A talk

Lucie urgently wanted to discuss the marriage threat with Ma'gina. She sent a message to the Apotheka asking the old woman to visit her as soon as possible. On her way to the Aviary she met Thomas lugging a sack of seeds for some of her birds. Helping him with his load, she asked: "Would you like to walk with me for a while, Thomas?"

"If I can pick up my walking stick at the aviary as we go by, I'd love to accompany you, Mistress Lucie."

A path led away behind the Aviary, down a gentle slope to a wilder part of the gardens: the bamboo plantation. It was one of her uncle's favourite places. He much preferred what he called the 'wilderness' of the bamboo plantation to the cultivated gardens of his fellow Patriciat. Slipping her arm in his, Lucie slowed her speed to match that of the old man.

"I have had very bad news," she announced.

Thomas stopped to look at her, worry written all over his face.

"It was that man in the canteen?" he said.

"Did you see him, Thomas?" Of course! She'd sent Thomas to get lunch in the canteen. Even if he ate in the commoners' part, he would still have been able to see and possibly hear the foreigner.

"Not a good man," he said, unwilling to go further.

"Why do you say that, Thomas?"

After years of habit, many older commoners were quite unable to say anything critical of the Patriciat. As he didn't reply, Lucie added: "I really need your help, Thomas. What you can tell me might make all the difference."

They'd arrived at a crossroads. Thomas suggested they take the narrow path to the right that ran alongside a small pond and then climbed back up between thick bushes of rhododendrons. Just beyond the pond a small bench lay secluded under low hanging branches. Privacy, Lucie thought. That's what he needed to be able to talk.

"Let's sit here for a while," she suggested. "You may sit next to me, Thomas, nobody will see us here."

Hesitantly taking a seat at the other end of the bench, Thomas began his tale: "At first the man was polite to your uncle: lots of compliments about the Gardens and the Aviary and about your uncle's reputation. But when your uncle refused to talk about marriage, the man became threatening. Said he had some secret means to force your uncle to agree. When your uncle laughed at him the man asked if he had heard of the Black Castle. That's where the Cellerini Clan live, south of here. Well they used to live there. The Castle was completely destroyed. Nobody survived. The foreign bloke said he had done that. Your uncle wanted proof. The man took out a tiny metal box and showed it to your uncle. I couldn't hear what was said then because the man lowered his voice. But I could see your uncle had gone terribly pale. That was when you arrived."

Lucie had heard of the catastrophe at the Black Castle. It was a mystery how the place could have crumbled so suddenly. At that moment a pair of ducks landed noisily on the pond, sending ripples across the water. Lucie called out to them in their dialect but they were only interested in each other.

Turning back to Thomas, she asked: "Do you think he can carry out his threat?"

"I don't know Mistress Lucie. All I know is that your uncle was really frightened."

Lucie stood and offered a helping hand to the old man. "You have been very helpful, Thomas. I thank you for all you've told me. Could I ask you not to tell anyone else about this?" She knew she could trust him, but it was better to be explicit.

"I won't say a word to anyone, Miss."

Flights of fancy

It was almost dark when Lucie entered the reception room in the Aviary. She'd been away longer than she planned. It was not good to leave new birds alone too long. Lifting down the cage from its hook she placed it on the table and handed the bird a mouse.

"I am sorry I was away so long," she apologised. "Something quite unexpected came up." She wondered if she should tell the bird about what had happened. Its attentiveness invited her to go on. "I'm to be forced to marry," she admitted, a tear rolling down her cheek. She had been able to keep a brave face up to now, but there, sitting alone with the bird in the dark, she felt the full weight of her loneliness. "I have devoted my life to the birds in this Aviary and now my work is to stop abruptly."

The owl hooted softly.

"So you can speak!" she exclaimed, wiping the tears from her eyes. "I have asked my friend Ma'gina to come. She will know what to do."

The owl hooted again gently.

On an impulse, Lucie leant forward and opened the cage. The bird hopped out and flew up onto her shoulder.

"Well my friend," she said stoking his head, "you are more than you appear to be."

The bird touched the lobe of her ear with its beak and jumped on top of the cage. "Yes," he said, articulating the word with some difficulty.

Startled, Lucie jumped up. "You can speak!" she said trying to calm her agitation. No bird had ever spoken to her in the language of humans, unless he had been a fellow Patriciat in bird form.

"Little," the bird replied.

"Are you a Patriciat?" She needed to know. She had told him some of her story and that could be dangerous. If the worst came to the worst, she would transform into an eagle and kill the bird. She hated the thought of doing it, but she had no choice.

"What?" The bird seemed confused. "Foreigner," he explained.

"Then you are the second one today. The first one wanted to marry me. Do you want to marry me too?"

The bird hooted mournfully.

She laughed. "I'm sorry. I'm so tense with all this business."

She told him the whole story, explaining how Patriciat marriages were organised. "Formally it's the father, or in my case my uncle, who decides for the daughter. But a suitor can force his hand by appealing to the Patriciat Council. That's what this foreigner says he'll do if my uncle doesn't accept."

The bird hopped from one foot to another. "Bad!" he said. It was more a hoot than a word.

She smiled at his efforts to talk. "How inconsiderate of me. Here I am telling you all my woes, when you have enough problems of your own." She wondered how he'd learnt to talk. "We must find a way to help you tell me your story."

The bird hooted mournfully in reply.

An idea germinated in her head. It wouldn't improve his ability to speak but it might help their relationship.

"I'm not always in this shape," she told him. "I can also take on the form of an eagle."

The bird moved nervously at the mention of eagles. He clearly knew what the word meant.

"If I shift into the form of an eagle we will be able to fly together. I promise I won't hurt you."

The little owl seemed more than hesitant. Its eyes were even wider than usual, if that were possible.

"Ok," it finally hooted.

Lucie opened the door so they could get in and out and then she changed. The owl immediately flew up into the rafters hooting wildly, no doubt scared by her size. She was an impressive eagle. This isn't going to work, she said to herself and changed back into Lucie.

"I'm sorry," she apologised to the owl that continued to hoot dolefully up in the rafters. "It would be easier if I could change into an owl."

An owl wasn't one of her shapes and she had always been told that the number of forms the Patriciat could adopt was limited. Still she thought she'd try. She had always been praised on her ability to transform and she knew owls well.

Shape-shifting had a very special feel to it just before the change took place. She evoked that familiar feeling and thought of herself as an owl. A change took place. But she wasn't sure which form she had adopted. She sensed that she was a bird but her current form was not familiar. She was wondering how she could tell when the other bird flew down and landed next to her.

"Owl," it said in owl dialect.

So now there are two of us, she thought.

"Fly!" the owl hooted.

"Fly," Lucie hooted back.

A short shower had left roofs and pavements glistening in the light of the rising moon. From above, the city sparkled like a many-faceted black jewel through which the Granwich canal wound its way like a fine necklace of light. Lanterns on barges navigated like glittering pearls along the river of light, stopping from time to time to negotiate lock gates. Here and there wisps of smoke rose from chimneys only to be scattered by a brisk breeze. Street lamps reflected off obsidian black walls and dripped in rich greens off the leafy trees along the avenues. Few people were out and about. It was late for humans.

The two owls flew wing to wing in ever widening circles, delighting in the sight of Granwich at night, delighting in the freshness of the air cleansed by the shower, delighting above all in the freedom to be on the wing and in the joy of flying together. Did not humans say 'as free as the birds'? Lucie let out a long trembling hoot of pleasure and the other owl hooted back.

"Follow me, my friend," she called out and she plunged towards a majestic building sprawling close to the canal. They landed side by side on the roof overlooking a large square crisscrossed with wide walkways that wound round small rose gardens, punctuated with the occasional statue.

"This is the Patriciat Council Building. It is here that they will hold the hearing to decide if the foreigner has the right to take me as his wife," she told him.

"When?" the other owl asked.

"In about four weeks, probably. I have said I will give my answer in three weeks at the annual concert in the Botanical Gardens."

Lucie turned to look at the other owl. He no longer looked so dejected as when she had seen him earlier that day. Maybe it was because she was seeing him with the eyes of an owl. In fact, he seemed quite handsome. Time to change back into my human form, a warning voice said in her head. She hooted with laughter.

"We fly away?" he asked.

"Not now, my friend. I must try to settle this as a human first," she replied, noting that he had said more than one word for the first time.

He gave a disappointed hoot and shuffled from one claw to the other.

"We must get back," she said launching into the air. "It is late." He flew after her as they followed the canal towards the Botanical Gardens and the Aviary.

Landing at the door they hopped inside and she shapeshifted into her human form. She was at a loss about what to do with the bird. She couldn't lock him back up in his cage. Not now they had flown out together. She could close him in the Reception Room. He'd be safe like that. But, to be honest, she found his presence comforting. Finally she decided to take him with her to her rooms in the main buildings.

"If you behave," she said, feeling as if she were talking to a child, "you can come with me. But you must remember that humans sleep at night, unlike owls. So you must let me sleep."

He hopped onto her shoulder and she closed the door behind them and headed for the mansion house next to the administration building by the main gates where her rooms were to be found. Situated on the first floor, her rooms were quite modest. They consisted of a small living room, the walls of which were lined with books, an even smaller kitchen that she used only when she wanted to avoid the canteen and a sizable bedroom that she also used as a place to read. There was also a tiny bathroom with a shower rather than a bath.

She prided herself on being a tidy person. Her clothes were all hung up in orderly rows in her closet. The books by her bedside were neatly piled with only one lying open at the page she was currently reading. The kitchen and bathroom were spotlessly clean.

She took down a bowl in the kitchen and put water in it for the bird that hopped off her shoulder and onto the work surface for a drink. She poured herself a glass and went into her bedroom to take her shoes and stockings off, singing softly one of the Gran songs she'd heard Mia singing. Her elders and fellow Patriciat would be horrified to hear her singing in Gran, but she loved the song and liked the language. She had always been one who walked the limits, although she had never protested openly about Patriciat ways.

She began undressing for bed when the bird hopped in at the door. Suddenly feeling shy about standing naked in front of the bird, she said half jokingly "Turn around you naughty bird. And stop taking advantage of the situation."

The bird hooted in protest, hopped up onto her armchair and resolutely turned his back on her. If he'd been a man she'd have said he was in a huff. Having washed her face and hands and brushed her teeth, she returned to the bedroom and lay down on her bed, pulling the covers over her. It was too late to read, so she turned off the light immediately and laid her head on her pillow.

"Goodnight, my friend," she said.

"Good night," he hooted back.

She slipped gently into sleep with the strange feeling of being watched over by a bird.

Learning to talk

Stretching after a good night's sleep, Lucie rose to pull the curtains. The sound of feathers ruffling reminded her that the owl was there. He was still standing on the armchair next to her bed.

"Thanks for letting me sleep," she said stroking his head. "Now fly into the living room while I get washed and dressed."

It was silly really, but the idea of this bird watching her get dressed made her feel uncomfortable. Maybe it was because he could talk. She decided she was going to help improve his speech and she mulled over plans for how she could do it while she had a shower.

Dressed and ready she stepped into the living room and invited the bird onto her shoulder. "Let's go get something for breakfast."

"Go hunting?" he hooted.

"Yes," she said laughing. "But only for bread rolls." She could feel his disappointment. "We'll go hunting tonight." And deciding to put her plan into action she began to question him: "Would you like that?"

"Yes," he hooted.

"You should say: Yes I would."

"Yes I would," he echoed.

There was a good bakery just down the road, so she set off in that direction. "We are going to a bakery. Do you know what we can buy there?"

"Bread," was his terse answer.

"Try to speak in sentences, if you can."

"Buy bread," he added.

"That's a little better, but I think you need to do even more."

"I can buy bread."

"Now that's excellent."

They had to stop their lesson because they were nearing the shop. People were used to seeing her with birds, but not with ones she could talk to. The smell of fresh bread was delicious. She hadn't realised how hungry she was. The bird nudged her ear with its beak.

"OK," she said quietly. "We need to get something for you too. But there aren't any shops here with food for owls in them." And she laughed at her own joke. On which he pinched her ear. "Oie!" she complained.

"Don't make jokes about owls," he whispered.

On her way to the Aviary, Lucie fetched a mug of coffee from the canteen that was just opening. Laying down her bag of provisions on the working bench in the Reception Room she searched for a plate and knife. The owl hopped across the bench and pecked at the bread.

"It's rude to eat other people's food," she said mockingly as she noticed what he was doing.

"I'm hungry," was his reply.

"Do you want a mouse or some bread?"

His answer surprised her. "Bread with butter and jam."

"Who are you?" she asked preparing tiny pieces of bread for him, spread with a little butter and jam.

"My name is Jake."

She almost fell off the chair she was sitting on. His answer filled her with alarm. "So you are Patriciat!" she said angrily. To think she'd let him sleep in her bedroom next to her.

"I don't know what Patriciat is," was his reply.

So she explained it to him, feeling increasingly perplexed at the situation.

"I am not Patriciat. I come from another world. I was here on a mission. That is finished, but I can't go home."

Lucie tore a bread roll in half and covered it liberally with butter and jam, hardly knowing what she was doing. "Well you'd better tell me your story." And she shifted to an armchair while Jake paced up and down on the workbench, occasionally taking a peck at the bread.

The story took a long time to tell. Jake struggled with words and concepts that refused to come easily. Lucie remained silent throughout, a piece of bread untouched in her hand. When he reached the part about Mia and the band of thugs and how Ma'gina had looked after her, tears began rolling down Lucie's cheeks.

"Mia is such a wonderful person," she spoke for the first time. "How terrible that such a thing should happen to her."

"So you see," Jake said, clearly feeling more confident with words now. "I am stuck as an owl."

"Maybe I can help you," Lucie thought out loud. "I'm very good at Shapeshifting. Maybe I can teach you."

Jake hooted loudly by way of warning as a knock was heard at the door.

"Come in," Lucie called out.

It was Thomas who limped over to her and handed her a letter. "It just arrived from the Apotheka. I thought you might want to read it immediately."

She thanked him and asked him to reserve a place for her in the canteen at lunchtime. Nodding, he limped back out of the door and across the lawn.

"This is from Ma'gina," she explained to Jake. Ripping open the letter, she read it out loud: "Ma'gina has gone with Mia in search of special flowers. They should be back in about a week. I will let her know you want to see her the moment she returns."

She laid the paper down on the bench and sat back in her armchair disappointed.

"That's a real set back," she told Jake. "I was hoping to get her advice on what to do with this man."

Jake flew to the arm of her chair and stood there staring at her. "What's this man like?" he asked.

She instinctively caressed his head until she remembered he was really a man. She stopped immediately.

"Please don't stop," he pleaded. "Your caresses are comforting."

She hesitated for a moment, having mixed feelings about stroking the head of a stranger, but continued all the same.

"What's he like?" Jake repeated.

She explained that she had only seen him for a short while but that Thomas had heard the whole conversation with her uncle. When she got to the part about the little box the man had threatened her uncle with, Jake rose up in anger, his wings splayed wide, completely startling her.

"What's the matter?"

"Do you know the man's name?"

"My uncle couldn't remember his name. Something like Lewschtly."

Jake took off with a wild hoot and flew up into the rafters.

"What's the matter?" she asked, frightened by his behaviour.

Circling several times round the room, he finally landed back on the arm of her chair. "Leuchtli," he said. "Dr. Leuchtli. He was the one that nearly killed Sally and was responsible for the destruction of the Black Castle."

"So what he said was true," she said groaning.

"Not exactly."

Jake went on to explain the workings of the Machine, as he called the little box the man had. There were many concepts that Lucie was unaware of so she had to stop him often asking for clarification. He told her about Sally's mission and the fact that Leuchtli had tried to use her as a conduit for an attack against the Littl' People. Lucie had heard of them. Some of them even came to Granwich from time to time. He described the waves of immense energy that had flowed through Sally because of the Machine, destroying all around until she had finally managed to deflect them with the help of a friend, making the Black Castle crumble to ruins, killing all inside. The owner of the castle had been responsible for the attack, so justice had been done.

Lucie sat silent for a long moment. "This man is mad," she finally said.

"Yes. And very dangerous," Jake added. "I wonder why he wants to marry you?" And then, as if embarrassed by what he had said, he added: "I mean apart from the fact that you are young and beautiful."

If birds could blush, she thought, the owl would have gone bright red, such was his apparent embarrassment.

"Don't worry," she said. "I understand what you mean. He obviously has a plan and I am a key part in it," Lucie said. "That is what we must find out."

Pleasure

"Undo two more buttons. Hmmm. And lean over backwards."

The position made her sway precariously, affording him a glance from time to time along her thighs and up between her legs.

"Come closer."

She was good at her job for all her relatively young age, but that didn't stop her being afraid of him. He could sense it. Unhitching her dress from her shoulders he let it slide down her body to the floor where it settled in soft mounds around her bare feet. She wore nothing underneath. Disappointed, he would have liked the undressing to last longer.

He ran his fingernails down her back and over her buttocks, digging into her skin, leaving faint red marks in her flesh. She was not one of those waifish girls, all bones and no meat. No. She had ample rounded hips and her breast hung full before her although her belly was smooth and flat.

"Lie down on the bed in front of me with your legs wide open so I can admire you."

He reached over and picked up his half-smoked cigar and re-lit it, sending clouds of pungent smoke billowing into the room. He picked up his whiskey, swilled the contents around the sides of the glass splashing some out over his fingers and then held the glass under his nose and sniffed deeply. Glancing over the top of his glass at the girl he imagined she was wet with anticipation. Quite a feat really, considering she looked rather bored. He gulped down a large mouthful and staggered over to the bed to join her.

"I'm going to give you a name," he said slurring his words slightly. "I'm going to call you Sally. Do you like your name, Sally?" he asked, putting his hand under her chin and lifting her head so she was obliged to look at him.

"Yes, Sir," was all she said in a small but husky voice, her eyes half closed.

"Now Sally. I want you to go to work on me. Get me so excited that I have to beg you to stop."

He staggered back to the armchair and slump down in it.

She stood up and sauntered over to him, getting down on her knees in front of his chair. One by one she unbuttoned his flies and folded back his trousers. Slipping her hand inside she searched for his manhood. As her fingers grasped his limp form, Leuchtli sighed and closed his eyes. She was good, really good. He ran an absent-minded hand over her hair, moaning "Sally" as he pulled her head closer to his crotch. His mind swam in a sea of whiskey and cigar fumes, untethered from worldly concerns.

"Is this how you spend your time?" a voice roared in his head.

Leuchtli cringed, causing the girl to stop her foreplay.

"Don't stop," he said breathlessly, knowing full well that it wasn't her that took his breath away.

"Have you found the girl?"

Yes he had.

"And what about the marriage proposal?"

She'll give her answer in about four weeks. "Achtung!" he shrieked when she accidently bit him.

"Get rid of the girl. You can't concentrate on what I'm saying."

Leuchtli shifted so he could push her away, but his sudden movement caught her by surprise, causing her to topple over and sink her teeth into him as she fell. He screamed. Warm blood was flowing freely between his legs. He screamed even more.

"You're hopeless," he heard in his head and then the voice was gone.

"Here. Hold this cloth on the wound. I'll run to the Apotheka to get help," she told him as she donned her clothes, picked up the handful of banknotes he'd laid out for her and ran out of the barge door.

I'm ruined he thought as he sank into utter despair before he blacked out.

Shapeshifting

She swung her feet back and forth over the edge of the bed, running her fingers through her hair enjoying the soft feel of it. Flat-chested and no hairs between her legs: how old must she be? Ten, maybe. She ran her hands over her body, unable to believe who or what she had become. The ambiguity of the situation troubled her. She blushed.

Jumping off the bed, she skipped to the clothes closet, humming a tune to herself. Better find something to wear. What if someone were to come in, she giggled. What if Lucie were to come back? She blushed at the thought. How could she possibly explain what had happened?

She caught sight of herself in a mirror. Bright blue eyes stared back at her as she tugged at her medium-length, red hair. That much had stayed the same. She turned left and right, peering over her shoulders to get a better look at herself from all sides. She was a bare slip of a girl although she wouldn't have called herself thin. She didn't know whether to cry or laugh. How was she to know that transforming from an owl she might turn into anything other than Jake?

Rummaging amongst Lucie's neatly suspended clothes she held up several pretty dresses against herself but they were all far too big. Finally she found a blue shirt that became a dress when she slipped it over her shoulders. Underwear was more difficult. Fingering through Lucie's private things made her very uncomfortable. In the end she found a pair of shorts that must have shrunk in the wash. Now she was ready to face the world. Well. Sort of.

Sitting in the armchair next to the bed, she picked up the book Lucie was reading. It was all about shapeshifting. Apparently, Lucie was reading up on the subject as she'd promised Jake to help him transform. She flicked through the pages, reading here and there. In

60

one place it said that women couldn't become men and vice versa. Well that was certainly wrong. Maybe it only applied to Patriciat. As an experiment, she searched her memory to see if she could remember things she hadn't known as Jake, but she found nothing lest it be the experience of her new body.

Her owlish meal had left a nasty taste in her mouth so she went to the kitchen to get some water to drink. Several bread rolls were left over from breakfast. Lucie had wrapped them in a cloth to keep them from drying up. The girl found butter and jam and spread thick layers of both on the bread. Mmm good, she thought, burping. Eating too quickly did that to her, she remembered. The food made her tired so she went back into the bedroom and climbed under the covers of Lucie's bed.

However she couldn't fall asleep. The faint perfume of Lucie troubled her. So she set to wondering what her name could be. One name came to mind immediately: Sarah. OK. That's a pretty name, she said to herself and she repeated it out loud several times to see what it felt like.

"So, Sarah," she said out loud to herself, "it's time to sleep."

Hearing her voice for the first time was a shock. A soft soprano song. She repeated the word "Sleep" several times trying to get used to it. But sleep still didn't come even though she was tired. How could Leuchtli possibly be there? she asked herself, turning over in the bed to see if the other side was more comfortable. Leuchtli couldn't travel between the worlds. That was why he had to get Sally to go for him. He should still be in Avan, unless time flowed differently between the worlds. Sarah finally decided to lie on her back and cupped her hands under her head. And what did he want with Lucie? Questions danced an endless round in her head with not an answer in sight until Sarah finally slipped into sleep.

Consultations

The Patriciat Council building rose regal above the Granwich Canal, its shining black form marking the city skyline. Inside, the main halls reserved for special receptions and major events were also majestic. But the narrow staircases, the interminable corridors half blocked with filing cabinets and the tiny rooms where the clerks worked on the upper floors and under the rafters were less impressive. Lucie marched along one such anonymous corridor at the top of the building, weaving her way between cardboard boxes full of

61

papers and overflowing filing cabinets, on her way to an appointment with one of the names clerks.

She passed door after door, each identical except for its number. 516. There it was, trapped between two immense cupboards. She knocked. No answer. She knocked again.

"Come in," a muffled voice called out.

Clerks were invariably commoners. Paradoxically, they kept order in the Patriciat world: receiving visits, filling out forms, filing those forms and other documents, searching for records when they were needed, making sense of the maize of files that they had accumulated, providing statistics and writing reports. Judging from the chaos in the corridors, 'order' was maybe not the right word. She turned the handle and pushed open the door. Something resisted her efforts. Peering round the half-open door she caught sight of a pile of annals blocking the way.

"Just push," the muffled voice called out.

So she pushed. The pile of records withstood a moment then tumbled over setting off a chain reaction that had a number of piles of documents sprawling across the floor.

"Don't bother about that. Come on in," the voice persisted.

Trying not to tread on the fallen papers or knock anything over, Lucie wove her way between waist high piles of records of all sorts along a narrow path that led her to a desk largely hidden under books and papers and files.

"Take a seat," the voice said from below the desk. "I'll be with you in a minute."

A large cardboard box full of newspaper-cuttings occupied the only seat available. From under the desk, she could hear the noise of someone rummaging through papers. Whoever it was had difficulty breathing because he or she was wheezing and coughing between muttered curses.

"Blast. Where could it be? It was always here." The voice broke off in a fit of coughing, stirring up a cloud of dust that rose above the desk. "Confound this dust. It makes my glasses filthy. I can't see a thing."

"Can I help?" Lucie asked.

"Here. Take this. I think I've found it."

And a wrinkled hand appeared from behind the desk brandishing a paper. Lucie leaned forward and caught the paper as the hand disappeared again. The old man - for a man it was - struggled to his feet with difficulty and brushed off his jacket and trousers.

"Good morning, Mistress Lucie."

Of course he knew her name: names were his business.

"I'm sorry," she replied. "I don't know your name."

"My name is of no importance," he said, recovering the paper that she was still grasping in her hand. "What is important is the name you've come to look for."

Picking up the box full of clippings, he indicated that she should use his chair. As she took her place in the swivelling chair he continued to speak.

"I thought you were wonderful the other night," admiration in his voice. At her perplexed look the old man went on: "At the Meet when you rescued that little girl."

"You saw me there?" she said, surprised.

"We all saw you, Miss. It's not often that someone from the Patriciat honours us with a visit at one of our Meets."

It was true that Patriciat didn't often mix with commoners, Lucie thought. She didn't usually bother about such distinctions, but she could understand that her behaviour might seem strange.

"I hope I didn't offend anyone."

"On the contrary we were all delighted to have you there. Everyone knows you are a good friend of Ma'gina and that you help commoners at the Gardens."

Lucie had never given much thought to her behaviour that, now she thought about it, must have been considered outlandish by many, especially amongst the Patriciat.

"So you want to know about this Leuchtli man?"

Lucie was shocked at the question. Did everyone in Granwich know about the man's offer of marriage? She must have looked worried because the old man tried to reassure her.

"You're wondering how I know, I bet. Well we commoners always keep a sharp eye open for anything that happens to the Keeper's Daughter."

Lucie wondered exactly what form a 'sharp eye' would take. She shuddered at the idea of being spied on.

"I have been able to find very little information on the man," the old man continued. "His name is Dr. Jakob Leuchtli. He is staying on a hotel barge on the canal near Grand Street. His name is not in the

Patriciat records. He claims he comes from a place called Jura that is beyond the waters."

"How do we know if he is Patriciat?" Lucie asked.

"He had a certificate from his home town."

"How do we know it is not a fake?"

The old man shifted uncomfortably as if he were wondering what to do in a tricky situation.

"OK," he said, apparently having reached a decision. "I will take you to a colleague. He's an expert in Patriciat law and he should be able to help you."

The colleague was three floors down and four corridors along. His office was impeccable: not the slightest paper was out of place. The man peered over his spectacles at them as they entered and stood as was proper when Patriciat entered the room.

"Mistress Lucie," he said with a slight bow. He offered her a chair but she remained standing.

"If you remain standing then so will I," she told him. She wasn't usually so demonstrative of her easy-going attitudes to customs.

"You can ask him your questions," the names clerk told her. "He knows all about this case."

Lucie had the feeling that her whole visit to the Council building had been orchestrated in advance. If such was the case, she was glad it was by people favourable to her cause.

"How can I get out of marrying this man?" she asked, having decided that directness was the best tactic.

"There are several ways. You could try to prove he is not Patriciat."

"How do I do that?"

"The easiest way is to challenge him to transform. If he succeeds, however, that may count against you later in the proceedings."

"You said there were several ways"

"Yes. Another way would be to show that he is already married or promised to someone else."

"I can't see how I could do that."

"You could argue physical incompatibility."

"What would be acceptable grounds?" Lucie asked.

"You should have been a lawyer," he said laughing. "His ill health, stinky breath, snoring, impotence, …"

"The latter might be a bit difficult to prove," she said grimly.

"You could also marry someone else," he suggested.

"I hadn't thought of that. Unfortunately there is no one."

"Or, of course, you could fight him."

"That is what I was planning to do. Although it doesn't seem a very good idea."

"There's another possibility. You could prove that he has been systematically going with other women."

"I wonder how I could do that?"

"I don't know. Maybe you can find witnesses or he keeps a diary in which he talks about the women he's slept with."

Lucie's head was spinning with all the possibilities. Things were less impossible than she had thought. At least that was encouraging. She thanked both men and was about to leave when the lawyer called her back.

"If ever you need legal council, I would willingly help out. I think all the commoners would willingly help you."

"Thank you," Lucie replied, moved by their support.

A pitiful specimen

"There he is," he heard the girl say as the door opened.

"Thank you. You did well to fetch me. You can leave now. Go back to the Apotheka. They'll look after you. I will take care of this one," an older woman's voice replied.

The door closed and he heard the woman move closer to him.

"Not unconscious I see," she commented.

Leuchtli groaned, hoping that would solicit sympathy. Proficient hands removed the cloth from his sex and examined it.

"I'm going to wash you and make sure there's no infection. You won't need sowing up. But sex will be out of the question for quite a while."

He swore as a liquid rolled between his legs. He wondered if he hadn't wet himself at the fright of it.

"Damn it woman! That hurts."

"Would you prefer amputation in a few weeks time?" she replied coldly.

He couldn't stop himself shuddering. He must be running a temperature, he thought. The girl was probably infected with some terrible disease.

"You are suffering from shock. Drink this herbal tea. It will help you relax."

Leuchtli did as he was told. He felt strangely distant, as if he no longer completely belonged to his body. It must be the liquid the woman had given him to drink. He shouldn't have accepted it. It might have been drugged.

"Hold out your hand," the woman said.

When he didn't respond, she grasped his right hand and smeared cream on his fingertips.

"Rub that gently on the wound. It will help it heal more quickly."

As he had some difficulties coordinating his movements, she guided his hand in the right direction. Touching the wound made it smart. He imagined that normally it would have been unbearable, but in his current fuzzy state the stinging was almost a pleasure. He continued to stroke himself completely forgetting that the woman was still there.

"I wouldn't do that if I were you," she commented. "If you get an erection it might start bleeding again."

Erection, he thought. He didn't get one with the girl, despite all her efforts. He began to giggle nervously. Maybe he would never be able to do it again. The giggles turned to tears and then sobs, his whole body wracked with desperation.

"Here. Drink some more of this liquid."

He vaguely felt the woman force open his mouth and pour a sweet liquid down his throat. Then she spread a blanket over him and said goodbye.

Once he was sure she'd gone, he thrust away the blanket, got to his feet and promptly collapsed on the floor, hurting his knees and elbows in the process. He lay unmoving for a moment trying to remember what he was supposed to be doing. Then he struggled to stand up. He managed to get hold of the armchair and used if for leverage. At his first step, he realised that his trousers were around his ankles. He collapsed into the chair and made a number of unsuccessful attempts to pull them up. It took him several minutes till he could button them up around his waist. The world was full of black holes, he noticed. Was his eyesight failing or was it the drug?

As he stood and swayed towards the door, he tried to avoid stepping on any of the holes for fear he'd fall into one of them. It was a narrow thing, but he finally made it to the door and stepped out onto the gangplank that linked the barge to the riverbank. It had rained earlier and the plank was wet and slippery and full of treacherous black holes. He had done so well up to then, how could anyone blame him for missing his step and landing right in the middle of one of those black holes.

A male voice shouted out: "Oie! You! Be careful?"

Leuchtli paid no heed to it. He was busy falling into the black hole. The bottom of the hole was wet and full of slimy things that coiled around him.

The cold brought him back to his senses immediately. He'd fallen into the Granwich canal.

"Help! Help!" he called out.

"Keep quiet," a deep voice said.

He felt a strong hand grabbing hold of his shoulders.

"No!" he screamed, fighting back with all his strength. Water seeped into his nose as he struggled against his attacker.

"Stop fighting against me, Leuchtli. You're hopeless. Just let me put an end to this."

Please, he pleaded. I did all I could. It wasn't my fault. But the solid hands held him firmly as he continued to struggle. His lungs were bursting for want of air. The voice rang out as the water rushed into his mouth and down into his lungs: "For God sake! Stop struggling!"

Uncovered

"Who are you?" Lucie asked as she stepped into her bedroom, startled to find a young girl lying in her bed.

The girl giggled nervously. "I'm Sarah."

"What are you doing in my bed, Sarah?"

"It's a long story. Have you got any more of that bread? I'm starving."

She'd never seen the girl before. How could she have got in when her flat was locked? Only the upper window was open for the owl to get in and out.

"Where's the owl?" Lucie asked, suddenly realising that Jake wasn't there.

The girl blushed and hid her head under the covers. Lucie moved over to the bed and, taking a firm grip on the girl's arm, pulled her out of the bed.

"Hey! That's my shirt you are wearing! Take it off immediately."

The girl turned her back and pulled the shirt off over her head.

"And those are my old shorts."

The girl burst into tears and threw herself on the bed face down. Maybe she'd been too hard on her, Lucie thought, sitting next to Sarah and holding her hand.

"There, there. Everything will be all right. Why don't you tell me how you came to be here?"

The girl continued to sob, refusing to face her. Lucie picked her up, surprised at how light the girl was, and cradled her in her arms rocking her backwards and forwards.

"You have lovely hair, Sarah. Do you want me to brush it for you?"

The girl began crying again, saying: "Please stop. You'll be so angry when you know the truth."

Lucie carried the girl across the bedroom and sat her in the armchair. Then, picking up her shirt, which had been abandoned on the floor, she helped the girl put it back on.

"I'll fetch you some bread and jam."

As the girl ate heartily, Lucie pulled up a stool from the kitchen and sat facing her.

"So Sarah, let's have your story."

Sarah pulled at her hair for a moment, not daring to look at Lucy.

"I tired to change," she said.

"Transform, you mean? So you must be from the Patriciat?" Lucie asked.

"No. I'm a foreigner."

"Not another one!" Lucie exclaimed. "Why do you all have to come to me?"

Sarah giggled. "Not another one. The same one."

Lucie looked at her uncomprehending.

"I was an owl before."

But that can't be, Lucie thought, guessing what Sarah meant.

"And what was the owl's name?"

Sarah bit her fingernails looking down at her feet. "Jake," she whispered.

Lucie roared with laughter. It was hilarious. She laughed so much it hurt and tears ran down her cheeks. Each time she thought of the person Jake had transformed into the laughter began again. When Lucie finally calmed, Sarah was making a disgruntled face.

"Is it really so funny?" she said and stomped into the kitchen.

Lucie could hear her pouring herself a glass of water. "Bring me one too, Sarah," she said.

When the girl reappeared carrying two glasses of water, Lucie took the glasses from her and laid them by the bedside. Then she took Sarah in her arms and hugged her.

"You have done very well for your first transformation, Sarah. I think you will be a good student."

And she kissed Sarah on the forehead. "Let's drink our water and then go and have some lunch in the canteen."

As Sarah drank she asked: "Can I really go dressed like this?"

The girl was right, of course. It did look a bit odd but Lucie had no alternative.

"It will have to do for now. We'll go and buy you some dresses this afternoon. Let's go and eat. I'm starving."

"So am I!" said Sarah skipping a dance around the bedroom while she waited for Lucie. And the two girls walked arm in arm towards the Canteen and lunch.

Chapter 4 - Class begins

Landscape

A straight line of poplar trees cut across the fields diagonally from the road. It spanned a winding stream and continued on to the foot of a small hill where it stopped abruptly. Above, on the crest of the hill, stood perched a church. Jenny sighed. She loved the way the country was traversed by lines of force that maintained the natural order. If only she could give form to that force in her pictures, she thought, she could maybe ... she wasn't quite sure what she wanted to say ... contribute to keeping that energy alive, that was it.

"I'm going to start painting again," she announced.

She hadn't really stopped. But the shock of having her fresco destroyed by Leuchtli's henchmen had been too much for her. The painting had taken her nine months to complete. With her boyfriend, Tom, they had organised their whole flat around it and planned to invite friends to admire her work but their plans had been brutally interrupted.

Tom was a journalist in the French speaking part of Switzerland. He'd been investigating about Leuchtli when the same henchmen had tried to get rid of him. Fortunately Jenny and her brother Martin had managed to rescue Tom. Fleeing from Leuchtli and his men they'd met Fran, a young scientist who used to work for Leuchtli. All four had travelled overland to see Jenny's friend, Sally in Avan, and seek refuge unaware that Sally was also in danger from Leuchtli. Now the four of them were on the road again on their way to rescue Sally.

"That's a good idea," Tom said, glancing at her then turning his attention back to the road. "Maybe we can fit your artistic work into the Dream Class somehow," he said.

She smiled at the way he had adopted the idea of the Class and frequently suggested additions and improvements.

"Soon we'll need a whole university to ourselves, just to carry out all our ideas in the Dream Class," she replied, laughing.

"Why not?" he said, "The Dream University."

Martin and Fran were on the back seat. Martin had spent a long time driving and now was fast asleep with his head resting on Fran's shoulder. Fran smiled at Jenny, winking. Jenny was happy for the pair. The short time they'd spent in Avan had been enough for the two to get to know each other better and a strong bond had sprung up between them.

"How much further?" she asked Tom.

"About four hours."

The stream now snaked its way parallel to the road, flanked on its other bank by a narrow path that in turn was lined with hawthorn bushes. Beyond lay fields of rye. She'd seen these forms before in a dream: bright, extravagant colours. She pulled her sketchbook out of her bag and traced the lines in the colours she remembered. The snake was yellow, spotted green. The wider line on one side was deep brown and the narrow line across the water was pale brown. They moved together slantwise across the paper. Yes. She told herself, she would paint again, as soon as possible.

Underground

Drops dripped from the ceiling of the tunnel, splashed on her sou'wester and cascaded in rivulets down her raincoat, forming puddles at her feet.

You remember, Vee, she said. We've been in this situation before.

Not quite the same, was his reply.

Lucky I had a waterproof torch with me, she thought as she rounded a bend in the tunnel.

Light ahead, Vee warned her.

She hurriedly put her hand over the light.

Let me go have a look, Vee suggested.

OK.

Switching off the light she edged closer to the tunnel wall. Just in case anyone peered into the entrance. Suddenly a siren went off followed by shouts.

Police! Vee said when he returned. They're staked out in several cars parked near the entrance. It's raining quite hard.

How are we to get by, she wondered? She smiled at the use of 'we'. Yes there were two of them. Can you sense any other way out, Vee? she asked.

No. I believe this is the only one for miles.

They probably know that. You'll just have to distract them while I get by, she told him.

Let me return first and check there are no others further down the track. I'll also find a good path to follow. If you look over there, he added, you'll find a cave. It is probably drier and you can rest.

Sally had stopped being surprised at the way she knew the direction he was indicating without him being able to point it out. More like one and a half, rather than two, she speculated about her earlier idea. But Vee had already left. That she could feel too.

He was right about the cave. She settled in, ate some dried fruit she'd had in her pocket and wondered if Vee could communicate with her even when he was away. They had never tried, but it could prove useful, she thought.

Leaning back against the rock face she thought about Jenny. She was looking forward to seeing her again. They had had so little time together in Avan before she had had to leave for the funeral. She mulled over the idea of the Dream Class. The thought of it filled her with force and hope. Her wish was that each of them would be able to develop their particular skills and share them with the others, strengthening the whole group. Then one day they might accept other 'students' or should she say 'voyagers'.

She felt Vee approaching. It was like being progressively complete again when she hadn't noticed anything was missing.

You're getting good at that, he told her.

What about the police?

They've set up trip-wires across the entrance. I don't think we can get out that way. However, there's an outcrop above the road a bit further down the track with lots of loose rocks. If we could get by, we could block the road with a rockslide...

Sally interrupted his thoughts: Jenny and the others should be here soon. I don't want them bumping into the police. I'll ring them.

"Jenny. It's Sally. I daren't talk too long. They might trace the call. I'm stuck in the tunnel. There are three police cars staked outside with tripwires across the entrance."

Tell them about the pile of stones, Vee reminded her.

"That's good. How long will it take that way?"

She pulled the phone under her sou'wester to protect it. Even in the cave, the water was beginning to get through.

"Oh. And Vee says to tell you there's a pile of stones perched above the track a little way from the entrance. If you want to have fun with the police." She nodded in response to Jenny's answer. "Bye. See you soon." And she hung up.

Do you think you can find the way back to the turn off where we are to meet Jenny and Tom? She asked Vee.

Sure. I had not bothered with that way out because we had no potholing equipment.

Before we leave, I'd really like to set up a system to trigger those trip wires later, she mused.

I can do that, he replied, pride in his voice.

Hey! Sally exclaimed. You've been keeping secrets from me.

Of course! And after a hesitation, he went on: I've been practicing.

Still got a mind of your own, she teased him.

The lamps on Tom and Jenny's helmets were the first sign she saw of her friends. After a quick hug they hurried back down a side tunnel until it widened out into a funnel shaped cave that stretched up towards the daylight above. Tom fixed a harness around Jenny's waist and hauled her up and out of the cave. She was to check if the way was clear. Then Sally was hauled up and finally Jenny and Sally pulled Tom up. Packing up their tackle, Tom took out his walkie-talkie and called Martin. "First phase complete."

Rockslide

Fran and Martin had made their way up the track towards the cave, stopping when they spotted the overhang Vee had talked about. Fran crept forward to check what the police where doing. When she hurried back she told Martin: "It's OK. They're still sitting in their vehicles."

When they went on potholing expeditions, Martin, Tom and Jenny always took along minute quantities of explosives that could be detonated at a distance if ever their way was blocked or they got

73

trapped somewhere. Martin climbed the outcrop and examined the stones perched there. He calculated the best place to set the charge. He was glad of the courses in explosives he'd taken in the Swiss army. It was about the only useful thing he'd got out of his military service. Checking that the mechanism was set, he climbed back down and joined Fran who was keeping an eye on the road.

He called Tom on the walkie-talkie: "Phase two complete."

"We're at the car and Vee is on his way up to trigger the tripwires."

Thank heavens these radios are encrypted, Martin thought. Taking Fran's hand in his they set off back down the track towards the car and the others. It was at that moment that shouts broke out behind them. At first they thought it was the result of Vee's work but glancing back they saw two policemen running after them. The men hadn't yet reached the outcrop so Martin triggered the explosives and a great pile of rocks and stones settled over the road sending up a cloud of dust despite the wetness of the day. More shouts went up as a siren went off.

"That must be Vee," Fran said panting as they ran down the track.

When they arrived at the car they jumped in and Tom started the motor.

"What about Vee?" Fran asked.

"He's back already," Sally replied.

"Let's get out of here," Tom said accelerating down the path. "If they radio the police station we'll have a hoard of hornets after us."

"Turn left here," Sally said. "Vee tells me it is a short cut. They won't expect us to take that way."

Thank heavens we've got such a powerful four-wheel drive, Fran thought as she snuggled up close to Martin on the back seat.

Who are these people?

"What!" Dieter shouted, bringing his fist down with a resounding crash on the table. "Who are these people?" He wiped the spittle from his mouth with the back of his hand. "I want the whole area sealed off." And he hung up.

So they had an explosives expert and specialists in rock climbing. Who were these people? An organised gang? A network of terrorists? Or just student pranksters poking fun at him? The Grand Master wasn't going to be happy. He shuddered at the thought.

74

The phone rang again.

"What now?" he said to himself. He picked up the phone and announced his name. "When did you find out?" He paced the Count's study that was somewhat more welcoming now that the bodies had been removed.

"So he just disappeared abruptly leaving no signs where he'd gone or how he'd got away?" Dr. Jakob Leuchtli had disappeared. They'd tracked him to a cheap hotel in Basel where he was under close surveillance, but he'd escaped from right under their noses.

"Thanks for keeping me informed. I'll do the same. Bye." Either the Swiss police were incompetent, Dieter thought, or something very strange had happened.

The phone rang once again.

"YES!" he shouted, unable to contain his frustration. The idea of visiting the Grand Master in his Centre unnerved him, not to mention the girl on the run that he couldn't get his hands on. "What do you mean they've got away?"

He gave a hefty kick at the dog's bone that was still lying on the carpet. It sailed across the room and smashed against a wall, splinters falling back noiselessly onto the rug.

"You told me there was no other road out." He listened to the man offering excuses for a moment then cut him short: "Meet me in my office at headquarters in an hour and a half." Weary with these affairs, he turned to leave knowing full well that where he was going would bring no relief: it was time to answer the Grand Master's summons.

In the library

Dieter shuddered. The place gave him the creeps. He could feel the hairs on his neck standing on end. It wasn't simply because the place had formerly been the site of a secret prison for political prisoners where torture had been a common practice. It wasn't just the sinister look of the brethren: dressed uniformly in overalls, their eyes shining bright, their body-builders' bulging muscles, their shaved heads that made them look like convicts and their fervent way of talking. It was above all something unpleasant in the air. It tasted rotten, even though it smelt all right.

He nodded to the man behind the reception desk. It was never the same person, he noted. He was about to step onto the stairs and climb to the first floor where the Grand Master had his office, when the receptionist stopped him.

"The Grand Master will receive you in his library. Do you know where that is?"

"Yes, thank you."

Dieter wondered if anyone knew the Grand Master's real name. He stuffed his hands in his pockets and headed off down a corridor to the right of the main stairs. The library was the first door on the right. He knocked and nervously checked if his flies were properly zipped up.

"Come in Dram."

The Grand Master was seated comfortably in a large armchair examining a parchment with a magnifying glass. Next to him on a low table several other parchments lay open.

"Knowledge is power," the man said. "You know that, Dram, don't you?"

Dieter felt uncomfortable standing in front of the seated man, but there was no chair to take refuge in.

"Let me be frank with you Dram. You have disappointed me. The girl has escaped. You have no idea where she is. With her friends she has made a laughing stock of the police."

Dieter didn't know what was coming, but it would surely not be very pleasant. He flexed the muscles in his back trying to ease the tension building up there.

"But I have decided to give you one last chance."

Dieter wondered what price he would have to pay for this reprieve. "Thank you Grand Master," he said, wishing his voice hadn't betrayed his anxiety.

"Do you know how the Brethren say thank you to me?" the Grand Master asked seemingly innocently.

Dieter shook his head, not trusting himself to speak again.

"They get down on their knees."

Dieter didn't immediately grasp what was meant. When understanding broke over him, he shrank at the thought. Slowly, reluctantly, he bent and knelt before the Grand Master.

"That's better."

And the man returned to reading his parchment, paying no further attention to Dieter. The police inspector felt utterly humiliated but he was powerless to get out of it. Where had he gone wrong? Ages ago probably, when he had mistakenly thought he could gain influence by pandering to the Grand Master's wishes. Some painful ten minutes later, the Grand Master put down the parchment and turned back to Dieter.

"My Centre is currently the focus of an intense investigation by the federal police. I need another month to put my plans into action. You are going to buy me that time."

"How am I supposed to do that?" Dieter asked, daring to speak up as the improbable perspective of intervening at such a high level left him feeling helpless. The man stood, looking down at Dieter as if he were something unpleasant someone had left on the pavement.

"I have arranged for you to be nominated at the head of that investigating commission. All you have to do is delay the work for a month."

Dieter's mouth fell open and stayed that way. How could it be?

"Our audience is over."

Relief rushed over Dieter. He would finally escape the crushing presence of the man, but it wasn't to be.

"Stay kneeling and meditate on what I have said. I will send one of the brethren when it is time for you to get up and leave." And he swept out of the room.

Half an hour later, his phone rang. The noise startled him. He'd sunk into a stupor of pain and distress that had numbed his responses. He struggled to find the phone. Flipping it open, he answered.

"Yes Sir."

It was the Head of the Federal Police Force.

"This is a great honour, Sir. Dare I ask why you chose me?"

He listened silently, desperately shifting from side to side trying to ease the pain in his knees.

"And when am I to begin?"

Using one hand for support, he leaned sideways till his hip touched the ground and he was almost sitting.

"So soon. What about the Sollarini affair?"

He rolled over onto his back and moved his feet backwards and forwards gently trying to ease his knees.

"I will pick up the papers and study them today."

When the man hung up, Dieter continued to lie on the floor. The idea that the Grand Master could orchestrate such a thing sent cold shivers down his spine.

The door opened abruptly and three of the brethren marched in. Stopping in front of him, the one in the centre stared at him with disdain.

"The punishment for disobeying the Grand Master is thirty strokes of the whip. But as you are not one of the Brethren I will be clement: ten should be enough. Take off your shirt."

Dieter stared at him aghast. Had he walked into a nightmare? As he made no move to remove his shirt, the two other men helped him. Then they held him, bent over the armchair the skin of his back pulled tight. He heard the whoosh of the whip as it descended on his back. He heard the crack as it bit into his skin. And he heard his own scream. He felt the pain as if it were miles away. And he fled deep into his mind...

Trapped

The steady tick-tock of the pendulum clock in the entrance hall rivalled with bursts of bird song that entered unannounced through the open windows. All else was silent. A gentle breeze stirred the curtains bringing with it a smell of newly ploughed earth and the more distant odour of pine trees warmed by the late afternoon sun.

Jenny, Tom, Martin and Fran lay on rush mats on the conservatory floor, eyes closed, breathing steady, wakeful. Sally sat silently in a nearby armchair watching them. She would soon need to call them back. For three days they had been working intensely in a secluded house in France that belonged to Jenny's aunt. Sally had concentrated on sharing some of the practical teachings of Rafter and Alo and Naniu, preparing them for their first outing in the Dream Realm.

She regretted the absence of Brent and Keira who had much more experience of the Dream Realm than her. She had spent very little time there, travelling almost immediately to the Reaches. Why had that been so, she wondered? Some people seemed to have developed the ability to be transported directly to the Reaches. Although she had no proof of it, she couldn't imagine Tyrell's uncle and his Clan travelling for ages through the Dream Realm to get to their castle in the Reaches. They must have found a way to go directly to their goal.

Vee chipped in with his own suggestion: Maybe it is easier if they've already been to the place; they can envisage where they are heading.

Vee had been quite quiet these last few days. He seemed to talk less to her when the others were around.

But how did I get there so quickly the first time? she asked him.

Family ties! was his reply. Didn't An come and fetch you?

And then there was the question of her body. It wasn't very convenient to leave her body behind as if she were asleep. It left her completely vulnerable in the Real World.

Brent and Keira must have found a way to take their bodies with them, Vee commented. That would explain why they suddenly disappeared.

"You are going to come back now. Close the door behind you and climb the stairs back up to this room."

She enjoyed taking them on these early excursions. It reminded her of Rafter. She realised that she'd adopted much of his style. He was both firm and yielding: like a Tai Chi master but with words rather than movements. They'd learnt that the Professor had managed to escape the clutches of the detective inspector and had made his way safely back to Avan. When she had spoken to him, he'd advised her to keep the class on the move and away from Avan. He'd also said that Anju wanted to join the class, so Sally was to go and fetch her when things were safer. Anju would be a great addition to their group. She had a sharp mind and had some experience of mystical practices thanks to her father.

Jenny and the others had opened their eyes and were stretching in wide slow movements. Fran yawned deeply, running her hand over her shaved head. Leuchtli had tried to use a sample of her hair to trace her and transmit devastating waves of energy into her brain at a distance with his Machine. If he'd succeeded she would probably have gone crazy like others before her. Cutting off all her hair had foiled his murderous attempts. Despite the fact that they knew Leuchtli was on the run and probably no danger to Fran, she said she would continue to shave her head, as she liked the feel of it. Martin agreed enthusiastically.

"What was that place?" Jenny asked.

"As far as I can gather," Sally replied, "it's a place in between. You can go from there to the Dream Realm, but I suspect you can also go directly to the Reaches from there. And maybe to other worlds as well."

"I like the way the place is malleable," Jenny added. "You can transform it easily with your thoughts."

Fran looked intrigued. "How do you do that?"

"I imagine the place like a canvas and use my mind and my thoughts like brushes and paints."

Sally was delighted. "That's a wonderful idea, Jenny. You must lead our next trip and take us through that together."

Jenny was about to protest when an alarm went off.

"Intruders," Martin said. He'd placed sensors and a camera down the track to warn them if anyone were to come. He checked the monitor. "Three police cars," Martin announced.

They had rehearsed this scenario several times and all knew exactly what to do. They were in the Landrover with all their belongings within a minute. Martin drove then away from the back of the house down a stony track through the forest. They'd deliberately left other car tracks earlier in the day to confuse any followers. The dry weather would help them now. He turned off at the entrance to a quarry aiming to take a track that led further into the forest and beyond to a road.

We can't go down there, Vee said urgently to Sally. There's a roadblock at the end of the track.

"Vee says to stop. There's a trap down there."

Martin brought the car to an abrupt halt.

"What shall we do?" Sally was worried, as Vee offered no solution. They looked nervously back down the track, expecting the police to arrive at any moment.

"Maybe there's a cave in the quarry," Jenny suggested.

Martin drove deeper into the quarry, although he didn't like the idea. They'd be completely stuck if anyone blocked the entrance. They reached the end of the quarry, which looked like it hadn't been used for years, but there was no cave or other place to hide.

Use the necklace! Vee said, breaking his silence.

How?

I'll tell you.

Sally rummaged through her backpack. The necklace was carefully wrapped at the bottom of the bag. Unfolding the cloth around the jewels, she held up the shining necklace she'd received from the Littl' People in The Reaches.

"What are you doing?" Tom asked, surprised at her behaviour.

"It's Vee," was Sally's only answer.

Put it on, Vee said.

She hung it round her neck, feeling it throb against her chest.

"Here they come!" Martin shouted.

Three police cars fanned out in the entrance to the quarry and came to a halt, blocking any possible escape. Car doors opened, and several policemen climbed out.

Mist, said Vee.

The policemen had drawn their guns.

I don't know how? She hissed.

Yes you do.

Two of the policemen had begun striding towards them. The others hung back, covering their colleagues.

"Let's try and run for it," Martin urged them.

"No!" was all Sally could say.

She concentrated on calling up the mist but nothing happened. Vee was silent. Sally felt abandoned and hopeless.

I can't do this, she pleaded with him.

The two policemen had already covered half the distance and were closing the gap rapidly.

Let go, Vee whispered. You are trying too hard. Remember how you changed the ceiling at An's place.

She remembered that all right. It had been so easy.

"Oie! You! Get out of the car with your hands up. No funny business." The policeman stood only a stone's throw away, waving his pistol at them.

"Get a move on," his colleague called out.

"We should do as he says," Martin whispered, moving to open the door.

"Wait," Sally ordered him. "Got it," she said sighing with relief.

A thick mist rolled between them and the police. Sally gasped at what she'd done as her friends all turned to look at her, shocked. Jenny burst out laughing. They could hear the muffled voices of the men calling to each other but none of the police emerged from the mist.

Now take us to your family in the Reaches, Vee ordered.

How?

With the power of the necklace! Call your family.

Sally thought of An, her sister. Conjured up her picture in her head, smelt her characteristic vanilla perfume, felt the smooth skin of her back and the taste of her lips as they embraced.

Nothing's happened, she said to Vee, doubting herself once again.

Look! was his only reply.

She stared out of the window and saw that the mist was rising. She expected to see the police poised to pounce but all she saw was a fifteen year-old girl standing in a clearing in the forest smiling at her. She ripped open the car door and ran towards her. Flinging her arms around An, she embraced her lingeringly on her lips.

Drawing back An said: "Welcome Cian'la, Princess of the Littl' People." And she bowed. "Who are your friends?"

Sally turned to see her friends approaching somewhat timidly. "This is my sister, An." She told them. "And this is Jenny, the artist." Jenny smiled at An who stepped forward and embraced her. "This is Tom, the bringer of news." Tom bowed a little stiffly at which An took his hand and pulled him towards, embracing him too. "This is Fran, who works with bodies and minds." The two girls embraced.

And finally Jenny said: "And this is Martin…" and An completed "… a strong man with a gentle heart." Martin looked surprised but boldly stepped forward and embraced An, saying "Thank you."

Sally wondered if her friends were as bemused by this self-assured young girl as she had been during her first visit to the Reaches. An looked from one to the other, and then taking Sally's hand she said: "In your world, you know my sister as Sally, but here in the Reaches she is known as Cian'la." Putting her arm around Sally's waist, she added: "Come and meet my parents. My mother has prepared a meal for you."

A mystery

He never ceased to wonder at the speed of the old lift. Once the sliding trellis gate had been closed and the tiny button pressed, the narrow lift cage shot up rapidly only to stop abruptly just before his floor and then shudder slowly up the remaining few inches. Dieter pushed back the sliding gate and opened the lift door. With his foot he shunted the box he'd brought from the office out onto the landing, trying to avoid the doors swinging closed on his whiplashed back. Once inside his flat he laid the large box of papers on the kitchen table and poured himself a beer. As a bachelor, he prided himself on the tidiness and the cleanliness of his flat. The Putzfrau came in twice a week. The flat was spacious. His sparing attitude towards furniture accentuated the feeling of space. Not that he spent much time there. His work had him on the road and staying in hotels much of the time.

His phone rang as he was about to settle in one of the kitchen chairs.

"Yes, Dram speaking."

He swallowed a mouthful of beer, listening to the person who'd replaced him on the Sollarini affair. His successor on the case wouldn't have been his choice. He'd have chosen someone younger and more alert. Such a man would never catch Sally.

"Astonishing!" he responded.

Listening with only one ear, he wondered how Sally had managed to disappear with three other people and a large car right in front of three police squads.

"Yes. I appreciate that. Do continue to keep me informed. And a good day to you too."

This was no ordinary girl. He wondered why the Grand Master wanted her so badly. Maybe the papers in front of him would provide a clue. His predecessor on the Brethren case, as they called it, had not managed to muster much information. Many official documents about the group were no longer available, having mysteriously disappeared just when they were needed.

He set aside the records about the house where the group had their headquarters and likewise dismissed papers about lectures given by the GM. GM! He disliked using the abbreviation because it seemed to imply a degree of familiarity that made him shudder. He extracted from the box the synthesis of the case that his predecessor had handed him. In doing so he uncovered an audiocassette. No label indicated the nature of its contents. Probably got there by mistake he thought, hissing as he accidentally leaned against his chair sending a searing pain up his back. The deep gashes were a permanent reminder that he was in the grips of the GM.

He turned the cassette over in his hand, hesitant. But instead of throwing it back into the box as he intended, he rose on an impulse and walked into the living room. He slid the cassette into the stereo system and switched it on. The quality of the sound was dreadful. He slipped a pair of headphones over his head and rewound the cassette to the beginning. It was a man's voice in what must have been a recorded phone conversation. Bad reception drowned out the words for long moments leaving disjointed fragments that Dieter noted on a sheet of paper:

… I can't say … dangerous … bridge to the other place so we can … everybody is to … no! money mainly and some jewels …. we need the ... first ... don't know who the girl is ... escape by the tenth ....

A dreadful scream brought the recording to an abrupt end. Dieter reread what he had written several times. Hadn't that girl Sally not said that the Sollarini case was about a catastrophe on another plain. Maybe that was the other place the man referred to. And the girl could well be Sally. Hadn't the GM said she had something he needed?

He slipped the cassette into his pocket, planning to hide it somewhere safe later. It might prove useful. He returned to the kitchen and opened his colleague's report. Half an hour later he closed the folder with a sigh. There were hints, but no concrete evidence, that the Brethren were involved in a series of major holdups and wide-scale extortion. There was also circumstantial evidence of political intrigues and intimidation. The last point was confirmed by his nomination as head of the current investigation.

Why had the GM said he needed a month to put his plans into action? If only he could get hold of Sally, he was sure she'd have the answer. Leuchtli would have been a second best, but he'd disappeared. Professor Rafter might know. Dieter had to figure this out if he was to have the slightest chance of staying alive. So he decided to leave immediately for Avan to visit the Professor.

Not knowing who was in the pay of the GM, Dieter informed nobody of his departure. He changed out of his suit, donning more informal clothes for the journey, and slipped away with only a holdall for luggage into which he'd carefully packed a few bare necessities. He walked briskly to the station, leaving his Mercedes in the garage. He was sure he would be less conspicuous on a train than a bus or plane. He paid cash for a single ticket to the next main town. From there he'd travel on to Paris and then over into England on his way to Avan. As the train pulled out of the station, he opened a side pocket of his holdall and withdrew a wad of papers: the lectures of the Grand Master. Easing himself into the softly-padded first-class seat so as not to put too much pressure on his wounded back, he began reading.

Entities

Insects buzzed in the warm early evening air. All else was still. Jenny closed the door of An's house quietly behind her and made her way slowly to the nearby forest. She needed to get out. She felt strangely lethargic. Food sometimes did that to her, but An's mother's food had been light and excellent. This was different: it was as if she weren't really herself, not unlike the few out of body experiences she'd had as child. At the time she'd been alarmed when she found it difficult to get back into herself. Unfortunately the fresh air didn't seem to make the difference she'd hoped for. The lassitude continued.

On the edge of the forest stood a half ring of stones that resembled the standing stones she was familiar with in Switzerland although they were much smaller. She rounded the first one, wondering if she'd see any of the elementals she was used to seeing in her own world. Not that she made a habit of looking for such beings. On the contrary, she generally tried to avoid them. The nightmares of her childhood had made her wary, not so much because of the nature of elementals, but because of the way people reacted to her seeing them. All the same, she was intrigued to know if such things existed in the Reaches as well. Opening up her senses, she reached out and cast around the clearing between the stones. To her surprise the place was full of all manner of beings, some sitting or standing sedately, planted where they stood, others scampered around like children or floated in the air, slender and sylph-like. She withdrew her senses with a gasp.

"You should be more careful," a female voice said.

Jenny spun round trying to see who'd spoken. As a child she'd been plagued by voices. It was as if they passed the word that she could communicate with them. As a result, she rapidly found herself besieged by a crowd of voices seeking her attention. This was no disincarnate voice, though. It came from an old woman squatting at the base of one of the stones. Easing herself to her feet with some difficulty, the old woman moved unsteadily towards her. Jenny felt no anxiety. She could clearly sense that the person was benevolent.

"Earth and air?" the woman queried.

Jenny nodded. "Water too," Jenny added. She felt slightly less affinity for fire and ether although she could still see them.

"So you are not so aware of the dragon?" the woman mused.

Jenny looked at her quizzically, not replying.

"Fire," the woman clarified.

"I can see them," Jenny replied. "It's a bit like ether, I am aware of them but I am not so familiar with them."

The woman nodded, thoughtful. "And you feel tired?" the woman asked after a while.

Jenny nodded, surprised at the woman's perspicacity. "Who are you?" Jenny asked, feeling impolite for being so direct.

"A good friend of An's," was all the woman replied.

The old woman turned as a group of sylphs flew around her, tugging emotionally at her to follow them. She beckoned to Jenny to come too and they all set off across the ring. Just beyond in the shade of the trees she discovered a bubbling stream with a group of undines playing in the fresh water. They all turned to look when Jenny and the old woman arrived.

"Can you see the spirit on that flat rock over there?" the woman asked.

Jenny nodded.

"Go stand next to him for a while. He'll tell you something about this place and you'll feel better afterwards. And I'll have An talk to you."

Jenny did as she was told. The spirit towered above her and billowed out embracing her. It was a bit like being in an updraft, not of air though but of energy. When she closed her eyes and settled in to enjoy the feeling, images began to flit through her mind tracing out the history of the site and the beings that lived there. As the story unfolded she felt better and better until she finally opened her eyes and found herself lying on the flat stone, next to the stream. She was completely alone and felt rather cold and stiff. She must have been lying there for quite a while. She tried to recall what she had been told by the spirit but the memories were already beginning to fade just like a dream.

Behold, the Land!

The sun had not yet risen as An led Jenny along a well-used path through the forest. Their destination was a hill that overlooked the countryside beyond. An carried a lantern to light their way. All was quiet except for the occasional rustling of a small creature scuttling out of their way. The birds had yet to wake. Since they had arrived the day before, Jenny had felt subdued. She'd noticed the others, with the exception of Sally, all seemed to be similarly constrained. They talked little, were reserved and, what was the word for it, they appeared "tern" as if a light in them was dimmed. An and her family

86

were charming and made them all feel very welcome, but Jenny had a profound feeling that they didn't belong.

She glanced at An who was walking silently beside her, a cool morning breeze ruffling her short hair. She liked the girl although they had spoken little to each other since she arrived. She wondered why An had suggested they go for a walk together at such an early hour. Could it have been the influence of the old woman she'd met the day before near the ring?

"An," Jenny said, turning to address her companion. "I can't help feeling I don't belong here. It has nothing to do with you or your family. You have all been wonderful. It's the place that doesn't feel right. I feel it in my body. It is as if I didn't have the same connection to the land."

An stopped walking and turned to look at her, a broad smile on her face. "Your grasp of the situation is outstanding, Jenny. I knew you'd understand, that is why I chose to bring you with me this morning," the young girl replied. "When Mia and Jake travelled here – you know them as Keira and Brent - their road led them through the Dream Realm and a long and painful initiation that anchored them properly in the Reaches the moment they set foot here." She began walking again as she continued speaking: "Although that experience was at times pleasurable, it was also very dangerous and risky. We need to find a different way for you four who have travelled directly here."

The occasional bird was awaking around them, sending out brief bursts of song. Dawn was close. The path rose sharply at that point and the trees fell back to reveal a small grassy slope that ended abruptly in a large rocky outcrop. Beyond, the land was laid out like a giant map that progressively took shape and form as the sun neared the horizon.

An sat on the outcrop and indicated that Jenny join her.

"Behold! The Land!" An said solemnly and then remained silent for a while contemplating it. "This outcrop is one of the key nodes in the trelliswork of nature. Lines of force range out from here providing vitality for all you see below us. In your world, a long time ago, wise men and wise women knew these things. It was their task to tend that trelliswork. They also fed energy into the nodes to nurture and protect it. They mostly used music, but music is not your way."

Jenny shifted her attention from the countryside that was coming alive in the first rays of the rising sun, and glanced at An. "I work with paint and pictures," she explained.

"You work with much more than that!" An said laughing. "Your material is the land itself."

Jenny was confused. "I don't understand."

An took her hand. "Feel the rock beneath you. Let your mind sink down into it. Can you feel how warm and alive it is?"

Jenny nodded, trying not to loose her concentration.

"Can you feel the flow of the energy out under that river down there?"

Jenny nodded again. A strong current flowed from somewhere below her, sinking down into the rock and then out across the countryside in line with the river.

"Follow it. Watch how rivulets flow off to the left and the right. Don't follow them now. But move on until you reach that mountain peak over there. It is another major node of the trelliswork."

It was an odd feeling, Jenny thought, as she was both looking with her eyes and her body. She had never before had such a strong perception of the land.

"Now feel the warmth of the rising sun and gently feed that energy into the trelliswork as a gift to the land."

Jenny did as she was told. She was startled to see the land responded immediately with flowers bursting open here and there and trees pushing vigorously upwards, sprouting new leaves. Even the earth itself seemed to sing with pleasure.

She sat quietly contemplating the land both with her eyes and with her inner sense of the Trelliswork, continuing to feed energy from the sun into the ground beneath her. Along the lines of the Trelliswork she became aware of a solid pulse that rose and fell in a slow, dignified cycle that matched that of the sun's warmth.

As she watched, she sensed a faint counter-current that flowed back from the land. It entered her at the base of her spine and rose up her back until it reached the crown of her head where it continued upwards to the sky above. The more she concentrated, the stronger the current became until the sense of self faded and she felt at one with the land below and the sky above. Tears flowed freely down her cheeks, such was the beauty of feeling at home at last.

"Thank you" she whispered full of emotion, not knowing if she was addressing An or the Reaches or the land itself.

An, who'd been silent for quite a while spoke up: "Now you must anchor your friends too. Reach out across the Trelliswork till you find them."

Jenny closed her eyes and plunged into the energy source beneath her and, turning away from the now familiar landscape in front of her, headed back towards An's house. It was easy to identify because it was built on a powerful node in the Trelliswork. She fed a small amount of energy from around her to the node below the house and was surprised to sense three bright spheres glow in the house. Sally and An's parents, she thought.

Approaching closer, she carefully fed energy into the spaces around the spheres until three dark forms became apparent. She knew Martin and Tom well enough to recognise them immediately. She guessed the third must be Fran. Her first attempts at feeding energy to them made their forms even fainter. Alarmed, she stopped immediately. Concentrating on Tom, she moved even closer and examined his nebulous form. He was like a dull brown cloud that retreated from anything that came near. The contrast with Sally's firm oval shape was startling.

There must be some connection between Tom and the land, she guessed, however tenuous it was. Without it, something told her, he couldn't survive. And sure enough, a thin thread curled out of the cloudiness that was Tom and reached down into the Trelliswork. She concentrated on that thread and strengthened it with her energy till it was strong enough to vehicle energy into his form that, little by little, gained shape and clarity, brightening progressively as she dared ease more energy into him.

Something was wrong, however: the more he gained strength, the weaker she felt. She stopped her ministrations for a moment so as to sense the state of energy flowing in and out of herself. In her efforts to help Tom she'd been giving him her own energy rather than being a conduit for the energy flowing into her. Her own sphere, which she sensed now for the first time, had shrunk to a third of its size. Once her own balance returned she continued her delicate work, this time using the energy from the Trelliswork and the sky above.

Intuition told her that it would be insufficient just to boost his energy. There needed to be a two-way flow. She examined him once again, paying particular attention to his anchorage in the Trelliswork. And then, sure enough, she saw what she was looking for: a faint trickle that flowed against the predominant current that she'd set up, moving back down into the Trelliswork. She coaxed that trickle, encouraging it with what might be called caresses as she rotated around it in an infinitesimal dance.

Taking great pleasure in what she was doing, she went on to experiment with adding colours to her movement, letting herself be inspired by the feelings the person gave off: mainly deep blues and bright greens with flecks of brick red here and there. Unlike a normal painting, this 'picture' was in constant flux. When she finally pulled back from Tom, the flow of energy continued of its own accord.

About half an hour later, there were now six glowing spheres in the house. Jenny let out a deep sigh and opened her eyes to discover An watching her closely.

"Wonderful!" the girl said, congratulating her. "I knew you could do this." And she flung her arms around Jenny in a big hug. "Now let's go and have some breakfast, I'm starving."

The young girl's spontaneity delighted Jenny who grasped her by the hand as they helped each other stand up. "Let's go home!" Jenny said, grinning as she realised what she'd said.

"You know, An," Jenny said, unable to contain her enthusiasm as they strode back in the direction of the house, "I could use what I have learnt here not just to nourish and help the land, but also to heal people. I'm sure I could do that." She hadn't given it much thought. The idea had come as she spoke.

"That's an excellent idea: a soul doctor!" An replied, laughing. "I'll have to ask my parents if they know someone who could help you."

Jenny pondered on the expression 'soul doctor'. "I think it would be more accurate to call me a 'connection artist', one who shapes people's connections to the world."

From across the clearing they could hear bright laughter as they broke from the trees and neared An's house.

"See what you've done," An mocked her in a friendly way.

Despite her success, Jenny had mixed feelings about using the Trelliswork to anchor people. She felt uncomfortable with the thought that she'd meddled with her friends without them knowing, even if it had done them good.

"Don't look so glum," An said. "You may well have saved them."

"It's the power of intervening in other people's lives that troubles me. I could just as well have harmed them as do them good."

An stopped walking and contemplated Jenny a long moment. "You are right. This requires more serious thought."

Even if An hadn't transformed into one of her older forms that Sally had told her about, Jenny felt that the young girl was speaking from that more mature stand point.

"We need to find someone with more experience of this work that you can talk to."

An's thought was echoed later within the house as her parents were busy talking about where best to send each of them.

"Martin might work with birds with Lucie." An's father was saying. "She's the niece of the Keeper of Granwich Botanical Gardens and renown throughout the region for her expertise with birds."

Chapter 5 - The Watchers' Dance

Grace

The darkened beams of the roof hung low over the kitchen table. Steam curled slowly up from a large stockpot placed squarely in middle of the table out of which Ma'gina ladled generous helpings of vegetable soup into three bowls. Mia leaned forward and broke off large chunks of homemade bread, laying them next to the bowls on the timeworn wooden tabletop.

A sudden gust of wind cut across the room threatening to snuff out the candles as a striking young woman dressed in a long emerald green robe, pulled tight around her chest just below her breasts, stepped into the kitchen from the garden carrying a bunch of parsley. She hastily closed the door on the darkness that had fallen outside. The wind had whipped her short blond hair into confusion, contrasting radically with the sculptured lines of her high cheekbones and her prominent chin.

Clearly she was someone who knew what she wanted, Mia thought, as she admired the young woman's firm breasts and ample lips. After many months steeped in a profound disgust of anything to do with sex, this re-awakening of her desire caught her by surprise. Embarrassed, she forced herself to look elsewhere. Out of politeness both for their host but also for Ma'gina, Mia reigned in her desire for the woman. On several occasions she had made veiled advances but the young woman showed no signs of being interested in Mia other than as a friend and fellow singer.

"Do you know why my name is Grace?" she asked Mia as she took her seat opposite the two women, sprinkling the fresh parsley on their soup.

Mia and Ma'gina glanced at each other. After two days in Grace's company they were getting used to her enigmatic questions. Mia shook her head.

"Because of the thanks people offer up before they partake of something good, like this meal." Mia must have looked perplexed because Grace burst out laughing. "My parents loved to play with words. I was born at mealtime. They saw me as an offering of thanks but they also saw me as the promise of poise and agility. They imagined me as a dancer. But they were partly mistaken. My future lay not in the gracefulness of my movements, but in my voice." Placing her down-turned hands outspread above her bowl, she sang a short but poignant blessing for the food.

"This place is really beautiful, but I don't understand," Mia said, "why you chose to live in such a secluded spot."

Mia could have sworn she saw a pained looked flit across Grace's face, but the young woman did not answer and continued to eat her soup. Mia blushed with embarrassment as the three of them ate on in silence. She had been unaware that she was broaching an awkward topic. When Grace had finished eating she put down her spoon and laid her hands on the table.

"I was deeply in love with a man who was much older than me," she began. "And although he was attentive and kind to me, he didn't return my love and refused to leave his wife for me." Unwelcome tears brimmed up in her eyes at the memory. "The situation was unbearable, I had to get away. When my aunt died leaving me this cottage, I seized the opportunity and moved here immediately."

"I'm so sorry," Mia replied. "I didn't mean to pry into your private affairs."

"Don't worry," Grace said, as she rose to put her bowl in the sink. "There is another more important reason why I came to live here. My Aunt didn't just leave me this cottage, as you will see tomorrow morning. We will need to set out around five, so I suggest we all get some sleep." She bowed almost imperceptibly and left the room.

Mia lay awake in bed thinking of Grace. She couldn't help being moved by the young woman's story. Although she had not experienced such a disappointment herself – she'd always managed to get what she wanted – she found it easy enough to sympathise with someone suffering from unrequited love. She felt drawn to Grace, but it wasn't just physical attraction. There was more. Sleep came with difficulty as she repeatedly went over all that she knew about the woman, which turned out to be surprisingly little. When Grace knocked at her door, calling out that it was time to get up, Mia had the impression she'd been asleep for only a moment.

The cottage had been built at the edge of a large wood, but their destination did not lie in that direction. Mia was relieved. She didn't fancy making her way through the closely planted trees in the dark. Instead, Grace led them at a brisk pace out into the open along a narrow path across the rolling hills that bordered the other side of the cottage.

As she strode ahead of them, Grace quietly sang a haunting song in a language Mia didn't recognise. Mia hummed along with her, adding the words of the refrain as she managed to make them out. With help from Grace, who repeated some of the words for her, Mia learnt the whole song.

"It's Gaelic," Grace explained, when they finally ceased singing. "The lyrics tell of the love of a stag for a beautiful woman who lies dying at his feet her breast pierced by an arrow, shot by the hunters who mistook her for a deer."

A thoughtful silence fell as the three women marched forward.

On the other side of the rise a startling sight awaited them in the first rosy glimmer of the coming dawn: a circle of odd-shaped standing stones rose majestically from a grassy meadow. Mia counted more than twelve of the larger ones that would have towered above her had she been next to them. None of them were upright or had regular shapes. They may have seemed haphazardly laid out there, but somehow together they hinted at inner harmony.

"As guardian of this sacred place, I ask you to follow my instructions closely." Grace said quietly, authority in her voice. "Do not speak or make a sound lest I ask you to do so."

They threaded their way across the meadow in single file, penetrating between the stones and into the heart of the sanctuary where an intense silence surprised Mia. Grace placed Mia and Ma'gina at precise points within the circle, where they stood waiting. Then she moved away to the centre and turned to face the rising sun. Raising her arms slowly upwards till they formed a 'V' above her, she began to sing. Gently at first, but then with growing strength and intensity, she greeted the coming day.

Mia was astonished to notice that the air around her had begun to swirl in eddies, as if moved by Grace's song. And in the heart of those eddies were all manner of strange sounds that couldn't possibly have come from Grace. How odd! It was as if the standing stones were accompanying Grace in her song. Alarmed and delighted by what she heard, Mia felt an irresistible urge to sing but she curbed her desire out of respect for the sacred place they were standing in. As the sun rose above the horizon casting long shadows behind the standing stones, Grace brought her song to a close and lowered her hands in front of her till they joined each other in what seemed like a gesture of prayer.

"Now you may sing, Mia, if you would like to" Grace said as she led Mia to the centre of the circle. Mia felt intimidated by her surroundings and remained silent for a long moment.

"Try various sounds and pitches," Grace suggested quietly.

Mia experimented with different notes, sending them out like messengers to the stones. At first nothing happened, then here and there her notes came back embellished by the stones they'd met. She discovered that the notes that worked best formed a pentatonic scale, so she improvised a song in that scale borrowing words from the Gaelic song she had learnt from Grace on their way there that morning. The standing stones responded to her song in a strange counterpoint resembling a choir that rang in tight vortexes swirling about her and about her friends.

When she finally ceased singing she felt completely elated. Her whole body rang with an energy she never knew she had. She had no idea how long she had been singing; it might have been hours. Grace, who stood at her side, linked arms with her and led her to Ma'gina who stood unmoving, a look of amazement on her face. All three women left the circle in silence, following Grace to a small lean-to that Mia had not noticed before.

Mia, who was feeling quite hungry after their long walk and her singing exploit, sat down, expecting Grace to spread food and drink on the makeshift table under the lean-to. But the woman stood still, her head leaning slightly to one side as if listening to an unheard voice.

Finally she turned to Mia. "Your song was most beautiful and the standing stones thank you warmly for your gift, but now you must leave. Your destiny lies elsewhere."

Mia was shocked and hurt at this abrupt dismissal. Tears sprang unbidden to her eyes. She thirsted to experience singing in the stone circle again and felt she had a lot more to learn from Grace. What's more, she hadn't completely given up on winning over the girl's heart.

"I would have willingly taken you on as my assistant," Grace added, "but that is not meant to be. You must hurry back to Granwich. You will be needed there."

Ma'gina had already stood and was saying goodbye to her friend.

"May my blessing go with you, Ma'gina. Take care of yourself in the difficult times to come."

Grace withdrew their few belongings from her bag and laid them on the table between them.

"Goodbye, Mia," she added unsmiling and gave a rather stiff bow before she turned and left.

Mia sank back on the bench, resting her head on her hands. She remained so for a long time.

"Come on lass, we need to get going," Ma'gina said impatiently.

"Did I do something wrong?" Mia asked, worry in her voice. "This is all so abrupt." Could the young woman have been put off by her advances? Grace had made no mention of it.

"I don't think so," Ma'gina replied, placing a kindly hand on her shoulder. "As guardian of this sanctuary, Grace has powers you couldn't imagine. What she sees is best not ignored. If she says you are needed in Granwich, then we'd best hurry back there."

Mia rose wearily to her feet, picking up her things from the table and stuffing them absent-mindedly in her bag. In so doing, an object fell to the ground and rolled under the table. Getting down on her hands and knees, Mia found a small locket and chain lying in the grass. She recognised it immediately as the one Grace had worn the evening before. Pressing it to her lips, she smelt the faint, but distinctive smell of Grace that lingered on it. Opening it carefully, she discovered a small piece of stone inside which she guessed came from the standing stones.

Standing once more, she showed the locket to Ma'gina, saying: "Grace must have left it here by mistake."

"The Guardian of the Stones never does anything by mistake. This is her gift to you. You are very fortunate to be able to carry her mark with you."

Mia unclasped it and, with Ma'gina's help, she hung it around her neck, the locket nestling snugly between her breasts.

Inspiration

Sarah lay on her stomach on a makeshift bed in Lucie's bedroom engrossed in a book. She swung her feet gently backwards and forwards in the air in time with a tune she was humming. On the floor next to the bed her new clothes were arranged in neat piles of bright colours. She had discovered to her surprise that she enjoyed wearing dresses, but even if the hem did reach below her knees she felt rather vulnerable in them, so she'd taken to wearing breeches underneath that she fastened below her knees. Lucie had laughed at the sight of her with such colourful breeches under her dress, saying she would set a new fashion in Granwich.

Tucking behind her ears the braids Lucie had woven in her hair that morning, Sarah put down her book with a sigh. She had unearthed the treasure in Lucie's library. The oldness of the tome had attracted her attention, and, opening it carefully, she had been delighted to discover a series of accounts depicting the lives of Lucie's forbearers. She was surprised to learn that Lucie came from the foremost family in Granwich. Her great grandfather had been the architect of the canals that criss-crossed the town, bringing water transport for the first time, further enhancing the prosperity of an already thriving market town known throughout the region for its craftsmen and inventors.

Sarah rolled over, slipped off the bed and skipped across the room to the living room where a pile of paper lay waiting on the table. A deep urge to write had taken a firm hold of her. She hadn't written for ages. It was almost as if she had never written before. The story of the tall, dark-haired man with the prominent forehead striding through the construction site of the canals had sparked her imagination. Lucie, who was busy caring for her birds in the Gardens, had left her several pens and a stock of ink along with the wad of paper. Sarah sat down, placing the heel of one foot on the chair and hugged her knee as she stared at the blank paper. Images jostled to be expressed so she picked up one of the pens and began to write.

She was still writing when Lucie returned several hours later. Pages and pages of neat handwriting were spread across the table, weighed down by an odd assortment of small objects: a misshapen pebble, half a saucer, a giant nut, a silver ring, a tiny doll's head, ... She glanced up briefly at Lucie, who was unbuttoning her coat, saying "Almost finished," and returned to her writing.

She could hear Lucie bustling about in her small kitchen, but paid not attention to her until the story was finished. "There!" she said finally, looking up at Lucie who had just returned from the kitchen carrying a platter of cheese and pickles and fresh bread. "Done it." She stood and stretched and then picked up a shawl that she threw around her shoulders. Lucie had apparently opened a window but Sarah was so engrossed in her writing that she hadn't noticed how cold it had become.

She grabbed a large chunk of cheese dipped it into the bowl of pickles and stuffed it unceremoniously into her mouth.

"You are not always very lady-like," Lucie teased.

Sarah pretended she hadn't heard the comment. Licking her fingers as she struggled to get her teeth into such a large piece of cheese. It wasn't her fault if she'd been a man and then a bird before she became a girl. None of that was of much importance at the moment though as other thoughts were uppermost in her mind. She picked up one of the pages on the table and turned to Lucie saying: "Let me read you a bit." Not waiting for an answer, Sarah began pacing the room, her manuscript held out in front of her and she read:

... The Council hall clock sounded five strokes, a distant welcome to the rising day as James picked his lone way amongst the freshly dug clods of earth along the future towpath of the Granwich canal. His hands plunged deep in his trouser pockets, the tails of his coat trailing behind him buoyed up by a dawn breeze, his thoughts turned to the day's work. He breathed in deeply, savouring the heady aroma of upturned soil, his homeland laid bare by pick and shovel. Only two more miles and they could do away with the makeshift dam that held back the river and let the water course through the new waterways.

Several shouts arose behind him, harsh voices and angry noises directed at him. He stepped up onto a mound of earth and turned to face the pack of commoners surging across the fields and along the canal side. He stood still following their rowdy progress till they came to a halt at his feet.

"We in't paid enough!" one shouted.

"Yer gives us slops fer nosh!" another hurled, waving his fist.

James held his ground, remaining silent a moment longer. Then he raised his arms and the swirling mass fell silent and came to rest, anxious at what he might do.

"Men of Granwich!" he called out, passing an outstretched hand over the crowd. "Are you proud of your town?" Several voices called out that they were, others started to complain again. "Are you proud of Granwich?" More joined the ranks, cheering their support.

Taking them by surprise, he suddenly switched languages and addressed them in the rich idioms of Gran: "You have worked hard and well. Your grand task is nearly complete. The Granwich canal will be the glory of this country. For years to come, all those who live in the town and the land around will reap the riches the canal will bring. And you have done this. You have built this marvel. And you will all benefit from it. Each of you will receive a deed giving you a share in the profits of the canal."

As he stopped to study their reactions, a tall man in the front row called out: "Three cheers for the Granwich Canal and the men who built it. Hip. Hip. Hoorah."

Wild cheering broke out all around as James moved amongst them shaking their rugged hands, receiving friendly pats on the back, greeting the many men he knew personally. As he finally passed beyond the crowd he turned and call out: "Now let's get on with the work. Only two miles to go." And he walked back towards the town.

Sarah stopped her pacing and looked expectantly at Lucie, a flush on her young face.

"Wonderful!" Lucie said as she clapped enthusiastically.

Sarah was struck how much younger Lucie looked when she was so fervent. Tears of joy burst from Sarah's eyes. Ignoring them she ran to Lucie and hugged her.

"Writing is such a wonderful experience," she said returning to the table where she picked up another piece of cheese and breaking off a small piece put it delicately in her mouth, making a funny face at Lucie.

"You know," Sarah added, "as I told that story I had an odd impression." She paused as she figured out how to express what she had experienced. "I felt that I could tell stories in such a way that the story would embark the listener with it."

"How would you do that?" Lucie asked.

"I'm not sure. When I was in the Dream World I was able to move from place to place by telling a story. I suspect it has something to do with the position of the storyteller and how she relates the story to the listeners as if they were actually in the story."

"Well you certainly captured my great grandfather in all his splendour."

Lucie abruptly turned and disappeared into the next room where Sarah could hear her opening and closing cupboards. Then she returned proudly carrying a small picture.

"This is a drawing of my great grandfather at the height of his glory. He was the first Keeper of Granwich."

Sarah took the picture, moved closer to the window and studied the man.

"He's not as tall as I imagined, but his clothes are rather similar," Sarah commented.

"He might not be so tall," Lucie replied, taking back the picture and examining it closely too, "but he was the greatest man of his time. They awarded him the keys of the City because of his part in building the canal and he was later officially named Keeper of Granwich and all his descendants have that honour."

Sarah, who was busy gathering together all her manuscripts, laughed and said: "So you're the Keeper's Daughter."

"I am, but it is more complicated than that. Since my father died, my uncle acts as Keeper till I get married."

The idea of Lucie getting married trouble Sarah. "So you will have to get married?" she asked.

"Not yet. Not if I can avoid it," Lucie replied.

"So you are the most desirable and powerful woman in Granwich," Sarah remarked mischievously, as she sorted her manuscripts into a neat pile.

"I am."

Sarah fell on her knees at Lucie's feet saying mockingly: "Your majesty. But why is your castle so small?"

"You will be punished for your rudeness, young lady!" Lucie said, brandishing her fists. Both of them laughed as Lucie unclenched her fists and helped Sarah get to her feet. "This flat belongs to my uncle who runs the Botanical Gardens. But my house is in the centre of town. It is one of the largest in Granwich. I don't go there so often since father died. But I will take you there to visit it."

"What does it mean to be the Keeper?" Sarah asked.

"Amongst other things, it means you are the head of the Patriciat."

Ballet

Abandoned wet trousers hung forlorn over the back of a broken chair. Men's they were. If their owner had hoped they would dry, he was mistaken. Heavy drops fell from a multitude of tiny holes in the poorly thatched roof and splashed inexorably onto the floor. It had been raining all day. Growing puddles had formed here and there between the broken flagstones.

"You are lucky I was there." The voice was male. The accent was foreign. The tone was one of authority. "And you fighting against me. What got into you? Another minute and you'd have drowned." If anyone had braved the weather to eaves drop, not a word of what was said would have been understood. Nobody in the Reaches spoke German.

"Stand up and put this cape around you."

So there were two of them. A soggy mass rose from a makeshift bed. Unclear about itself, it dripped its way to the cloak. And cast the thing, dry on wet, as instructed, over its shoulders.

"Take him to the cart, Jorg." If there had been a door, it would have opened at that point. Instead, a figure stepped through the empty doorway, hard lines and shaven head.

"This way, doctor." Normally the title would have indicated respect. Here, even the most casual observer would have sensed the scorn.

The bald man took the reins, seated on a bench at the front of the cart. Next to him sat a tall man, upright, shroud in a black coat and cap. Behind, huddled on the floor of the cart lay the doctor in confusion.

Nobody turned to cast a last glance at the ruin they were leaving. Nobody saw the bedraggled eavesdropper slip away into the nearby wood. Nobody noticed the owl perched on a sodden branch, eyes wide open, watching. The reins cracked. The two horses ceased munching grass and took a tentative step forward. Nothing happened. The cartwheels were firmly stuck in mud.

Abandoning the bundle of doubt where it lay, the two more solid men applied their shoulders to cart. Their efforts were rewarded with a good deal of mud and subsequently by the cart moving off down the track. The noise of the rain covered the veiled laughter that broke out in the wood beyond the hovel.

The Waymakers' Inn stood on the outskirts of Granwich. These days, people seldom used the road that ran passed its doors, especially in such weather. People rarely ever came there, as if it had slipped off the map one bad day and never managed to crawl back again. The tall man dressed in black entered first. The bald man followed. The tottering doctor was the last to enter. The three occupied a table near the blazing fire. They had the place to themselves. In a far corner, next to the bar, narrow stairs wound up to the floors above.

"What can I do fer yer?" The voice was that of the barman. Greying at the edges. Suffering from too much alcohol. Somebody had to drink the stuff, there being no customers and all. The German's didn't understand Gran. From under his black hat, the tall man replied in English.

"Your best ale all round."

The barman grunted. Foreigners! Better that than nothing though. Flog 'em a good bed for a few nights, if he woz lucky.

The bowls now lay empty. Spoons licked clean. Fingers too. But the glasses were full, once again. Clothes had dried and the rain was forgotten. Cloaks and jackets had come off, some strewn, others neatly folded on nearby benches. Spirits had risen. The ale helped. The barman had climbed the stairs to prepare three rooms for the night. Floorboards creaked as he moved from room to room above. Huddled together, the three conspirators spoke quietly in German. The silent eavesdropper still didn't understand, but watched all the same, mentally noting everything.

"So what did you find out?"

The ale had worked miracles for the doctor. Even the unseen watchers noticed the shift: he was beginning to take on a human appearance again. And he felt less confused. Feeling was creeping back into his body that tingled in unfortunate places.

"You were right: she is the daughter of the head of their ruling group – the Patriciat they call it – but her father died in an accident. Her uncle acts as Keeper until she gets married and then her husband will become the new ruler of the Patriciat."

Unwanted memories surged into his mind as his cock began throbbing painfully between his legs. He'd completely forgotten the bite. Maybe it was infected. Panic began to take hold of him. That wouldn't do. Not now. He hurriedly swallowed several mouthfuls of ale to deaden his feelings.

"What about the prospect of marriage?"

"She's not interested: more concerned about her birds and the aviary. She prefers to live there in a tiny flat than in her family mansion."

The tall man was about to ask a question when the barman reappeared. "Your beds are ready sirs."

All three rose in unison. Clothes were gathered up. Lanterns distributed. Keys given. Goodnights wished. Breakfast would be at eight. Night had long fallen.

The clock struck eleven. An eavesdropper slipped unseen into the kitchen, exchanged a few words with the barman and disappeared again. Upstairs all seemed quiet. The watchers waited, patient. The doctor slept in borrowed pyjamas. Snoring softly, he dreamt of mermaids with sharp teeth.

Next-door sleep was not on the agenda. The tall German quelled his urge to pace the room. Something was out of joint. The ancient manuscript clutched in his hands offered no explanation. He was not one to let himself be bothered easily. The situation frustrated him. No one was around to blame. No one was there to get angry with.

Jorg had slipped away to clean their boots. Smart guy. Knew how to survive. The boots lay on Jorg's bedroom table untouched. He felt unwell. Couldn't pinpoint the problem. He'd never felt so lost. Not since his initiation into the Brethren. He'd tried meditating. Didn't work, despite his skill at it. He'd tried sleeping. Didn't work either. Depleted! That was how he felt.

If the tall German next door had compared notes with Jorg he'd have known he had the same affliction. But he made a point of not comparing notes with the likes of Jorg. The doctor slept on, untroubled. Watchers and eavesdroppers exchange silent signs as they waited.

Dawn came with hushed exchanges and renewed silent signs. Both the tall German and Jorg were in a sorry state. Neither had slept. Neither was aware that the other suffered. Behind closed doors both struggled with the incomprehensible in silence. Alone, but neither unseen nor unheard.

It was eight o'clock and breakfast called. The watchers had eaten earlier, taking turns in the kitchen. Unknowing, the doctor made his way hungrily down to the dinning room, greeted the barman and ordered a full breakfast. Jorg, unsteady on his feet, negotiated the stairs with caution, his vision blurred. An unseen watcher would have noticed how pale he looked. He remained blind to the fact. No mirror informed him on the subject. Odd that. There were no mirrors in the place.

The tall German didn't get as far as the stairs. He crumbled in a heap on the landing. The thud of him falling had the barman running up the stairs, closely followed by the doctor. Groan was all he could do. Jorg called out in a croaky voice from the foot of the stairs: "Master. Are you all right?"

Interesting, thought the eavesdropper. The heap was beyond replying. Jorg laboured up the stairs, alarmed, sheer willpower at work. What devotion, one watcher thought. The bald-headed Jorg collapsed on the landing next to his Master. The symmetry of the situation pleased more than one.

Side by side the Master and Jorg lay in adjacent beds. Curtains had been pulled. Buttons undone. Shoes removed. Potions given. Temporary poultices applied. The doctor sat nearby, attempting to decipher the manuscript he'd found abandoned on the floor. To no avail, it wasn't a language he knew. The barman had sent out for help. Watchers and eavesdroppers drew closer. Only the faint rasps of hard-won breath troubled the silence. Suspense held all in its tight grip.

An old woman and a young girl climbed the stairs preceded by the barman. The women's clothes were mud-smattered from travel. They spoke sparingly in Gran. Her look resolved, the old woman nodded to the hidden watchers and listeners. She carried a small leather case. Vials filled with tinctures and elixirs rattled softly from within. The young girl studied her new surroundings. She noted a faint smell of decay. Was it the inn or the patients? The three halted on the upstairs landing. A cocked thumb indicated the room to enter. The barman stepped back to let them in.

The old woman crossed the breach and approached the patients. The 'doctor' rose to greet her. The younger one hung back in the doorway. Her eyes flew to the doctor. A look of disbelief flitted crossed her face to be quickly replaced by one of fear. She withdrew quietly, stepping backwards into the shadows, wishing herself invisible, hoping the man had seen nothing. She signed to a watcher to follow her as she retreated to the stairs. The barman was to tell the older woman where she was. The third man was Leuchtli, the sinister doctor. She knew him well. His presence meant trouble, serious trouble. Hadn't they learned he'd drowned? Her knees trembled despite herself. The watcher offered her a chair and a glass of ale. The chair she accepted. The drink she declined. Runners were sent off. Watchers and listeners shifted positions to adjust to the changed circumstances.

In the sick room, multiple pulses were felt, eye whites examined, skin texture plied between finger tips, muscle tension tested, ... The situation was pronounced grave. Tiny drops of potion were forced between tight-shut lips by firm fingers. The patients slept on, their breathing easing with time. The old woman went to the door, opened it slightly and leaned out calling "Bartender!" A watcher made a sign that she acknowledged before turning to the barman. Special help was needed. She alone could not save them. Instructions were given. A potion was handed over. And leave taken. The old woman joined the younger woman in the kitchen and together they stepped out into the rain. A watcher closed the door behind them.

"That was Dr. Leuchtli." Mia told Ma'gina, unable to conceal the fear in her voice.

Pulling a cape tighter around her shoulders Ma'gina asked for explanations.

"I never told you about where I come from or why I was here," Mia said, apologetically.

"Well, now might be a good time," Ma'gina told her. "We have a very long journey ahead of us."

They walked on in silence as the rain poured down around them.

"I come from another world," Mia began.

By the time she'd reached the end of their adventure with the Littl' People and her kidnapping by the band of thugs they'd arrived at a friend's house where Ma'gina planned to procure horses for them. Ma'gina had remained silent throughout most of the story. Interrupting only when she didn't understand something from the other world.

Once they were mounted, their saddlebags bulging with provisions generously provided, it was Ma'gina's turn to tell Mia a story.

"... so you see, Leuchtli threatened to marry Lucie, by force. Lucie is very important to us. Not only because her future husband will be the Keeper of the Patriciat, but because she is a close friend of us commoners."

When she stopped talking Mia voiced her surprise: "But you received a message that he had drowned."

"Someone must have pulled him out of the canal before it was too late."

The two women lapsed into silence, deep in thought. The rain had eased up as they approached the foothills. Clouds were scudding across the sky, driven by a cold wind. The road was deserted. Despite her warm clothes Mia hoped they would soon stop and light a fire. But when she suggested halting, Ma'gina insisted they push on. She wanted to arrive at the Way House before nightfall.

Their path skirted a range of mountains the peaks of which remained shroud in cloud. Mia wondered if it was in these mountains that her adventures with Nala and Jake had taken place. She had been so engrossed in life in Granwich that she rarely thought of her former friends. It seemed like years since she'd been dragged away from the blackened valley where Nala had saved the Littl' People from a cataclysm. She shuddered at the memory of what had happened to her at the hands of those thugs. Instinctively her hand sought out the locket that Grace had given her. It brought comfort. Mia wondered if Nala had made it home to Avan.

"There's the Way House," Ma'gina said, pointing towards to a place at the edge of a forest. Mia peered forward into the gloom and could just make out what she guessed must be a house. As they drew closer, it took shape and form, and grew till she was surprised at the extent of it and all its outhouses.

"We'll stay here for the night," Ma'gina told her. "Tomorrow we'll travel on to visit a friend who might be able to help us with our two mysterious patients."

As they entered the Inn, a lot of noise could be heard coming from the dining room. The Inn Keeper greeted them, leading them down a long corridor.

"We're unusually busy tonight. A whole group just arrived. But I have a couple of rooms for you, if it doesn't bother you that they are rather small."

Ma'gina indicated that that would suit them fine. "We are leaving very early tomorrow morning, anyway," she added. "Meet you in the dining room in a short while," Ma'gina said to Mia as she stepped into her room.

Reunion

Mia followed the long corridor they had taken earlier. She felt much better now she'd washed and changed into a clean dress. She could hear laughter in the dining room at the end of the corridor. There seemed to be many voices, too many. She wondered how many people were staying in Way House. Feeling a little uncomfortable at the prospect of finding herself in a crowd after so much time spent alone with Ma'gina and Grace, Mia slowed her pace and approached the doorway with caution.

As she crossed the threshold, a large round table came into view with about ten people sitting around it chattering in small groups. She glanced at the faces trying to see if Ma'gina was already there when she stumbled on a face so familiar it almost hurt. There, sitting in the middle of the group of people, sat Sally or should that be Nala, a broad smile on her face as she talked to an elf-like girl with sparkling green eyes. Jealousy surged unbidden as Mia stood frozen on the spot, her eyes wide, her mouth slightly open.

At that moment Sally looked up, saw her standing there, recognised her and let out a cry of joy as she rose from her seat and ran towards her. Mia was whirled off her feet by Sally who swung her round and kissed her full on her lips. As her joy at rediscovering her friend calmed, Sally turned towards the group seated around the table and presented Mia.

"This is my best friend Keira, although I believe she's called Mia here in the Reaches. We've been without news of her since she was abducted by a hoard of thugs in the Lost Meadows."

Mia felt her body stiffen at the mention of the ordeal. But she had no time to mull over the pain it caused her for Sally had begun introducing everybody.

"… this is Jenny, a friend of mine from Switzerland. She's an artist. And this is her boyfriend Tom who is a journalist. And that is her brother Martin and his girlfriend Fran."

Mia noted the girl's shaven head and was surprised at how attractive she found the form of her head without hair as a distraction.

"The four of them make up the Dream Class. It was Jenny's idea. We work together sharing our knowledge, in particular about the dream world and the Reaches."

"We want it to become a Dream University" Martin added.

The five of them laughed. Sally continued her round of the table, her arm around Mia's waist.

"And this is An, my sister," she said blowing An a kiss.

Sally's sister: the girl troubled Mia. She was so young and yet she seemed so self-assured and mature. She was also very attractive. But now was not the time for such feelings.

The only person remaining in the room who hadn't been introduced was Ma'gina. She sat apart at a small table in a corner.

"And this is my dear friend Ma'gina," Mia said pointing to Ma'gina, "the person who saved my life, the person who helped me rediscover singing and who taught me how to heal others and so heal myself."

Ma'gina bowed, a broad grin of pleasure spreading across her face. An stood and bowed to Ma'gina.

"I have heard lots of tales of your work, Ma'gina. You may not know it, but you have cured many a friend of mine in Granwich. You are most welcome. Why don't the two of you join us at our table? We were about to eat."

An pulled over two chairs for Mia and Ma'gina to sit on either side of her.

"Maybe Mia would like to sing grace for us," Ma'gina suggested.

Mia was surprised at the suggestion. However at the mention of grace she remembered how Grace had blessed their meal in her little cottage. Stretching out her hands, palms down, as she'd seen Grace do, she let song well up in her using the pentatonic scale she'd discovered amongst the standing stones. When grace was finished, a hush had fallen as all looked in her direction, transfixed by the beauty of her brief song.

It was An who broke the spell, surprising Mia with the question she asked: "Can I see the locket you have around your neck?" When An had examined it, she turned to the others and told them: "Our guest this evening is much more than she seems. It is my pleasure to greet a member of the Sisterhood of the Stones."

Mia had heard Ma'gina call Grace the Guardian of the Stones but this was the first time she'd heard the Sisterhood mentioned. It made her wonder what exactly had happened in the ring of standing stones. Had it been some form of initiation? Was that what An meant? Grace's gift suddenly took on a new significance.

An handed back the chain and locket and helped Mia fix it around her neck. Mia could feel the sliver of stone in the locket between her breasts and it brought her both strength and comfort. Unknown to her it would seem she'd become a member of the Sisterhood of the Stones.

A job to do

Coffee and tea had been served in the Inn Keeper's living room as a favour for his special guests. The change of rooms had led to much laughter as everyone milled in the corridor waiting for the man to open the door. Now everyone was reclined lazily in comfortable armchairs listening to Mia sing. At the invitation of An, she'd sung several songs in Gran. Sally wondered at her friend's ability to learn a new language so quickly. She couldn't remember her being good with languages. Finally Mia had sung a song in Gaelic that she said she'd learnt from Grace, Guardian of the Stones.

Sally had picked a chair that was slightly withdrawn from those of the others so she could observe them better. Mia had changed. She'd lost a lot of weight and although her face shone with the joy of singing, Sally thought she could detect deep-seated suffering beneath.

She looks more mature, Vee commented in her head.

It was then that Sally noticed the scars on Mia's arms and legs. Something terrible must have happened to her, she thought, turning her attention elsewhere, embarrassed, when Mia looked in her direction.

A really deep hurt, Vee whispered.

Ma'gina was seated near Mia. The little old woman smiled at Mia singing, clearly proud of her protégé. When the song was over and the applause had died down, Ma'gina spoke up.

"It is time we told you why we came here. We received an urgent call to treat two men who'd fallen into a coma. Their pulses were very weak, their skin cold, damp and flaccid. I had never seen anything like it before. As their clothes were not like ours and they smelt strange, I guessed they were foreigners or maybe even people from another world. We are on our way to visit a friend who might be able to help us."

Sally noticed the way An and Jenny glanced at each other. The two had said nothing of their early morning trip into the forest. Judging from the excited look on An's face, it must have something to do with Ma'gina's problem.

"Then we are well met," An said laughing. "For you won't need to travel any further. Let me explain," she pursued. "One of the difficulties for people coming to the Reaches from other worlds is that they cannot anchor successfully in our land and they start to get ill. It was happening to Jenny, Tom, Martin and Fran, although not to the same degree as the men you had to treat."

Tom, Martin and Fran looked startled. "But I feel fine," commented Tom.

"You do now, my love," Jenny spoke up, taking his hand in hers.

"If Jenny had not anchored you three, you'd be feeling far from well now." An added.

"I don't understand," Fran said, rubbing her shaved head. "I have hardly spoken to Jenny all day."

"Jenny has the ability to work with the energy of the land," An explained. "She has connected you three to the land. Neither touch nor words are necessary."

"Where did you learn that?" Martin asked his sister, who looked embarrassed.

"She didn't need to learn," An replied. "It came naturally to her once she'd discovered the way."

Suddenly the idea of the Dream Class had taken on a tangible form in a most spectacular way, Sally thought. She was delighted at the news.

"Congratulations, Jenny," Sally said. "This is one of the first of many successes of our Dream Class."

Ma'gina waited patiently for the enthusiasm of the young ones to calm before she continued. "Then will you come with us, Jenny, and help these two men?" Jenny looked at An, who nodded almost imperceptibly. "I will," was her reply.

"We could all go, we were all headed for Granwich anyway" Tom added.

"That may not be such a good idea," Mia said, the tone of voice putting an immediate dampener on their ardour.

"Why not?" An asked.

110

"Because those two men were accompanied by a third man some of you know quite well: Dr. Leuchtli!"

Sally gasped, horrified at the thought of the hateful man who'd nearly killed her with his insane experiments. Fran rose terrified, glancing all around, looking as if she was about to run for it. She only calmed when Martin took her in his arms and whispered soft words in her ear.

"So you understand why Sally can't go near those men," Mia concluded.

"I don't need to be with them physically to treat them," Jenny explained. "Anchoring is done from a distance."

"All the same," Ma'gina said, "it would be too risky."

Sally could see her friends were torn at the prospect of being separated.

"Whatever you decide, I have to return to Avan to fetch Anju who wants to join the Dream Class," Sally said.

Ma'gina stood and addressed them all. "Here is what I suggest. Jenny and Tom join Mia and I and return to Granwich. You cure the two men, Jenny and then the two of you stay a while with Mia and I. Sally returns to Avan and brings Anju to Granwich so Jenny can make sure she is correctly anchored in the Reaches. An might like to accompany you when you come. There are people in Granwich I'd like you to meet, An. And finally I suggest Fran and Martin visit the Littl' People. An could guide you there, if she agrees. What do you think?"

"Is it a good idea to send An off across country? She's so young," Mia commented.

An startled them all, except Sally, by transforming into an older woman. "Would this form do better?" An asked mischievously.

"So you are from the Patriciat?" Mia retorted.

"That is what they call people like me in Granwich," An replied, explaining the word to the others once she'd transformed back into the young girl they were familiar with. Sally saw Mia stare questioningly in her direction.

Ma'gina interrupted their discussion: "So do you agree?"

They did, although Sally could read some misgiving on faces here and there. No doubt her friends were apprehensive about confronting the unknown.

"Good!" Ma'gina concluded. "We need to leave very early tomorrow morning if we want to save the lives of those two men."

"We must find out why they are here. If they are with Leuchtli it is not a good sign." Sally commented.

"Don't worry," Ma'gina replied, turning to Sally. "People are keeping an eye on them."

Reassured, all rose and prepared in their different ways to go to bed. Sally wondered at the strength and character of Ma'gina who, for all her little size, was a born leader.

After emotional leave-takings under the porch of the Way House, the journey to Granwich was uneventful. The rain had stopped and the wind dropped. Jenny and Tom took it in turns to tell Mia and Ma'gina about all that had happened in their world: how Leuchtli had tried to kill Tom; why Fran's head was shaved; what happened at Tyrell's funeral; how they'd been chased by the police; and how they came to be in the Reaches thanks to Sally and the necklace. When their tale was finished, Mia told them about Granwich, in particular about the commoners and the Patriciat. And Ma'gina told them about the Apotheka.

They stopped within sight of the Inn and Jenny slipped away into the nearby wood to concentrate on the energy of the land. When she returned she told them that she had succeeded, that the two men should be OK now, although she said she felt they may never be really at home in the Reaches. They withdrew back down the road to wait for a messenger to come from the Inn.

While they waited, they speculated about why the three men had come to the Reaches. Their quiet conversation was interrupted by a man running down the road, calling out to them.

"They've disappeared," he said, breathless, when he got close enough.

"What do you mean 'disappeared'?" Ma'gina asked.

"They have disappeared leaving no trace."

"But couldn't they have slipped away without you noticing?" Mia asked.

"Impossible! One of us was watching them all the time. The slightest move and we'd have seen it. No. One minute they were there and the next they were gone."

Chapter 6 - The Necklace

A bright light

Brilliant sunlight streamed in through the open windows of the Common Room. The young girl standing on her own in the middle of the room must have been the most striking woman in the Department, he thought. Tall and slender, she wore a pale green sari that offset her short pitch-black hair and her sparking blue-green eyes. A sea of sloppy greys and smudgy browns milled about her, un-noticing and un-noticed. The girl had closed her eyes till they were mere slits and was peering around the room at the academics chattering quietly in small groups. Too young to be one of the teaching staff, too young even to be a student, yet clearly composed and confident amongst a crowd of professors and researchers, he wondered who she could be.

As he observed the young girl and mused about who she might be, he noticed that the chatter in the room had decreased and he felt a presence next to him. Turning to see who had caused the stir, he was confronted with a tall man dressed in a grey suit over which he wore an academic gown.

"To what do we owe this pleasure, Inspector Dram?"

Dieter immediately recognised the Professor he'd sought to interrogate about the mass death of the Sollarini Clan.

"Good day, Professor Rafter," he replied, and, not wanting Rafter to get the better of him, he immediately asked: "Who is that delightful young woman over there in the sari?"

Rafter waved to the girl who waved back and came to join them. "This is Anju, the grand-daughter of Professor Outman, the world renowned specialist on Chaos Theory."

The girl scrutinised Dieter with piercing eyes.

"Anju," the Professor continued, "Meet Inspector Dieter Dram. He is the man who is investigating the mysterious deaths of some thirty people in a Castle in the Black Forest in Germany."

Dieter shook her outstretched hand. Her grasp was firm, her skin soft and warm. "Delighted," he managed, feeling strangely moved by the girl.

"And how is your investigation going?" she asked amiably.

"I don't know," he lied, for once feeling uncomfortable about doing so. "I am no longer responsible for that case."

Rafter excused himself, smiling broadly, and went to speak to colleagues across the room leaving Dieter alone with the girl.

"It always intrigued me, Inspector," she said still studying him, "how detectives sift through seemingly unrelated pieces of information until some of those pieces suddenly fit into place providing a picture nobody had seen before. That cusp must be an almost magic moment."

He guessed she must be about fifteen, but her grasp of the world around her and the language she used went way beyond her age. He decided to do battle with her.

"Do you like to dance?" he asked, trying to throw her with his unexpected question.

"I love it," she replied, unperturbed. "And you Inspector, do you get much chance to dance?"

She's good, he thought. He appreciated how she shifted the emphasis in redirecting his question at him. It was his turn to move, but he was not sure where to go next. She didn't allow him any respite.

"How do you think all those people came to die?" she questioned him.

"I've no idea," he replied, surprising himself by his honesty. She waited. He didn't want to continue, but she just stood there smiling at him completely self-confident. He had some difficulty hiding his discomfort.

"To be honest, I find it incomprehensible," he replied.

It was indeed, he thought. Nothing that he'd unearthed really made any sense of the whole affair.

"Why don't you tell me about it? Maybe a fresh perspective might help."

Alarm bells sounded in his head. Was she bewitching him like Rafter had done during the interrogation Dieter had tried to carry out in Germany? It didn't feel the same. For one, he felt quite free to act. And what's more he could make out no struggle within himself like he'd experienced with Rafter. Yet here he was on the point of confiding in a complete stranger.

"Maybe you'd prefer to talk outside," she suggested. "Hoyt Park is a most beautiful place for a stroll and a talk."

Why not he thought? Maybe she knows something about Rafter and Sally. You're just trying to convince yourself, his conscience berated him.

"I must talk to Professor Rafter," he told her. "It's urgent."

She glanced in the direction of Rafter. "I'm sure he'll be delighted to talk to you. But right now he's got to chair a meeting of the Department."

All right, he thought. Let's try to regain the initiative.

"OK. Let's go."

"Excellent" she said. "If you'd like to make your way outside, I will join you on the bridge opposite the entrance. I just need a quick word with the Professor before he leaves."

And she was gone, weaving her colourful way through the thinning crowd to where the Professor stood near the entrance to a large meeting room. She'd out-manoeuvred him again, he thought laughing to himself as he turned to leave the room and headed for the exit.

In the park

"It was Madame Blavatsky who designed the building," were her first words as she drew along side him on the bridge.

Her voice startled him. He was deep in thought, wondering what he might learn from her.

"I love the way the river flows around the curves of the Theosophy department," she pursued. Not giving him any time to reply, she linked arms with him and led him across the bridge and into the park. "So how did you come to be given the Sollarini case?"

No preliminaries, he thought, straight to the point. Well not exactly. She'd chosen a slightly tangential route to get there.

"Because I was the best," he said laughing, pleased that he'd managed to shrug off her gambit.

"Come now Inspector. You don't need to play with me. I have no doubt you are good, but there must have been another reason."

He suddenly saw himself from the perspective of someone watching them from a nearby bench: a middle aged man strolling though a public park arm in arm with a fifteen year old girl talking earnestly together.

"You realise there are things I can't tell you or anyone else," he said adopting a slightly paternal air, wondering how that would work with her.

"That's no bother. Tell me what you can. And we'll see what we can do with that."

They were moving closer to the sea. Not only was there a salty tang to the air but also the number of gulls circling overhead had greatly increased.

"Just give me a fragment," she suggested.

He saw the opportunity for an opening in her defence and jumped at the occasion. "On the mantelpiece in the study of Count Sollarini I found a visiting card of a man called Leuchtli and on the back of the card the Count had written two names: Rafter and Sally."

There was not the slightest hesitation in her stride or her conversation at his revelation.

"I believe you met both of them in Germany. What did they have to say?"

Clever, he thought. A damn good move.

"I was unable to talk to them much as they both left before I had finished my questions."

As he expected, she ignored that avenue of thought. Instead she asked: "What connects the Count to these three people?"

"A young man called Tyrell," was his succinct reply.

She continued walking in silence, waiting for him to go on. He took the opportunity to think over the connections between the young victim and the other three. As he glanced absentmindedly at rhododendrons that lined their path, he voiced his doubts.

"The links between them and the late Tyrell Sollarini are intriguing. For example, Tyrell was a close relative of the Count, yet the Count kept him locked in his room. On the mantelpiece in the Count's personal study there was the visiting card I mentioned from a certain Swiss doctor called Leuchtli. Apparently the doctor was working here at the university with Professor Rafter. Not surprising then to find Rafter's name written on the back of the visiting card. But there was also a girl's name: Sally. Both Tyrell and Sally were assistants of Professor Rafter. Grasped in Tyrell's hand on his death bed, we found a note from him to Sally indicating that she might understand why he'd died."

He stopped abruptly realising that he'd been thinking out loud. "Did you know Tyrell?" he asked, letting go of her arm and turning to face her with his back to the University.

"I met him once at a dinner with Professor Rafter. The young man seemed distraught and somewhat disoriented. I remember him shovelling food into his mouth in a way that was hardly polite."

"And I suppose you know Sally?"

"She's a very good friend of mine. I have known her for a number of years, although we don't meet very often as I live mostly in India," Anju answered.

Didier thought the time had come to play a key card. "And do you know where she is now?"

"Right behind you, Inspector!" a voice said.

He spun round, startled. He'd been unaware that anyone had crept up on him, so much for his finely tuned senses. There stood Sally, wearing what looked like a medieval costume, grinning at the effect she'd had on him.

"Sorry if I made you jump, Inspector," she said, shaking his hand. "Professor Rafter told me you were in the Park with Anju. So I came immediately."

On the defensive, he retorted: "So you came to save her from me and spirit her away like you yourself disappeared in Germany."

She laughed. "I had no fears for Anju. She is quite capable of looking after herself," she said, as she greeted Anju with a kiss. "I was more worried about you, Inspector," she added, laughing. "But I admit that I do have to spirit her away, as you put it. We have important things to discuss. I'm sure Anju will agree to meet you later and pursue your discussion."

Anju nodded her approval. Hand in hand, the two young women started to move away, back to the University. Glancing over her shoulder, Anju called back to him: "Maybe there is another person in the equation who has yet to become apparent."

And they were gone, leaving him alone amongst the rhododendrons watching them disappear across the distant bridge and into the waiting Department building.

If he'd been a child he might have stamped his feet in frustration. Instead, he turned his back on the two of them, crossed the local railway line and walked the short distance to the sea. It would help clear his thoughts.

The Promenade was almost deserted. Along the beach the occasional dog owners walked the water's edge, their footprints washed away by each successive wave. Didier was about to make his way down the steps to the sand when his phone rang.

"Inspector Dieter Dram," he said automatically.

"Good day Inspector." The voice was familiar, but Dieter didn't immediately recognise it.

"Where exactly are you Inspector?"

Of course, it was the GM. He sounded somehow odd – what was the word for it? – 'diluted', that was it. Dismissing the idea of a walk on the beach, Didier retreated to the nearest of the benches that lined the front and sat down.

"I've heard your new boss has been looking for you."

As Didier had suspected, he was being closely watched.

"You asked for me to delay the enquiry. That's what I am doing."

Unable to hide his irritation, the GM responded: "You need to be credible, Inspector, otherwise people will begin to talk. What are you doing anyway?"

"Following a hunch."

"And what's her name?"

The question surprised Didier, for he wasn't aware that he had a reputation as a womaniser.

"Sally."

"Ah! So you've found the girl." The GM sounded excited at the news.

"Yes. She's here at the Avan University. She just arrived."

"Good work, Inspector." And the GM added as an after thought: "Make sure you're back at work by tomorrow." And he hung up.

Attack

The bay window in Professor Rafter's study opened over the River Avan providing a fine view of the town centre and the cathedral across the water. Sally and Anju had pulled two armchairs under the window, both reclining at ease, sipping beer from a bottle. The Professor sat opposite them, astride an upright chair his arms crossed, leaning on its wooden back.

"... and so Jenny was able to anchor them in the Reaches and avoid the whole Dream Class getting ill," Sally said.

She had already explained much of what had happened to her and the members of the Dream Class despite the innumerable questions Rafter and Anju had fired at her.

"I still can't understand why Leuchtli was in the Reaches. It doesn't make sense. He hardly seemed the adventurous type," Rafter said puzzled.

"He's quite cowardly, if you ask me," Sally said with vehemence, adding: "He preferred to send others to take the risks instead."

"If his being there is so out of character, it looks like someone or something forced him to go," Anju put in.

Rafter stood and leaning on his chair back, addressed Anju: "I think you're right. Do you still want to journey to the Reaches?"

"More than ever," was her reply.

Rafter was about to say something but instead he glanced over his shoulder at the door. "Someone is coming. I suspect it is the Inspector. Do you think we can trust him?"

Sally shook her head, looking a little worried. Anju however nodded, grinning meaningfully at Sally.

"Come in Inspector," Rafter called out as a knock was heard on the door.

Sally watched the man closely out of the corner of her eye as he stepped into the room and noticed the two girls at ease sipping bears. Greeting the Professor, the Inspector said: "I need to speak to you urgently, Professor." Glaring at the girls, he added pointedly: "In private!"

Sally wondered if Rafter would ask them to go.

Maybe you should offer, Vee suggested.

"Would you like us to leave Professor?" Sally asked, deliberately not looking at Dieter.

"Thank you, Sally. I suggest the Inspector briefly outline what he wants. Then we can decide if your presence would be useful or not."

Turning to the Inspector, Rafter invited him to take a seat, saying: "Do you agree?"

He's not going to sit down, Vee whispered in Sally's head.

She nodded almost imperceptibly in agreement as if Vee were really in the room talking to her. And sure enough, the Inspector began pacing the study.

"I have two very dangerous cases on my hands. One wrong move and I'll get killed and maybe others will die too."

Nobody spoke as he continued to pace the room. When he got closer to Sally he stopped in front of her somewhat threateningly and said: "You probably have the answers I need, but I don't think you will tell me what I need to know."

Sally looked up into his eyes. She thought she caught glimpses of anger and despair, a mixture that irritated her intensely. But she chose not to speak. It was true she had been angry with him for quite a while, though she could no longer recall why.

This situation reminds me of you and Tyrell, Vee commented, almost to himself.

Don't you start, she retorted. Struggling to keep her annoyance from showing, Sally turned her back on him and looked out of the window.

The Inspector must have moved away because his voice came from across the study. "I have two questions to ask you all. The first is: How did the people in Sollarini's Castle die? The second is more difficult to explain. I am investigating a German sect ... called the Brethren ..." A violent bout of coughing interrupted him. "Their leader asked me ... to hand over ... Sally," he continued, gasping as he struggled to breathe, "... to him ... I want ... to know ... why ..."

Alarmed both at what he said and the way he was trying to say it, Sally spun round just in time to see him collapse in a heap on the floor. All three of them rose in unison and gathered around his prostrate body. Rafter felt his pulse.

"Shall I call an ambulance?" Anju asked.

"Do," was all Rafter said as he tried to bring the Inspector round. "He's out, but I don't think he's in danger."

With Sally's help, he made the man comfortable on the carpet and covered him with his jacket. All three sat back into their respective armchairs and continued to stare at the unconscious police inspector.

"When I questioned him in Germany, a powerful force stopped him answering. I suspect the same force is at work here. Someone doesn't want him telling us about this Brethren Sect."

When the ambulance arrived, Rafter offered to accompany the Inspector to the hospital suggesting that Sally and Anju prepare their journey to the Reaches.

Out patients

Rafter was fascinated by the way life continually bustled in the hospital without ever being noisy. He wondered if the nursing staff received special training so as to go about their work quietly or whether it came from an innate respect for the ill and suffering. He sat on a chair by the Inspector's bed waiting for the doctor to come on his round. A series of thin tubes and brightly coloured wires cascaded over hooks hung from the ceiling, making their way to drip-feeds and electrodes and an oxygen mask. Dieter's breath rasped in his throat as he struggled to breathe. Rafter watched the rise and fall of the unconscious man's chest, reassured at the relentless effort his body put into pursuing life.

Outside the cubicle, a woman in her forties wearing a regulation hospital nightshirt shuffled back and forth along the corridor, pushing a wheeled support bearing various apparatus that were attached to her body by a bunch of wires. A young assistant nurse hurried from room to room, dispensing drugs, administering injections, replacing drip feeds, taking blood samples, consulting temperature charts, … Yet despite her busyness she found time to exchange a few friendly words with each patient as she went about her work. She shot a smile in his direction as she passed the cubicle where Dieter was installed, pushing a trolley piled up with a stack of patients records, her ponytail bobbing from side to side at the sway of her walk. Sometimes Rafter wished he were younger.

A bevy of serious young men and women in white coats crowded round the doctor as he entered the cubicle. He shook Rafter's hand and enquired about his relationship to the patient.

"He was visiting me at the University when he began to have difficulties breathing. Then he collapsed," Rafter explained.

The medical students had fanned out at the foot of the bed while the doctor placed his stethoscope on the Inspector's chest.

"There seems to be no obstruction of the lungs," he informed his young audience. He shifted the oxygen mask and peered into the Inspector's mouth with the aid of a small torch that he extracted from the lapel pocket of his white coat with a flourish. "No signs of infection or unusual growth, although the throat appears to be constricted," he continued. Rolling back the patient's eyelids he shone his light into his eyes as he examined them. "No untoward dilatation of the pupils." He briefly felt his pulse, shaking his head. "There is no apparent physical cause for his condition," he concluded.

Turning to Rafter, who had retreated against the wall to leave room for the doctor and his entourage, he asked: "Is there anything that might have frightened him?"

Rafter hesitated over how to answer. "I had the impression that something was stopping him saying what he was trying to tell me."

The doctor replaced the torch in his lapel pocket and folded the stethoscope into the ample side pocket.

"Hypnosis," was all he said.

"I don't understand," one of the bright students spoke for them all.

"I once had a patient with similar symptoms. It turned out the person had been hypnotised and told not to say a particular word. Every time she tried to use the word, it caught in her throat and almost strangled her."

Rafter had suspected as much, but he wanted to be sure there were no physical problems first. This was a case for Alo.

"I have a friend who is a specialist in hypnosis," he told the doctor. "I'll ask him to come and see if he can do anything."

The doctor was already heading for the door as the students filed out. "Good," he commented. "In the mean time, I'll prescribe something to help relax his muscles. That should help." And he left.

The pretty nurse with the ponytail entered the cubicle, swaying her hips as she negotiated the narrow passage between the bed and the visitor's chair.

"I just need to give him an injection," she explained, unwrapping the syringe.

"OK. I'll step outside and phone while you do your work," Rafter replied.

"There's a phone just down the corridor if you need one," she told him, smiling deliciously as she flicked her nail against the syringe to ensure that there were no air bubbles trapped in the needle.

The phone was further down the corridor than he'd imagined. It was one of those old fashioned contraptions that only existed in such out of the way public places.

"Alo?" he asked, as the coins fell into the waiting metal box.

Alo was a well-known shaman who lived in Avan. He and Rafter were part of a small circle of friends who had helped Sally and her fellow voyagers on their first journey to the Reaches. Rafter explained the situation briefly to his friend over the phone, and Alo said he would come immediately, although he had misgivings about using hypnosis on someone in a coma.

That's the ticket

The massive doors to the castle had been replaced by a single pane of glass tinted slightly green in which a narrow glass door lay open.

"This way, Sir," an aging attendant said beckoning to him, his back humped, no doubt from years of stooping to greet visitors. "Tickets down there," he wheezed.

As Dieter turned his back on the man he heard him break into a prolonged fit of coughing. A wide corridor led down a gentle slope of cobblestones. A thick glass wall from floor to ceiling ran almost the whole length of the corridor dividing the passage in two. Only here at the beginning of the corridor did he have a choice: left or right.

"To the right!" the old man said, almost choking on the words.

And candles fixed to the walls spluttered with him, giving off thin columns of black smoke that rose to the ceiling where they curled around awaiting stones and hung silently like a pack of predators.

Dieter didn't get far. A long queue of silent people stood waiting to gain access to the main building. The air was thick with cheap perfume mingled with assorted body odours: animal, fish, vegetable, … Bile rose in his throat leaving a bitter taste in his mouth that caused him to cough uncontrollably.

A squat man with a thick neck and massive hands turned to stare threateningly at Dieter. The man cleared his throat making a noise somewhere between a cough and a gurgle, spat copiously at Dieter's feet and then wiped his lips with the back of his hand. Disgusted at the slimy splodge steaming in front of him, Dieter looked away.

Examining the tiny sheets of paper stuck to the glass wall, he had to lean close to read what was written. Even then he could barely make out the words that seemed to shrink the closer he got. In addition to the visit to the Castle, he managed to decipher, they offered treatment for people with lung problems. It was a long-standing tradition in the place. The price was exorbitant. It was the

123

only word written large enough to read with ease. It was so big, he couldn't believe it. In the mean time a crowd of people had joined the queue behind him bringing reinforcements if ever the smells threatened to ease off.

No one spoke. The only noises were the spluttering of the candles, the slow shuffling of feet and the frequent cough or wheeze. Imperceptibly the entrance drew closer, till finally it was Dieter's turn to pay. The prohibitive price made him hesitate. He wasn't even sure he had enough money on him. His musings were interrupted by a sharp prod in the ribs. Turning to see what the trouble was, he was shoved violently against the glass partition knocking the breath out of him, as the remainder of the queue shuffled hurriedly by and through the door.

Bent over double he tried to recover his breath as he succumbed to wave after wave of spasms in his lungs. Desperate for air, he thought he was going to die. But with time, the waves retreated leaving him cast ashore, run aground in front of a firmly closed door. He was alone in the corridor. Pulling himself upright with the help of the door handle, he tried to push his way through. But the door wouldn't give. He was too late.

Desolate, he turned round and plodded wearily back up the corridor to the entrance. Stretching out his hand to open the small door in the massive glass pane, he suddenly realised that the door was gone. Well not completely gone. It had shifted to the other side of the corridor but access to it was blocked by the glass wall that divided the corridor. Where before he'd been able to choose which side he wanted to use, now the glass wall stretched right up to the front pane. There was no longer a way out. He sank to the ground, his back against the glass wall, his knees pulled up, leaning his arms on his knees and his head on his arms. A distant voice in his head invited him to relax and close his eyes.

Out for the count

"… Turn around now and look behind you. A path stands there, a long path that stretches away into the distance. Begin walking along it. Take your time. You are moving back in time. Slowly at first, ever so slowly, then little by little you move quicker, slowly you go quicker, and the further you move away the closer you come and the faster you go. Year after year whizzes by, and further and further you go back. Twenty, nineteen, eighteen, sixteen, fifteen, … one birthday

124

after another ... twelve, eleven, ten, nine ... and you continue on backwards, but slower now, slowly slower you go ... seven, six, five ... until you finally come to a halt. And halted, you turn round, you turn round several times until you are facing back the way you came, the way you must go. Your eyes are wide open, your ears, your nose, your mouth, your skin, all your senses are alert. And you begin to walk, slowly, alert and open. You are on the look out for something, something familiar, something deeply familiar, a voice speaking to you. And at each birthday you stop a moment and turn several times, your eyes wide closed, looking all around, listening for that something. Then you move on, turning at each birthday until you come to that familiar voice. Soft and strong, it speaks deeply in your head, persuasive, convincing it speaks to you and only you. And you begin to turn on the spot, your arms outstretched, slowly at first, then faster and faster. And as you turn, a whirring sound begins quietly and grows, beginning from your heart, flowing out to your outstretched hands and moving beyond to fill all around. No place is free of the sound. It enters every empty space. It empties all the spaces that are full. Till only the whirring exists. All else if of no importance. Just the whirring. Listen to the sound of your body turning and let go of all else. Feel yourself sinking as you rise and fall with the music of your body. The deeper you go the higher the music rises till all is dark and silent. Peaceful. Reposing. Relaxing. Your whole body is relaxed and you feel good. And in a moment I am going to count from one to three and on three you will awake feeling relaxed and full of energy, refreshed and full of energy, ... one ... two ... three."

Alo sat back in his chair by the bedside, slid his hands deep into his jacket pockets and studied the sleeping Inspector. Dieter's eyelids began to flutter as if they were about to open but then he coughed violently and sank back into the coma.

"It worked once on another patient. There was a slim chance it would work with him. The post-hypnotic commands must be too deeply ingrained."

Rafter nodded in agreement. "Someone will have to go into the Dream Realm and bring him back," the Professor commented.

Alo agreed. "Could Sally do it?"

"No!" The Professor was emphatic. "Her relationship to the Inspector is unclear and what's more she should get back to the Reaches."

"Then I will go," Alo offered.

"I think that would be the best solution," Rafter agreed. "I will let Sally and Anju know where you have gone."

Their discussion was interrupted by the arrival of the Doctor making his rounds.

"We tried hypnosis," Rafter explained. "But as you can see it didn't work. We are now going to try to contact his mind in other ways. Can you keep him under observation and relaxed for the next few days? It would be better if you didn't give him drugs that stimulate the mind or produce hallucinations. That might make our work more difficult."

Rafter was surprised and pleased at the way the Doctor readily accepted them and their ways of working. He mentally noted the man's name for future reference and wished him good day.

Gone

Two bulging rucksacks lay neglected on the bed. Unfastened, their contents had spilled out onto the floor revealing assorted underwear, warm socks and a small selection of books. In the kitchen, no one had bothered to pick up a chair that had been clumsily knocked over. Fragments of a cup were scattered over the otherwise spotless floor. Sally might not have been as well organised as Keira but her flat was invariably clean and tidy. Something was out of joint. He could smell it. The place reeked of males: aging sweat, dried semen and cheap alcohol. Not at all smells you'd expect to find in Sally's place. The girls should have been there preparing for their journey to the Reaches. But they'd gone, spirited away by unknown forces.

A wave of weariness washed over him leaving him drained. Rafter suddenly awoke to the fact that he'd had enough of adventures. Never before had he felt such a longing for peace and quiet. Was it age or was he just tired? He righted the kitchen chair and sat down, pensive. Pushing away the lethargy that weighed him down, he steadied his breath, closed his eyes and searched. Neither Sally nor Anju were close by. Stretching his senses farther afield he finally traced Sally's complex presence. She was very far away. He could not track Anju, however, maybe because he knew her less well.

Blindfolds

The blindfold could not mask the constant bustle around them. People were on the move on every side. She could hear heavy boxes being dragged here and there across what sounded like a stone floor. She heard the grunts of exertion as large objects were heaved up and carried off elsewhere. And then there was the constant rustle of paper mingled with the sound of tearing all of which was capped by the crackle of a fire. Destroying the evidence no doubt, Sally thought. People around her spoke a multitude of languages in hushed tones but German was predominant.

Nobody spoke to them directly, however. Ignored, they were trussed up in cords and sacking, dumped unceremoniously in two armchairs, where they had been left for more than an hour. They'd been transported by car then plane and finally car again. Judging from the noises that greeted them when they were finally carried out of the car at their destination they must have been in the countryside somewhere.

"Free them and take them before the Grand Master," a rough male voice barked.

Their cords were cut and the sacking removed, leaving only the blindfolds in place. Strong hands grasped her upper arm, pulled her up out of her seat and pushed her forward down what must have been a corridor. She almost fell as her foot caught on an unseen threshold, but the man who accompanied her kept a firm grip on her, almost wrenching her arm from its socket. The further they walked the more the bustle and movement fell away leaving only their footfalls to accompany them. Then they halted as someone knocked and a door opened. They were pushed forward into a room that smelt of age-old books and manuscripts and dust. It could have been a library were it not for the echo suggesting a large empty space. And the door closed behind them with a faint click.

"So we finally meet," a man said.

Judging from his voice he must have been somewhat younger than Rafter.

Be careful, Vee warned her, the man is powerful and dangerous.

It was true, he gave off an intoxicating presence. She felt a shiver of fear run down her spine. His English was impeccable, but there were still faint traces of a German accent. Whoever it was, he apparently had no intention of removing the blindfolds. Why were men so intent on making her blind, she wondered, thinking back over the blindness Tyrell had inflicted on her in the Reaches.

She could feel the necklace of the Littl' People pulsing strongly around her neck. She was in half a mind to grab Anju's hand and transport them both to her sister's home. Instead she chose to speak.

"What do you men fear from the eyes of a woman that you invariably need to plunge her in darkness?"

She heard footsteps approaching from across the room and the blindfold was removed. So this is the Grand Master, she thought as she stared at the thickset German who stood in front of her. He was dressed in a grey suit, under which he wore a white shirt and tie. He could have been a banker if it hadn't been for the intense, almost predatory look on his face.

He returned her stare unblinking. Not a good time for a battle of wills, she speculated as she turned away to see if Anju was OK. She too had had her blindfold removed and was busy rubbing her eyes. It was then that she noticed Leuchtli slumped on a large wooden crate.

"You know Dr. Leuchtli, I believe," the German said.

The sight of the Doctor would normally have filled her with dread, such was the threat he had been to her life and that of her friends, but his emaciated face and his withered form were so pathetic that she felt little for him, lest it be disdain. He looked as if he were recovering from an ordeal or a prolonged illness.

Leuchtli had recently been in the Reaches her friend Keira had told her, in the company of two other men who had been gravely ill. Her mind began to race, calculating possibilities, weaving threads together, jumping to all manner of conclusions. So this German must have been the man Jenny had gone to save in Granwich. The key question was why he had been doing there.

"I have a task for you," the Grand Master began.

Sally was about to challenge him with some choice caustic comment, but decided against it.

"My men and I are about to go on a journey and you are going to help us get to our destination."

She suspected they wanted to return to the Reaches, but she remained silent. Let him talk. The Grand Master lapsed into silence himself, crossing the room to look out of one of the windows. Was he trying to draw her out? Probably. To hell!

"And how am I to do that?" she asked.

Spinning on his heels to face her, as if he'd been waiting for her cue, he continued: "With the necklace you wear around your pretty neck."

So it was the Reaches they were headed for.

"You are to transport myself and my men to a place in the Reaches. We will travel in batches."

"I could never transport so many."

"If you can transport your friends and a car, you can surely transport us."

He was well informed, Sally noted.

There must be a catch, Vee said.

She agreed.

"Your pretty friend will stay here with Dr. Leuchtli to make sure you don't play any tricks on us. You will fetch them last." And the Grand Master turned away, addressing Leuchtli. "And you, Jakob, will hand over your Machine. Let's call it an assurance that you don't do something silly while I'm gone."

Leuchtli unwillingly withdrew a small box from his pocket and handed it to the Grand Master.

"Be careful with it," Leuchtli pleaded. "It's the only one left."

If I were the Master, Vee said, I'd use that machine once you have returned here to fetch Anju and Leuchtli. That way he can get rid of all the evidence in one blow and stop anybody else following him.

But how can I possibly deflect such energy. Sally wondered. I only managed in the Reaches thanks to Tyrell.

We'll find a solution, Vee replied.

Nodding almost imperceptibly in response to Vee, she turned to the Grand Master and said: "I agree."

Off with their heads!

Sally ran up the stairs two at a time in search of the library where Anju was waiting for her.

To the left, Vee said.

Panting she pushed open the door and burst into the room.

"Come!" she said to Anju.

"But we can't leave the doctor alone her," Anju protested.

"Bring him too, then," Sally called out, retracing her steps to the door.

Anju half carried, half pulled the ailing doctor along the corridor and down the main stairs.

"We must get outside and as far away as possible," Sally hissed urgently. She returned to help Anju drag the doctor across the courtyard. "We don't know which of us he will target with that Machine," she explained once they'd reached a nearby hill. "As soon as Vee and I sense the energy rising we are going to try to deflect it onto the Mansion of the Brethren. We can guarantee nothing. But we'll try."

Leuchtli had crumbled in a heap on the grass complaining that he didn't want to die.

"Stop whining!" Sally spat out the words. "You weren't bothered when others were killed by your infernal contraption!"

"Tell us," Anju began in a more placating tone as she addressed Leuchtli, "is there no way to stop the waves of energy?"

Leuchtli continued whining.

"For God sake, man," Sally swore, "make yourself useful for once. We have very little time. When that monster realises that I have dumped all his men in the Dream Realm he's going to hit us hard."

Anju chuckled. "What a neat idea," she said, delighted. "They'll take quite a while to find their way out of there."

"You did what?" Leuchtli asked in a high-pitched voice, horrified.

"Only the Grand Master and his assistant made it to the Reaches. The others are lost in the world of dreams where I left them."

Leuchtli started to tremble. "He'll kill us all," he muttered.

"Off course he will," Sally retorted. "He was going to kill us all anyway."

Anju put her hand on Leuchtli's shoulder to calm him. "Help us, doctor," she said softly, pulling him up till he was standing. "Is there no way to stop this machine?"

"No," he admitted, pouting. "The technology is still very rudimentary. It homes in on its target by resonance."

Anju stood opposite him, her hands squarely grasping his shoulders. "What frequency does it resonate with?" she asked urgently.

"A series of harmonics of the body's frequency. It is a complex waveform specific to the person being targeted."

Anju let go of Leuchtli who slumped to the ground again. Drawing Sally some distance away, she whispered: "Maybe we can beat it by singing, if we can find the right harmonics. A slight difference of frequency might be enough to destabilise the incoming waves and dissipate a good part of their energy. If we can diminish the flow, you can try to reflect part of the waves back the way they came and destroy the Machine."

They knew the moment the attack began because the hair on their heads stood abruptly on end and their teeth began to chatter as if they were cold. The Grand Master was targeting Sally. The cowardly bastard, she thought. She'd get him back. Wave after wave of terror swept over her as she remembered the devastation the Machine had caused in the Reaches. She fought to set aside the memories and concentrate.

"Sing!" Anju ordered. And the two girls began trying different notes searching for the right frequency.

"You ... tell me ... when we get the right note ..." she said to Anju. "I must ... deflect ... as much energy ... as possible ..."

One of the outhouses burst into flames as she channelled energy towards the former lair of the Brethren.

Anju had narrowed down the choice to three adjacent notes. They concentrated on moving up and down by quartertones from the lowest to the highest. And all the while the energy grew and spread, threatening at any moment to burst through her defences and rip her apart. More that half the mansion was on fire and the roof and several walls had crumbled under the assault.

I can't hold out much longer she gasped to Vee.

You deflect, I'll sing he said.

And all of a sudden she had the impression that she'd lost control of her voice as it emitted high-pitched notes several octaves above the note sung by Anju. Anju looked at her alarmed, but continued to sing.

"There!" shouted Anju. "We've found it" as she sang a particular note.

Vee's falsetto spun minute variations close to the note Anju had discovered. The air around them began to pulse, laying waste to a large area but leaving them unscathed. Sally could feel the force waning as she continued to channel the remaining energy towards the Mansion.

Now the force is decreasing, see if you can't send a small dose back the way it came, Vee suggested.

Rather than oppose it directly, Sally let a part of the energy spin round her several times and then she released it back along the incoming flux. Nothing happened for a long time, then, suddenly, the waves of energy stopped as abruptly as they had began. Anju and Sally sank to their knees and hugged each other, tears streaming down their cheeks.

Thanks, Vee, my love, Sally said in her head. She hadn't called him "my love" for a long time.

The grey world

He sat crossed legged on the floor, doused in grey. No matter where he looked the same monotonous colour stared back at him. Well at least it was an improvement on the cold, damp place he'd been stuck in before. He began to wonder if he looked long enough at this greyness whether his thoughts would become grey too. He closed his eyes but the inside was just as grey as the outside, although there were hundreds of tiny veins branching here and there in a complex web of greyness.

"What colours is grey made up of?" a voice asked, startling him.

The shock of it threw him "off centre" making it difficult for him to collect his thoughts. He looked around nervously, but he was alone.

"Well?" the voice insisted.

"Who are you?" Didier asked.

"I'm a friend," came the reply.

"Do you really expect me to trust you?" he asked out loud.

"Trust your feelings. Do I feel malevolent?"

Well, no, he concluded, but then again in that place he wondered if he could even trust himself. His mind drifted back to the problem of the all-present greyness. Black and white, he thought.

"Exactly!" the voice replied, clearly delighted.

How come this voice could read his thoughts? Fear coursed through his veins at the thought of being so exposed.

"Thought and words, they all the same here."

So you can hear all my thoughts?

"Not all of them."

The grey turned threateningly darker.

"Let me show you how to hide your thoughts. That should make you feel more comfortable."

Dieter could see the potential advantages of being able to mask his thoughts, so he agreed.

"Think of something you do not want me to know about," the voice suggested.

That's a clever way to get me to reveal things, he muttered in his head.

"You are cautious. That's good. But my reason for asking you to hide a secret is because doing so only makes sense if you really have something to hide."

Dieter decided to accept the explanation. He didn't want to waste his time in fruitless arguments.

"Good. Now draw up a mist around it."

How the hell could he do that? At the mention of mist, it was true that a faint mist had appeared. He tried to think the mist denser and to his surprise it swirled around the girl's naked body he was trying to hide till she was no longer visible.

"Well done," the voice concluded. "So what is the colour grey made of?"

Black and white.

"Set aside the black and inspect only the white."

He must be going nuts, Dieter thought. It was like being in a surrealistic school.

"And?"

He hated those teachers who set out deliberately to teach you a lesson, leading you down their path to their conclusions. Despite himself the answer formed on his lips: "All the colours of the rainbow." And as he said it, the grey disappeared and he found himself sitting in a most spectacular garden full of tropical plants.

Homeward bound

The wail of several sirens brought them back to themselves. The fire had been spotted and the fire brigade was on its way, probably with the police as well.

"We can't stay here," Sally said to Anju, ignoring the Doctor who had sidled closer.

"Can't you use the necklace to take us to the Reaches?"

"Not yet," Sally said, making off along a path away from the burning buildings. "I need to inform the Professor of what has happened and we need to get rid of the Doctor."

"Take me with you," Leuchtli pleaded. "There's only trouble waiting for me here."

Sally spun round to face the Doctor, furious. "You killed Tyrell along with many other people and you tried to kill me. How could you possibly imagine I would spare you a little trouble with the police?"

Anju touched Sally's arm. "He might cause us more harm if we leave him here," the young girl suggested.

Why don't you use the necklace to get home to Avan? Vee asked.

I've only used it between this world and the Reaches, Sally replied.

"What does Vee say?" Anju asked, presumably sensing the private conversation between the two.

"Give me your hand," Sally said, "and take Leuchtli's. Hold on tight, we are going home."

The way

The floor began to tremble violently. He tried to keep his balance as the world swayed backwards and forwards. How could you make sense of the world if the very earth beneath your feet became uncertain? It was his ultimate reference. He had been cut loose and was completely lost. Terror seized him, cutting short his breath. Sinking to his knees and falling forward on all fours, he gasped in a desperate effort to get air into his lungs.

The earthquake had diminished in strength, only the occasional aftershock continued to ripple through the ground beneath him, but his breathing still came with difficulty. He had to get out of there as fast as possible. It might collapse on him and crush him forever. He moved forward, still on all fours, frequently rounding fallen objects, trying to find the way out.

"This way," a distant voice called out.

It was the same voice he'd heard earlier. He turned to head in its direction.

"Good," the voice encouraged him. "More to the left."

The place was littered with broken furniture, upturned bookshelves and all manner of obstacles.

"Keep going," the voice pursued.

He had the impression it was getting nearer and as he got closer he also found it easier to breathe.

"Almost there."

He reached a bed that blocked his path. It wasn't the exit he'd expected but he knew he had to climb up onto it. Once he'd heaved

134

his body up onto the bed, he rolled over on his back and opened his eyes.

"Welcome back, Inspector. My name is Alo. You were lost and I have been guiding you back."

Dieter immediately recognised the voice as the one that had spoken to him in his dreams.

"Thanks," he said.

At that moment the door of the hospital room opened and he saw Professor Rafter walk in followed by Sally and Anju both of whom looked like they'd been a fight. Their hair was dishevelled, their clothes torn and their faces smudged with soot.

"What happened to you?" he asked propping himself up on one elbow.

"We had a fight with a man calling himself the Grand Master," Sally told him.

Dieter collapsed back on the bed wondering if he was going to pass out.

"Don't send him back to the Dream World," Alo said jokingly. "I had to work very hard to bring him back."

Anju came and sat on his bed. "I told you there must be a third party missing in your clues. It was the Grand Master. But you suspected that, didn't you?" she asked.

"Do you mind if I give you a hug?" the Inspector asked, somewhat embarrassed about asking. But Anju didn't wait to answer. She simply hugged him.

Chapter 7 - The Company of Watchers

Vigilant

Tom shifted uncomfortably from one foot to another in an effort to ease the weight on his legs and hips, but it didn't do much to alleviate the growing muscle ache. He'd been standing still in that dark recess for nearly an hour. He signalled to a colleague further down the corridor that all was OK and returned to listening for sounds from the room next to him. All was quiet. The intruders had arrived several days earlier and he was part of the group appointed to watch over them, mainly because he was the only one who understood German. Little was known about the two men apart from the fact that the watchers suspected they were the same two Jenny had treated earlier and who had disappeared so mysteriously once they were healed. The only difference being that one of the men looked much younger.

As he listened, his thoughts wandered to his training over the last few weeks. The Watchers were a secret company of commoners dedicated to keeping an eye on anything unusual or threatening that happened in Granwich and the surroundings. It was their way of protecting the commoners both from the Patriciat, but also sometimes from themselves. On Ma'gina's recommendation they had willingly taken Tom in, giving him the basic training each new Watcher received. This was his first real mission. In a way, his job as journalist had not been so different. Had he not spent much time watching out for news that might be worthy of a story? He wondered how many journalists would have the dedication and the patience to be a Watcher. Unlike journalists, the Watchers reports were spoken rather than written down and published. He had found memorising the details difficult at first. He'd constantly wanted to pull out a notebook and jot things down. The details themselves were also a problem. The Watchers prided themselves on being attentive to even the smallest detail. He'd been told that details could sometimes save lives.

A noise from the room next door called his attention back to the present. He signalled to his colleague that he'd heard movement, they'd taught him a special sign language, and then he pressed his ear against the wall to listen.

"... Damn that woman! What did she do to all the others? They were supposed to meet us here."

The other voice was inaudible.

"We've lost more than thirty men because of her."

The mumbled response this time lasted much longer. Tom signalled that the people were talking and listened again.

"I don't like the idea of recruiting here. There are too many unknowns in this society."

Shuffling of boots then heavy footfalls indicated the people were on the move. He signalled again to his colleague and shifted to a safer vantage point. Watching successfully, he'd been told, had a lot to do with being constantly on the move from one vantage point to another. His colleague shifted too just before the two men opened the bedroom door and walked away down the corridor. You needed to anticipate where people were likely to go. He could hear the two men descending the stairs of the inn where other watchers would take over the vigil. He whispered a few words to his colleague about what he'd heard, such regular sharing was also part of the technique, and repositioned waiting for signals from downstairs.

A place of his own

"This place gives me the creeps," the Grand Master said quietly as they stepped out onto the road and headed at a brisk pace for Granwich. "I continually feel like I'm being watched. The sooner we find a place of our own the better."

That Sally woman had thrown his plans into chaos. Not only had she spirited away all his men, wasting years of his work selecting and preparing them, but she'd also caused the Machine to be wrecked.

He'd been very lucky he'd placed the thing on a table just before it exploded, otherwise he'd have lost his hand and arm. The two of them had had a hard time extinguishing the fire that the explosion caused. No woman had ever got the better of him and he wasn't going to let it happen now.

His first port of call was a tailor's. He needed to be well dressed for what he had to do. The tailor was efficient and knowledgeable, taking the necessary measurements with a minimum of fuss. The cloth he proposed was excellent. These people had good taste, he noted. He had his haircut and then visited the baths while the suit was being made. Basking in the warm water he admired his body. The potion he'd taken had caused him to look considerably younger than he was and he'd lost weight too. The effect would not last for long, but it would suffice for what he needed to do.

Sporting his new suit and his slick hairstyle, a much younger looking Grand Master strode confidently through Granwich searching for an agent that sold property in the region. The shops and other services, he discovered, were run exclusively by those commoners who had been intelligent enough to learn a trade. The idea of the superior ruling class pleased him immensely, although a number of those he'd noticed in shops and at the baths didn't seem so superior. He was sure he'd be able to set that right once he was properly installed and introduced into society.

Amongst the various houses for sale, he chose a large house that had once belonged to a Patriciat family that had been wiped out by the tragedy that had caused so many people to die in the Black Castle to the South. The irony of it amused him, and he silently thanked Leuchtli. It was one of the few things the Doctor had done that had had a positive result. The house was not up to the standards of his Mansion in Germany, but it still had several reception rooms and a well-stocked library. He looked forward to uncovering more about the culture of Granwich. In the mean time he hired several servants via an agency and had them clean and freshen up the house. He left the work in the hands of the new housekeeper he'd taken on. She was in her late forties, she'd told him, as they visited the house together and he gave orders about what he wanted changed.

Alone now, as he'd sent his assistant off in search of news of the Brethren, he went to dine in a select restaurant where his housekeeper told him the Patriciat were in the habit of eating. From the outside, the place didn't look very special, but inside it reeked of opulence: thick plush carpets, carved oak chairs and tables, delicate china and sparkling silverware on spotless tablecloths and a bevy of serving girls in delightfully enticing costumes. He was shown to a small table in an alcove from which he could see most of the restaurant. He couldn't have wished for a better position.

Few tables were occupied, but the waitress explained that most people arrived a little later. The girl had tried to flirt with him, but he'd politely discouraged her, wishing to be seen as well behaved and respectful of the other sex. By the time the main course was served the restaurant was almost full. It was then, as the waitress spooned a generous helping of a thick sauce over his meat, that he saw the young woman he'd been waiting for. Lucie was her name. As she passed amongst the tables, people greeted her with almost ostentatious politeness. Even if he hadn't known she was an important member of the Patriciat society he would have guessed it from the attitude of those around her.

The only person who didn't pay any attention to this unspoken protocol was the young girl who accompanied her. She couldn't have been more that ten years old. Once they were seated, the two chatted animatedly not paying much attention to those around them. For all its animation, their conversation remained delicately restrained, such that he could hear not a word of what was said. From time to time Lucie laughed at something the child said, her face lighting up with pleasure. It was a sight that would have most men weak at the knees, he thought.

The child would be a nuisance. The two seemed very close. From time to time, Lucie would lean forward and brush the hair out of the little girl's eyes. Leuchtli had made no mention of a sister. He wondered who the kid could be. Of course he might try to gain access to Lucie by making friends with the child. It was worth a try; but not tonight. This required time and patience. He paid his bill and left.

The evening meeting

Watchers slipped unnoticed into the building through different entrances, one at a time, or in pairs. Tom had left the inn much earlier where he'd been on watch and had gone to visit Jenny who was working with Ma'gina and Mia at the Apotheka. Now it was time for the evening meeting of the Watchers so he too made his way into the building where the Watchers were to meet. They often changed venues, he'd been told, so that no routine was perceptible. It was not his first attendance at such a meeting, but it would be the first time he had something to report and the idea of doing so made him nervous. Some thirty people were gathered quietly in a large room. Many of them greeted him as he arrived. Their watches were organised in such a way that you were often with someone different. So he'd met nearly everybody. Other watchers were still out watching and would report at some other time or place.

Once he had delivered his report and answered the many questions his fellow watchers asked, he was able to relax and listen to what the others had to say. Apparently the man he'd been watching had gone into town and done some shopping, spending a considerable amount of money on clothes. He'd then bought himself a house and hired servants. One of the watchers was given the task of finding where the man got all his money. The housekeeper the man had hired was close to the Watchers and would be a useful relay with news from within the house.

The man, who'd sent his assistant away across country, presumably in search of his lost men, had spent the evening in a Patriciat restaurant. He'd kept to himself, refusing the flirtations of the waitress that they'd deliberately sent to test him, but the watcher reported that the man had taken a particular interest in Lucie, staring at her for long periods at a time.

"Excuse me for asking," Tom said, "but who is this Lucie."

They told him that she was the Keeper's Daughter, the Keeper being the head of the Patriciat, and that, given that her father was dead, whoever became her husband would become the new head of the Patriciat.

"Do you think our mysterious man is after Lucie?" Tom asked.

"Could be," someone said. "We'll have to keep a close eye on this one."

Everyone agreed and several watchers were appointed to spy on him the next day, Tom being one of them.

Reunion

"So this is your real house," Sarah exclaimed as she spun on her heals taking the place in during successive turns.

Although she knew who Sarah really was, Lucie couldn't help being enchanted by the girl's enthusiasm and joy of life.

"You've come a long way from the speechless bird you were before," Lucie commented soberly.

Sarah stopped her dance and stuck her tongue out at Lucie. "But you haven't change one bit," Sarah riposted, "you are still so serious." And the girl skipped out of range as Lucie threw a cushion after her.

Following her and picking up the cushion, Lucie defended herself saying: "I have one or two very good reasons to be serious, young lady." Sarah took hold of Lucie's hands and danced her round the room. "You're not at all as serious as you think," the little girl corrected.

A servant served them tea in one of the smaller reception rooms. When the servant had finished placing plates of biscuits and sandwiches and filling cups of tea, she curtsied and left Lucie and Sarah alone.

"In a short while, my friend Ma'gina will be visiting us with her assistant Mia and a new girl called Jenny," Lucie told Sarah. "I would like you to meet them. Both Mia and Jenny come from another world according to Ma'gina. She wondered if it was the same one as yours."

A distant bell rang and shortly afterwards the servant returned to announce that three women had arrived on a visit.

"Show them into the Winter garden," Lucie ordered. "Serve them refreshments and tell them we will be with them in a short while."

The servant curtseyed and left. Sarah rose and imitated the curtsey.

"You're getting more feminine every day," Lucie casually remarked, knowing that the comment would irritate Sarah. Predictably Sarah stuck out her tongue and grabbing one of the biscuits, stuffed it whole into her mouth. Lucie had to laugh. "I wonder if I would love you so much if you were in the form of a man," she mused, almost to herself. Sarah's only response was to cuddle up on Lucie's lap. "Come on, you're getting too big to sit on my lap," Lucie said pushing Sarah to her feet and rising herself. "We've got visitors to entertain."

Ma'gina and the two young women were waiting for them, standing as was appropriate for commoners when a member of the Patriciat was present. Ma'gina was a spritely old woman with greying hair who greeted Lucie with an energetic hug as if she were her daughter. Mia also greeted Lucie warmly, they'd apparently met before, Sarah gathered. She remembered the tale of Mia's songs at the commoners' Meet. Ma'gina then presented Jenny to Lucie explaining that Jenny was working with her for a short while to learn more about healing.

Sarah hung back near the door, shy, nervous and quite confused. She recognised Mia immediately. She had been her lover when Sarah had been in a man's form. The last time they had been together both of them had been in a pitiful state. Sarah preferred to forget the details.

"What's the matter with you, Sarah?" Lucie asked. "It's quite unlike you to be shy."

Lucie came over to her and, taking her by the hand, led her up to the three women and presented each in turn. Sarah kept her eyes on her feet as she shifted uncomfortably from one to the other. She prayed that Lucie would not reveal who or what she really was.

"Where do you come from?" Ma'gina asked. "Lucie told me she thought you might come from the same world as Mia and Jenny."

This is going to be a nightmare, Sarah thought, desperately seeking a way out. Her churning stomach gave her an idea.

"I think I'm going to be ill," she told Lucie in the smallest of voices.

Her ploy wasn't going to work though because she'd forgotten that she was standing in front of three of the best healers in Granwich. Ma'gina pulled out a small vial from her bag and poured a few drops into water in a glass that she handed to Sarah.

"Swallow this. You'll feel much better." And turning to Lucie she added: "It could be the beginning of her periods."

Sarah would have fallen in a faint of absolute embarrassment if Mia hadn't caught her at the last moment. Sitting down in one of the ample armchairs, Mia cradled Sarah against her breasts, rocking her gently backwards and forwards. The girl broke into tears.

She could see Lucie looking at her knowingly, a bemused smile on her lips. Before she became a girl, when she was still a bird, Sarah had told Lucie her story. So Lucy must know or guess that Mia was the girl from that story.

"Why don't you tell Mia who you are, Sarah? She has a right to know."

Sarah couldn't stop crying. And when Mia gently kissed her forehead, she burst into sobs. Through her tears she could see Ma'gina and Jenny waiting patiently. Extracting herself from Mia's arms, she stood before the four women. Pulling herself upright, she wiped her nose with a handkerchief Lucie handed her and took a deep breath.

"In the form of a man, my name is Jake, at least it was in the Dream World."

Mia gasped. Let's hope she doesn't laugh like Lucie did, Sarah prayed.

"Mia and I travelled from our world through the Dream World to save our friend Sally that you may know as Nala." She turned to Ma'gina. "You know me as an owl, but now, as you can see I am a little girl called Sarah. I have no control over the form I take. All I know is that I want to stay with Lucie." Sarah looked up to find Lucie grinning at her.

"And you can stay with me as long as you like," she told Sarah.

"Sally is going to be delighted to know we've found you," Jenny said. "She and Professor Rafter were so worried about you. Nobody knew where you were."

Mia rose from her chair, tears brimming over from her eyes. "So you were the bird with me during my ordeal."

Sarah was crying again, but softly this time. "I could do nothing to help you, Mia. I felt so useless."

Mia took the girl in her arms. "You helped me much more than you know. I was able to tell you my problems, even if you couldn't answer."

Ma'gina invited them all to sit down and take tea, saying: "You have a lot to tell each other, so why not make yourselves comfortable. It could take a long time."

Sarah cuddled up in Lucie's arms and listened to Jenny tell them everything that had happened since Mia and Jake had set out on their mission.

Brute

Sarah made her way along the Canal back to the Botanic Gardens from Lucie's town house. She liked that particular path because it reminded her of her first flight with Lucie. It looked quite different, of course, on foot and in daylight. This morning there were very few barges navigating the canal, so she shared the place only with the birds and a few stray cats. The evening before, she'd been so engrossed in the stories that Mia and Jenny had to tell that she'd forgotten her notebook when she and Lucie returned to the Botanic Gardens. Having just fetched it, the book was now safe if her pocket.

She was in no hurry to return because Lucie would be busy catering for her birds all morning, so Sarah chose her favourite bench that overlooked a bend in the canal and sat down. What had Jenny said? Sally had been chased across Europe by the police because of the explosion in the Black Castle. What intrigued her most was the spectacular escape from the police using the necklace to travel to the Reaches. It meant that, the time come, if ever she wanted to return to Avan she would be able to go with the help of Sally. Of course she could hardly go in her current form. They'd force her to attend a girls' school all day long and even possibly put her in an orphanage because she had no parents. She clenched her fists at the idea of having to sit still at a desk supposedly to learn. It made her furious. There were no schools in Granwich, thank heavens. People learnt differently ...

"Excuse me. Could you tell me the way to the Botanic Gardens?" a man asked.

"It's down there," she replied, pointing along the canal without even bothering to look at the person. Where was she before she was interrupted? Ah yes, schools.

"I'm a stranger here and I don't know Granwich so well," the man pursued. "Could you show me the way?"

Blast the confounded man! She'd thought he was long gone. It was then that she turned to see him. Young. Well relatively so. Smart. Both his hair and his suit. Shoes too.

"Where do you want to go, exactly?" she asked, somewhat rudely, deliberately making it clear his intrusion was unwanted.

He smiled. If Sarah had really been the little girl she appeared to be, that smile might have convinced her of his well-meant intentions. But Sarah had seen more of the world. There was a hint of greed, if not perversity in that smile. It made her shiver. And there was the faint German accent that only someone from her world could identify.

"The Botanical Gardens," he replied, patiently.

If she gave full reign to her feelings she'd kick him in the shins and push him in the canal, such was the dislike he inspired in her.

"Come on then," Sarah said, getting up unwillingly from her bench. "I'll show you the way."

The man, who said his name was Horst, tried to engage her in conversation but she said as little as possible.

"What's that large building over there?" he asked her.

"Dunno!" was all she replied.

Changing his tactics, he questioned her about herself.

"Where I come from, a little girl like you would normally be at school at this time of the day. Where do you go to school?"

Sarah pondered what to reply. "I'm too dim to go to school," she finally replied, deciding that being an idiot was an amusing way of annoying the man. But it had quite a different result. Horst must have thought he could take advantage of her, seeing as she was a bit simple, so he tried to get hold of her hand. She saw it coming and scratched his hand with all her force. He yelped and struck out with the flat of his hand sending Sarah backwards into the canal.

Sarah was in no danger because she was a strong swimmer. She and Lucie often went swimming together, although not in the filthy canal. All the same, she screamed with all her might. Horst just stood there looking at her for a while, unbelieving. The man had obviously had other plans, she thought. He'd clearly figured out that she was in no real danger. But when people came running, alerted by her screams, he took off his jacket and made a show of preparing to throw himself into the water to rescue her. He didn't need to get his clothes dirty though, as one of the barge people dived passed him into the canal and pulled Sarah to the bank. That must have been quite a relief to the German, she thought, seeing as his suit looked new.

Alerted by the barge people, Lucie arrived shortly after, immediately taking Sarah in her arms. She was now wrapped in a large blanket thanks to one of the barge people.

"There, there, my love," Lucie crooned. "Everything is all right now."

Muffled as she was in a thick blanket she couldn't turn to see what was happening behind her, but she heard Horst address Lucie.

"My name is Horst. I was about to jump in to save her when this brave fellow sprang into the water."

Not bothering with introductions Lucie questioned him. "Did you see what happened?"

"I think she slipped on the bank and fell in," was his reply.

What a liar, Sarah thought, furious at the cheek of it. She guessed the man was counting on the fact that she was supposed to be simple-minded and that no one would believe her if she said he'd pushed her into the canal. After all, there was no apparent reason why he should do such a thing, she realised. Lucie thanked Horst and turned to leave, holding Sarah close to her.

"I have a carriage nearby," he told Lucie. "I can drive you home. It wouldn't do for the little girl to get cold."

So much for being lost, Sarah thought. The whole situation must have been carefully planned. Sarah whispered in Lucie's ear that she was OK, but to no avail, Lucie accepted the invitation.

Sarah sat huddled in her blanket in one corner of the carriage, shivering and miserable. What's more, her face hurt terribly for the blow she'd received. There was sure to be a bruise. Then she realised that her notebook had been completely destroyed by the water and with it all the notes she'd painstakingly collected for a new book. She looked to her friend for comfort, but Lucie was in animated discussion with the stranger, who happened to know quite a lot about wild birds. Sarah felt completely neglected. Blast the man, he was clearly making a play for Lucie and Sarah could do nothing to stop it. When they got to the point where he invited her out to dinner at the restaurant, Sarah thought she was going to throw up. She could see exactly what would happen. Once they were back at the Botanical Gardens, Lucie would insist that Sarah go to bed and keep warm while she went alone with the stranger to the restaurant.

A watcher's view

"... yes! He slapped her on the face. The blow was so hard it propelled her into the canal..." the woman watcher related.

"Where did he come from?" someone asked.

"He was waiting in the shadows. He'd been there nearly twenty minutes when the girl arrived. The moment she sat down he moved closer."

"And you say he just stood there staring at her trashing about in the water?"

The watcher nodded.

"It seems difficult to understand his behaviour. I'm not sure he planned to throw her in the canal, but he didn't seem to have any intention of saving her. He just made a lame demonstration of preparing to rescue her once he saw somebody else about to do so."

"What happened then?"

"Lucie arrived and was about to take Sarah away when the man, whose name is Horst, offered to drive the two home in his carriage. And Lucy accepted."

146

"I was watching the carriage," another watcher put in. "Before he went to the canal, he told the driver to wait saying he'd be back with a couple of passengers that they'd take to Botanical Gardens."

"So it was planned in advance," Tom ventured. "But I don't understand why Sarah didn't tell Lucie what happened."

"I may be able to explain that," a watcher told them. "I heard the little girl tell the man she was too dim to go to school. I remembered you told us that schools were places were young people in your world went to learn. Of course he can't know that we have no such thing here. But the point is, he must have thought she was a little simple-minded. So he might have calculated that even if the girl said he threw her in the canal, nobody would believe her."

The door opened at that moment as another watcher entered accompanied by Ma'gina. The new arrival immediately spoke up. "I have been watching the German who took Lucie to the restaurant. I overheard him trying to talk Lucie into thinking that Sarah might not be quite right in the head. He had some convincing arguments. So I left a colleague to pursue the watch and went to fetch Ma'gina. I think the little girl may be in serious danger."

They briefly recapitulated the story for Ma'gina and debated what course of action to take. It was decided that Ma'gina should fetch Mia and Jenny and then go immediately to the Botanic Gardens and convince Sarah to leave, explaining to her what was happening if necessary, although Ma'gina would have preferred to keep the details from the girl for fear of upsetting her. A watcher was dispatched to the restaurant to try to delay Lucie, hopefully to give more time to Ma'gina. In addition a round-the-clock watch would be set on both Horst and Lucie, and should there be a threat to Lucie's life they were to intervene immediately.

Desperate

The crocodile slid silently through the muddy waters of the canal heading for Sarah who was lashed to a post in the middle of the canal, her feet only inches above the waterline. She could hear the mocking laughter of Horst from the bank as he delighted in the scene. If only she could transform into another shape she might be able to escape, but it was too late, for the beast was upon her...

A sharp knock at the door woke her, dissolving the crocodile but not the fear that went with it. Her sleep must have been agitated because the bedclothes were all in knots. A second knock reminded her that someone wanted to get in. For a brief second she wondered if this too was a dream, but the cold of the floor on her bare feet as she stood convinced her that this was probably real.

"Who is it?" she asked cautiously from behind the door.

"It's Ma'gina and Mia," a muffled voice said. "We need to speak to you urgently."

Pulling Lucie's shawl around her shoulders, she opened the door just enough to see who it was. Seeing that it was indeed Ma'gina and Mia but also Jenny, she opened the door fully and let them it. Saying nothing by way of greeting, she simply returned to Lucie's bed and sat down leaning against a pile of pillows, waiting for an explanation. Ma'gina remained standing but the others sat on two chairs.

"I have urgent things to tell you, Sarah, and what I have to say is not going to be easy for you."

Ma'gina's words filled Sarah with apprehension. "Well, get on with it," Sarah said. "I've just been chased by crocodiles in my dream and before that I was thrown in the canal by a liar and a thief."

"We believe you are in serious danger from the man who pushed you in the canal," Ma'gina began.

"Not half the danger Lucie is in," Sarah retorted. "I have to protect her."

"The situation is much more complex than you know, Sarah. We know you led that man to believe you were a bit simple-minded. Well at this very moment he is convincing Lucie that you have a problem in the head and need treatment."

Sarah laughed. "Lucie will never believe him," she scoffed.

"That's where you are wrong, Sarah. Lucie will believe him, sooner or later. He will stop at nothing to separate you from her. You are in the way of his plans. He might even go so far as to drug you to make you look mad…"

"But what about Lucie?" Sarah protested.

"There is nothing you can do for her at the moment," Ma'gina said firmly. "The best thing you can do is to get to safety. Know that Lucie has many friends in Granwich and none of us will ever let harm come to her."

A part of Sarah wanted to argue with Ma'gina. Had she not already let a close friend down when she hadn't been able to protect Mia. Now she was to abandon Lucie. Desperate tears sprung in her eyes, but she wiped them away.

"We need to hurry," Ma'gina continued. "Lucie and that man will be back very soon. You must not be here when they return."

Lucie clambered off the bed, pulled off her nightshirt, not paying any attention to the others and began dressing as quickly as possible. Extracting a backpack from a cupboard she stuffed various clothes into it and added some jewels Lucie had given her and several empty notebooks. When the bag was full, she turned to Ma'gina.

"I must leave a note for Lucie."

"I am afraid we can't let you do that," Ma'gina insisted. "Anything you write will be used against you and Lucie by that man."

A piercing whistle interrupted their conversation.

"They're here," Ma'gina said. "Our time is up. Is there no other way out of here?"

Sarah shook her head.

"Then I'll have to stall them while you get away with Mia and Jenny. They will explain what is planned." And she turned and left.

With Mia and Jenny they slipped out of Lucie's apartment and crept downstairs. Sarah showed them the backdoor that led out into the Botanical Gardens. They could hear Ma'gina talking to Lucie.

"… Yes. I heard she fell in the canal and I wanted to see if she was all right."

"And is she?" Lucie asked.

"I don't know," Ma'gina replied. "She's not in your rooms…"

The last thing they heard was Lucie running up the stairs as Sarah led her two companions along the shelter of the house wall till they could get away into the forest where, some distance away, Ma'gina had parked her cart.

"We are to take the cart to the Apotheka and from there we'll go on by horse," Mia whispered.

"What about Ma'gina?" Sarah asked.

"She'll be alright," Jenny replied.

Abandoned

Lucie searched everywhere in her tiny flat, pulling open cupboards, looking under the bed, rummaging behind curtains, but to no avail. Sarah was gone. There was not even a farewell note. Lucie sank down on her bed, sitting amidst the disorder of the covers with her head in her hands. She felt as if a large segment of herself had been wrenched out leaving her sore and vulnerable.

"I told you she was unstable and untrustworthy," Horst said smugly, pushing passed Ma'gina to gain access to the room. "I only wish I could have warned you earlier. It would have saved you a lot of suffering."

Ma'gina rounded on him and blocked his path. "You must leave her alone now. She needs rest," she told him.

Horst pushed her roughly out of the way. He was clearly set on making the most of the situation.

"If you don't leave immediately," Ma'gina told him, "I will have you thrown out bodily."

Pulling up to his full height, he towered over her as he spluttered: "Who are you, commoner, to threaten me?"

Ma'gina was not about to let herself be intimidated, especially when she saw the two burly watchers slip silently into the room.

"I am a healer, Sir. And as such I tell you that you must leave."

He raised his hand to hit her but his blow never reached its mark as he was dragged from the room by the watchers.

"You cannot hit me like you hit unprotected little girls, Horst. Now leave."

"I'll get you back for this, woman," Horst spluttered as the Watchers forced him back down the stairs.

"I'm sure you'll try," replied Ma'gina turning away to care for Lucie.

"Has someone hit Sarah?" Lucie asked.

"Don't worry about her, she'll be fine. It is yourself you should worry about," Ma'gina said, pouring a potion for Lucie. "Here! Drink this. It will help you rest. And I will stay with you to be sure you come to no harm."

"But Sarah?" Lucie asked, having swallowed the liquid.

"She's quite safe," Ma'gina reassured her. "You have a difficult time in front of you and it is better that the little girl doesn't get between you and this man." Ma'gina helped Lucie lie down as the potion began to have its effect.

Some time afterwards, one of the watchers returned. "He went straight back to his house where he was joined shortly afterwards by his assistant. Several colleagues are keeping an eye on them."

Ma'gina thanked him for the news. "Tell me, did the little girl get away all right?"

He nodded. "I was told they left on horseback immediately after they reached the Apotheka. A couple of our colleagues have accompanied them on their journey, just in case."

Ma'gina was relieved to hear Sarah had made good her escape. She thanked the watcher who slipped back into the shadows and she pulled up an armchair in which she settled for her own vigil.

She hadn't meant to oppose the man so frankly, at least not yet. It meant that she would not be able to work as openly as she'd intended. If this man was prepared to use violence to get his way they might have to train the Watchers and others in unarmed combat. She didn't personally know anyone who was an expert, although she'd heard Tom say that Martin had learnt such things in the army. Maybe he could help, but for the moment he was with the Littl' People further south.

Attached

Ma'gina had taken her leave of Lucie a while earlier saying that she had work to do in the Apotheka. Not feeling at all hungry, Lucie skipped breakfast in the Garden restaurant and wandered across the lawn next to the hot houses, greeting the pheasants as she went. She would have liked to talk to Thomas, but the old man was in bed ill. She hadn't seen him for days. One thing Ma'gina had said puzzled her.

"Know that whatever happens in the coming months, you will always have the support of the commoners."

To the best of her knowledge nothing special was planned in the near future, lest in be the annual concert in the Gardens. What's more, she could see no reason why she would have to call on the commoners for their support. It was true that she appreciated them much more than her fellow Patriciat and that she knew they liked her too, but she had never thought in terms of sides. She was on nobody's side.

Everything she saw in the Gardens reminded her of Sarah. They had walked almost all the paths together as they discussed a great variety of subjects. If a casual observer had been able to listen in to those conversations, she would have been startled by the breadth of Sarah's experience and knowledge. In her brief stay at the Botanical Gardens, Sarah had been an avid reader and had devoured much of Lucie's library. Lucie was surprised to realise how deeply the girl had entered her life and her heart in such a short time. Was she in love with the girl? Or was it a more motherly instinct? Whatever it was, it was a potent attachment that she felt all the more strongly now Sarah was gone. She didn't believe Horst's theory that the girl was somehow deranged, but she could forgive him for being mistaken. He didn't know the whole story about Sarah and she was in no hurry to reveal it to him. She hoped he would desist with such a line of thought when he realised how much it distressed her.

"Lucie!"

It was him. He probably couldn't see her amongst the trees. On a whim she decided to remain hidden for a moment and observe him. It was true he was a handsome man although she didn't feel attracted to him. She liked the passionate way he talked and admired the extent of his knowledge. She liked less his ideas about the superiority of the Patriciat.

"Ah! There you are," Horst said, finally finding her on a narrow path amongst the bushes.

It was the sort of private meeting far from any witnesses that many a man, both Patriciat and commoner, would take advantage of, but Horst limited his advances to gently kissing her hand and enquiring about her health.

"Would you like to visit my new house?" he enquired.

"I would like to," she replied, "but first I must care for the birds."

He remained silent for a moment and then suggested she ask a commoner to look after the birds that morning.

"After all," he added, "you have had a trying time and you need a rest and a change of scenery."

He had arguments for everything, she noted, but she wasn't sure it was a quality or a defect in him.

"I will join you early this afternoon," she said, tacitly accepting his invitation.

He left almost immediately saying he must prepare the house for her visit.

Poison

Good. Things were going according to plan. He unlocked the door of a tiny cupboard in the wall of his room and took down a flask from within. It had cost him a fortune to procure it from a neighbouring town. He'd sent his assistant on the mission the day before. He didn't want people in Granwich knowing he bought such things. Unstoppering it, he sniffed the contents and immediately replaced the cork, putting the bottle back in its place. He locked the door and slipped the key in his waistcoat pocket. It was exactly what he needed. A little of that mixture each day concealed in a drink and she would wither like a blighted flower but in such a subtle way that no one would suspect a thing.

He'd have to get rid of that woman from the Apotheka too. He didn't want her meddling in his affairs. She was quite capable of detecting the poison and producing an antidote, although the person who had sold it to his assistant had assured him there was none. Scandal might be a good idea. If people were to think untoward things were happening in her "establishment" she could easily be discredited.

How convenient that little pest had suddenly disappeared. His hand still hurt from the scratches caused by her filthy nails. At least he wouldn't have to dispose of her. Still, he wondered where she'd gone and why, all of a sudden, she'd decided to leave. Surely a little girl like that couldn't just leave unnoticed. But maybe the idiot had fallen into the canal again and drowned this time.

As soon as he got Lucie on his hook, he needed to gain more influence amongst the Patriciat. There didn't seem to be a leader amongst them so it was unlikely any individual would oppose him once he'd become the Keeper. All the same, it would be safer to get as many under his influence as quickly as possible. He'd read that there was an age-old tradition amongst Patriciat men of meeting regularly to discuss issues about the town and its surroundings. That tradition had fallen into disuse, but he would resurrect it. He'd already taken to walking the streets of the town in search of things to improve…. A cough startled him from his musings.

"Excuse me, Sir. Would you like me to have your waistcoat cleaned for you before the lady comes this afternoon. I noticed it had a slight stain on it."

He hadn't noticed, but then he'd been busy with other more important things. Still musing about improvements he wanted to have made to the town, he unbuttoned his waistcoat and handed it to her. She took it, bowed and left. He was pleased with her work, although he'd never tell her so. She got the house up to a standard that was close to what he was used to in an extremely short time. And she was meticulously careful about cleanliness. What's more, he had tested her discretion and found her flawless. No. Unlike most of her fellow commoners she was all he could expect.

The spiral stairway was just wide enough for her to make her way down. This place hadn't been used for years. It dated from the period when the canals had been built. The commoners who had worked on the construction of the waterways had also built much of Granwich and, in provision for more difficult days, a small group of them had added a network of underground passages and rooms beneath the town. Ma'gina was glad that Mia was there to help her. She was getting too old for capering around in dark tunnels.

"To the left," Ma'gina whispered, holding up the lamp. Even though she hadn't been down there for ages, she remembered her way around very well. Her Grandfather had insisted she learn all the passages off by heart. She would have to do the same with Mia.

"We're going to a place just below the German's house," Ma'gina whispered.

"Why do you whisper?" Mia asked quietly.

"Because sound down here moves in funny ways and a voice can carry a long distance," Ma'gina explained. "Do you have the things I asked you to collect?"

"Yes."

They hurried on down the passage, not taking any of the side passages they came across.

"Here," Ma'gina said, pointing to a door in the tunnel wall. She peered throw a spy hole in the door. Several of the watchers were gathered inside. She knocked gently and opened the door.

They joined the watchers around the table.

"You know Mia, I'm sure."

They all nodded. Of course they did. It was there job to know everybody in town.

"Are Tom and Jenny OK with the little girl?" Mia asked.

"Yes," a woman watcher replied. "They arrived safely at their destination."

Ma'gina interrupted their conversation. "We need to hurry, I believe."

"Indeed," one of the watchers said producing a small flask from his pocket and placing it on the table. Ma'gina examined it closely.

"Interesting. This type of flask can only come from Ginger's. Horst must have sent his assistant over to Smeth'ick to buy it." She turned to Mia and said: "Give me the things you brought."

Mia placed a small bag on the table and Ma'gina extracted a pair of gloves from it. Slipping them on her hands, she cautiously opened the flask.

"Hm."

"What is it?" Mia asked.

"I don't recognise it. I'm going to have to take a small sample to analyse."

Taking a clean flask from Mia's bag she transfer a very small quantity of the liquid into it. Then she corked the original and handed it back to the watcher who left immediately.

"Where did you find it?" Ma'gina asked.

"Locked in a secret cupboard in his bedroom. We had to copy the key to get access to it."

"Good work," Ma'gina said putting the sample in her pocket and standing to leave. "I'll keep you informed."

Once they were back in the tunnel, Ma'gina handed the lamp to Mia and said: "Go and explore the tunnels. I want you to know them by heart."

"But what about you," Mia asked.

"I can find my way around down here without a light. And while you are down here I'll prepare us a trip to Smeth'ick to see my old friend Ginger."

Memories

Mia had progressively drawn up a mental map of the tunnels and underground rooms adding and adjusting parts as she went along. She'd learnt the technique from Grace during their short stay with her. Grace used the technique to memorise the topology of sounds in a landscape. Surprisingly few of the tunnels were in bad condition and all the doors she discovered worked perfectly. She was about to head back to the Apotheka when a noise caught her attention. It was very faint. If she hadn't had the extraordinary experience with Grace at the standing stones she probably wouldn't have noticed it. It pulsed rather like the sounds she'd heard there. Closing her eyes, she listened carefully. She couldn't detect the source of the sound but she could feel in which direction she should go to reach it. Making her way slowly along a corridor she hadn't visited so far, she realised that the sound was laid out in waves along the tunnel. There were places where it was almost inexistent and others where it was much stronger. When she stood at the stronger nodes, the locket Grace had given her began to vibrate. The Sisterhood of the Stones, she thought. There must be a temple of stones nearby. She pressed on, intrigued to see if she was right.

Unlike the other tunnels this one wove its way beyond the walls of the town and out into the countryside. Although Mia had no reference points by which to judge, she was convinced of it. And the further she went, the stronger the signal became and the shorter the distance between the crests of the waves. The tunnel abruptly ended at a door that was locked but there was no key. There wasn't even a keyhole. Frustrated, Mia had no idea how to get beyond the door. She placed the lamp on the floor and sat down staring at the door. The locket around her neck was pulsing much more strongly now so she took it out and held it in her hands. Instinctively she honed in on the predominant note in the sound she could hear and she sang it gently. The door sprang open with a resounding 'click'.

Jumping to her feet she moved through and found a staircase leading upwards towards a faint light. Turning off the lamp she made her way slowly up the stairs till she came out into a small cave. The light was coming from outside, filtered by a large bush that blocked the entrance. Peering through the branches she caught sight of several large standing stones in the moonlight. She hadn't realised it was night time. Getting down on her hands and knees she was able to scramble under the bush and get outside. She found herself on the top of a large hill some distance from Granwich. Right next to her stood a magnificent ring of standing stones. She walked reverently amongst them, not daring to make a sound. There were twelve main stones and a number of smaller ones. After an hour of mapping out all the stones in her mind she began softly singing the note she'd found in the tunnel. She shifted within the main circle, sensing the reaction of the stones. The hub of the whole system, she discovered, was slightly off-centre. When she sang there the stones resonated much more strongly. The sky in the east was tinged pink with coming sun as birds around broke into the dawn chorus. Mia joined them, singing the same song she had sung for Grace and the stones sang with her. Never before had she had such a strong feeling of being in the right place at the right time. Tears streamed down her cheeks as her song came to an end and the rising sun's rays touched the first stones. She stood their silent, transfixed.

Chapter 8 - Sparing Partners

Setting things straight

The meal had been delicious. Anju certainly knew how to cook Indian food! Dieter leaned back in his armchair and closed his eyes, relaxing for the first time in ages. In the next room Sally was singing a song in a language he'd never heard before. Anju accompanied her on the piano. Rafter had invited them back to his country house for an evening meal. They were to stay the weekend so that, as Rafter put it, they could clear up one or two points together. He must have dozed off because it was to a strong smell of coffee that he awoke. All the others were settled in armchairs talking quietly, waiting for him to wake. Considerate, he thought. Seeing he was awake, Rafter offered him a coffee.

"Where shall we begin?" the Professor asked. "The other day you said you had two questions, Inspector. One was about the mysterious death of so many people in the Sollarini Castle." Standing the Professor offered to refill Dieter's coffee cup. Dieter declined. "The second question you were unable to complete, but it concerned a Sect called the Brethren. We can provide you with information about both these subjects, but for reasons that will become apparent, you will not be able to use those explanations in your reports, you will not even be able to talk about them outside this little circle."

The Professor glanced at Sally then turned back to Dieter. "In a way, what we can tell you will be of no use to you at all, although it might satisfy your curiosity. Beyond that, it will probably bring you more trouble than it is worth. So now is the time to turn back if you don't want to get caught up in something that you will mostly likely regret." He stopped talking and stared at the Inspector for a long moment, giving him the chance to think things over. "So Inspector, do you want to go on or would you like us to drive you back to your hotel?"

Dieter cast a furtive glance at Anju who was grinning at the Professor. Seeing Dieter's look she laughed.

"You should have been in film-making, Professor," she said.

Everyone laughed, especially when the Professor made a show of not understanding what she meant. When the laughter had died down, Dieter replied.

"I will go on, Professor. I have always been curious and have lived dangerously because of it."

So, Leuchtli had been behind the death of all those people. Ironically it had been the Count himself who had instigated his own death and that of much of his family and entourage. Rafter was right, though, there was no way he could prove such things and they would never be accepted in a court of law. What astonished him even more was the news that the Grand Master had fled to another world leaving his mansion a flaming ruin.

"I'm really sorry about you two being kidnapped. It was my fault," he explained. "I told the Grand Master that you were here. I never imagined he would move so quickly to get you."

"Don't worry about it," Sally replied. "At least now we know who the enemy is."

Feeling restless, Dieter stood and walked to the window. The idea that the GM was at loose and unrestrained in another world troubled him. Who knew what manner of damage he could do from there? Night had fallen while they had been talking but no one had bothered to close the curtains, no one was concerned that people might be watching them from outside. The garden was shroud in long shadows between the narrow bands of light streaming from the windows.

"What are you going to do now?" he asked.

"Sally and I are to return to the Reaches as soon as possible," Anju informed him. "Our trip is all the more important now that we know more about this man. Your information was very useful, Inspector."

Dieter couldn't help but admire these girls. He wasn't sure he would have the courage to do what they were about to do.

"What do you think about them returning to that place, Professor?" he asked Rafter.

"The Reaches is Sally's second home," the Professor replied. "Not only does she have a great deal of support from the local people, but she also has a team with her of very competent people like Anju here."

That night, Dieter couldn't sleep. No one had asked him what he would do now, probably out of tact, but that question was uppermost in his mind and going over possible courses of action kept him from sleep. He could hardly return to Germany and his work with the police. He couldn't face the idea of having to investigate the disappearance of the GM and the fire at his country mansion, knowing all the time exactly what had happened but not being able to reveal it. Deep down he knew exactly what he wanted to do: go with Anju and Sally to counter the GM. But his mind was working overtime, producing arguments why such a move would be foolish if not dangerous.

He got up and went down to the ground floor of the house that was shroud in shadow and silence. Thinking he'd go for a walk, he headed for the front door. It was there that he noticed the light in the basement. Concerned that there might be intruders he eased his way down the stairs. The distant sound of a struggle made him hasten his pace. He reached the basement at a run and pushing open a door, rushed into a large room that looked like a gym. Before he knew what was happening, capable hands caught him up, spun him in mid-air and threw him across the room where he landed on his back, winded. Rolling over and crouching, he turned to face his assailant. Anju! He burst out laughing, as did she.

"Well Inspector, are you looking for a fight?" she asked, still smiling.

Dieter rose slowly, cast aside his jacket and moved towards her, seeking to intimidate her with his size and weight. In no time, he found himself lying on his back again. Anju stood nearby, quietly observing him.

"You're good!" he had to admit, rolling over and springing to his feet. "Can you show me how to do that?"

Anju continued to observe him from a distance. "Can I trust you with my best moves?" she asked.

He pondered the question a while as the two of them observed each other like two wild cats.

"Probably not," he replied with a grin.

"You look so much more alive when you smile, Inspector," she commented.

"Don't call me that," he said. "I don't think I am an inspector any more. You can call me Dieter."

She turned a cartwheel and in mid-flight pushed out her foot sending him sprawling to the floor. Folding herself neatly into a ball, she rolled several times across the gym floor and stood up with ease.

"OK, Dieter."

She was not even out of breath while he was wheezing from the effort.

"I used to think I was good at unarmed combat, at least that is what my colleagues in the police told me, but I see I still have some things to learn," he told her.

Squatting down she sat cross-legged opposite him. "I will teach you Dieter, but I warn you, I will work you very hard."

He would have laughed at the idea of a fifteen year old girl training him in combat, but seeing her in action he realised she was deadly serious.

"OK!" he replied. "Then I will come with you two to the Reaches... if you will have me."

The suggestion took him by surprise. He hadn't planned it like that, but he liked the girl and enjoyed being with her. What's more, he had unfinished business to settle with the GM.

"Good. That's settled. I wondered when you were going to offer," Anju said. "See you here tomorrow morning at six for meditation and practice, Dee."

Dee

Dieter helped himself to several large slices of toast.

"Hungry Inspector?" Sally asked.

"Sure. I had a rough workout this morning," he replied, glancing at Anju.

Sally looked questioningly at Anju.

"I took Dee through his paces in unarmed combat. When I'm finished with him, he'll be excellent," she said with a grin.

"You don't waste any time," Sally commented.

Dieter wasn't sure if she was talking to him or to Anju or to both of them.

"Morning, children. Slept well?" Rafter asked as he stepped into the dining room.

Calling them children, Dieter had learnt, was Rafter's little joke.

"And how about you, Inspector?"

Anju didn't leave any time for Dieter to reply. "He's not called Dieter anymore. I've baptised him 'Dee'."

Feeling tension in the air, Dieter changed the subject. "I had a very strange dream," he said. "I was riding on a model train railway. In places the rails were almost inexistent. The train stumbled from one block of wood to another. At times it ran precariously on only one rail. I can't remember the rest. What do you think it means, Professor?"

Rafter sat down, poured himself a tea and began buttering some toast. "Those people who interpret dreams do so because they see them as bringers of messages. There is a long tradition of dream interpretation that goes right back to the oracle and beyond. I personally see the world of dreams as a place. As such it is not to be interpreted but lived. Most people's experience of dreams is extremely fragmentary possibly adding to their feeling that they are more like hidden messages. But when you begin to travel more extensively in the Dream Realm you see things differently. My students learn to voyage in that World. You too have travelled there, Dieter. That was the place Alo brought you back from."

Dieter had never thought of dreams as a place. "That would mean dreams have as much substance and reality as the world we live in," he mused out loud.

"More or less," Rafter agreed. "Of course you can both live in them and interpret them as well if you like."

"Tell me, Professor, are you going to the Reaches too?" Dieter asked.

Rafter chuckled. "No. I leave that sort of thing to my younger associates. Anyway, we have some bother in the university. A couple of those zealot economists on the University Board of Governors have decided we need an audit, as they call it. There are even some people who are beginning to question the existence of a Theosophy Department within a "modern" university. So you see, I have other battles to fight."

With the sun setting, a stiff wind began to blow from the east. Sarah sat huddled under a cloak, holding her hands out to warm them by the fire. Not only was she cold and tired, but also her legs and backside were sore from so much horse riding. They had hardly stopped all day. The others were in a hurry to get Sarah to her destination and return rapidly to Granwich. They were all worried about the situation there. Jenny and Tom stood some distance away talking quietly to the watcher that had accompanied them. Sarah preferred to avoid their endless debate about Horst and what he planned to do.

Closing her eyes, she listened to the sounds around her. A bevy of birds were celebrating the setting sun while further afield a couple of beasts slunk through the undergrowth, keeping a safe distance from the noisy humans. Much closer she could hear the patter of tiny feet as a mouse hurried past. It was not quick enough though as an owl plunged on the rodent, digging its claws firmly in its back.

"Got you!" it said as it tore bits of fur and flesh from the bone amid the shrieks of the dying mouse.

"Pardon?" Sarah said.

"You don't need to ask pardon," the owl replied somewhat unintelligibly as it continued to eat.

Sarah knew that she had lived for a while in the form of an owl but she hadn't realised she could still speak Owlish. Lucie had no owls in her collection and they had not gone out in the country during her stay at the Botanical Gardens.

Finishing its meal with a flourish, the bird began pruning itself. "You wanna come for a flight?" it asked.

"I can no longer fly," Sarah replied.

"Course you can," the bird retorted, strutting around the remains of the mouse looking for one last piece. Having decided there was nothing left worth eating, it said: "Follow me," and launched into the air.

Sarah felt a sickening lurch inside herself as if she was being ripped in two and she found herself winging after the owl. They spiralled up, catching an up draft that carried them high above her fellow travellers. Glancing down she was shocked to see that her own body was still were she'd left it, slumped by the fireplace. The shock was so great she almost fell out of the sky.

"Silly thing," the bird called as it plunged after her. "You didn't think that big hefty body was going to fly, did you?"

Sarah turned several times surveying the scene below trying to get used to being outside her own body.

"Can people see me?" she asked the bird.

"Dunno. I can see you," it said.

It was then that she saw a couple of men she hadn't noticed before creeping up on Jenny and Tom. She let out a screech of fright and plunged towards her friends to warn them, but they clearly could neither see nor hear her, so she flew straight at her body, hoping she would somehow become one again. It worked, but the change provoked an extremely uncomfortable lurching feeling that made her think she was going to throw up. Pushing the feeling aside, she rose unsteadily to her feet and began to run on shaky legs towards her friends.

"Look out," she shouted. "There are two men creeping up on you!"

Jenny and Tom grabbed broken branches from the ground nearby and turned to face their assailants. The watcher, however, slipped away, unnoticed. Sarah guessed he was trying to get behind the men.

Jenny and Tom were having a hard time fighting off the men. Tom's arm was bleeding where it had been cut by a knife and Jenny was in the grips of the other man who had clasped her by the throat.

"Help them!" Sarah called out to the owl that she could see flying above.

It must have understood because it squawked loudly and plunged at the man holding Jenny, digging its claws in his scalp. He screamed and let go of the girl in an attempt to protect himself. Sarah called out again for help, in the hope that other birds might respond. Several did. Each attacking the intruders as best they could. It was at that moment that the watcher burst from the bushes with a large club, dealing fierce blows at the two men. The two must have decided they'd had enough because they turned and fled. Sarah thanked the birds and ran forward to tend to her wounded companions.

"Good morning, Professor Rafter," the Rector greeted him, indicating that he should take a seat. "Sherry?" the Rector offered, pointing to the decanter on his littered desk.

Rafter declined. Professor Burthwaite had become Rector some three years earlier. Malicious rumours had it that the University Board and the Town Council had chosen the weaker man so that everybody could have some peace. But peace wasn't to be. A series of bitter skirmishes between departments fighting for greater power and influence coupled with a wave of so-called modernisation in universities that swept across the country had led to the departure of several key professors, sickened by the general atmosphere of the place.

Rafter had been so engrossed in the work of his own department, that was generally left alone by the others not to say shunned, and the adventures of Sally and her friends, that one day he'd abruptly woken to find his university in serious decline and his own department threatened.

"You wanted to speak to me, Rector," Rafter reminded the man.

"Er, yes. It's about the Faculty meeting this afternoon." Burthwaite served himself a generous glass of sherry and sat down across his desk from Rafter. "What do you plan to do?"

Rafter pondered the options. Life in the university had never been a problem for him. In a way, it had always been his element. But now he felt like a stranger. He no longer recognised the signs around him and wasn't sure how to react.

"This audit is absurd," Rafter finally answered. "It makes no sense in my department. Economic criteria don't apply to theosophy. But if I refuse it, people will think I have something to hide."

The Rector nodded but made no other comment.

"I have spoken to the Blavatsky Foundation and they fully support my work and that of the Department. My salary and that of my assistants is assured. They at least understand. But these young economists, new as they are to University Board, have no idea what we do…"

Burthwaite swigged down the remainder of his sherry and stood somewhat unsteadily.

"Well at least you have only a few years to retirement," the Rector commented with a slight slur in his voice.

"That's not the point," Rafter countered. "What matters is the life and survival of my department."

The Rector had given up ages ago, Rafter realised. Burthwaite must have long since known he was just a pawn in other people's games. He was just coasting towards his own retirement hoping the place wouldn't fall down around him before he got there.

"Good for you, Rafter," the Rector said, dismissing him. "I hope you succeed".

The Faculty meeting took place in the traditional Faculty Hall, a vestige of the earlier constructions built when Avan University had been much smaller. A quiet buzz of conversation filled the air as Rafter entered, only to lessen as he moved to his seat. He wondered how many of the people present would be happy to see him and his department forced out of the university. He had to admit that in the current climate in universities across the country, a department of theosophy was really an anachronism. People were wildly enthusiastic about anything to do with technology. That was where all the money went.

The Faculty President called the meeting to order.

"First on the agenda today," the woman began, "we have the plans for quality control beginning with an audit of the Theosophy department." She glanced at Rafter possibly expecting him to oppose the idea, but he didn't respond. "Dr Frick from the University Board has kindly accepted to attend our meeting and explain his plans for ensuring quality in our university."

Frick stood. He was tall and surprisingly thin with a narrow moustache and a balding head. Rafter had never spoken to the man before. Maybe he should have.

"The town council, the national government and beyond them the taxpayers are increasingly demanding clear indications of return on investment from universities. If we are to continue our mission and keep our independence, we need to provide them with tangible proof of the quality of our work…"

The argument was flawed, Rafter thought. By accepting the logic inherent in the discourse of return on investment the university had already lost its independence. But he kept quiet. Arguing that point would get him nowhere. Frick droned on about the criteria by which to judge quality and the statistics that would be a measure that those criteria were reached.

"Tell me, Dr. Frick," Rafter said interrupting the man's unending monologue. "Theosophy is about the direct experience of the transcendent. How do you plan to measure the efficiency of that experience?"

A couple of people sniggered. Rafter wasn't sure if it was at him or Frick.

"The important thing, Professor Rafter," Frick replied, "is the extent to which these studies are seen to contribute to life and work in society."

Rafter knew the battle was pointless, there was no point in arguing with people sealed away in their own logical bubble, but he had to wage it all the same.

"Your logic and those of the people who support you, Dr. Frick, is based on that of the modern market place. It arbitrarily attributes quantifiable value to unmeasurable quantities under the cover of the myth of supply and demand and a blind belief in self-regulation. The advocates of the market place seek to extend their logic to everything: to the living, to knowledge, to beauty, to the transcendent. The logic your audit subscribes to is part of a cancer against which my colleagues and I have fought all these years, Dr. Frick. That is why we will oppose your audit with all the means we have at our disposal. That is what the independence of the university is really about."

A number of people present burst spontaneously into applause but most sat looking embarrassed, fidgeting with their hands or pretending to be taking notes. A couple of people looked downright scared. Rafter had to smile. At least his reputation as some sort of dark wizard had its uses at times. Clearly Dr. Frick was unsettled by Rafter's words judging from the beads of sweet forming on his brow. Pulling himself together, Frick closed the discussion saying: "You have no choice in the matter, Professor Rafter. The University Board has agreed to the audit and it will take place as planned."

Rafter smiled. "That we shall see," he said sending a shiver of fear through the room.

"Ladies and gentlemen," the head of the Faculty said after a prolonged silence, "let's get on to the next point on the agenda."

Rafter sat at his desk alone in his office. The bay windows were open over the River Avan letting in all the sounds and smells of the afternoon. He remembered the faces of the many different students that had taken courses with him in that room. Although he was convinced that the logic of the audit was wrong not only for his department but for the university, he could see quite clearly that the battle was lost. A Theosophy department had no place in a university in the so-called modern world. The change was inevitable.

That didn't mean that society didn't need people doing the work they did. Universities everywhere were increasingly based on accountancy principles such that each student's studies was sliced up into conveniently packaged segments that could be weighed, measured, controlled, re-controlled and subsequently sold. That the process of fragmentation made nonsense of learning and knowledge not to mention the experience of transcendence was of no concern to most people. Theosophy had always been at odds with much that took place in the university but they had always managed to exist side-by-side. This new homogenisation left no room for such immense differences.

Tales unfold

They had ridden all night. Jenny and Tom had been too worried there would be other attacks that they had decided to press on, hoping to arrive at An's place at dawn. No attacks had come, but now that they were in sight of their destination, a fight seemed to have broken out right on the front doorstep of An's house. Four people were struggling on the lawn, sending each other flying in spectacular moves. Things were happening so quickly that Sarah couldn't figure out exactly what was going on. Abruptly, the fight came to an end, the assailants bowed to each other and turned to greet the new arrivals.

"Welcome!" a young girl said. She was a little older than Sarah and seemed somehow familiar. "Anju is teaching us unarmed combat," she added by way of explanation.

Sarah glanced at Anju and finally recognised Professor Outman's granddaughter. Then she turned to the other woman and suddenly realised it was Sally. She immediately felt shy and vulnerable, not knowing how to approach a one-time would-be lover. Jenny introduced her to the others as Sarah from Granwich. And Anju introduced Dieter. Sarah guessed that the young girl must be An, so, as they hadn't been introduced, Sarah went up to her and offered her hand in greeting. An took her hand and pulled her into a warm hug then took her by the arm and led her into the house.

"You must be tired," An said showing her to her room. "You have not slept all night."

"To be honest, I am more hungry than tired and more worried about my friend Lucie than I am hungry."

An laughed at Sally's cascaded description of herself. "Then let's have breakfast with the others before you decide to eat me instead. You can tell us all about Lucie's problems once you've eaten."

Sarah really liked An. She was that sort of person that immediately made you feel at ease, and she was amusing too. Sarah took An's offered hand and followed her in the direction of the dining room.

"We have the house all to ourselves at the moment," she said, winking in a conspiratorial way as from one girl to another. "My parents have taken Fran and Martin to visit the Littl' People."

Without thinking Sarah replied: "So they will see D'rick and El'na." Sarah realised she'd revealed more than she intended the moment she said it, but it was too late.

An stopped to stare at her. "You really are a mystery Sarah, aren't you?" An said, clearly intrigued. "How come you know the Littl' People so well?"

"I was not always in this form," Sarah explained. "A long time ago I was a man called Jake and before that I was Brent. I travelled in search of Sally and helped save her from a disaster in the country of the Littl' People."

An's reaction was quite unexpected. Most people laughed at her predicament, but An gave her a kiss on her lips, and then said "Well met. I thank you for helping save my sister's life."

When Sarah had recovered from the kiss that had given her a strange fluttering feeling in her stomach, she quickly added. "Please don't tell Sally who I am. I'm very embarrassed to appear before her like this."

"You shouldn't be. I'm sure she'd be delighted to have you in this form," An added, grinning mischievously.

Sarah had some difficulty concealing her discomfort at the multiple implications of An's joke.

"I'm sorry," An said, "I was only teasing. It is a great gift to be able to change form."

"But I can't control it," Sarah explained. "I have no idea how to change back. And I'm not even sure I want to. If I could continue living with Lucie I'd be very happy."

An grinned at her. "You know, you make a very attractive girl," she teased.

Sarah blushed. The pleasure such a statement procured threw her into confusion.

"I'm sorry," An said. "Now I really have embarrassed you." In the mean time they had reached the dining room and kitchen. "I will say nothing of our little secret."

"What secret is that?" Sally asked as she emerged from the kitchen carrying a tray of food.

"Secrets are not made for telling, especially not those between two little girls like us," An joked.

The two kissed tenderly causing Sarah to be even more embarrassed.

"I think we are embarrassing Sarah. She's had one shock after another."

Sally took Sarah's arm and led her out onto the veranda where they were about to have breakfast. Jenny, Tom and the watcher were already seated. Dieter and Anju were standing nearby.

"When Sally returned to us from a long stay in your world," An told them as she poured drinks, "we taught her how to transform the world around her. Do you still remember what you did?" An asked Sally.

Sure she did. It had been just after Teresa had admitted she was her mother. She still hadn't really come to terms with that news.

Sally glanced at the ceiling and it was immediately transformed into a riot of many coloured flowers filling the air with their rich perfumes. An applauded and everyone joined her in congratulating the young woman. Sally stood and bowed theatrically.

"Enough," An said. "You'll be getting a big head and you won't want to have anything to do with us lowly girls!" she mocked, putting her arm around Sarah's waist and pulling her closer.

"Have you girls finished?" Dieter said half jokingly, causing An to make a face at him.

"Anyway, I believe Sarah has a story she wants to tell," An said.

Her choice of words caused tears to spring to Sarah's eyes. The Storyteller. Yes, that was what she was, irrespective of the form she took. Wiping the tears from her cheeks, she stood and began thus:

"The Granwich Canal was one of the greatest feats in modern times. It was to change the face of the whole area..."

And she told the magnificent tale of the building of the canal by Lucie's ancestor and how the role of the Keeper of Granwich had come into being and was perpetuated through a long line of people stretching right up to Lucie's father. She described Lucie's father's death and the legacy it left Lucie as the Keeper's daughter. Sarah portrayed her life's work with birds and Lucie's ability to change into the form of several birds and talk to them.

"When I came to Lucie I was not the little girl you see now, but a bedraggled owl that had completely lost its voice. And she took me in and cared for me. She loved me and I loved her. I think it was that love that made it possible for me to find my voice again and to change into the little girl you see before you now. Lucie's love and generosity helped me rediscover the pleasure of life and gave me the will to start writing stories anew."

When Sarah began to tell of the dramatic events that occurred as Horst burst into their lives, she let herself slip into the story and briefly took her listeners with her. She let them feel the shock of the bitterly cold, filthy canal water when Horst pushed her in. She had them feel the exasperation and fury she felt as Horst used the supposed accident as a pretext to get close to Lucie. Then releasing her listeners from the tight grip of the story so that they could come back to themselves, she continued: "Lucie is in terrible danger with that man. He is not interested in her. He just wants to become the Keeper himself. He is evil. I fear for her life. I fear for all of Granwich." And she burst into tears. Sally took Sarah in her arms and held her tight, stroking her hair. An came too and gave her kisses.

"We will do all we can to protect Lucie," An reassured her. "She is dear to us, too, for many reasons."

"What a wonderfully well-told story, rich in detail, full of passion and gripping too," Tom said. "When you got to the part about the Canal, it was amazing. I could actually feel the water. It was disgustingly cold!"

"And that Horst," Jenny added. "He made me so furious, I thought I was going to strangle him."

Everyone laughed. They agreed that the story had been gripping and congratulated her. In her sadness, Sarah was happy to have pleased them and she was also pleased that her experiment in storytelling had worked so well. She picked up a piece of bread and stuffed it into her mouth. The gesture reminded her of her first meeting with Lucie when she'd become a little girl. She couldn't help but smile. Turning to Sally who still held her in her arms, Sarah kissed her forehead.

"I believe I must tell you the secret I told An and that Jenny knows already."

Sally pulled away, intrigued.

"Before I was a bird, I was in the form of a man you knew well. One of my names was Jake. Another was Brent."

Sally stood suspended in her astonishment for a long moment and then flung her arms around Sarah saying: "I'm so glad you're back. And I'm so glad you've found the love of your life."

Once the emotion was over and everyone had eaten and drunk, An led them out into the garden and they settled leisurely in reclining chairs in the shade of the trees.

"So you were attacked?" An said examining the cut on Tom's arm. "There are a lot of bandits further south and sometimes they find their way as far as here," she added. "Most of them come from the remains of gangs that used to be associated with the Black Castle before it was destroyed."

"We were lucky to escape them," Jenny said. "If those birds hadn't helped us, we might well be dead now."

"What you need is a good combat teacher, like Anju," Dieter said, clearly proud of Anju.

Everyone laughed. "You are not wrong though," the watcher put in. "We have little experience with violence in Granwich and we are ill armed to counter it. We've lived in peace for so long. If this Horst guy were to use force against us, for example, I'm not sure how we would survive."

A long silence ensued as each person thought about the problem. Finally it was Anju who spoke up. "Then maybe Dieter and I should come back with you to Granwich to train the Watchers in unarmed combat."

Tom was enthusiastic as was the Watcher. "That would be excellent."

"When do we leave?" Dieter asked. Sarah suddenly felt abandoned. They were all going to return to Granwich while she would be condemned to stay so far away, unable to help or protect Lucie.

Sally must have noticed that Sarah was crest-fallen because she said. "I think you should stay on a few days here so the travellers can rest. Anju and Dieter can use the time to teach An, Sarah and myself some of the basic moves so we can continue to train when you are gone. I will stay here. I want to catch up on news with Sarah and An. What's more, this Horst would recognise me if I came to Granwich with you. I don't think he is very happy with me as I cost him all his men and his precious mansion in Germany."

Rumours

"Have you seen the papers?" Alo asked as he entered Rafter's office, not bothering with greetings. He was followed by Naniu, the renowned singer and good friend of the Professor.

Of course he had. He'd seen the headlines on the billboard on his way to the Department: Local Girl Disappears in Theosophy Department. "Yes," was all he replied.

"Where did they get hold of the information?" Naniu asked.

"No idea," Rafter muttered. Standing, he moved to the window and looked out. He'd been in this town for years, ever since he got the post in the Department. It had never looked so ugly and unwelcoming as it did now. Turning to face his friends, he said: "I didn't think they would hit back like this. It seems disproportionate. What are they up to?"

"So you think it was the same people as those who want to do the audit?"

"It would make sense in a fearful sort of way. But it may just be a coincidence."

"The only way to put an end to these rumours would be to get Keira back," Naniu commented.

"We can't do that. She's caught up in other stories elsewhere," Rafter retorted.

"And you can't deny it," Alo commented. "They might have concrete evidence."

"I have an appointment with the Rector in a short while. He wants explanations. Apparently the press has been in contact with him," Rafter added after a long silence.

"It's a nightmare!" Alo complained. "As a specialist in dreams I never thought I'd hear myself calling life a nightmare."

Rafter picked up the newspaper that lay open on his desk and read the article again. Under a large picture of Keira taken during one of her recent concerts, the journalist explained that Keira, well known in the local community both as a successful singer but also as librarian in the main library, had taken leave from her work to take

172

part in an experiment at the Theosophy Department. Since then no more had been heard of her. Her boss at the library admitted she'd not returned to work. A neighbour, interviewed by the newspaper, went into great detail about how he'd noticed her absence. The police said that nobody had been reported missing. The journalist finished his article regretting the great loss to Avan and hinting that a police investigation might be a good idea.

"Good," Rafter said, startling his friends with his joviality. "It is not as bad as I first thought. I think I can handle this." And strolling to his door, he left saying: "See you in half an hour. There are fresh drinks in the fridge. Help yourselves."

The Rector was not alone. Several members of the University Board including the obnoxious Dr. Frick were comfortably installed in armchairs leaving nowhere for Rafter to sit. Calling on his shamanistic skills, Rafter turned to Frick and said: "Run along next door Frick and fetch a chair."

The man looked astonished and then alarmed, but he stood and did as he was told. Rafter took his seat and greeted the others present with a broad smile.

"You wanted to see me, Rector?" Then he kept quiet waiting for the Rector to lay down his cards.

Burthwaite waited for Frick to carry in his chair. In his haste, the man clumsily knocked a pile of books off the Rector's desk and went down on his hands and knees to gather them all up. Frick was obviously furious, even more so when he looked up and saw Rafter watching him placidly.

"I have been contacted by the head of Avan local council asking for an explanation of the disappearance of a young girl last seen in your department Professor Rafter. He was not at all happy and insists on organising an enquiry. What have you to say?"

Rafter leant forward in his chair and asked: "On the basis of what evidence did he reach those conclusions?"

"Everyone knows you carry out weird experiments in your buildings," Frick interrupted.

"Don't let you anger get the better of you, Dr. Frick. You are more intelligent than that," Rafter retorted.

Frick spluttered, trying to conceal his confusion by making a show of coughing.

"Professor Burthwaite?" Rafter pursued. The man looked embarrassed and not a little drunk. "Shall I spell it out for you,

Rector?" Rafter asked. The man remained silent. "Hearsay and rumour. That was all the journalist had to offer."

"But surely," Frick said, finally getting a grip on himself, "the disappearance of this girl is sufficient cause for concern."

Rafter laughed, shocking most of the people present.

"How can you take such accusations so lightly?" Burthwaite asked, indignant.

"If there is one thing people abhor it is the unpredictable especially in people they think they know." Rafter let his words have their impact. "A successful, attractive, well-liked girl fails to return to work after a short absence. What could possibly explain such unpredictable behaviour? In the circumstances, fast thinkers reach sinister conclusions in the blink of an eye. I don't need to enumerate those conclusions. I'm sure you can imagine your own. But what if she simply met someone she liked and didn't want to leave that person? Or what if she suddenly realised that there was more to life than classifying dusty books and singing popular songs to drunken audiences? Or what if she journeyed to another world and decided she would tarry there because she was convinced it was where she should be at that moment? There are many plausible explanations that, taken in the larger context, are in no way out of character with an extremely intelligent, passionate young lady." Rafter rose and pushed his chair aside. "If there are no more questions," he asked, waiting a moment for an answer, "then I will go. I have work to do. Good day, Gentlemen."

Split in two

Sarah dangled her bare feet in a large basin of warm water and watched the birds frolicking in the trees nearby. She had not had time to consider what happened with the owl. Somehow she'd managed to split herself in two and leave her body. A part of her had soared above in flight and had been capable of seeing what was going on from a quite different angle than that of her body. What's more the bird had been able to see her and speak to her. She had no idea if she could do the same again without the help of the bird. As she recalled the feeling of leaving her body, she felt the same wrenching sensation and realised that she had once again quit her body.

She flew across the lawns to where she saw one of the servants collecting herbs. She recognised the girl immediately. It was the same one who'd poked fun at her earlier when she'd lost her way in An's house. Clearly the young woman was oblivious to Sarah's presence. She tried talking but that had no effect either. The girl continued selecting herbs and placing them carefully in her basket. Maybe she wasn't going about it the right way, Sarah thought. An idea crossed her mind: instead of talking, what if she whispered directly in the girl's head. The girl started in surprise and dropped her basket, looking left and right as if expecting to see someone. Finding nobody nearby, she calmed down and eventually continued her work.

Delighted at the success of her experiment, Sarah decided to push it a little further. She whispered very quietly in the girl's ear, telling her a story in the way she had done earlier with Sally and her friends. The girl was walking through a dark forest, she had to deliver her basket to someone but she had lost her way. Night was falling and panic began to seize her ... Sarah ceased her story when she realised that the girl was terrified. The moment that Sarah released her from the story, the girl fled into the house, leaving her basket and tools scattered across the herb garden. The impact of her experiment alarmed Sarah too, making her fly back to her body as fast as she could. Her thoughts were interrupted by the arrival of Sally. Reintegrating her body more abruptly that she wanted to, she took her feet out of the water feeling disorientated.

Picking up a towel, Sally began drying Sarah's feet with firm strokes. The ambiguity of the situation was not lost on Sarah. I'm not really the child I appear to be, she told herself, in a vain attempt to calm the confusion she felt at having Sally's touch her so.

"Would you like me to massage your feet?" Sally asked. "An gave me a massage oil that is particularly relaxing."

Sarah nodded her approval, feeling somewhat uncertain about expressing herself with words. The moment Sally uncorked the bottle, Sarah could smell a powerful scent of lavender. Sally's fingers were warm and soft on her skin as they slid between her toes and along the inside arch of her instep. Sarah couldn't help moaning faintly. Sally didn't stop at her feet, but encircled her ankles twisting this way and that until her hands glided to her calves, massaging the muscles in firm circular movements. When Sally's hands reached her knees it was too much. Sarah thought she would burst with a mixture of desire and fear. She began trembling gently. She wasn't sure exactly what she was afraid of: maybe of exploding. It was then that it happened. She stepped out of her body and stood nearby watching Sally progress sensuously up her thighs.

"I have learnt to step outside my body," her body said, possibly trying to deflect the inevitable. Her voice sounded deep and husky to her surprise. "I have done so now. My spirit, if I can call it that, is standing over there, watching."

Sally stopped her massage, but didn't take her hands off Sarah's thighs. Looking at her with passion in her eyes, Sally asked: "Did I ever tell you about Vee?"

Sarah shook her head.

"He's a voice I hear in my head. A man who is always with me, a close friend, a lover too, an excellent adviser, but who can also travel elsewhere and do things in the physical world even though he has no body."

Sarah in her spirit form saw a man rise up from Sally and move towards her.

I'm Vee, he said, bowing slightly. You are the only other person that can see me.

I'm honoured, Sarah's spirit said, holding out her hand to Vee who took it and moved it to his mouth. You too can see me, Sarah's spirit said as Vee sucked the tender flesh between Sarah's thumb and forefinger.

When he changed to nibbling the inside of her wrist she felt uncontrollable shivers running up and down her spine. It was at that moment that Sally chose to move forward and kissed Sarah firmly on the mouth, insinuating her tongue between the girl's lips. And Sarah's spirit laced her arms around Vee's neck and pulled him into a passionate embrace, feeling their bodies pressed tightly together.

"Ah! Here you are!" An said finding Sally and Sarah entwined in each others arms.

To her relief, Sarah found that she was one again. She wasn't sure she would survive that double explosion of passion a second time.

I'm sure you would, Vee said in her head, laughing.

So you can talk in my head, Sarah said.

And both of you in mine, Sally added.

"This is all too much for me," Sarah said out loud.

An looked intrigued. Giving both Sally and Sarah a kiss on their lips she sat cross-legged opposite them. "So is anyone going to share the news with me? What have you discovered?"

"Amazing!" was all An had to say when they had described what had happened and Sarah had told about her experience with the owl. She chose not to mention the episode with the servant girl, though.

She felt guilty about what she had done and, what's more, she imagined people might not take kindly to the idea that she could get inside their heads.

"I suspect those of us who can transform here in the Reaches – what the people in Granwich call the Patriciat – have become somewhat lazy or maybe we have not had so many outside influences as you. Whatever, you far surpass us in your abilities."

Tears were running down Sally's cheeks. "Did I ever tell you about the Dream Class? It was Jenny's idea and all our little group have vowed to make it a reality."

Sarah could see that Sally's face shone with excitement and inner contentment.

"Each of us develops our abilities as we have been doing here and we share them with the others, learning as much as we can from the world around us and each other."

Sarah clapped her hands in delight. No comments from you Vee, she thought. I really am a little girl as well.

He just laughed inwardly as did Sally.

"Later we would like to extend the class to more people possibly making a 'university' of a completely new type."

"I have one complaint," An said, pretending to pout. "I am jealous of how you two or should I say three or four are able to talk to each other in your heads."

Sarah took An's hands saying: "Then I will try to teach your spirit how to move out of your body so that you can talk to us in our heads and in return you can teach me transformation for, although I want to remain the little girl I am now and return to be with Lucie, I would also like to be able to change form too."

Sally came and hugged them, saying: "It looks like our class just gained two new members."

Experiments

Sarah sat under the trees at a large oak table, a broad boater on her head, writing the beginning of her first book. She wanted to get down the story of Lucie and her family. It wasn't easy to keep a grip on what she was doing, mainly because the story had a way of telling itself, independently of her. Sally sat across from her reading, a dark silk cloth cast over her head and shoulders making her look like a wayward Madonna. The late afternoon sun was still warm and tiny insects buzzed around them playing noisily in the sun's rays.

"May I disturb you?" Sarah asked, breaking a long pause in their sporadic conversation.

"Sure," Sally said, looking up from her book.

"I've been wondering about what happened earlier today."

Sally grinned. Realising that Sally had something else in mind, Sarah clarified: "I mean my being able to separate from my body." She put down her pen and leaned her chin on her hands. "I've been wondering about whether my body can continue to function normally while I am out of it."

"With Vee, it's different, of course," Sally replied. "He began by being completely separate from me. So it seems normal for me to continue being who and what I am whether he is with me or elsewhere. I suppose he progressively became a part of me."

Sarah remained silent for a moment thinking over how the separation had begun for her.

"Maybe we could carry out an experiment," Sally suggested. "You separate and I talk to your body while your spirit talks to Vee."

"I'm not sure I can separate at will," Sarah pretended, hoping Vee couldn't hear her thoughts. "I've never done it deliberately."

Maybe I can help, Vee said. I could invite your spirit self to come for a walk.

Sarah felt the strange lurching feeling that went with separation and realised that her spirit self had walked away with Vee. If she listened she could hear their conversation quite clearly, but Sally was talking to her bringing her attention back to her body.

"… what does it feel like then?"

Sarah surveyed her body from within before answering. "I feel numb, as if my senses were deadened and I was half asleep."

"Give me your hand," Sally ordered.

Sarah wasn't sure she wanted a repetition of their earlier lovemaking, not now at least.

Sally must have sensed her hesitation because she said chuckling: "Don't worry, I'm not going to take advantage of you."

Sarah stretched out her hand and Sally took hold of it and pinched Sarah's thumb between her own thumb and forefinger "Tell me what you feel." "Pain in my finger," Sarah said grimacing. "And in the background I can hear Vee and my spirit self talking."

"Come on," Sally said standing and pulling Sarah to her feet. "Let's go for a walk."

Sarah was reluctant but she wasn't sure why. She pulled on Sally's hand, resisting.

"What are you afraid of?" Sally asked.

Sarah had to give it some thought before she recognised the cause of her concern. "I'm afraid I will lose my spirit self; that we will no longer be able to get back together."

An joined them at that moment saying: "I heard what you were talking about. It might be a mistake to believe Sarah's spirit self is in any way like Vee. It sounds much more like the practice of a Shaman who can send a part of herself out on a journey. I don't think you can force things." She took Sarah's hand and went on: "I suggest you tell Vee to bring Sarah's spirit self back. I imagine the forced separation could be the cause of a lot of anguish .... Until Sarah has got used to doing such things."

Sarah was grateful for An's explanation. She had been feeling increasingly anxious. A familiar lurch told her that her spirit was back. Her relief was so great that she burst into tears in An's welcoming arms.

"I'm so sorry," Sally apologised. "I had no idea that the separation could be so distressing."

Chapter 9 - The Dawn of Chaos

Well met

"You can't come in! The gates are locked!"

None of them recognised the voice that refused them entrance to Granwich. It sounded foreign.

"The gates have never been locked before," the watcher retorted. "Why are they closed?"

They could hear a heavy weight shifting on the other side of the gate. Jenny hoped it meant they would soon be able to get in. She was tired after the long ride home and it was late.

"There's an outbreak of withering sickness over at Smeth'ick. We have orders to keep everybody out."

"But we haven't been to Smeth'ick," Jenny protested.

"Don't matter. Orders is orders!"

Jenny and Tom looked at each other in the half-light, both wondering about who could have ordered such a thing.

"Who gave the orders?" Tom asked.

"The Council for the defence of Granwich. Now go away and let people get some sleep."

Jenny was about to protest but the watcher pulled gently on her arm. When they were at a safe distance from the gate he said: "The watchers will know. They'll send someone to fetch us, if it is possible."

"What's this Council they talk about?" Tom asked.

"Never heard of it," was the Watcher's reply.

"Where shall we go?" Jenny asked.

"We can head for that hill over there," the watcher suggested. "The trees will hide us from view and we can see what is happening in and around the town below."

"But first we must go back and fetch Anju and Dieter." They had left the two in hiding a short way back down the road, as they didn't want to reveal their presence yet.

Having briefly explained the situation to the two, they set off in the direction of the hill under the cover of night. The upper half of the hill was densely planted with trees amongst which there were no apparent paths. They struggled upwards forcing their way between the trunks and branches till they came suddenly to a clearing that hadn't been visible from below.

Dark forms lurked in the open space making Jenny and the others crouch down in fear. It was then that they heard the noise of footsteps, but they could see no movement in the moonless night.

"It will soon be dawn," Jenny whispered. "Then we'll be able to see what's going on."

As the first faint rays appeared in the east, a weird sound rang out making Jenny shiver. It was not so much frightening as penetrating. The voice, for she realised it must be a voice, seemed to enter her chest and resonate there, inciting her to sing with it. She found it difficult to resist its call. As the voice grew stronger other voices began to respond to it till the air around them vibrated in wild eddies that brushed against her face and stirred her hair. Then, as abruptly as it had begun, the voice ceased. The scene before them was now illuminated by the red glow of the rising sun revealing a young woman standing still, her arms outstretched, her head upright, silent. She stood in the middle of a circle of majestic standing stones that reminded Jenny of circles she had visited in her own world. No one spoke, no one moved.

"Come on Mia," a woman whispered. "We must be gone before there is too much light."

"Ma'gina," the watcher whispered as strongly as he could, recognising the voice.

"Well met, Jon," she replied. "Who is that with you?"

"Jenny, Tom and two friends," Jenny answered, rising and moving towards Ma'gina.

"Do not come any closer," Mia said, for it was she that had sung. "This is a sacred place. We should not disturb it any longer. We will come down to you."

After the hasty greetings were over, Ma'gina spoke up. "We are on our way to Smeth'ick. We must leave immediately."

"But they told there was some sort of illness there. Why are you going there?"

Ma'gina had already set off for the far side of the hill and the slope the furthest from the town.

"Come with us, at least some of the way, and we will tell you on the road."

"I can't come with you as I must return to Granwich," Jon said. "And these young people are going to help train the Watchers in unarmed combat."

"Good," Ma'gina said.

"Tell the Watchers we are on our way to Smeth'ick." And she turned and left followed by Mia, Jenny and Tom.

Ma'gina refused to talk or to let them talk for a while, forcing them to set a brisk pace as they silently crossed woods and fields by small paths. Just as Jenny was thinking they must have reached a safe distance they heard voices from the main road, several hundred feet away.

"Why the 'ell do we 'ave to stay in this forsaken place," a man swore.

"Cause the boss told us to," another replied. "We're to make sure no one gets by from Smeth'ick or anywhere else."

The men were concealed behind a large rock and anyone coming along the road wouldn't have seen them, but from their vantage point across the fields the two were clearly visible.

"I ain't got no boss," the first one complained.

"'Course you 'ave, you silly git. It's that big guy wot pays the money."

Ma'gina took the lead indicating silently that they should follow her. She apparently knew the place well for the path she took led to a shallow dip in the ground that hid them from the men on the road. Following each other in single file they snaked their way through fields and bushes till they judged they were far enough from the road to talk.

"You need to give us an explanation," Jenny whispered, feeling increasingly anxious at not knowing why they were stealing their way through the countryside like thieves.

They had reached a copse situated in a fold in the ground within which they were completely hidden from view.

"Let's have something to eat and drink and we will tell you our story," Ma'gina said taking a seat on a log and opening her bag from which she extracted bread and cheese and wine.

"We have a little cheese left from An's place," Jenny said, placing the remains of their food with that of Ma'gina. "We didn't expect to have to continue travelling. That's all we have left."

"Don't worry, we'll find things along the way," Ma'gina reassured them.

Everyone ate in silence. When they had finished Ma'gina handed around the bottle of wine. Despite the sun getting higher in the sky it was still cold. Jenny cuddled up in Tom's arms making the most of his warmth. He didn't seem to suffer so much from the cold as she did. His reassuring strength and his warmth were amongst the things that appealed to her most about him.

"Most of what I am about to tell you I learnt from the watchers during a secret meeting. That new man, Horst, went with Lucie to an emergency meeting of the Patriciat that she had convened. Horst explained that his assistant had been to Smeth'ick on business, but had not been able to enter the place because a plague had broken out there. He described the symptoms in gruesome detail that both convinced and terrified the Patriciat. As it is not so far away, Horst told them they needed to protect themselves by not letting anyone in or out of the town. Apparently the Patriciat were so frightened they were prepared to do all he suggested. He set up a Council for the defence of Granwich with him at the head of it. They decided to block the entrances to the town to stop people coming in and going out. He offered the services of his own men to keep watch at the gates. No one had ever seen them before. Judging from their accents they come from the south and look pretty wild."

"We were attacked by two such men on our way to An's place," Tom explained. "Thanks to Sarah's help we managed to fight them off. Jon told us that they sounded like people from bands that used to work from time to time for the people in the Black Castle. Maybe these are the same lot."

"So why are you heading for Smeth'ick?" Jenny asked.

"Because we suspect Horst of not telling the truth," Ma'gina said, her voice revealing the intense dislike she felt for the man.

Jenny was surprised to discover such vehemence as she had come to know Ma'gina as one of the most open and tolerant people she had ever met. "As we can't get into Granwich, I suggest we accompany you to Smeth'ick, if Tom agrees," Jenny said looking to Tom for his approval. He nodded.

Like Granwich, the buildings of Smeth'ick were predominantly black and the town owed much of its development to the building of the canals. Smeth'ick, however, was a much smaller town whose main craft was producing stained glass windows. Local glass blowers had the secret of some of the most beautiful coloured glass in the country, Ma'gina told them. Her friend Ginger had first worked developing the salts used in creating stained glass, but his interest turned to medicinal herbs when his wife fell seriously ill. When she died some years later, he had dedicated himself to researching cures.

"I learnt a lot from him," Ma'gina explained. "I think he hoped I would take over from him here in Smeth'ick, but I was always a girl of Granwich."

As the path they were following crested a low hill they got their first view of Smeth'ick.

"Ginger lives near that pond," Ma'gina told them, pointing to the small expanse of water at the edge of the town. "I will go down alone to see him. That way if there is any danger of infection you will be spared."

Mia insisted she go too but Ma'gina refused.

"People know me in Smeth'ick. It won't seem odd me visiting him. But if an unknown young girl comes on a visit, people are likely to talk."

Ginger's Apothecary

Ginger's Apothecary, as he called it, was very similar to Ma'gina's. Not surprising, she thought, as she had built her Apotheka on the same principals. As Ginger was old now and had no assistant to help him in his work, he spent most of his time writing about his work and discoveries rather than treating people. Most young people weren't so interested in learning healing, Ma'gina bemoaned. Thank heavens she'd found Mia to help her.

As she pushed open the door of the Apothecary an unpleasant smell of decay overwhelmed her. Covering her mouth and nose with her shawl, she ventured further into the building, calling out Ginger's name. No answer came. She found him on the first floor lying exhausted in his bed. His face was grey and withered but he was still alive.

"Keep away," he warned her as best he could. "I've caught the withering sickness!"

Ma'gina set her bag on the table and pulled out one of her simples. She poured a couple of drops on his lips and watched as he licked the substance. He must have recognised what she was giving him because he said: "Good."

"Save your strength," Ma'gina told him.

There was no known cure for withering sickness. Most people died within days of the first symptoms, although a few managed to survive. It began with aches and pains all over and a high temperature. Within a day or two, the muscles would begin to shrivel rapidly until the heart finally gave up its efforts. It was believed that direct contact led to contagion, which was why people with the sickness were generally locked away and left to die.

Ma'gina went to the well outside with the intention of fetching water to try to reduce the man's fever. The well was in the front of the house, next to the entrance. As Ma'gina stretched forward to reach the pail to pull up water, she could not help notice the odd smell coming from the well. Something was not right. Glancing down the well she saw tiny splashes of a red substance against the side of the well. The water must be contaminated, she thought. That would explain why Ginger was ill. Judging from the marks she'd seen, someone must have poured something down the well. Horst! She thought. The bastard. He'd sent his assistant to see Ginger to buy that poison ... but also to poison the well and add credence to his claim that the people of Smeth'ick had the withering sickness.

Hurrying back into the Apothecary, she headed for the storeroom where she found a tiny glass bottle and sharp knife. Back at the well she scraped a small quantity of the red substance from the side of the well and transferred it into the bottle. She couldn't manage to do what was necessary alone. She needed help. Placing the bottle in the laboratory she returned to Ginger's bed side.

"I don't think it is really the withering sickness," she told him. "You've been poisoned, or rather your well has been poisoned."

He groaned by way of response as she continued.

"I think I can save you, but I need to fetch help. I'll be back in a short while." And she left him, hoping he would hold out till she got back.

Help!

Mia looked up expectantly when she saw Ma'gina arrive. She stood and was heading to greet Ma'gina when the woman warned them all to stay back.

"Ginger is ill. He has all the symptoms of the withering sickness. But I found a substance in his well that makes me think he has been poisoned. Mia I need your help, but I can't force you to take the risk of contamination. You must decide for yourself."

Mia didn't hesitate she stepped forward, asking, determined: "What can I do to help?"

"First I have work for you others," Ma'gina replied. "We will need fresh water. Can you get buckets of water and leave them near the entrance of Ginger's house? But use only running water. Don't take water from wells. They may also have been contaminated. Ask the people of Smeth'ick to loan you the necessary buckets. Tell them I sent you and explain that Ginger has been poisoned, then warn them not to use the water from their wells until we are sure they are not contaminated."

They nodded that they had understood.

"I may also need herbs. I don't know what Ginger has in his stock. You know enough now Jenny to be able to find them. I need another thing from you, Jenny, which is much more important. I need you to send energy from the earth into that house so that those who are ill and those who heal are protected."

Jenny looked concerned. "I have never done such a thing before, but I am certain it is possible," she replied.

"Make sure you maintain your own level of energy," Ma'gina insisted. "And don't let any of the dark energy in the place flow back into you."

Jenny's face was furrowed with worry. "Thanks for the advice, Ma'gina," was all she said.

"We must hurry," Ma'gina said. "Keep away from the well in front of Ginger's house and don't enter his house either. If I need anything more, I will call out to you from within." And with that she turned and hurried in the direction of the town closely followed by Mia. Jenny and Tom also headed for the town taking a different path.

Ma'gina sent Mia to fetch coals so as to light a fire in Ginger's room, for although he had a fever, the loss of muscles left him completely vulnerable to the cold. Taking a clean cloth Ma'gina dipped it in the fresh water and gently washed the man's face and neck.

"You are a strong man, Ginger," she told him. "You will last this out. I'm sure of it."

He was having difficulties breathing and when she tried giving him a drink she discovered he could no longer swallow properly causing him to almost choke. Ma'gina helped him sit till he stopped coughing and then she continued to drip droplets of water on his lips.

"Continue to moisten his lips, but avoid touching him, if you can," Ma'gina told Mia. "I am going to his laboratory to try to examine the substance I found in the well."

Demon from the well

Ma'gina sat on a high stool by a large wooden bench on which she'd placed the small bottle. The red substance shone in the lamplight, its colour deceivingly welcoming. She had too little of it to examine the material and no time to carry out tests. There was only one possibility and it was fraught with risks. The technique was generally used to glean information about medicinal plants. It involved communing with the essence of the plant. It was generally used with plants that were beneficial or at worst innocuous. Here the substance was lethal.

She took a deep breath and closed her eyes. A swirling red mist surged up in front of her, threatening to suffocate her. She brushed it aside. And stepping beyond she saw three open vials on a workbench. One was deep purple. The second was a yellow green colour. And the last was pitch black. She bowed to each in turn and then turned her attention to the deep purple one. She could feel intense heat radiating from it. If she listened carefully she could hear a high-pitched note resonating in the substance. It was familiar but she couldn't immediately place it. A door opened before her and she stepped inside only to find a new workbench on which lay several flowers of Belladonna. That would explain the difficulties swallowing, she thought, and the high fever.

Next to it on the bench lay a seed pod and a couple of deep chocolate-brown beans. Calabar. A risky antidote, she mused. Pulling back she returned to the previous room and approached the yellow-green substance. As she came closer she had a clear vision of a stream cascading over shingle as it wound its way towards Smeth'ick.

She knew the place well. Ginger had often taken her there in search of flowers. Her vision refocused on a tiny plant growing amongst the roots of a tree. Its flowers were like little green and yellow buttons. Instinctively she knew she had to mix the petals of both colours for the remedy.

Hastening back to the third vial, she felt a threatening dark sound than wove its way around her trying to force her downwards. She resisted.

"Reveal yourself!" she ordered.

One didn't normally give orders to essences, but this one was clearly malevolent. A violent flash blinded her. It was all she could do not to stagger and fall, such was the force that hit her.

"Show yourself!" she ordered again.

A clap of thunder preceded a second brilliant flash. There was nothing she could do to oppose it. She felt herself falling followed by a searing pain as her arm hit the ground breaking her fall.

"You are unmasked!" she cried between clenched teeth. And there before her stood Horst laughing at her, his white teeth flashing threateningly, the glint in his eye frankly evil.

She must have blacked out at that moment for the next thing she knew was Mia stroking her face trying to bring her round. She felt dreadfully cold and empty.

"I know what is in that well," she said.

"And I know you have broken your arm," Mia told her. "I will have to reset it, before you think of doing anything else."

Ma'gina refused. "Help me to my feet and let me lean on your shoulder."

With Mia's help she struggled up and staggered along the narrow corridor to the front entrance. Once outside she called the others. She asked Jenny and Tom to get the yellow and green flowers she'd seen in her vision, explaining exactly where to find them. She sent Mia back into the Apothecary to search for Calabar seeds. Before Jenny and Tom left, she turned again to Jenny.

"I have a very complicated mission for you. First we have to make the antidote and administer it to Ginger. But there is another component to his illness that comes directly from that Horst devil. You must use the earth energy to break the link between the two or at least to shield Ginger from the man's influence. I'm not sure how you can do that. Maybe a shield would suffice. But you need to be very careful. This man is extremely dangerous and he must not know you are working against him. Tom you must stay with Jenny all the time and give her all the support you can. I will ask Mia to sing for protection as well. When she begins singing you will know you must do your work."

Healing song

"No you won't! You'll sit down and let me set that arm of yours," Mia insisted.

She was well aware that Ma'gina was quite capable of letting her own arm knit together incorrectly to save the life of someone else. But Mia was having none of it.

"It won't take long. I have already prepared the splints."

She felt her way along Ma'gina's arm, noting the position of the bones and pressing here and there to ease them back into place. The arm was broken in several places, with one of the fractures quite badly misaligned.

"This is going to hurt," she apologised as she pulled sharply on Ma'gina's arm and the bone snapped back into place.

What an incredible old woman, she thought. Most people would have screamed at such a treatment. Ma'gina sat quietly watching Mia at work as if studying the treatment of someone else.

"There," Mia said. "Now the splints."

When she'd finished, Mia tied up the arm in a sling warning Ma'gina not to use it. She knew the woman didn't need to be told, but then again she was quite capable of using the arm to help a patient, ignoring her own pain.

"You are an incredible woman," Mia said, kissing Ma'gina on the forehead.

"And you are an incredible pupil," Ma'gina replied, pale but smiling.

They climbed the stairs to Ginger's bedroom. His condition had deteriorated, as he struggled to get air into his emaciated lungs.

"We must hurry," Ma'gina said, a look of concern on her face. "We are going to give you a special potion, Ginger. But alone it will not be enough. Mia, here, and her friend Jenny outside, are going to help you in their own ways. All you need to do my friend is to hold on to life."

His eyes blinked. No other sign came to indicate he'd understood. Mia carefully forced open his mouth and, using a small pipette, she fed small quantities of the bright green potion into his mouth. Ma'gina massage his throat gently with her free hand, in an attempt to help him swallow the liquid.

"That should be enough," Ma'gina said after they'd repeated the operation three times. "Sing now, Mia, and save my friend's life." And the old woman sat down next to Ginger on the bed, holding his withered hand in hers.

Mia stood in the middle of the room. Pulling the locket Grace had given her from under her blouse, she grasped it firmly in her right hand and began to sing. Closing her eyes, she visualised the circle of standing stones, imaging them closing around her. She sang first for them, letting her voice go out to them and they responded to her call. Whirls and eddies of sound swirled around the room filling it with music.

To her surprise she saw Grace standing nearby, exalted, her eyes closed, her voice curling around the stones, reaching out to her. Then one by one all the sisters of the Sisterhood appeared, each singing amongst their own stones yet present there in that room with her in a musical prayer for Ginger. The more they sang, the closer they seemed to come, till Mia could no longer tell where her body ended and those of her sisters began. They stood united, one powerful woman of sound, radiating outwards and upwards, knowing no limits.

As the singing finally came to an end and her sisters withdrew leaving Mia once again to herself with a feeling both of loss and profound belonging, she opened her eyes and look in the direction of Ginger. He had a broad smile on his lips. He must have heard the music they made for him, but it hadn't been enough. For despite it all he had slipped away. Ma'gina sat still by his side, clasping his hand in her bony old hands, tears streaming down her cheeks.

"Goodbye, my friend," she said as she leaned forward to close his eyelids. Mia helped Ma'gina to her feet and they made their way slowly down the stairs, along the narrow corridor and out into the front of the house where they were surprised to find a large group of people of Smeth'ick had gathered. Seeing the grave look on Ma'gina's face they bowed their heads and some began to cry quietly. Ginger was much loved in the town.

It was then that Mia noticed Jenny prostrate in Tom's arms. Leaving Ma'gina in the hands of some of the local woman she hurried over to Jenny's side.

"What happened?" she asked Tom.

"She was in a trance for a long time and suddenly she went stiff and collapsed in my arms."

Mia felt her pulses, listened to her chest and decided it was not too serious. All signs of life were strong. She might simply be exhausted. Mia extracted a small vial from her leather bag – she'd taken to imitating Ma'gina's habit of having such a bag of medical supplies with her at all times – and, unstoppering it, she waved it gently under Jenny's nose several times. The girls' eyes fluttered and then opened.

"You sang so wonderfully Mia, but I could hardly hold Horst off." She paused a moment nestling back in Tom's arms. "Ginger's dead isn't he? I saw it happen. I couldn't stop it." And she burst into tears.

Ma'gina came to join them along with a group of local women. "It was his time," she told Jenny. "It is not your fault. Both you and Mia worked miracles here today." And she stepped forward, taking Mia and Jenny into her arms as best she could with only one free arm. "We are so lucky to have you here with us." Then she straightened up and said: "Come you must tell us what happened, Jenny, and we must prepare the funeral and then there will be a meeting with the Smeth'ick Council."

New ways

The air underground was stuffy and a little musty. Anju didn't like being closed in for long periods. She was a child of the sunshine. That was one of the things that appealed to her most about India. They hadn't been above ground since they'd arrived a few hours earlier. She flexed her muscles in an attempt to ease the tension that prolonged immobility had caused. She sat next to Dieter in a large underground room in which most of the Watchers were now gathered.

Dieter seemed fascinated by the Watchers. As a former police inspector, especially as he'd been in the German police force, the activities of the Watchers must have been troubling at best. From the little Anju had learnt of this group, they functioned without a leader or any apparent form of hierarchy. A number of sensible principles guided their actions. Their daily practice led to an excellent flow of information and a safe measure of redundancy without any external control. She could imagine Dieter replying that it only worked because it was such a small town.

The beginning of the meeting tore her from her reflections.

"Tristan was to keep an eye on Horst from a warehouse across the street. He was caught by three of Horst's thugs and beaten to death with clubs. When they'd finished, they dragged him to the east gate and flung him into a pit some way down the road beyond the walls."

Clearly many of the Watchers had already heard the news, but they were not any less shocked by hearing the brutal facts again.

"What sort of club did they use," Dieter enquired.

The watcher described it meticulously.

"May I ask why you enquire?" another watcher asked.

"Because it is important to know what sort of weapons they use if we are to teach you how to defend yourselves against them."

People seemed satisfied with his answer. Anju guessed that Jon had already told them of their plan to teach them self-defence. Discussion returned to the attack.

"How did they know he was there? Tristan was an excellent watcher. He wouldn't have been caught easily."

"They seemed to know that someone was hiding nearby."

"Could they have a spy amongst us?"

"I doubt it," several people said.

Dieter stood and walked round the table that most of them sat at. "Are you sure that no other watchers are missing?" he asked.

"You mean torture?" Anju speculated.

"We have no written list of the members of the Watchers but all of us know each other. Six of us are not present at the moment. Two are still watching Horst. Two have been sent to the gates. Tom is away with Ma'gina and Mia. That leaves one person unaccounted for: Brian."

A shocked silence filled the room.

Anju could see that for all their dedication and skill they were not used to this kind of situation.

"May I say something?" she asked standing and pacing around the table. Any form of movement was a relief after sitting still so long.

"Of course," someone said.

"Is this the first time you have been confronted with this kind of violence?"

Several people said: "Yes."

"I have two suggestions to make," Anju pursued. "First that you learn to defend yourselves from such attacks. I can help you there. Secondly, you need to reconsider your ways of working. This may well be the first time you have had to face people who are frankly evil. It may well require a different approach on your part. These people are not going to react in ways you are used to. Maybe Dieter can help you there. In his job he had to deal with such people in our world."

She was pleased that Dieter remained silent at that moment. These people were probably frightened and perplexed. They needed time and space to think.

Echoing her thoughts, someone said: "We need time to think."

It must have been a special signal to them because they broke up into small groups and continued discussing. Some groups approached Anju and Dieter with question, but they mostly spoke amongst themselves.

A scream shattered the peaceful conversations as Brian burst into the room closely followed by two of Horst's henchmen. Clubs waving, they struck out at Brian giving him several vicious blows to his head that sent him crashing to the floor with blood spurting from his head. One of the henchmen went to kick the wounded man, but his foot never reached its mark. Anju sent him flying across the room, crashing into the opposite wall and crumbling to the floor. Dieter took care of the other one who was trying to back out the door waving his club in front of him.

"Use the pressure points," Anju called out to Dieter.

She had been teaching him their use during their journey from An's house. Both henchmen slumped unconscious onto the floor. Anju and Dieter dragged them together in a heap and then stopped to look around them. The company of Watchers stood silent watching, as if tetanised by what they had seen.

"Quick! This man needs your help," Anju said to no one in particular as she bent over Brian's bloodied body.

Several watchers started forward while others went to fetch water and bandages.

"It looks worse than it is," Anju said. "The head always bleeds a lot. The wounds only seem to be superficial, but I am no healer."

One of the women watchers was a healer and she tended to Brian. The others retreated to the table and sat dazed around it.

"You need to check the tunnels to be sure that nobody else got in." Dieter said. "And if you can find out where they got in, you should block that up if that is possible. We don't want any more of them finding their way down here."

He didn't need to say any more, several people ran off to follow his suggestions. Anju and Dieter compared notes quietly about their respective combats, discussing what they might have done better.

When the watchers came back from the tunnels they reported that no new intruders had been found. They had also discovered where the men had broken into the tunnels chasing after Brian. Steps had already been taken to block the hole and stop anybody else getting in that way. Once their report was over, all faces turned to Anju and Dieter.

"It would seem that both your suggestions were right," Jon said. "We cannot defend ourselves against such people and we are unable to anticipate their moves because we cannot understand their way of thinking. Your offer to help is most appropriate and timely. We accept and thank you both whole heartedly."

Adieu

Ernan had been the innkeeper of Smeth'ick's most reputed inn for years and before him his father had filled that role. He was also Mayor of Smeth'ick and was much respected for his practical, common-sense way of sorting things out. As she watched him put down brimming tankards on the table in front of her and her friends, Ma'gina wondered how he would handle the chaos that was about to break over them.

"Food'll be here in a moment," he told them and he hurried away into the kitchen.

"You still haven't told us what happened to you back there, Jenny," Ma'gina said by way of invitation. Jenny unlaced herself from Tom's arms, and swallowing a large mouthful of ale she made ready to describe what had happened to her.

"It was easy enough to identify the bright energy coming from both Mia and yourself, Ma'gina. I found it interesting to see the resonance between your different colours. You are not similar, but you go well together. I imagined it was because you have worked so closely. At first I couldn't find any trace of Ginger. I searched closely around you two and finally I found a very dim light smothered under several layers of dark colours. Little by little those layers slipped away leaving him like a withered apple, all greens and browns and dirty yellows. I tried to feed him energy from the earth but something resisted. As I looked closer I caught sight of a thin black thread coiled tightly around the lifeline that connected him to the earth. The thread and the lifeline were so closely wound together that I could find no way to separate them. I thought I might be able to get at the black thread where it was attached to Ginger's form, but it wasn't attached, it was plunged straight inside. At that moment, the intensity of Mia's song suddenly increased. I don't now how, but the vibrations forced the head of this thing out of Ginger's form. It was like a tapeworm, all sickly black and sinister with a flat, ugly head. The thing must have sensed my presence because it turned in my direction and started moving rapidly towards me. I was sure it was going to attack me. I could feel its pure malevolence."

She broke down at that point and started crying. Tom took her in his arms.

"I think it was me that killed Ginger," she admitted, pulling free of Tom's embrace. "I was terrified. To protect myself I threw a mass of energy at the beast producing a brilliant flash. After that I can recall no more."

Having said that, she slumped back in Tom's arms, her hands over eyes.

"It's too hard," she muttered. "I told An I was afraid of this ability of mine because I knew that someday I would have to use it to attack and not to heal."

"We will never know what really happened," Ma'gina said, thoughtfully running her hands through her hair. "Sometimes we have to do ill. We have no choice. But in the larger scheme of things that ill may turn out to be good. I believe that was the case here."

Ernan, who had brought their food a while ago, had been listening to Jenny's tale. "Ginger was a good friend of mine," he began by way of explanation. "I think he would have chosen to do what you did. He often said that healing was not always easy. When things got complicated, he'd say, you have to follow your instinct. Don't fret then, Miss, I believe Ginger would have approved of your choice."

After the meal was over they followed Ernan outside, returning to Ginger's house where women had been busy preparing his body for the funeral. Dressed in his best clothes and decked in flowers, he was carried out on a wide plank by four men, one at each corner. A large crowd had formed in front of the house. They stepped aside to let the procession pass between their ranks and then joined the growing file of people following the makeshift coffin. The road to the market place was lined with hundreds of people, many of whom threw flowers. Few people had dry eyes as they wiped tears from their cheeks. The only sound to be heard was the shuffling of feet as the procession made its slow way through the town. A large pile of branches and sticks had been built in the middle of the market place. It was there that they laid Ginger.

Ernan stepped forward and spoke of Ginger and his work in the town.

"Many of us standing here owe our lives to him," he reminded them, bringing his oration to an end. "Yet for all his great knowledge, he was modest and easy-going. Many of us counted him as our friend. Thank you friend for all you have done for us," the Mayor finished, unable to retain his tears.

Many others stepped forward and said a word or placed flowers next to Ginger on the pyre. Ma'gina spoke too.

"I learnt much of what I know of healing from you, Ginger. Above all, you taught me to listen to people rather than getting caught up in the techniques of healing. I will dearly miss you my old friend."

The four men who had borne the body came forward with torches and lit the pyre. And as the flames started to lick their way up towards the body, Mia began to sing. Ma'gina had heard her sing many times, but never had she sung with such emotion and beauty. There was so much richness in what they heard it was as if a great choir of women's voices were singing. Ma'gina had the impression that Mia's wordless song was lifting Ginger up into the skies above. The whole crowd was completely transfixed by the music, heads bowed, eyes closed, listening. When the song finally ceased and people looked up at the pyre they gasped to see that the body of Ginger was no longer there. All that remained was a blazing fire that would soon consume all the wood.

A meeting with fate

The town hall couldn't possibly have been fuller. All available chairs were occupied and people were sitting on the floor, blocking the passageways between the rows of chairs and many more stood against the wall at the back of the room. Everybody knew that something serious was afoot. Many rumours were circulating about the death of Ginger and the people who had come to help from Granwich and farther afield.

Ernan climbed the stairs to the small rostrum that stood at the front of the hall and invited Ma'gina to join him. Holding up his hand for quiet, he greeted the citizens of Smeth'ick. Not wishing to waste time, he got straight to the essential.

"We have reason to believe that Ginger was killed as part of a wider plot to gain control in this area. We also know that a rumour has been put around in Granwich that we have the plague here. The gates of Granwich have been closed to all comers. We do not as yet know exactly why Smeth'ick has been singled out in this way, but we need to find out rapidly as our town may be in far greater danger than we think."

He paused for a moment to let what he'd said sink in. Many people looked concerned, Mia thought as she looked back over the crowd. There was nothing worse than a threat that you could neither understand nor locate.

"I have asked Ma'gina, whom you all know, to give us news of the developments in Granwich which seem linked to what is happening to us here."

"People of Smeth'ick," Ma'gina began. "Recently we have had a number of visits from people come from far away. Mia and Jenny and Tom you have already met," she said pointing in their direction. "They are gentle people who have helped us a great deal. But there are others who come not to help but to plunder, who are interested only in their own gain. One such person is a man called Horst who has seized control in Granwich on the pretext that there has been an outbreak of the plague here in Smeth'ick. We know that it was him that had the water in Ginger's well poisoned and who used black magic to make Ginger look like the victim of the withering sickness..."

She didn't get any further because there was a disturbance at the back of the room. Panic had broken out for no apparent reason and people were pushing their way forwards. It was then that someone called out "Fire!!!" and smoke began to billow around the door at the back. Everybody stood and started pushing towards the other entrance that was near the rostrum. Mia noticed that smoke was also creeping under that door too. Someone must have set fire to the place. Ernan pulled himself up to his fullest height and shouted for quiet. It took some time for the noise to die away.

"Stop pushing," he ordered. "People will get hurt."

"Is there no other way out?" Ma'gina asked him.

"Yes," Ernan replied, "but it is only a narrow tunnel and it will take time to get all these people out that way."

Someone will have to hold off the fire to give time for people to escape, Mia thought. She wasn't sure that her songs could do it, but she was prepared to try. Glancing at Jenny she realised the girl had had a similar idea.

"Send strong men on ahead," Ma'gina said. "We may have to fight our way out even if we use the tunnels."

Ernan turned to the waiting people of Smeth'ick. "We will escape by a secret route," he told them, clearly not wishing to say exactly where for fear their attackers could hear. He pointed to a group of farm workers and builders. "You will go first and make sure the passage is clear. You may have to fight your way out. The others will all follow you. You must remain calm throughout and above all, make no noise. No one must know where we are."

He stepped down from the rostrum and was about to show the way to the tunnel when Mia spoke up.

"Jenny and I will use what powers we have to try to hold back the fire. Your thoughts and prayers will help us."

Ernan thanked them. Then he hurried over to the group of men and showed them the secret passage concealed under a set of benches.

Mia found a space that had been left free by the fleeing people who were lining up to descend into the tunnel. Jenny came and joined her.

"I will try to use the earth magic to stifle the fire," Jenny told Mia.

"And I will try to call for rain," Mia replied although she had no idea how she was going to do it.

Tom, who refused to leave without them, stood quietly nearby intent on watching the exodus. The last thing Mia saw before she concentrated on the music was Jenny closing her eyes. The notes that came were quite unfamiliar. A series of soft, almost liquid sounds rose and fell resonating off the woodwork of the ceiling of the hall. The smoke had increased considerably and began to smart her eyes and irritate her throat. She set those feelings aside and concentrated on the singing, mentally seeking the link with the sisterhood. They were all there, she could feel them coming closer and getting stronger all the time.

A sudden clap of thunder startled her. She thought the ceiling was falling in, but the sound of rain falling on the roof told her otherwise. Their song had worked. Before she felt the sisterhood retreat she clearly heard Grace's voice in her head.

"Did I not tell you that you would be needed elsewhere, sister," she said. "But now you must get out fast. The roof is about to collapse."

Breaking off her song she turned to Jenny and Tom. "Quick we must get out. Now!"

Ominous cracking noise came from the roof as they rushed to the entrance to the tunnel. Jenny plunged inside and Mia followed. Tom insisted on being the last. It was at that moment that whole building folded inwards and the beams came crashing down on Tom, who held back deliberately till he was sure the girls were safe.

Mia and Jenny struggled to push their way back out and help Tom, but several large beams had fallen on him, blocking the entrance. Mia heard Jenny scream as they clawed at the charred wood, burning their hands in their desperate efforts to free a passage. Several Smeth'ick men came running back down the tunnel and helped them heave the beams away one by one from the entrance till they were able to squeeze through into the ruins and remove the rubble that covered Tom. He was still breathing but he was very badly injured. Other people joined them and helped transfer Tom onto a plank and carry him away from the ruin and into one of the nearby houses.

Rescue

Jenny looked ghastly. Her hair was a wild mass of knots that stood up on her head. Her hands and face were smeared with soot, her clothes were torn and scorched in places, her eyes were sunk in their sockets. She looked haunted and haggard. She had not slept for nearly two days. Mia was getting as worried about Jenny as she was about Tom. The girl sat unmoving, hunched up in a chair by Tom's bedside, his hand clasped in hers. She said nothing, lest it be the occasional groan, and she refused to eat. Tom had not yet recovered consciousness. Ma'gina and Mia had worked together all the first night to set the broken bones but Ma'gina reckoned that one of beams had crushed the small of his back which might well mean he would be paralysed and unable to walk for the rest of his life. Jenny had taken the news silently, no emotions visible on her face.

When Ma'gina returned from her rounds tending those injured in the escape, she stood quietly at the back of the room observing Jenny. After a while she came forward and pulled up a chair opposite the girl.

"You must stop this, Jenny," she said firmly. "You are dragging both yourself and him downwards. It is not at all what is needed now."

Jenny cast an angry glance at Ma'gina and then returned to her silent vigil.

"You have the ability to save him, Jenny. You know it. But you are terrified that if you give him back his life, it will be one of pain and suffering and eternal regret. You are a healer, Jenny, like Mia and myself. It is not up to you to choose whether this man lives or dies. You must heal him if you can. That is your responsibility; that is your duty. You love him with all your heart whether he be hale or handicapped. Save your loved one, Jenny."

Jenny gave off a heart-wrenching cry that was midway between a groan and a growl. Tears were coursing down her cheeks as she clenched her fists together till her knuckles turned white.

"Why did I have to bring him here? It's all my fault."

"It is nobody's fault," insisted Ma'gina. "We go where we have to. Even those who are too cowardly to go where they must end up being driven to the place they deserve."

Jenny sobbed as she turned back to Tom. "I love you, Tom," she said through her tears, leaning forward and kissing his hand.

She slid forward on her chair till she was kneeling on the floor by the side of the bed. Placing her two hands together as in prayer, she closed her eyes. She remained unmoving in her meditation for more than an hour, but neither Mia nor Ma'gina intervened. Both could feel that something important was happening. Silence prevailed. Watching Tom's face and chest, Mia had the impression that his breathing had improved and his face had recovered some of its natural colour but he remained unmoving. Finally Jenny opened her eyes and struggled with difficulty to her feet, Mia giving her a helping hand.

"I tried everything I could imagine, but I couldn't heal the injury to his back," she said, her voice distant as if she was still in a trance. "I had more success with the rest of his body. It is healing well."

She went on to describe what she had attempted to do to Tom's back with Ma'gina asking many questions.

"It would seem the nerve has been severed," Ma'gina concluded, remaining silent for a moment. "I know relatively little about the earth energies," Ma'gina began again. "But if I remember rightly Grace told us that they worked best when you didn't deliberately try to manipulate them. It is possible that your wanting so badly to heal Tom is hindering those energies from doing their work. Maybe you should try again but just accept what they do and not try to impose your will on them." Ma'gina fell silent and returned to her chair as if she had said all there was to say.

Jenny stood staring at Tom's face for a long moment then she knelt once again and closed her eyes. Mia was startled by a strong rushing sound that filled the room. She looked at Ma'gina whose eyes were closed too, but whose face wore a broad grin. Everything must be all right then, Mia thought. The sound grew in complexity and strength, resembling the eddies she created when she sang for the Stones and they sang back. Here the sounds were deeper, as if the earth were shifting under her feet. The dance was slow and sedate, more swaying than an outright movement, but it was accompanied by a more playful set of sounds like water cascading over rocks.

She also noted a ball of light glowing just above Tom's stomach, slowly descending and ascending, each time becoming one with him before it rose again. Mia was troubled by a strange feeling that the whole sisterhood was watching what was happening through her eyes. She could distinguish most of the sisters in that presence, Grace being the strongest. She immediately recognised Grace's voice when the woman began humming gently. Mia hummed too echoing the sound of the earth energies and harmonising with the music from Grace and the other sisters: a quiet, unobtrusive music accompanying Jenny's work.

A startled gasp from Jenny had Mia turning her attention back to Tom again. He'd opened his eyes. Jenny eyes were still closed and she had not moved from her position, so she must have perceived something from inside. Whatever it was she saw, her face was transfigured by it. When the elements had calmed down and the choir of the sisterhood fallen quiet, Jenny leaned forward and kissed Tom who smiled in return.

"Don't try to move for a while. Don't even try to speak," Jenny warned him. "You have been gravely injured, my love. If you want to have a chance of recovering fully you must keep completely still."

Ma'gina rose from her chair with some difficulty and came to congratulate Jenny. "Well done, my girl. You have done an excellent job."

"Hold on to your praise for the moment," Jenny said to Ma'gina. "Let's wait and see what I have managed to do."

Chapter 10 - Women's business

In praise of women

Women were one of the major driving forces behind the growth and development of Granwich. Contrary to popular belief, the project of building a canal for the transport of merchandise had not been due to James, the first of the Keepers raised to that status as the beginning of a long line of male heads of the Patriciat, but to his wife, Maria who had presented him with detailed plans and drawings to demonstrate the feasibility and utility of such a construction ...

How ironic, Lucie thought, to read what Sarah had written about her ancestors when she had been left behind by Horst who had called a meeting of the Patriciat without any women present. She had had an argument with him about the subject but he had insisted in his infuriatingly unemotional way. She remembered exactly what he had said.

"Such subjects are not for women to discuss. You have little experience of these matters and will only get in the way. What's more, it's dangerous and you have other important things to do."

She'd been so furious with him that she been at a loss for words. It was true that many Patriciat men harboured such ideas and attitudes, but no one before had dared speak of them publicly.

She returned Sarah's notebook to the secret draw in her desk and paced the library. She had moved back into her town house after Horst had insisted that living in cramped quarters in the Botanical Gardens was below her status. Even though she travelled to the

Gardens to work every day, she missed being able to visit her protégés at any hour of the day or night. Coming to a halt at the window, she glanced out over the trees and shrubs that were the work of her grandfather. She hadn't realised how alone she felt. Thomas was still off ill, Sarah had disappeared and showed no sign of returning and Ma'gina too seemed to have disappeared. In fact, she doubted she'd ever be able to see Ma'gina again after what had happened at the last Patriciat meeting. Horst had announced that his men had unearthed a plot involving a carefully organised group of commoners. They had caught one of them snooping around his house. When the man had been questioned he'd revealed that there was a secret organisation of commoners called the "Watchers" who were continually spying on the Patriciat. He revealed that a woman called Ma'gina was at the head of that organisation which she ran from a basement in her Apotheka.

The Patriciat were shocked. They all knew Ma'gina well and no one could imagine she would do such a thing. They protested that they had almost all been healed at some time by her. Horst made quite a show of sharing their disappointment, but then went on to reveal that the man they'd been questioning had escaped and that the guards who'd chased after him had been severely beaten up by a gang of commoners and left to die in a deserted building.

Luckily some of his men had found them but they were in an extremely confused state as if they had been drugged. When he questioned them, they'd been unable to say what had happened to them. He'd ordered a search of Ma'gina's Apotheka, but someone had tipped the commoners off because much of the material had been removed and they'd found only a young girl alone in the offices. It was then that he'd had her brought into the meeting room.

The girl had been in a terrible state. She was terrified and Lucie had the impression she had been beaten. None of that seemed to bother Horst. He questioned her sternly, violently shaking her from time to time till she confessed that Ma'gina had left for Smeth'ick. When the girl broke down and started trembling uncontrollably, Lucie couldn't stand it any longer. She left her place as daughter of the Keeper, went to the girl and led her out of the room. It turned out that the girl was not at all one of Ma'gina's staff but someone who was lodged there because she'd been threatened by a certain Dr. Leuchtli, the very same man who'd taken an interest in marrying Lucie.

The girl, whose name was Molly, was now resting in one of the servants' rooms in the basement of Lucie's house. Of course, Horst didn't know that. It hadn't been easy to smuggle the girl into the house. She'd taken every precaution because she suspected that one of her servants who had been appointed by Horst was there to spy on her and report back to him. Despite the ransacking of Ma'gina's place, Lucie had managed to find a healer to help the girl and Molly no longer seemed in danger. The girl had many small burn marks on the insides of her arms and on her thighs. Lucie had never seen the likes of it before. It was revolting.

Reaching Molly's room, she knocked gently and pushed the door open. Molly looked up at Lucie and struggled to get to her feet.

"You need not stand in my presence when we are alone, Molly," Lucie told her. And helping the girl sit back in her armchair, Lucie asked: "How do you feel?"

Despite her insistence that she was OK, Lucie suspected the girl was suffering more than she wished to admit.

"My name is Lucie. You have my permission to call me by my name."

"Thank you, my Lady."

Lucie had to laugh. "I suppose it is not easy," she said thinking out loud. "Have you had anything to eat and drink?" Lucie asked.

Molly nodded.

"Do you think you can tell me what happened?"

The girl immediately cringed and started to tremble, no doubt imagining she was in for another interrogation.

"I'm sorry," Lucie apologised. "I didn't mean to distress you."

"You're with that man, aren't you?" Lolly blurted out.

"Which man?" Lucie asked, confused by the girl's sudden outburst.

"That big foreigner. The one what questioned me."

Lucie thought for a moment about how to respond. Was she with Horst? She had begun wondering if she really was.

"Yes I am 'with' that man, as you put it. But that doesn't mean I agree with what he does or how he does it."

The girl remained silent.

"Ma'gina is a very good friend of mine," Lucie added, hoping to convince the girl. "I cannot believe that she would mean anybody ill."

"It wasn't 'er. It was 'im. He sent those men to the Apotheka. They carried away a lot of papers but they also planted arms 'ere and there. I 'eard 'em laughing saying everyone'd think she was plannin' somethin'. They took me to that foreigner. He had me take off all me clothes..." she began trembling again and tears ran down her cheeks. "And he burnt these marks on my arms 'n legs with a hot poker. I didn't want to tell 'im where Ma'gina was but it 'urt so much I couldn't 'elp it." Molly broke off, wracked with sobs.

Lucie came closer and took the girl in her arms.

"We must get you away from here quick. You won't be safe here with Horst around," Lucie said.

"Maybe the Watchers could 'elp," the girl said.

"So they do exist!" Lucie exclaimed, startled and worried at the confirmation of Horst's story.

"They're really good people," Molly explained. "They saved me from that Leuchtli bloke wot wanted to do me in. They protect us all, 'ave done for years."

Even if these people were good, Lucie still found it alarming that a secret force had worked for years in Granwich without her or her fellow Patriciat knowing.

"Well maybe you would be safer with them. But I have no idea how to contact them," Lucie admitted.

"No sweat," the girl said, smiling for the first time since Lucie had seen her. "There's probably one of 'em listening to us now."

The thought of it sent shivers down Lucie's spine, but she pushed the feeling aside.

"Well if they are listening then they should know that we need to get you to a safe place. They should also know that I am very concerned about Ma'gina. If this situation continues we are going to need her help."

Nothing happened. Nobody stepped out from the walls or from behind curtains. In a way she was disappointed, but she was also relieved. Maybe there was nobody watching over them.

"Don't worry Miss. They'll 'ave 'eard. They mightn't come immediately. But they'll do somethin'. You can count on 'em."

Between men

"Despite all the love I have for her," Horst said, looking knowingly around the gathered men, "the behaviour of my future wife at our last meeting is a clear illustration of how women can get

206

in the way of men's work. They can't understand the importance of what we do or the reasons behind it."

"But women have always attended the meetings of the Patriciat," one elderly man protested.

"Yes. I know," Horst replied, understandingly. "But times change, and we are facing a grave crisis with our own society infiltrated by a dangerous group of commoners that wishes the Patriciat ill."

His speech was interrupted by one of his men who knocked at the door. Perfect. The timing was just as he'd planned.

"Excuse me," he said as he went to the door. He spoke briefly with his man and then moved back to the centre of the room. "I am sorry to have to tell you that I have just learnt that your wife was attacked and killed," he said addressing one of the younger Patriciat that went by the name of Harry. "My men were unable to save her, but they did catch the two commoners that did it. Unfortunately in the fight that ensued both men were killed."

Harry slumped back into his seat, his face a ghastly white. "But it doesn't make any sense," the man said echoing the incomprehension of many present.

"I suggest my men search the town for any more of this dangerous group of criminals," Horst pursued. "The quicker we act, the more likely we are to catch them."

The old man who'd spoken earlier stood and addressed the assembled men. "As Harry said, none of this makes sense. Granwich was never like this before. We need more time to investigate this closely for something is out of joint here."

Horst realised he would have to deal with the old man later. The old fool might manage to rally the others against him.

"I understand your incomprehension," Horst countered. "At your age it is difficult to understand how some young people react and how society changes. And I warn you, it has changed," he said, stressing the word 'has'. "If you knew all that I knew you'd be more than shocked. But let's not dwell on these matters. Harry has to take care of his wife's body and all of us must make sure our houses are secure. Who knows who could be the next victim?"

And with that hardly veiled threat he dismissed the Patriciat, saying a few words of consolation to Harry in private but making sure everyone saw him do so.

Horst needed to check on Lucie. Her outburst earlier about not being allowed to attend the meeting of the Patriciat was not a good sign. He needed to make sure she didn't do anything foolish. Not that she could do much against his carefully laid plans. He wasn't to get to see Lucie immediately, however, because his man came to see him on urgent business.

"We can't talk here," Horst said, aware that they might well be being watched. Although he knew that the group of Watchers really existed, he had no idea what they really did or how they did it. It didn't really matter. Their existence was enough for his plans. Moving out into the centre of the square, he stopped near the fountain, telling himself that the noise of water would prevent anyone eavesdropping on them.

"So?" he asked, impatient to get on.

"Things didn't go as planned," the man admitted rather sheepishly. "After our men had done in that woman like you said, they went to round up the two commoners you suspected of being part of that group. But the commoners defended themselves with all sorts of clever fighting techniques we'd never seen before. Our men had no chance against them. Not only were they beaten but they were kidnapped and carried off too."

Horst was furious. What a bungling load of idiots he had to work with. "I presume you had someone there spying on them."

"Sure, but his instructions were not to intervene. So he just watched."

"Thank heavens someone obeys instructions," Horst retorted. "Take me to that man."

Horst's men were housed in a number of empty houses that he had requisitioned specially for them. It was in one of these that the man he wanted to interrogate was holed up. Coming, as many of them did, from the wilds in the south, most of the men were used to living rough. Horst had given them clean clothes to wear and insisted they wash regularly because no one would take them seriously the way they looked and smelt when they first came.

Despite this fact, most of the men were still quite untamed. The man he came to see was one of them. His hair was matted with filth that a simple bath had not been able to remove. He didn't smell good either and his breath stank.

"You need to smarten up if you want to continue working for me," Horst snarled. Not waiting for a response, he continued: "What happened with those watchers?"

The man described how Horst's men had approached the two watchers, quite confident about getting what they wanted. But the watchers had refused to stop. When Horst's men had tried to attack them the two watchers had laid them out in no time. One knocking the feet from under one of the man with a sweeping movement of his legs and the other seemed to spin in mid air sending Horst's man sprawling on his face. "They must have used magic," the man concluded his description, "because they touched each of Horst's men briefly after that and both of them lay unmoving not opposing the watchers as they dragged them away."

Horst had a pretty good idea how the 'trick' had been done but people from the Reaches couldn't know such things. Someone from his own world must be there teaching these people what to do. Rather than being annoyed at such an intrusion, he was excited at the idea of the forthcoming battle.

"Did you follow them?" Horst asked.

"I tried," the man admitted, looking embarrassed. "But they disappeared almost immediately. I could find no trace of them anywhere."

Supporters

Horst walked in silence back to his house, his man pacing alongside at a slight distance. He wanted to change into something more appropriate before he called on Lucie. Once again he regretted the loss of his men. Curse that Sally! Several of them had been quite proficient at unarmed combat. As it was, he had to find someone to train his men as soon as possible. It would be amusing to capture the person training the watchers and force him to train his own men. But that wasn't on the cards for the moment.

"Do you know any combat skills?" he asked his man.

"No Grand Master."

"How many times have I told you to no longer use that name here," he hissed. "You never know who might be listening. "

He could try to get someone from his own world, but he was not sure he could bring the person back with him. He'd need Sally for that, and he'd heard no more about her since he'd left her in his mansion in Germany.

When he reached home a report came in that he'd been expecting all day: his men had managed to set fire to the Smeth'ick Council Hall burning all the Council and a good deal of the population with them. Well that ought to distract them for a while and would make sure no deputation arrived from Smeth'ick in the near future claiming there was no plague there. A further piece of good new was that Ma'gina and her assistant had also perished in the fire. They had apparently tried unsuccessfully to save the apothecary's life. That would explain the interference he'd felt in the tight noose he'd tied around the man's life. A very useful trick that. He'd discovered it by accident while manipulating the minds of the Brethren. He wasn't sure how it worked, but it did and that was all that mattered.

He was about to leave for Lucie's house when several of members of the Patriciat arrived. Unable to send them away without offending, he felt obliged to ask them in and welcome them in his drawing room. Offering refreshments he asked them why they had come at such a late hour, barely managing to conceal his irritation at being disturbed.

"We wanted to make it clear that we support your move to set Granwich back on the right footing. We approve of the firm hand with which you handle the women and are now going to deal with these watcher people."

Supporters, Horst smiled inwardly.

"I'm so glad," Horst said, all smiles. "I was wondering how much support I'd get. It is not always easy to set things right when they have been going progressively askew over a number of years. I imagine there must be some opposition."

Let's see if they rise to the bait, Horst wondered. The youngest, Greg, was particularly enthusiastic.

"Most people agree with you although not all will say so openly. Very few are opposed to what you suggest."

"I imagine they have their reasons. People often have vested interests in opposing change," Horst continued, hoping to push Greg to say who was opposed to him.

Half an hour and several stiff drinks later, he knew all the names of those who opposed him and some of the reasons why.

"Well thank you gentlemen. Our discussion has been most fruitful. I look forward to your help and support in the future." And he went with them to the front door to wish them goodnight.

Damn, he thought, it's too late now to go to Lucie's place. But he felt uneasy about her. His intuition told him that she might have done something foolish, so despite it being improper to arrive so late, he hurried through the darkened streets to her house. When he knocked at the front door, a servant woman in a nightshirt and nightcap answered not daring to take the door off the latch, surprised to see him so late.

"No sir, I believe she's gone to bed and must surely be asleep. If you would like to leave a message I will see she gets it first thing in the morning."

Something told him the girl was lying, but he could hardly force his way in so late at night.

"I understand," he said, doing his best not to look too annoyed. "Please tell her I called. I apologise for coming so late, but I was retained by urgent business. I will come and see her tomorrow morning."

Illicit meetings

Lucie breathed a deep sigh of relief. She had been terrified that Horst would insist and push his way into the house, discovering her in an illicit meeting with a couple of members of the watchers. Such behaviour on his part wouldn't have surprised her now she'd seen proof of the violence he was capable of. Molly, who was with her and the watchers in one of the small back rooms, had been trembling ever since Horst had knocked at the door.

It alarmed Lucie that he could play court to her while torturing young girls in the basement of his house. In one short moment the veil had dropped and she'd come to see him as the monster he really was. She couldn't understand how she could have possibly found him charming or attractive.

One of the watchers, whose name was Jon, repeated the question he had asked earlier: "Will you not accompany us? It is far too dangerous for you to stay here."

Lucie was adamant. "I will not run away from danger. My duty is to stay and try to do what I can for Granwich."

Clearly Jon didn't agree but she could see he respected her decision. "OK," he said. "But I would like you to meet someone before you go to bed tonight."

Going against her better judgement that pleaded for her to go to bed so as to be fresh and rested for tomorrow, she gave in.

"Provided it doesn't take too long," she added.

"We will take you with us, Molly. You will be safe where we are going and you will also be able to help." He pulled two blindfolds from his pocket.

"Is it necessary?" Lucie asked.

"It is safer this way. They will not be able to force you to give away what you do not know."

Lucie felt the air get colder and damper as they descended stairs. She stumbled when they reached level ground but Jon held her arm and stopped her from falling.

"Not far now," he whispered.

Despite his reassurance, she had the impression they walked a long way before she heard a door open and she was guided into what must have been a room. When the blindfold was removed she found herself in a small windowless room that was sparsely furnished. She was standing face-to-face with a tall, slim girl who couldn't have been more than fifteen. Her appearance was startling. She had short pitch-black hair and her eyes were a bright blue-green, the like of which Lucie had never seen before. But most striking of all were her clothes. She wore a brightly coloured cloth wrapped several times around her body under which she wore loose-fitting trousers.

"It's called a sari where I come from," Anju said, smiling. "My name is Anju. And you must be Lucie. Sarah told me a lot about you."

"You've seen Sarah?" Lucie exclaimed, unable to conceal her joy.

"Yes. Quite recently. She told me that if ever I was to see you I was to tell you that she loves you deeply and is busy writing the history of your family."

Lucie wasn't sure if she should laugh or cry, but Anju left her no time to decide between the two.

"We must hurry," Anju said. "We have very little time before you return home. Jon tells me you have decided to stay in your house and brave what is to come."

"I won't be driven out of my world for fear of a man!" Lucie retorted.

"If you agree, I will teach you a few moves that you can use to protect yourself in an emergency. An hour should be enough. I can teach you more later."

Here was another young girl, albeit older than Sarah, who spoke with far greater assurance and knowledge than befit a girl of her age.

Lucie wondered if she might also be the transformation of an older person.

"So with those three pressure points and the few moves I've shown you, you should be able to defend yourself if you are attacked."

Lucie was out of breath after so much exercise.

"You might do well to find an excuse to get more exercise," Anju advised, "a morning walk, for example, or climbing stairs or lifting weights."

"You have given me an idea," Lucie replied. "I'm going to begin helping the women of Granwich. If I am to be excluded from discussions with men, then I will rally women to my side."

The door opened and Jon stepped in. They had been alone till then. "That's an excellent idea," Jon commented. "I've heard that the mother of Gwen is ill. You will remember Gwen, you saved her at the Meet from a couple of thugs by changing into an eagle."

She had indeed. And she knew Gwen's mother Gloria quite well.

"Eagle, hey!" Anju said admiringly. "That aught to help protect you."

"It's not always easy to transform when you are threatened," Lucie said. "It requires time and concentration."

"Well maybe you should practice changing rapidly," Anju suggested.

"In return for your lessons, I will teach you how to transform, Anju. I'm sure you could," Lucie concluded.

Taking her leave, Lucie asked Anju to say goodbye to Molly for her. She let Jon blindfold her and he led her back to her house.

Early morning

As the first rays of the sun caught the top of the trees in the garden Lucie got up, washed and dressed. It was still very early and none of the servants were yet up and about. Breaking off a hunk of bread in the kitchens and taking a bottle of beer with her, she stepped out into the garden to be greeted by a joyful chorus of birds. Although she could speak many bird languages, there was not much you could add to the morning song so she contented herself with listening to its diversity as she made her way to the Botanical Gardens.

She walked at a brisk pace, remembering Anju's advice about exercise. Anju had also advised her to wear clothes in which she could move freely. Rather than wear one of the long dresses and petticoats she frequently wore, she had donned a shorter dress under which she wore loose fitting pants. It was the sort of thing that Sarah preferred to wear and now she understood why. It was much more comfortable and she felt like she could run or jump or even roll over without the slightest encumbrance.

As the Gardens lay beyond the city walls, Lucie had to negotiate her way through the blockade manned by Horst's guards to get there, but they knew she was favoured by Horst and generally caused no problems. Their fear of Horst had its uses, she thought. The gardens were shroud in a fine mantle of dew that the rising sun had not yet had the time to dissipate. As she walked towards the aviary, the droplets shone like tiny rainbows each time they caught the suns rays.

Checking that the birds were OK, she headed down the steep path at the back of the aviary that led to a concealed gate into the woods outside. Once under the cover of the trees she practiced the moves Anju had taught her as best she could without a sparing partner. She also practiced transforming into an eagle and an owl as fast as she could. It struck her that she hadn't transformed since Sarah left. Although transformation was one of the distinguishing features of the Patriciat they had little need for it except possibly in teaching their children how to transform. She wondered how many of them could still transform if they had to. It was an alarming thought that maybe the Patriciat were loosing the ability to transform.

The beginnings

After freshening up she headed for Gloria's house. Lucie had decided that she would continue to wear the short dress and loose trousers. She even stopped in at the tailors on her way to Gloria's to order a number of pairs of such clothes made of lighter but stronger material.

"Lucie! How good to see you," Gloria exclaimed as she opened the door and discovered Lucie on her doorstep. "Come inside quickly."

Lucie could not understand the furtive, nervous way Gloria glanced out into the street before closing the door.

"Where are you servants?" Lucie asked, surprised to find Gloria answering the door herself.

"I had them smuggled away to our country house after what happened."

"I must have missed something," Lucie commented, perplexed. "I was unaware that anything special has happened."

"Oh dear!" Gloria said, ushering Lucie into her private study and locking the door. "There's been a murder. Petra, Harry's wife, was killed last night by a group of commoners going under the name of the watchers."

Lucie let herself slip into a waiting chair. "This is dreadful," she said. "Did anybody see it happen?"

"Some of Horst's men."

They could just as well have done it themselves, she thought. They probably did. She couldn't believe it was the watchers. She wondered if she could confide in Gloria. Better not, she thought. Too dangerous! Gloria's husband was one of the admirers of Horst.

"Why did nobody tell me?" Lucie asked.

Gloria went red with embarrassment. "Um…. Er … People were afraid to talk to you about it."

"But why?" Lucie said, beginning to get irritated with the growing mystery.

Gloria still hesitated and finally she blurted out: "Because you're with that Horst guy. None of the women trust him. They're afraid you'll tell him."

Lucie laughed and the sound of her own laughter frightened her. It sounded alarmingly crazy.

"Have you got anything to drink?" she asked Gloria.

"Oh I'm so sorry, how clumsy of me not to offer," Gloria apologised. "All this business has got me in such a state."

And she left briefly in search of refreshments. While she was alone, Lucie stood and paced the room. What a dilemma! She needed these women so she was going to have to trust them.

When Gloria had poured drinks and offered biscuits, Lucie asked: "Are we alone in the house?"

"Yes."

"Are you absolutely sure?" Gloria looked at her in a quizzical way and then suggested: "We could retire to the basement. Nobody ever goes there. And there's only one door which we can keep an eye on."

Lucie stood, suddenly feeling that she had to act urgently. "Let's go."

Gloria seemed startled but stood and led the way. Once they were safely concealed in the basement, Lucie asked a question: "Where exactly is your house in the country?"

Gloria was clearly getting more alarmed than ever.

"Let me explain," Lucie said. "The murders are not the work of the watchers but of Horst's men. He has a plan but I don't yet know what it is. I asked where your house is because I want to be sure your children and servants will be safe there."

Gloria had gone a sickly pale colour. "It's just over an hour's ride from Granwich," she admitted in a strangled little voice.

"We need to find a safer place for them. There are bands of wild men roaming the country side and any or all of them could be in the pay of Horst,"

"But where?" Gloria asked, slumped in her chair.

"I'm going to tell you a story," Lucie began, "but you must keep it absolute secret. Above all not a word to your husband." And she went on to tell Gloria about the torture of Molly. Gloria was horrified. Lucie then told her about the watchers and her meeting with them. "We must ask them to help us get our children to safety," Lucie said, convinced that it was the only solution. "But tell me, Gloria. How many other women have sent their children to the country or are thinking about doing so?"

"I'd say about half of the Patriciat women."

"Good. We need to act quickly," Lucie said, standing and helping Gloria get up. "Here's my plan: we meet the watchers and explain our problem to them and see if they can help us. If they can then we will contact all those women we think we can trust. We will need a few others to help us. Do you agree?"

"I do," Gloria said, having regained some of the colour in her face.

The messenger came quicker than Lucie expected. She had not yet left Gloria's place when a boy came to the service door. Luckily they had left the basement otherwise they might not have heard his knock. Ushering him in, Gloria asked him why he came.

"I'm to take mistress Lucie to see Anju."

It could have been a trap, Lucie had thought, but no one else could know Anju's name. Stepping out of her hiding place in the room beyond, Lucie simply said: "Let's go."

It was then that a second urgent knock came at the door. Lucie pulled the boy back with her into the shadows while Gloria went to the service door. A distraught girl stood in the entrance.

"I didn't know who to turn to," the girl sobbed. "Men came during the night and killed my mistress and one of her children."

"This is terrible," Lucie said, coming out of hiding. "Did you see who did it?" she asked.

"No, I was so terrified I hid in a cupboard. But I heard their voices, they sounded foreign to me."

"Your mistress has three children, hasn't she?" Lucie asked. When the girl nodded she continued. "What has happened to the other two?"

"Servants are hiding them in the house of a commoner in town." And she described where it was.

"Good," Lucie replied. "We'll get you all to safety very soon. You should return to that house, stay with the two children and wait for us to come and fetch you. Keep out of sight if possible."

Plans

Once the girl had left, she turned to the boy. He led Lucie and Gloria down the garden path to a small shed where the servants kept tools to tend the garden. The shed backed onto one of those strange black rock formations that protruded abruptly from the earth here and there in Granwich. Opening the door, the boy indicated they should go inside. Lucie couldn't help feeling apprehensive, knowing the deviousness of Horst. But Anju called out from within, reassuring her.

"Come on Gloria," Lucie whispered and stepped into the darkened shed.

"I'm going to have to blindfold you," Anju explained.

Lucie had expected as much. The watchers were cautious even though they now knew she was not opposed to them.

This time the underground walk was much shorter. It ended in a similar room to the one she had already visited the night before. Removing their blindfolds, Anju greeted her properly and then, turning to Gloria, she said: "Greetings Gloria. I am Anju and this is Jon."

Jon stepped forward from a corner in which he had been standing, unseen by them.

"Greetings," he said. "Take a seat."

Once the four had sat around a small table Jon asked smiling: "So you want to leave Granwich?"

Thinking he was referring to her declaration that she would not leave her town, Lucie retorted: "It's not for me. It's for the women and children." She went on to explain that they suspected there was nowhere near Granwich that was safe for the woman and children who seemed to be the expendable victims of Horst's plans, whatever they were.

"There are three major difficulties," Jon pointed out. "First, where are we going to take them that we can guarantee their safety? Second, how are we to transport them safely across the countryside with so many dangerous bands of men roaming around. And finally, how do we get the women and children out of Granwich under the noses of the men, especially Horst's guards?"

"I may have some answers to your questions," an old woman said, stepping out from a door Lucie hadn't noticed before.

"Ma'gina!" she exclaimed, realising who it was. Rising from her chair she moved forward and embraced the old woman. "And Mia too! Well met!" Lucie continued. Then she noticed another young woman move into the room pushing a young man in a funny little chair with wheels on it.

"This is Jenny and Tom," Ma'gina explained. "Now let's sit down. We have little time and a lot to tell and discuss."

It took some time for Ma'gina to tell them what had happened in Smeth'ick and for Jon and Lucie to inform Ma'gina and her friends of events in Granwich.

"So you want to evacuate women and children?" Ma'gina asked Lucie.

"Two women and one child have already been murdered," Lucie began. "And a servant girl has been tortured."

"Yes. It does seem that women and children are Horst's favourite victims," Ma'gina said bitterly.

"But where are we to go? Nowhere near here is safe," Lucie said.

"I have an idea," Mia put in. "Why don't they go to the Lost Meadows with the Littl' People. The place is difficult to access and easy to defend," she suggested.

"Martin and Fran are already there," Jenny added.

Mia described the place to Lucie and Gloria, although she omitted to mention that the Meadows had been completely devastated before Sally put things right.

"And how are they to get there?" Jon asked.

"Maybe Sally could transport them all there," Jenny suggested.

"I'm not sure she could handle so many," Tom said, speaking for the first time.

Lucie noted the look of both pain and joy on his face. She wondered how he had come to be handicapped. Ma'gina's story hadn't explained that.

"No. I think you'll have to go over land to An's place and then on to the country of the Littl' People," Ma'gina concluded.

"But we are sure to be attacked," Gloria worried.

"And everyone will know where they have gone," Lucie added.

"If we can make it to An's place," Jenny said, "maybe she or Sally will have an idea how to conceal the remainder of the journey."

"The best would be to travel by night," Jon chipped in.

"But how are we to be able to get away with so many people?" Gloria asked.

"That's where I come in," Ma'gina said. "I will prepare a mixture that must be given to all Patriciat men and Horst's guards. It will make them sleep all night and spend the next day on the toilet."

"How do you plan to give it to them and make sure they take it?" Lucie asked.

"We could put it in the water supply, but that would not be a good idea. It might mean the wells would be contaminated for a long time. No. I suggest we organise a great celebration especially for the men, all the men, with music and dancing, for which we women prepare food and wine and beer. That is how we'll give it to them."

Anju, who had been silent all this time, had what seemed the final word on the subject. "And if any of them refuse to drink or eat, we'll have to deal with them physically," she said flexing her fingers.

Jon laughed. "It'll be Horst's birthday in a few days, we could say we were celebrating that," Lucie said, delighted at the idea of getting back at him at least in some small way.

"Excellent idea," Tom said. "That will give you a cover to do all the organising you need. You'll even be able to get supplies for the voyage."

"In which case I'll have to prepare an antidote if ever some women are forced to drink the stuff," Ma'gina said, thinking out loud.

"We need to draw up a list of all those women we are sure we can trust, both Patriciat and commoners," Lucie continued. "I'll need your help with that Ma'gina."

The old woman nodded her agreement,

"And then we'll have to contact them individually and explain the plan."

"I suggest you don't mention how we are to get away nor how we are going to fool the men," Ma'gina said.

"You and Mia will have to stay in hiding, Ma'gina," Jon said. "Horst thinks you died in the fire in Smeth'ick."

Ma'gina got to her feet and indicating that Mia should go with her, she asked Jon to show them where they'd stocked all her material from the Apotheka. Before Jon could leave, Tom called him back.

"We need to send a messenger to An so she and Sally know what is happening."

"You are right. I'll ask three of the best watchers to go," he replied and left with Ma'gina and Mia. Jenny followed them, pushing Tom in his wheelchair.

Lucie sat back down at the table with Gloria and Anju. Anju poured them a drink and taking a big swig said: "I have an idea and I'd like to know what you think of it. Even if we get away under the cover of dark there is still a considerable risk we'll be attacked by bands of men on the road. I offer to teach all the women the rudiments of unarmed combat over the next few days till the party. That way they'll have some means to defend themselves. There's a much larger room in these tunnels that we can use to practice in. Access is quite easy from the outside and you can bring the women there in small groups each day. What do you think?"

Lucie was pleased with the idea because not only would it help them defend themselves but it would also allow women to assert their role in society more fully and not be pushed around by bullies like Horst and his men.

"I agree," Lucie replied. "Providing you make it quite clear that they are not to use these techniques till they know how to use them properly. I am afraid that women could get badly hurt clumsily trying to defend themselves."

"They will get hurt anyway," Anju pointed out, "if they are attacked and they don't defend themselves. I will do as you say but I will set out to teach them techniques they can use immediately, like I did with you." Anju stood and flexed her muscles. "I suggest we call it the FF, for Feminine Force."

Gloria giggled at the name.

The FF

Three hours later, Lucie, Gloria and three other young women were comfortably installed in Gloria's private study.

"We need to make sure the children we sent to the countryside are OK," Gloria said, clearly worried about her children. "And we need to plan how we pick them up along the road," she added.

"Do we know how many children and servants have been sent away?" Hilda asked. Lucie didn't know the young woman so well. Apparently she had two little children that she'd hidden with relatives outside town.

"The trouble is that everyone has been very secretive. They're afraid that Horst's men might find out. It's illegal. The Council has decreed that we're not allowed to leave the town," Gloria replied.

"Then we'll have to find out by asking each woman, but only once they agree to take part in our plan..." Lucie said.

A knock came at the door and one of the watchers stepped inside. "Horst's on his way here. He'll arrive in about five minutes. Would you like to use the underground passages?" the watcher asked.

"No," Lucie replied. "We have nothing to hide from him. Except that we are preparing his birthday party." She paused a moment. "On second thoughts, you three should get away. It might be safer if he doesn't know who we are organising the party with. Take them to see Anju." Hilda and the two other women left immediately with the watcher. Gloria and Lucie hastily removed glasses and cups and cleaned up. No need to cause unnecessary suspicion.

Thinly veiled anger

Gloria answered the door and let Horst in. From the tone of his voice, Lucie, who had remained in the reception room, could hear that he was annoyed although he was trying hard to control his temper. He certainly didn't like to be crossed.

"Ah there you are! I've been looking for you everywhere. I was beginning to wonder if you'd run away."

Lucie felt an involuntary shudder go down her spine. If only you knew, she thought. "I've been very busy," Lucie said, smiling, as best she could.

"I wonder what you could have been doing all this time. I heard that you left your house at dawn," he said striding into the room as if he owned it.

"I'm afraid I can't tell you," she said, figuring that he was likely to get a little more annoyed before she finally admitted she was preparing a surprise for him.

"We've never had secrets from each other before," he commented.

What a lame effort, she thought. He hardly knows me. Does he really think I'm so dim? "Even people who know each other very well, have their little secrets..." She wondered how far she could push him before the game became dangerous.

"It is not a time for secrets," Horst retorted, moving forward till he was standing right in front of her. "We are in a very dangerous situation and I learn you've been wandering the streets of Granwich on your own. You could have been killed."

So that is how he intimidates people, she noted.

"If you have to run such risks I'll have to appoint one of my men to be your guard."

Yeah and have him spy on everything I do, Lucie thought wondering how long she could hold out without getting really angry with him.

"That won't be necessary," she said. "On your advice I will be much more careful in future. And I will ask for a guard when I need one."

He took hold of her hands and said earnestly: "You must understand that my concern for you is just part of my love and affection."

Lucie wanted to pull her hands away, but instead she said: "Yes I know. I'm sorry," and she gave him a brief kiss on his cheek before freeing her hands from his and walking to the window. Glancing outside, she decided she must play her trump card.

"Oh well! I suppose I would have to tell you sooner or later. The secret I was keeping is that we women are preparing a celebration for your birthday."

A strange mixture of emotions flitted across his face: relief, greed, triumph, lasciviousness. She saw it all.

"How thoughtful," he said.

So much for enthusiasm, she thought. "I thought it would a good way to take people's minds off the troubles." As she said it, she realised that he didn't want people's minds taken off the troubles, on the contrary. But it was too late, she'd said it.

"I can think of a far better reason for having a celebration," he said, clearly following a completely different strategy. "If it were to celebrate our marriage."

She felt like a chess player who hadn't seen checkmate coming till her opponent sprung it upon her. She glanced at Gloria who was standing near the door. The woman looked stricken with worry. In that moment Lucie made up her mind that she should risk her future to save the others.

"What a good idea, Horst. You are right that a marriage and a birthday together would be excellent reasons for a celebration." She looked straight in his eyes and found nothing that could give her a clue as to what he thought or felt.

"Does that mean you accept my proposition?" he asked feigning apprehension and excitement.

How silly of him, she thought: it is so out of character.

"I may well," she said trying to avoid capitulating. "But please give me another day to think things over. It is after all a big decision."

"As you wish," he said and then he took his leave saying he had important things to deal with.

Trapped

Lucie sank heavily in an armchair and laid her head on her hands, trying to stem the tears of exasperation that sprung into her eyes. Gloria was about to say something when Lucie urgently signalled that she should keep quiet. Horst might well have arranged for someone to spy on them in his absence. Pulling herself together, Lucie stood and with Gloria they headed for the basement and the watchers tunnel. She desperately needed to talk to Ma'gina. The thought of marrying Horst was disgusting. She couldn't bear to think of being linked to him for life. And then there was the fact that she'd have to get in bed with a man who had tortured a young girl by burning holes in her legs and arms. Bile rose in her throat along with hot red anger.

One of the watchers materialised from the shadows and offered to take them to Ma'gina. Mia had set up a laboratory in one of the underground rooms and the two women were busy mixing a potion when Lucie and Gloria entered.

"Give me a moment!" Ma'gina ordered.

They had apparently arrived at a difficult moment in the making of the potion. Ma'gina poured a few drops of a foul smelling liquid in the potion and then stoppered the large bottle.

"Good. Now I can greet you. What's the matter?" Ma'gina asked presumably noticing the stricken look on Lucie's face.

"We'd be better off next door," Mia suggested. "The air here is a bit thick with chemicals."

Once installed around a small table, Lucie told them what had happened with Horst.

"He's a very clever man," Ma'gina said. "I understand you feel frustrated and put down."

Lucie had hoped for more support or commiseration from her old friend.

"The first thing I will do," Ma'gina pursued, "is add another ingredient to my potion that removes men's desire."

Lucie didn't get the point at first then she saw the purpose of it.

"But I don't want to marry him," she said almost petulantly.

"You may not be able to avoid that," Ma'gina said.

"What if you plan the wedding at the end of the ceremony so they are all under the effects of the potion?" Mia suggested.

"I don't think he'll ever agree," Lucie replied. "He absolutely needs to marry me if he is to become the Keeper of Granwich." He'd got her cornered and there seemed no way out.

Chapter 11 - Preparations

Numbers and more numbers

Rafter tossed the letter and the questionnaire on his desk where the bunch of papers landed face up, mocking him. How many students are enrolled? How many students drop out during the course? What is the success rate in examinations? What is the per capita spending in the department? What is the ratio of students to teaching staff? What is the student to computer ratio? How is student satisfaction measured? How many students find a job? Numbers. Numbers. Numbers. As if everything could be reduced to numbers.

Rafter poured himself a glass of water and went to stand in the bay window of his office, looking out over the River Avan. An obsession with numbers was a form of selective blindness: such people found it difficult to see anything else. As a result they were unaware there were other possibilities, they were even unaware that their vision might be limited. Ironically numbers hadn't always had such a constraining sense. They had long been an integral part of transcendence. It was the subject of one of his lectures.

A knock interrupted the train of his thoughts. His secretary opened the door and peering round it asked: "I've organised the meeting of the Department for this afternoon as you asked. Would you like me to organise refreshments?"

"Yes please, Mae," he replied and she slipped back out of the room.

Mae had been working with him for several years. She had seemed so young at the time, but she had rapidly understood what was required of her and now much of the day-to-day organisation of the department rested on her shoulders.

Staff meeting

"Colleagues," he said, calling the meeting to order. "And friends," he added.

The teaching-staff of the Theosophy Department numbered some twenty people, counting professors, lecturers and assistants. Not so many really, he thought. The fundamentals of Theosophical thinking and practice were taught by Professor Wolf Greenacre and Professor Liam Lettrot taught dreams and dream travelling. Professor Chris Dryman taught the history and practice of shamanism while Lyra Enquist was professor of the healing arts and her colleague, Martina Aschlyman, was professor of occult sciences. Finally there was Professor Gavin Trundle who taught comparative theology and the history of religion and paganism and Rafter himself who taught transcendence and its relationship to science and religions.

"As you know, we are to undergo an audit," Rafter said.

"Is there no way we can stop this?" Professor Dryman queried.

"We don't have that option, I am afraid," Rafter told them. "The university administration is convinced of the necessity of the exercise and they are under considerable political pressure to demonstrate return on investment."

Professor Aschlyman snorted in disgust. "What nonsense," she retorted. "You can't apply economic principles to our work."

Rafter smiled. Martina was the youngest professor in the Department. She tended to be impatient but she was also a motor for change and development.

"I agree entirely, Martina. And I have told them so. But they can't understand. No, we won't be able to stop the audit and we wont be able to change its nature. Those are givens as far as they are concerned."

Professor Trundle leaned forward in his armchair and turning to face Rafter, he asked: "So what do you plan to do, Professor?"

Rafter stood and strode around the common room. Movement was conducive to thought he felt. "There are several possibilities. But before I talk about them, I will ask Professor Dryman to make sure we are not overheard."

Chris laughed. Rafter particularly liked him for the jovial way he went about life.

"Of course, Professor."

The man, who was in his early forties, closed his eyes. Rafter could see quite clearly what Dryman was doing. He could easily have done so himself, but he preferred not to display his status as a shaman, even in front of his close colleagues. After a brief silence, Dryman reported that they could talk safely.

"I see several possibilities," Rafter began. "First of all I think that directly opposing the audit is not a good strategy. Those of you who practice Aikido will understand what I mean. We have to use their energy."

"How do you plan to do that, Professor?" Professor Enquist enquired.

"Their main thrust will be in gathering facts and figures and subsequently in analysing the results..." Rafter began.

"According to their logic," Martina spluttered, interrupting him.

"Exactly!" Rafter reacted.

The young woman looked at him astonished. Apparently people didn't always react so favourably to her interruptions.

"You've got ahead of me there, Professor," she said.

"Well, at first I thought that we should also carry out our own 'audit' to bring additional evidence of the impact and benefit of our work. But the more I thought about it, the more I realised that the difficulty was not in bringing more data to the table, however different it might be, so much as the fact that there are several radically different approaches, or logics as you call them Martina, to this question."

Martina still looked perplexed. "I'm not sure I catch what you are getting at Professor."

Rafter smiled. He liked the way she took the risk to say she didn't understand. Not all the professors in the department could do that.

"Let me try to approach the question from another angle. What if collecting data were part of the problem? If that were the case, then our collecting more data would not help solve it, on the contrary."

"And how could collecting data be part of the problem?" Martina asked.

"Those who gather data assume that if they then put all that data together in the correct way they are going to understand what is going on and that ultimately they will be able to reach a decision."

"Isn't that how science works?" one of the assistants asked.

"Yes and no, John," Rafter responded. "If we were to pursue this conversation we would need a whole day if not more to come to terms with the failings of the so-called scientific method," Rafter added. "Remind me to organise a seminar about it. Suffice it to say that the field we study cannot be understood by gathering data alone. The transcendent has to be experienced in its fullness. The moment you try to analyse it, it's gone. Gathering data can't help people experience and understand transcendence. That is how our approach is different from those who want an audit. What we need to do is to make apparent those differences of perspective."

"I think I grasp what you mean, Professor," Enquist said. "I see it as making differences of perspective explicit as a force for healing conflict. And I really would like to work on the subject with my students and anybody else who wants to be involved."

"It would seem we have found our champion," Rafter said, congratulating Lyra.

"The second avenue I see," Rafter went on, "involves charm."

"You surely don't want to bewitch the auditors?" Chris Dryman said, beaming at his little joke.

"You are right I don't. We can in no way use our occult knowledge to influence people against their will," Rafter said firmly. "They are already wary of us and what they believe we can do. Any hint of such interference would come back at us like a boomerang."

"Those that are meant to kill don't come back," one of the assistants whispered to his neighbour, but everybody heard him, making him blush with embarrassment.

"You are right Tommy. But I don't think our situation is so dire, yet, that we need to resort to such means."

A number of people laughed making the young man even more embarrassed.

"What I meant by seduction was to help the rest of the university and the townspeople to better understand what we do by involving them in the experience of transcendence. There are many paths to transcendence: music, dance, theatre, storytelling, meditation, ritual, …"

Professor Trundle was particularly enthusiastic at the idea: "I'd love to have an opportunity to have people experience how the subjects we deal with are a key part of the history of Avan and its surroundings."

"That's an excellent idea," Rafter responded.

"Sounds like what you need is to organise some form of festivities," Mae put in.

"Could you bring our ideas together, Mae, and make a first draft of a programme for our festival," Rafter asked.

"Sure," was all the secretary replied.

"Ok. Describe your propositions for the event to Mae and Professor Enquist will coordinate the work on multiple perspectives," Rafter told them.

When the meeting finally came to an end an animated group gathered around Mae talking about ideas for the festival. Amazing how a crisis brought out the best in people, Rafter thought, as Professor Enquist came to talk to him about the work they were to do.

News from Granwich

Sarah walked alone, deep in thought. She made her way several times around An's house, following a narrow path that wound its way from flower beds to vegetable patches and on to the main drive, taking the longest strides she could. Something drove her to stretch her young body to its extreme.

Irritated by the monotony, she broke the round and walked out along the road in the direction of Granwich till she came to a small bridge over a noisy stream. Climbing down the bank she plunged her hands in the ice-cold water and splashed some over her face. It made her skin tingle, which went some way towards relieving the feeling of numbness that had progressively gripped her since she left Granwich.

It wasn't just being separated from Lucie. It was deeper: as if she weren't in the right place, but she didn't know where she should be. Clambering back up to the road she spotted a cloud of dust in the distance. Someone was coming. Fast. Suddenly terrified, she turned and ran at full speed towards the house. She reached the front door at the same time as the riders thundered along the drive. Hammering on the door, she pushed it open in a panic and plunged into An's waiting arms. The young woman had come to see what the noise was about.

"Welcome," An greeted the riders, not releasing Sarah from her arms. Sarah blotted her head in the scented folds of An's dress. "What news brings you here?" An asked the men.

Dismounting the three riders hastily tied up their horses and replied: "We come with a message from Ma'gina."

"Come inside then," An said, keeping her arm comfortingly around Sarah's shoulders. She led the visitors into the reception room and called for drinks. Once they were seated, each with a fruit juice to drink, An sat too, indicating that Sarah should sit next to her on the sofa.

"Can we talk safely here?" one of the men asked.

An cocked her head to one side as if listening then she replied: "Yes. The place is now shielded against unwanted eyes and ears."

The man explained that they were part of the watchers of Granwich.

"The situation in Granwich is alarming. Several women and one child have been murdered in the last few days. It is no longer safe for women there. Lucie and the other women have decided to get the women and children as well as the old people out of town. They are going to travel overland to here and then on to the Lost Meadows."

An asked the men many questions about the escape plans until finally one of the men concluded: "Ma'gina asked if you could send a message to the Littl' People to let them know the people are coming and to prepare for them."

Sarah hadn't realised that Sally had joined them till the young woman spoke up. "We were planning to leave for the South anyway," she said.

"Good," the man said, nodding greetings. "If you have no more need of us we must get back as quickly as possible."

An stood and Sarah followed suit. "Rest a short while, the time to feed and water your horses and for us to prepare food for your journey," she suggested.

Although they were reluctant, the men finally accepted. Sally showed them to the stables while An took Sarah to the kitchens to supervise the preparation of food for the return journey. She also ordered the preparation of food for their own journey to country of the Littl' People.

On the road again

Once the men had left, Sally joined An and Sarah in An's study.

"Are you alright now, Sarah?" An asked.

"I was so frightened earlier," Sarah admitted, shuddering at the thought. "I couldn't stop trembling. I had visions of being dragged off by a band of savages. I've been having nightmares ever since I left Lucie's place. Maybe it was the attack on our way here."

230

"Tell us about your dreams," An suggested.

"I haven't had such dreams since I left Avan, if you discount the passage through the Dream World itself. They are not so much about being attacked though. I am invariably on the road either in the countryside or in a town. The way is complicated and tortuous. I have to go somewhere, but I have no idea where. Something drives me forward: a deep urge or sometimes the awareness of a veiled threat. There are moments when I think I know where I must go or someone with me knows, then I lose the path or the person. One thing is sure: wherever it is I have to go, I haven't got there yet," Sarah sighed. "I feel so restless. I just want to travel on."

"Well," An commented, "if its any consolation you'll get to travel a lot today."

"If Jenny were here," Sally suggested, "she might find something in your connection to the worlds that would explain these dreams of yours. Maybe you are rooted elsewhere," she wondered.

"You think it might be physical?" Sarah asked.

"Just an intuition," Sally replied.

"I am concerned about something else," An said, changing the subject. "The exodus of the women of Granwich will surely lead Horst and his men here, putting us all in danger."

The mention of Horst made Sarah angry. She couldn't think of the man without wanting to stick hundreds of needles in him. If she'd been a witch she'd have changed him into a squealing pig or, even better, a fat toad. She giggled at the thought and the others shot her strange looks. But the thought gave her an idea.

"I heard you can transform the appearance of things, Sally," Sarah said. "Couldn't you hide this house?"

Sally looked pensive. "I've never transformed anything so big."

"At least you could try," Sarah encouraged her.

Camouflage

Sarah and An had gone off on a cart with the servants to get food for the crowd that was to arrive in a few days. The pretext they were to use with the people in the village was that they were having a large number of guests to stay. Sally sat at the wooden table that stood at the edge of the forest and stared at An's house.

What had An's father, Vic, told her the first time she'd come to their house? That transformation was rather like prayer: effortless wanting. She'd had no idea what he meant at the time. She'd had very little experience with prayer. At the time, she'd found her own road to transformation that travelled via sound and vibrations.

Taking a deep breath, Sally sought out the vibrations of a small outhouse in which tools were stored. She'd decided to start with something smaller. It was not easy to shut out all the rest. The place was particularly full of vibrations. Not surprising really; had not Jenny told them the house was situated right on a node of the earth's energy grid.

The trick was to picture the little building and pair it off with the vibrations that went with it. Once she had that double 'vision' she could begin to shift the vibrations and change the form and colour of the thing. She tried changing it into a clump of trees, but they didn't look right. They seemed artificial. She let her grip slip and the outhouse transformed almost of its own will into a grass-covered mound. The change didn't come from her, she was simply tuning into something that had been there earlier, much earlier.

Casting her glance at the rest of the house, she saw instead a more extensive mound of earth. So that was what had been here a long time ago, a tumulus. The presence of the ancient burial place would explain the high energy of the place, she thought.

Standing, she made her way to explore what she had created. She was intrigued to know if she could walk through such a creation. The place was astonishingly realistic. Silly me! she told herself. Of course it's real, she had simply temporarily shifted this place back to the way it was before.

The entrance to the barrow was cunningly concealed at the side of the mound behind a large boulder most of which was also cover in grass and moss. Venturing inside she found a large cavern with a stone altar raised in its middle. The place was lit up by a number of tiny openings in the upper parts of the walls. Cautiously avoiding the altar and the ground around it, Sally made her way across the cavern and found a second exit on the far side that led to a narrow path through the dense forest beyond.

Worried that she might not be able to shift it back to the house it was, Sally hurriedly returned through the barrow and transformed the mound into An's house. No problem. To test how other people would perceive the place, she returned it to the barrow and waited for the others to return.

A surprise

Sarah laughed heartily at the story An was telling her as the cart rumbled along the last stretch of road to the house. An had a way of imitating each of the characters in her story that made it come all the more to life. Sarah very much liked An. It wasn't the same as Lucie, but she felt relaxed and safe with the girl.

To her surprise, An broke off her story and sat staring in front of her, her mouth fallen open. Sarah was tempted to make a joke about the risk of swallowing flies, but that might seem a little childish. Instead she turned to see what An was looking at, it was then that the cart screeched to a halt and the servants gasped in fright.

"What has happened to the house Mistress?" the servant driving the cart asked, clearly troubled by what he saw. Where the house had once been, the ground rose in the form of an ancient burial mound. To everybody's surprise, An burst out laughing. When she recovered, she called out: "Come out Sally, wherever you are hiding!"

Sally stepped out from behind one side of the barrow, a broad smile on her face, clearly pleased with herself.

"Well done," An said. "Now give me my house back," and she pulled a face that was meant to indicate that she was angry but she couldn't quite conceal her pride in her sister. When Sarah glanced back at tumulus it had disappeared and An's house had returned where it should be.

"Wow!" she said. "Impressive! A useful trick! I wonder what happens to any people who are in the house when you transform it?" she mused.

As nobody volunteered to find out, she dropped the idea.

To the south

The journey south was surprisingly uneventful. There were none of the groups of wild men they had feared they'd meet. Their absence however was almost as worrying as their presence. Sally wondered where they could all have gone. Sally's little group went on horseback so that they could get back in time for the arrival of Lucie and the women of Granwich. As they rode, she told them what she knew of the Littl' People.

"They call me Cian'la," she explained to Sarah, "because when I first came to the Reaches I was called Cianala or Nala for short. But you know that already, don't you?" Sally was careful about not making any reference to the person Sarah had been before she became a little girl.

Changing the subject, Sarah turned to An, saying: "You promised to teach me transformation." "I did indeed and we will take some time off when we arrive to work on it."

The closer they got to their destination, the tighter the mountains on either side of the road pulled in around them till they were making their way through a narrow valley. Memories came flooding back of her last visit to the place.

"Oh look," Sarah suddenly exclaimed.

A short procession of the Littl' People was moving in their direction along the road. Some carried torches, others carried sticks or bows and arrows. Sally wondered where all the other people were. At the head of the procession she recognised D'rick, the leader of the Littl' People and El'na, the girl who had befriended her during her stay. Getting off her horse she handed the reins to Sarah.

The procession came to a halt and D'rick stepped forward. Drawing himself up to his full height, he said: "You are most welcome Princess Cian'la. And welcome to your friends."

"Greetings D'rick, greetings El'na and greetings to all the Littl' People," Nala said before she went forward to embrace D'rick and El'na. Then turning to her friends who had dismounted, she said: "This is my sister An. You know her already I believe. And this is Sarah. You have met her too, but she was in the form of an owl at the time."

Seeing El'na make a face, Sarah stepped forward. "I apologise, El'na. I was not very kind with you last time I was here."

El'na burst out laughing and hugged Sarah. "I prefer you as a g'rl," was all she said, still laughing.

D'rick raised his hand for silence. "Princess Cian'la is returned," he said addressing both the Littl' People and the visitors. "We should sing Cian'la the traditional song about her exploits, but doing so would be far too risky. We must hurry back to safety."

Sally tried to ask him what the danger was, but he refused to answer and only hurried even faster. To her surprise they did not head for the houses that the Littl' People had built at the end of the valley. Instead, D'rick led them into one of the many tunnels that dotted the side of the mountain. The Littl' People mined the mountains for gems and they made the most exquisite jewellery that was much in demand all around.

The entrance they were about to use was some ten feet above ground level and had to be reached by a narrow staircase cut out of stone.

"Let us look aft'r the 'orses. We'll st'ble 'em," D'rick told them.

As she reached the top, Sally turned and looked back over the village. What she saw horrified her. The wooden pillars that held up the Forum had been hacked down and the roof had collapsed over the fireplace and dining hall. Beyond, the w'men's 'ouse, as El'na called it, had been gutted by fire. Everywhere she looked she could see signs of devastation. She had loved that place for its restful peace. Seeing it ransacked made her both angry and deeply sad. El'na pushed her inside and others followed rapidly after them till they were all gathered at the end of a narrow passageway in a larger chamber.

"We have been repeatedly attacked by bands of wild men that once worked for the owners of the Black castle," D'rick explained. "As you saw, they have destroyed our village and made trade completely impossible. I am surprised you managed to make it here unmolested," D'rick said. "They have even tried to penetrate the tunnels several times, but we have been able to fight them off each time."

"What do they want?" Sally asked.

"At first it was just plunder and booty that drove them," El'na explained. "They were quite disorganised and attacks were at random. Some days several different groups came one after another, other days none came at all. But in the last week or so, the attacks are better planned and coordinated. It was then that they tired to break into the tunnels."

In the tunnels

D'rick invited them to follow him saying: "We must go deeper under the mountains. We will be safer and food awaits us."

He was right about the food. The Littl' People had set up a replica of their Forum in a large cavern and a delicious smell of vegetable soup wafted out from the central fire around which a number of people were busy putting the finishing touches to the communal meal.

When all were gathered and ready to eat, D'rick insisted they sing Cian'la's song. No instruments accompanied the singers who sang quite softly, presumably not to attract attention should the music happen to travel down one of the tunnels and reach the outside world. Sally thanked them for their welcome and wished them a good meal. For a while the only sound to be heard was eating.

"This is really delicious," Sally said to D'rick.

His only reply was to nod behind her. And there stood Martin and Fran. She got up and hugged them both and then presented them to Sarah who'd not met them before.

"Why don't you join us. This soup is really excellent!"

Martin laughed. "We know. We made it."

Ladling another spoonful of soup into her mouth, Sally said, not without difficulty: "You didn't used to cook, did you?"

"We've been taking lessons ever since we got here," Fran explained. "One of the old women has taught us what wild herbs to use, when to pick them and how best to prepare them. Another younger woman showed us how best to store and prepare the meat and vegetables and above all what frame of mind to be in to cook well."

"And many of the Littl' People have taught us their recipes," Martin added. "It's like cooking and healing and loving and meditating all rolled into one delicious dish," Fran said with a flourish of enthusiasm.

"Well the result is wonderful," Sally said, finishing her plate.

D'rick called for applause for the two cooks who bowed and returned to the oven to fetch cakes they'd baked.

Sally, An and Sarah were seated at the same table as D'rick and El'na. An questioned D'rick further about the attacks. The Littl' People had an efficient watch and nobody had been hurt in the early attacks. They had managed to get everybody to safety in the mountains, but they had had to abandon the village.

"It was such a beautiful place," Sally regretted.

Everyone remained silent and thoughtful for a while.

"Your situation here is not going to make our task any easier," An began. She went on to explain what had happened in Granwich and the decision of the women to flee the town with their children and the old people. When she told D'rick that they wanted to travel to the Lost Meadows, a number of the Littl' People gasped.

"Several of the bands of men have managed to clamber over the mountains and have gained access to the Lost Meadows, setting up an ugly camp there. They hoped they could better attack us from there, but we sealed the entrances to keep them out."

Sally listened in silence. Two contrasting memories of the Lost Meadows sprang to mind. First there were the gnarled, blackened forms of the trees and the scorched earth and rocks as she released the energy that was being channelled through her by forces she couldn't control. Second there was the ecstatic song she sang accompanied by all the Littl' People as she brought the valley back to life and all manner of flowers and grasses and trees sprung up and thrived where devastation had reigned.

"I have an idea how we might rid ourselves of those men in the Lost Meadows," she announced. She wouldn't tell them what she was going to do.

Better not let too many people know what you are capable of doing, Vee cautioned her.

"It is not without risk," she added. Turning to D'rick she asked: "Do you think the mountain could stand up to another battering like it got when Leuchtli threw all that energy at me?"

He did not reply immediately, apparently weighing up the possibilities. "I'm n't sure," he admitted. "This cav'rn m'ght coll'pse, fer ex'mple. I 'ave found a numb'r o' faults runnin' 'long the w'lls, prob'bly from yer last exploits," he said making a valiant attempt to smile.

"Can you lead your people away to a safe place for a short while?" Sally asked.

He glanced at El'na and then replied simply: "Yes."

"Good then get everyone together including Martin, Fran, Sarah and An and take them there immediately," Sally said. "If you agree El'na, I'd like you to accompany me. I need someone to show me the way. And to help me if anything goes wrong."

An wanted to accompany Sally as did Sarah, but Sally refused adamantly.

Déjà vu

When the others had all departed leaving only Sally and El'na, Sally said: "Take us as close as you can to the entrance to the Lost Meadows, El'na. I will explain what I plan to do on the way."

El'na had filled her little sack with food. "Just 'n case," she'd said.

When Sally had explained what she planned to do, the young woman was shocked.

"Oh no! Not again. I couldn't stand it."

Sally laughed. "It's not you that has to stand it, it's me."

El'na looked very serious in the light of the torch she was carrying. "Did I ev'r tell yer I lov'd yer, Cian'la?" the young woman asked.

"I don't remember you saying it in so many words, El'na. But I knew it. And I love you too."

"I couldn't bear t' risk loos'n yer ag'in," El'na said.

"Don't worry, El'na. None of us will get hurt this time. All will be OK. The only people who will suffer will be those men."

The two women crouched near a crack in the rocks through which a part of the Meadows was visible. An ugly grey tarpaulin hung over the branches of a tree, affording some shelter for the couple of men huddled together under it sharing a bottle of what must have been some form of alcohol. On a fire nearby, a brace of rabbits roasted.

Those poor animals, Vee exclaimed. They didn't deserve such a scorching end.

The first time she had been in the Meadows, Sally remembered, the animals had willingly communicated with her and her friends.

The animals are going to be a problem, if you want to carry out your plan, Vee commented.

I know, she replied. We'll have to get them out first, if we can.

Drawing back from the crack, Sally asked El'na: "Is there any way we can get out into the Meadows?"

"Yes. There's a place with a large stone th't c'n be moved fro' ins'de the tunn'ls, but no' fro' outs'de."

"Take me there, please."

The two young women rolled back the stone till they had enough room to squeeze through.

"Do you still have your horn to call the animals?" Sally asked El'na.

"It goes wi' me ev'rywh're," she replied.

"We need to get the animals out of the Meadows as soon as possible."

El'na looked worried. "If yer do th't, they'll likely g't kill'd by th'm men."

She's right, Vee put in.

"Maybe I can limit the transformation to the space just around their camp. I imagine most of the animals and birds will keep away from there."

238

The sun was low on the horizon and night would soon fall. They crept further out amongst the rocks that surrounded the valley. Sally needed to know how many men there were and what they were doing.

Can you check on them, Vee, she asked. Sure.

And she felt him slip away.

"I've sent Vee to spy on them," she explained to El'na.

"Amazin'" was all El'na said, her eyes wide in surprise.

There are five men Vee told her when he returned. Three are camped down there. One is further up the meadows on the look out and one more is higher in the mountains also on watch.

Night had fallen and the new moon afforded very little light.

I can't do this in the dark, she told him. How can I see what I am doing?

Maybe you don't need to see, Vee replied.

"So Vee's back?" El'na asked, somehow guessing that Sally was deep in conversation with Vee.

"Yes. He says there are five men."

And Sally repeated what Vee had told her.

You know where the three are, Vee pursued. Maybe its enough to get rid of them. Surely that'll frighten the others. They need to run and tell the colleagues elsewhere what has happened so no one else comes.

Sally nodded in agreement, although she knew doing so was rather silly because he could hear what she thought.

"OK. I'll do it. Now," she informed El'na. "I'm not sure if there'll be shock waves. We might not be safe behind these rocks."

"'ave faith that'll w'rk out right," El'na reassured her.

Half hidden behind a massive rock, Sally relaxed, breathing deeply. She listened for the vibration emitted around the camp, searching for something deeper, older; something painful and violent. It was there all right, surprisingly close to the surface. She let it slip slightly, letting the violence seep upwards and outwards. Opening her eyes she could see the whole area around the makeshift camp site was beginning to glow. Sparks arced downwards, striking the ground in ever wilder flashes. The grass was rapidly consumed and the tarpaulin caught fire. The three men screamed as the rocks around turned red and began to deform under the heat. A sudden violent shudder caused the earth beneath the camp to heave up, scattering near molten rock wider afield. Sally gasped.

"It's looking for me," she whispered, terrified. "It wants to flow through me like last time."

Let it go, Vee ordered. Release all hold on it. But if I do, she replied, getting breathless, it will spread everywhere.

Panic was threatened to overwhelm her.

A wild cry rang out overhead. Looking up they saw an owl plunging towards them. Before it had completely landed it transformed into a man.

"Brent!" Sally called out recognising him immediately. "Help me! I can't control it. It's starting again."

A thunder-clap rang out above.

"Sing!" Brent insisted. "Sing for rain and appeasement. This land is hurt."

And he began a deep guttural song that seemed to echo the voice of the gathering storm. Sally let her voice rise above his, like a wild bird tossed on the storm, but delighted to be aloft and free. El'na sang too: a prayer for rain in a long forgotten language. And Brent and Sally reined in their wild sounds so as to accompany her, twining their wordless song around the words of El'na.

A brilliant flash of lightening lit up the whole valley. In that moment they all saw that nothing was left of the encampment, only charred rocks, still glowing with the heat. The first drops of rain came fast on the heels of the lightening, thick heavy rain that pounded on the waiting ground, drenching it. Sally could no longer feel the pull of that former energy. As the rain fell steadily, she sensed the valley relax. They had finally put things right. Their first try about a year ago had not been enough.

Completely drenched, she realised that she was holding Brent's hand as he stood dripping and naked next to her. El'na was holding his other hand. Progressively the rain eased off and the three of them began to feel the cold. Suddenly Brent was gone and the owl he had become rose majestically into the air, pushing upwards against the remaining rain. Circling, rising all the time, in ever widening circles over the Lost Meadows. Then he glided down to them and transformed back into his manly form.

"The two survivors are terrified. They are fleeing, clambering up impossible mountain paths. Both have multiple burns and cuts. They won't readily forget what they have experienced here."

"Neither will I," Sally replied.

"We need t' git yer s'me clothes y'ng man," El'na said laughing. "'nd somethin' warm fer all o' us t' eat. Or we might 'ave to eat yer instead, y'ng man," she added laughing.

Brent gave her a kiss on her cheek and slipping his arm around Sally's waist he pulled her close to his side. She was still shaken by what had happened and was glad of his support as he led them back to the concealed entrance. El'na took them to one of the many store places within the mountains and found loose fitting trousers that were big enough for him. There was no shirt suitable, but a cloak served to keep him warm while El'na cooked up a soup.

"Where have you been?" Sally asked as she cuddled up in Brent's arms.

"On a journey," he replied beaming, brushing the wet hair from her eyes.

El'na was surprisingly quiet as the three made their way back to where the Littl' People were sheltering.

She's jealous, Vee said.

And you, Sally asked him, are you jealous?

Not really. I'm happy for both of you.

"El'na," Sally said, "come closer so I can put my arm around your shoulder."

The girl was pouting, she noticed, and refused to come any closer. Letting go of Brent she used both hands to grasp hold of El'na and tickle her.

Stiffly opposing the attack at first, El'na let go a little and began to giggle, saying: "Stop it, Nala."

"I can still love you, even if I am with Brent," Sally told her, ceasing her tickles and taking El'na in her arms. Their conversation didn't get any further because they had reach the cavern where the Littl' People were camped.

The story

"I'm so terribly sorry," An said, running up to Sally. "I was teaching Sarah how to transform. For all her complaints that she didn't know how to do it, she was surprisingly good at transforming once she'd got the knack. Then, all of a sudden, she changed into an owl and flew away. We've looked ever where for it. But we found no trace of it."

"Don't be sorry. That owl saved our lives and possibly yours too."

241

More and more Littl' people were crowding around them clamouring to hear the story.

"We will tell you the story once we've had something warm to eat. But first I must present an old friend to you."

Turning to Brent who had held back in the shadows, she beckoned at him to come forward. Taking his hand she announced: "This is Brent a very good friend of mine."

"But he's been lost all this time," Martin said.

"How did he get here?" Fran asked.

Giving Brent a kiss, Sally said mysteriously: "All will be revealed in due course."

It was at that moment that El'na intervened. "Enough for now. Let's have something to eat. I'm starving."

The tables had been placed in a wide semi-circle and torches lit the Littl' People and their guests who had just finished a delicious meal.

"I th'nk Cian'la 'as a tale t' tell," D'rick said, calling for quiet.

"I am not a storyteller," she clarified as she stood and faced everybody.

"But we do have a storyteller with us, returned from a long journey." And she gestured to Brent.

He'd donned one of Martin's shirts. It was slightly too big for him but the colour suited him well.

"I'm sure he will willingly tell us the tale of what happened."

The Littl' People hammered on the tables and whistled encouragement, calling out his name.

As he stood before them, a memory flashed through his mind: the time when he had read Lucie the story of her ancestor. It had been his first real story. He could still remember the fervour and pride he'd felt as he gave form to the story of the man who was wrongly supposed to have built the canals in Granwich. As Brent stood in front of the Littl' People he also recalled his journey with Mia through the Dream Realm and how he'd used stories to transport them from one world to another.

"The little girl was called Sarah. She was barely ten years old. Only a few hours ago she sat here amongst you all," he began, weaving the magic of storytelling around the gathered audience. "She had not always been a little girl, but that is another story." He drew on the images that flooded into his mind and used them to transport his listeners with him. "… Once she had transformed into an owl, a desperate call for help immediately became audible to her. Its pull was so potent on him that he couldn't resist it. Despite An calling him back and warning him of the dangers, he had to answer it."

He took his listeners headlong through darkened tunnels, skilfully navigating their way around twists and turns to a tiny exit that gave them access to free air. They soared upwards, delighted at the joy of flying in the night air till they rose above the mountains and were able to see the Lost Meadows far below. An intense glow marked the middle of the Meadows, and the closer they came the clearer they could see fire and sparks raining down on the glowing centre. They heard piercing screams and could smell the stench of burning flesh that clog their beaks and noses.

There, nearby, Cian'la stood, arms outstretched, struggling desperately with an invisible force. A violent shudder shook the earth and the fiery mass rose up into the air and spread outwards extending its grip on the valley. It sent fear through all their hearts

"Help!" Nala called out in their heads. And they were rushing down towards her. Landing on the grass they transformed into human form and urged Nala and El'na to sing for rain. The collected voices of all the Littl' People joined in song, buoying El'na up in an ancient invocation of rain. And each of them felt the rain answer, pouring down over them, drenching them till their clothes were soaked and the rain began chaffing their skin. And they looked out over the Lost Meadows and saw that the fire had stopped and each of them felt deeply inside that the evil force had finally gone from the place.

He brought them gently back to the cavern where they sat listening to him. And he bowed and sat back down next to Sally. People stared unbelieving about them, unable to adjust to the return to their normal state. Then one by one they burst into applause, standing in ovation to Brent who simply cuddled up in Sally's arms. It was the first time he'd used the gift of story telling for such a long story.

The return

A group of the Littl' People sporting bows and arrows with D'rick as their leader accompanied An, Sally and Brent on their return journey to An's house. Martin and Fran had stayed behind to prepare the Lost Meadows for the arrival of the women of Granwich. They saw nothing of the wild men along the road.

"Maybe what happened in the Meadows has taught them a lesson," Sally speculated.

She was glad they could travel unencumbered as they were in a hurry to return to An's house and, what's more, the narrow valley they were passing through with the high rocky walls rising on either side of it would have been ideal for an ambush. She didn't get any further with her thoughts. A shout went up further down the road and a large pack of filthy men slunk out from their hiding places behind boulders and started advancing cautiously along the road to meet them. The archers calmly took up their positions waiting for the men to come within range. A further shout went up behind them. Glancing over her shoulder, Sally saw a second pack of wild men following them at a distance along the track they had just used.

A trap! Vee said. They are more organised and better informed than we thought.

The group behind them was getting dangerously close and would soon be upon them. They couldn't defend themselves against both groups.

"Concentrate on those in front of us," she said to the Littl' People. "I'll deal with those behind." In a flash she tuned into the ground behind them but there didn't seem to be anything she could use against the men.

Try to the left in those rocks, Vee said urgently.

Ah yes, a vague memory of a landslide, a long time ago. She allowed the past to overflow into the present as a deep and threatening rumble announced the imminent arrival of a terrifying mass of boulders and earth and rocks. The wild men stopped in their tracks, horrified. They tried to flee back down the road, but they were no match for the deadly landslide. It rolled over them and continued a good way up the other side of the valley before it ground to a halt.

We need to get out of here, Vee urged her. We'll be swept away too if it overflows sideways along the path.

Turning to look forwards once more, she discovered that the archers had not yet fired a single arrow. The men were keeping at a safe distance and there were far too many of them. The men clearly realised that the Littl' People had no means of escape: the landslide had blocked any retreat. Her action had boxed them in far better than the force she'd driven away.

"Lay down your arms. Offer no resistance unless they try to do you bodily harm," Brent ordered the Littl' People. "Trust in me. We'll be all right."

Seeing that the Littl' People were giving themselves up, the wild men finally surged forward, blood lust and stench accompanying them.

"Stop!" a powerful voice shouted. The men faltered and then halted, obeying. Horst stepped out from behind a rock, smiling. "So we meet again, young lady," he said addressing Sally.

As he turned to talk to the group of the wild men, out of the corner of her eye Sally saw two owls rise up into the air and wing themselves to safety. Brent and An were escaping. She only hoped the two would be able to deliver herself and the Littl' people.

"Take them alive and tie them all up. I've got a job for them," Horst ordered. "Sally, isn't it?" he enquired, attempting to feign affability, as he came closer. "Tell me, how is Dr. Leuchtli?"

Humour him and gain time, Vee suggested, until the others can save us.

"He's in a mental hospital somewhere in Germany I expect, no doubt mulling over plans of revenge," Sally replied, returning his sham smile.

Horst grabbed her by the wrist, hurting her, and dragged her forward in the direction of the Littl' People who were being roped together by the wild men.

So much for his pretence of congeniality, Vee muttered.

"And how come you managed to escape my little gift?" Horst asked, clearly angry.

"The local fire brigade extinguished the fire," Sally replied, sidetracking his question, "but not before most of your former mansion was destroyed."

Easy does it, Vee warned.

But Sally was furious with the man.

"You realise that you cost me all my men. That was years of my work. I will make you pay dearly for that," he said, slapping her as hard as he could across her face, sending her flying to the ground. "Tie her up and rope her to the others," he snapped at his men. "Let's get going, we have a long way to go."

Escape plans

Flying wing to wing, Brent and An soared high above the sad caravan as it trudged wearily along the valley. Brent was about to talk to An when they both noticed that Horst had shielded his eyes from the sun and was peering up at them. Plunging away out of sight, Brent spoke into An's mind: He can sense us. Landing on one of the upper branches of a pine tree, they stood side-by-side pruning their feathers.

I will have to go in spirit form, Brent said. Sarah learnt how to do it. Maybe he won't be able to feel me like that. At least he won't be able to see me.

Show me how you do it, An asked.

I can't. I don't know how I do it, Brent replied. We need to be in a secure place because I will be vulnerable if there is any danger, he continued.

Over there, An said, there is a cave and I will watch out for you while your spirit is gone.

Brent's spirit flew lower over the cortege of prisoners and their sordid hoard of guards. Horst marched alone at the head of the cortege, apparently deep in thought while Sally trailed last of a long line of captives. Invisible to everyone, Brent landed lightly on Sally's shoulder and spoke to Vee. He explained that he and An couldn't follow too close because they suspected Horst could sense them.

Do you think he realised that you caused the avalanche? Brent asked. I ask because we might use some sort of transformation to trick him.

Sally didn't think he did. But we mustn't delay him too long, Vee said on behalf of Sally. He has to be back in Granwich for the festivities.

Then we need a means for you all to slip away, Brent suggested.

Careful, Vee warned him, Horst is coming our way.

Brent had no time to fly off so he sat still and silent on Sally's shoulder hoping the man wouldn't sense his presence.

"You don't need to pretend you're not involved in my future wife's plots," Horst said.

"Are you getting married?" Sally retorted. "How nice for you."

He ignored the biting sarcasm.

"She thinks I don't notice the way she huddles up with the other Patriciat women, whispering. I have spies watching her all the time."

He laughed. "And she expects me to believe they want to celebrate my birthday. How naive of her."

He moved away and was about to return to the head of the cortege when he turned back and said: "When we halt this evening at your friend's house, I'll get the information out of you, whether you like it or not."

Brent stayed silent until he was sure Horst was far enough away.

That's useful information, he said to Vee. We'll fly on ahead to An's house and prepare a welcome for him. We'll need your help to create an exit for you and the Littl' People, Brent said.

You remember the burial mound Sally called up to conceal An's house, Vee replied, couldn't we escape through there.

Good. Leave us an hour or two to reach the house and get the servants out, then transform it into the burial mound. Can you do that from so far away?

I think so, Vee said, replying for Sally.

Don't worry about the wild men, I'll deal with them, Brent said. Just warn the Littl' People. Have them pass the message along to be ready. And his spirit winged away leaving Sally to her thoughts.

When they reached An's house the two owls landed on the lawn in front of the veranda and transformed into their human forms. An hurried inside to get the servants out of the house and away to safety. Brent was to fetch food from the kitchens and carry it to the edge of the forest. Shortly afterwards the transformation occurred and the house was replaced by a barrow.

Lugging sacks of food and drink through the dark tunnels, they concealed the material on the opposite side of the mound amongst the trees.

Returning to the path, Brent said: "We need to give them a good reason to stop here even if there is no house to welcome them. What if we made a makeshift camp site here in the clearing in front of the mound with a large fire and food and drink scattered around as if the people settled here had fled in a hurry."

They had barely finished their preparations when Vee arrived to warn them that Horst and his men were only five minutes away.

Concealed in the trees, the two of them watched as Horst entered the clearing and halted astonished in front of the tumulus. He turned on the spot, looking in every direction as if he expected to find the source of the trouble, but nobody was there to be found. He was clearly confused and alarmed by what he saw, although he mastered himself rapidly. Turning his back on the mound, Horst ignored the campsite and ordered his men to continue.

"But we're starving and tired," several of the men complained.

"Then gather up the food as you go by," Horst insisted.

But a growing number of the wild men had already sat down by the fire and began cautiously sniffing the food.

"Seems all right to me," one said and took a bite.

"Mmmm! Scrumptious."

More and more of the wild men gathered around the fire and helped themselves to the food and drink. Horst shrugged and gave in, allowing the men to halt, although he didn't touch the food himself.

"Tie the prisoners up to a tree," he snapped, clearly irritated by their failure to obey him.

How long before the sleeping draught works? Brent asked from mind to mind.

About an hour, An replied.

What about Horst?

We'll figure something out was An's reply.

The men didn't all fall asleep at the same time giving the impression that they were succumbing to tiredness rather than a drug. For Brent, it seemed to take ages till the last of the men collapsed close to the fire. He then went from one to the next in spirit form whispering stories into their ears of ghosts from the barrow rising up and chasing the wild men away till he felt the panic like a tide rising in them.

In the mean time, Horst had got up from his solitary seat and sauntered amongst the sleeping men to where Sally was resting at the foot of a tree. Shaking her to waken her, he dragged her to her feet and bound her to the tree by her hands and feet.

"Now for our little business together," Horst said, running the tips of his fingers across her breasts.

Sally spat in his face. At which he slapped her, hitting her in the same place he had done before, sending a shot of pain through her body and causing her to whimper. He wiped the spittle from his face and cleaned his hands on her dress.

"There's nobody to save you here," he sneered. "You're all mine. And I intend to do with you whatever I will."

He blocked her with his body, pushing her against the tree trunk as he fumbled between her legs. Sally struggled, trying to bite him but he was able to avoid her teeth.

Brent couldn't bear to watch what was going on. He had to act immediately. The man disgusted him. He hovered in spirit form just behind Horst's head. It was a risky plan, but he had no other. Speaking into Horst's mind he began a story of a frightened little boy all alone locked up in a dark place and desperately in need of going to the toilet. Unable to escape, the boy made every effort to control himself but his body's needs were stronger than his will. He couldn't hold on much longer. What would his mother say if he returned home soiled? He'd surely be beaten and humiliated.

When the door suddenly burst open the boy fled as fast as he could across the grass and into the bushes beyond to relieve himself. Anxiety and disgust drove him to hide for fear he might have been seen and would still be caught and punished. He pushed his way ever deeper into the forest trying to find a safe place to hide. The sound of crashing branches of people in pursuit drove him further and further away till he finally came to rest exhausted and depressed on a tree stump.

At last he was free of the nightmare and could gather his wits. Opening his eyes he saw his men, terrified, fleeing through the forest, crashing into the branches, not heeding the scratches and cuts in their terror. What on earth had got into them all?

Meanwhile, An had freed Sally and the Littl' People and led them through the barrow to the forest beyond. They could hear Horst's men screaming as they fled in the opposite direction, the sound of their voices getting more and more distant. Brent joined them shortly afterwards, transforming from an owl back into his human form.

"We need to get further away," he whispered. "I doubt they will come back. But you never know. He's a stubborn man."

Indicating that they should pick up the supplies waiting for them, An led them single file along a narrow path to a house hidden deep in the forest. It was a one-storey thatched cottage with a large veranda on all sides protected by the roof that extended way out beyond the walls.

Looking at it, Sally had a curious feeling of déjà-vu that grew further when she entered the main door. Instinctively she knew that the kitchen was to the right and the living room was straight ahead. And there was something familiar in the smell of the place.

"Could I have been here before?" she asked An.

"I doubt it, my mother used to come here," An replied, "when she wanted to get away from us children. We were never allowed to come."

"Where are your parents?" Brent asked.

"They went south to seek help against the bands of wild men roaming the countryside," An replied.

"Are they likely to return in the near future?" Brent continued.

"I doubt it."

"Then we should leave your house transformed into a burial mound to protect it against reprisals," Brent suggested.

"So what d' we d' now?" D'rick asked.

"We've got to warn Lucie that Horst knows she's up to something," An said. "What's more, I can't see how they can possibly get through to the Lost Meadows with all these wild men on the roads."

"I will go," Brent insisted. "I will be less conspicuous flying there and I can travel faster than anyone on horseback."

"Then I will come with you, just in case you go all gooey when you see Lucie again and can't deliver the message," An said teasing him. "But seriously, it will be safer if there are two of us."

"I'm not sure it's safe to let you two little girls go together. You are likely to get up to mischief." Sally said looking pointedly at Brent who blushed. Sally wondered if she was most jealous of her sister or Brent.

"I'd come too to keep an eye on you if I could transform, but instead I'll stay here with D'rick and the Littl' People to prepare for the arrival of the women. We will need to clear a way through the avalanche ..."

With that decided, Brent and An left almost immediately for Granwich.

Chapter 12 - The rebellion

Practice

Ten women stood silent and unmoving at an arms distance from each other in a large room devoid of windows. The air in the room was in need of a change, but no welcome breeze came from the outside through the one door that remained resolutely closed. At a predetermined signal they all relaxed and began to flex their muscles.

"I don't understand," one of the women said, "How can standing here not doing anything help us learn to defend ourselves?"

Several of the other women laughed nervously at the question. Anju spun round gracefully on the ball of her foot, turning to face them.

"It's called 'effortless doing'. You need to be aware of what your body is doing ..." she said.

"But I know what I am doing: nothing," the woman exclaimed, interrupting Anju.

"I wouldn't say that," one of the younger women said. "I could sense a great many tiny movements as my body continually adjusted its position."

"Me too," several others agreed.

Anju smiled, happy that so many had grasped the point so quickly.

"Once you become aware of how your body moves, even in stillness, then you will begin to notice that making an effort is not the best way to move. When you make an effort you contract your muscles in preparation and that contraction works against the fluidity of the movement. Making an effort is the mind's way of expressing intention through your body. But in combat your movements need to be effortless. What's more, if your body contracts in preparation for an effort, it looses its ability to react in a different way should that prove necessary."

The woman remained thoughtful at her explanation.

"I will teach you a dance. You will be able to practice it on your own and no one will suspect what you are doing. But as you move you must listen to how you body reacts."

Anju took them through a series of steps that involved moving forwards and sideways and turning on one foot, echoing their feet movements with their arms and hands. After ten minutes practice, she called for a halt.

"I see what you mean," one of the youngest women said, excitedly. "If I just let my body move on its own it is so much easier."

Another of the younger ones' reaction was quite different. "For me it was not at all like that. The more I paid attention, the more I got stiff and was unable to move!"

"Paying attention can be like making an effort," Anju explained. "The mind tries hard to control the body and in doing so gets in the way. It will come. You will see. To help you relax and let go more easily you can use a massage."

Following Anju's instructions, the women paired off and spent ten minutes giving each other a short hand massage. Being massaged caused some of the women to giggle and Anju was obliged to ask them not to make so much noise, not only because it disturbed the others, but also because they mustn't be overheard.

When the massage had done its work, Anju had them go through the dance sequence again.

"Extraordinary," one woman exclaimed. "It really is easier."

Many people agreed with her. Bringing the session to an end, Anju suggested that they practice their movements whenever they could, pretending that they were practicing a new dance.

"You can also practice the massage too," an idea that met with general approval. "See you the day after tomorrow at the same time," she finished.

The women all thanked her as they left.

When the last of the women had filed out of the room, Dieter slipped through the open door.

"How'd it go?"

Anju was going through a series of rapid aerobatic movements that she brought to an end by rolling over and landing on her feet in front of Dieter.

"Fine. Some find it more difficult. They are not used to using their bodies. It is going to take a while to get them to feel what they are doing. How was your group?"

Dieter leaned forward and bushed a hair from her forehead where it had landed.

"OK. Most of the watchers are quite aware of their body. Maybe their training helps. They were less enthusiastic about the massage. People don't seem to have so much bodily contact here."

"How about you," Anju asked, massaging Dieter's neck. "How do you feel about bodily contact?" she teased him.

Dieter pulled away. "To be honest, it disturbs me."

Anju donned her jacket. Now that she was no longer moving, the room was rather cold.

"I imagine it feels like being attracted to a friend's younger daughter," Anju continued to tease him.

Dieter shot her a startled look then lowered his eyes, embarrassed. "Sort of," he grunted.

"I don't want our being together to be a torture for you," she said.

"It's not at all. I really enjoy being with you," he replied. "I like the way you move. I appreciate how you are always open to new experiences and learning. And talking to you is very stimulating." He hesitated for a moment before pursuing, presumably wondering how best to put his thoughts. "The only thing is that … you awaken something in me that troubles me."

She was tempted to tease him further, but she judged it was no longer the right thing to do. So she kept quiet and waited for more. When no more came and he stood there studying his shoes, she took his hand and saying: "Let's go get something to eat before the next group."

Imprisoned

Lucie paced her study furious, tapping her clenched fist in the palm of her other hand. She now knew how it felt to be a bird in a cage. As a bird keeper the irony of the situation was not lost on her. The man had upped and gone, leaving her under house arrest and no one to complain to about it. She'd lost count of the number of times she'd rehearsed the verbal lashing she planned to give him when he returned. She recalled his last words before he left.

"Be careful about flying out in bird form. I've given orders to my men to shoot at any birds or animals they see trying to smuggle in or out of the town."

Apparently he'd warned the Patriciat too, although she hadn't been present when he did because he wouldn't let her out. For her safety, he'd exclaimed. She'd heard that he'd talked of new security measures to the full Patriciat meeting. According to Horst, the threat had extended beyond the infamous watchers, who were now being supported by a number of renegade Patriciat members. People were being encouraged to spy on their neighbours and denounce any strange behaviour.

Hearing the telltale distant bell ring in the basement, she checked that none of her servants were around (she was convinced that several of them were there to spy on her at Horst's orders) and made her way by a roundabout route down to the cellar. It was Gloria come to fetch her.

"Can you attend the session with Anju?" the woman whispered, standing half concealed in the doorway to the passages.

"Yes. I don't think anyone is watching me at the moment," Lucie said as she joined Gloria and they closed the door behind them.

To avoid anyone unwittingly using the door, it remained locked at all times. Lucie relished the chance to get away from her house for the first time in the day. Horst would only let her out accompanied by himself or several of his men.

Presumably sensing Lucie's tension, Anju suggested they begin with some warm-up exercises that allowed her to let off steam: running, jumping, rolling and finally pushing and pulling in pairs with the other women. After ten minutes Anju stopped them.

"Last time we looked at how we move even when we are standing still. Today I want us to look at balance. Get in a comfortable stance with your feet shoulder width apart. Good Gloria, that's fine. And now lift one of your feet slowly off the ground and keep it there. Watch how your body shifts weight and uses muscles to compensate."

She walked amongst the women making a comment here or there.

"You remember we talked about your centre of balance. Make sure it is in your belly and not between your shoulders."

Several of the women laughed.

Try as she would, Lucie couldn't stay more than a few seconds on one foot. Watching the other women happily balanced like cranes she felt incapable. Tears of anger and frustration welled up in her eyes. She disliked herself intensely for being so helpless and hopeless. She was quite unaccustomed to such a feeling. Anju came and stood next to her.

"Your centre is up here," Anju said lightly touching Lucie's forehead. "Worry and concern does that. So does anger and frustration." And the young woman took Lucie in her arms and gently massaged the nape of her neck. It was just too much. Lucie burst into tears despite her efforts to hold them back.

"Let go," Anju whispered in her ear. "You're carrying a great weight on your shoulders. No wonder you can't balance on one foot."

It was true, she thought, she was bearing the brunt of Horst's assault on Granwich. She was at the eye of the cyclone. She laid her head on Anju's shoulder and let her tears flow.

"Now change to the other foot," Anju told the other women over Lucy's shoulders, keeping Lucie firmly in her arms.

After a while she called the other women to form a circle around them.

"Lucie needs our help," she explained. "Move in closer and put both hands out in front of you till you can touch her." And shifting to join the circle herself, she said. "Now, Lucie, close your eyes and let yourself lean on those hands and we will pass you gently around the circle."

Lucie couldn't help being afraid they might let her fall, especially as she had her eyes closed. But as the many hands passed her leaning form around the circle she began to relax. Anju must have made some unseen sign to the other women because all of a sudden the group picked her up and laid her in their waiting arms, swaying backwards and forwards. When finally they placed her back on her feet and she opened her eyes she saw many a tear filled eye around her.

"You need to know that we all care for you, Lucie. And will do what we can to help you bear the load that is yours," Anju said.

"Now let's go back to our balancing act," Anju quipped, "but this time you will draw large circles with your foot above the floor."

Lucie was astonished to find it was much easier now. Still standing close to her, Anju said: "You must learn to get your centre down into your belly whenever it tends to creep up into your chest or even higher. Practice standing still and feeling where it is, then let it sink as low as it will go. If it helps you can try swaying very gently from side to side as you do so."

Anju shifted away and went to watch each woman in turn.

"Good. Now I will teach you some new moves to add to our dance."

Swinging one foot forwards and backwards, she had them turning on one foot using their outstretched hands for balance and momentum. Then shifting their weight to the other foot they did the same again. Lucie was so engrossed in the movements she was surprised when Anju announced that the session was over for today.

With Gloria, they then went to visit Ma'gina who was in her improvised laboratory with Mia.

"He's driving me mad, shutting me up all the time," she complained to Ma'gina.

Rather than commiserate with her, the old woman rebuked her: "We are also condemned to stay here underground without the slightest daylight. These are no easy times for any of us."

Lucie was indignant at Ma'gina's reaction. She would have preferred consolation, but she had to admit that Ma'gina was right.

"How are the preparations going?" she asked.

"We've gathered a large quantity of food and drink down here," Mia told her. "And the Patriciat women have continued to prepare food for the festivities."

"We still have to sort out the means of transport," Ma'gina added. "Many of the children and the older people will not be able to walk all the way."

"Couldn't we have the people of Smeth'ick drive a convey up to the other side of the Stone Circle Hill?" Mia suggested.

"It's an idea," Ma'gina conceded. "But any movements on the roads will immediately attract the attention of Horst's men. And even if those here are put to sleep by our potion, the others outside the town will still be wide awake."

Lucie was having serious doubts about their plan. The last thing she wanted to do was to put the women and children in unnecessary danger.

"Is there no other way we can move from here to there?" she asked. "The Patriciat women and children could fly, for example."

"Your Horst has given order to slay any animal or bird entering or leaving Granwich," Mia pointed out.

"He's not my Horst!" Lucie spluttered. "If it were up to me, I'd strangle him with my bare hands."

Then remembering what Anju had said, she calmed down and let her energy centre sink slowly from her throat were it had lodged itself, almost strangling her.

"We've got to get everybody out of here," Ma'gina recapitulated. "That's clear. But we need to find a better way of doing so."

If the women couldn't get away then sacrificing herself to marry Horst would have been for nothing. Feeling increasingly shut in on all sides, the only issue Lucie could think of was going to bed. She felt exhausted.

"I have to get back," she said wearily and rose to go.

"Here! Drink this before you leave," Ma'gina said. "It will restore some of your energy."

The liquid was not unpleasant but didn't seem to have any effect. Thanking Ma'gina, all the same, she left for her house accompanied by Gloria.

Snapping point

Listening carefully behind the locked door, they could hear no noise.

"Won't you come in a moment," Lucie pleaded with Gloria. "I can't bear to be locked up in my own house all alone."

Gloria refused, not wishing to take the risk of getting caught. But Lucie insisted and finally Gloria gave in.

"Only for half an hour," she conceded.

Lucie led Gloria to her bedroom, one of the few places where her servants wouldn't disturb her. The two women were sitting on Lucie's bed discussing how to get all the women away when a knock came at the door.

"Who is it?" Lucie called out, indicating to Gloria to hide in the dressing room.

Judging from the voice that said "It's me Miss", it was Angela, the very woman that was in the pay of Horst. Hastily removing her blouse and throwing a shawl around her shoulders, Lucie went to the bedroom door.

"What is it?" Lucie asked, unable to veil her irritation.

"I've brought your medicine Miss."

"Put it there on the bedside table. I'll drink it just before I go to bed."

"The Doctor said I was to make sure you drank it," the woman insisted.

"OK. Give it to me," and she leaned forward to take the glass when a movement out of the corner of her eye caught her attention. It was probably that distraction that caused her to let the glass fall to the ground where its contents spilled all over the carpet.

"How silly of me," Lucie said. "Please get me another glass of the stuff." Lucie couldn't understand the strange look the woman gave her at that moment.

"Of course, Miss. I'll be back straight away." And she hurried out of the door.

"How long have they been giving you that stuff?" Gloria asked in a whisper from the clothes cupboard.

"Almost a week," Lucie replied. "Why? My doctor said I was over worked and need a pick-me-up."

"It's poison!" Gloria said. "The watchers found out. That's why Ma'gina's been giving you the antidote."

A knock came at the door and the woman didn't wait to be asked but walked straight in. Seeing Gloria in the room she stopped in her tracks.

"What are you doing here? No visits are allowed. I shall have to call the guards." And she turned to leave the room when Gloria moved forward and grabbed the woman by the hair.

"You're not going anywhere, young lady!" Gloria said.

"Let me go or I'll tell Master Horst about you," the woman threatened.

"Of course you will," Gloria said, tightening her grip on Angela's long hair. "But in the mean time, give that glass of medicine to Lucie. We don't want to spill a second glass do we?"

Lucie was astonished at Gloria's decisiveness. She was discovering a completely different facet of her friend.

"Take the glass, Lucie. Put it in a safe place, we'll need it later. And find something to tie this woman up with."

They tied her legs and arms to a chair and stuffed an old scarf in her mouth when she started to shout for help.

"What do we do with her?" Lucie asked.

"We question her, of course," Gloria said. "But what if she won't talk?"

"I'm certain she will," Gloria replied, determined. "But first let's move her somewhere no one will hear her if she calls out."

They pushed and shoved the woman attached to her chair till she was firmly planted in the middle of the dressing room. It had no windows and only one door into Lucie's bedroom. As a precaution, Lucie locked her bedroom door and made sure all her windows were closed. Closing the dressing room door, Gloria removed the scarf. Angela immediately started to shout. Gloria hit her hard across the face causing the woman to stop the noise she was making.

"We can't do that," Lucie said. "I wouldn't do that sort of thing to anyone. I abhor violence."

"Don't forget, Lucie," Gloria replied, "this women was slowly poisoning you!"

Turning to face the woman, Gloria asked: "Do you know what is in this glass?"

The woman, whose nose was bleeding copiously, shook her head. "It's just medicine," was all she said.

"OK. Then I'll give you some of this 'medicine' as you call it and we'll see what effect it has on you."

As Gloria moved forward with the glass the woman started to struggle violently in a desperate attempt to escape.

"Hold her head, Lucie," Gloria ordered. Seeing Lucie hesitate, she added. "This is war, Lucie. These people are out to destroy everything we know and love. They've already killed several women and a child. And now they are trying to kill you."

Lucie moved forward but remained undecided.

"Pull her head back by her hair," Gloria told her.

Something suddenly snapped at that moment in Lucie's head, because all of a sudden all hesitation was gone. She grabbed the woman's hair and pulled it back with all her force. When she screamed, Gloria poured a part of the poison into her open mouth. The woman choked and tried to spit it out, but Gloria and Lucie held her mouth shut till they felt her swallow the liquid.

"Good. Nothing like a little cooperation," Gloria said as she pulled a small bottle out of her pocket. "This is the antidote to the poison you just swallowed. I will give you some if you answer our questions satisfactorily."

Lucie was shocked. How much did Gloria know and the others too, but had not told her.

"So you knew and you had that with you all the time?"

"Yes. We needed to make sure you were not really poisoned but we couldn't tell you about it, as we believe Horst could force the information out of you. But more about that later."

"Who are the other servants in the house working for Horst?" Lucie asked.

"I don't know. He never told me," Angela confessed.

"OK," Gloria said. "Let's give her some more of this medicine. I don't think she's had enough."

Lucie grabbed hold of her hair and Gloria moved threateningly close with the glass.

"Wait!" the woman said, terrified. "I'll tell you. Abigail and Zania."

Lucie was surprised. She would never have imagined that those two would work for Horst.

"And what are they doing now?"

"Waiting for me to bring them news. It's a precaution. In case anything happens to one of us."

"And what will they do," Lucie asked, "if you don't turn up?"

"One will come looking and the other will go and fetch the Master's men."

"One more thing," Lucie pursued. "Where is the rest of this medicine hidden?"

Angela hesitated till Gloria raised her glass threateningly. "In a secret cupboard in his bedroom here."

"You go in his bedroom?" Lucie asked, surprised.

The woman must have thought it was a good way to get back at Lucie, as she said: "I often spend the night with him."

"Better you than me," was all Lucie had to say.

"Now you call Abigail. Tell her you need help with Mistress as she has collapsed," Gloria ordered. "And remember, no trying to double cross us. Only we have the antidote. Your precious Horst has none."

Gloria released Angela from the chair but kept her feet bound and her hands tied behind her back. Taking a heavy stick that Lucie used to keep the door open, Gloria indicated that Lucie should lie on the bed and pretend to be unconscious. Taking up her position by the doorway, Gloria told the woman to call Abigail.

Abigail, who was younger, came running up the stairs and stepped cautiously into the room but she saw the stick too late as it crashed down on the back of her head. She crumbled to the floor and Gloria and Lucie rapidly tied her up and gagged her, disposing of her in the clothes cupboard.

"Now call Zania. Tell her the mistress is poorly and you need her help. Tell her to bring a bucket of water with her."

A short while later they could hear Zania puffing up the stairs with her heavy bucket. Gloria dealt with her in the same way.

"Now what do we do?" Lucie asked.

Games people play

Stepping out on the landing, Lucie heard the front door click closed. Hurrying to the window she saw two of her servants running down the drive to the waiting guards at the entrance. Lucie swore. The woman had tricked her. The two servants now trussed up in the cupboard were not in Horst's pay. She should have trusted her intuition. Jumping down the stairs two at a time, she bolted and barred the front door then bound back up the stairs.

"Get Abigail and Zania out of the cupboard and untie them. That woman lied to us. They are not the traitors," Lucie said.

"What can we do? The guards will be here in a short while," Gloria exclaimed.

"Let's get you and the other two women to the basement and away from here," Lucie replied.

"What about you?" Gloria asked, clearly worried about her friend, as they helped the two servants down the stairs.

"I will stay. If they find me gone, they'll search everywhere and are sure to find the tunnels sooner or later."

"What will you do with the other women?" Gloria asked when they reached the door to the tunnels.

"I'll give her the rest of the poison. I doubt if it will be enough to kill her, but she'll have a very uncomfortable time," Lucie said, and before she locked the door the friends wished each other good luck.

Lucie had just time to return to her room and administer the poison when the guards managed to force their way into the house. She could hear them running up the stairs following the instructions of the two women. She'd untied Angela who now lay unconscious on the floor of her bedroom. She gave the men no time to talk when they burst into her room.

"Ah, there you are. I've been waiting for you. Why have you taken so long. This woman has been taken poorly and urgently needs a doctor. You should take her there immediately."

The men hesitated a moment, but Lucie confused them, saying: "Horst will not be at all pleased if you do not do as I say."

The men briefly examined the prostrate woman and then carried her out, saying to Lucie: "You remain here. And you two, keep an eye on her."

Lucie ignored the two women who stood rigidly like guards on either side of the open door. Taking a deep breath, she began the dance Anju had taught them earlier in the day. As she went through the movements she was surprised how calm and clear headed she became. She thought over her situation. She could overcome the two women using the technique Anju had shown her. Then she really would be a renegade and would have to flee. But she already was an outcast. She was forbidden to attend Patriciat meetings of which she should be the acting head. She couldn't go out or receive visitors without the presence of two guards. So she was mostly confined to her house with only people in the pay of her future husband as warders of her prison.

The only thing that was lacking for her to cross the line as an outlaw was for her to declare her position. The game she was playing was a bit silly really because Horst clearly treated her as if she were waging war against him. She had refused to outlaw herself for fear that her actions would drive Horst and his men to retaliate, hurting or killing even more innocent victims. But her choice had made little difference. Only the day before several women from amongst the commoners had been found dead, raped and strangled, Gloria had told her.

Her thoughts hung between two options: declared rebellion or continued deceit, as she stood there a long moment, suspended on her right foot, her left leg extended out in front of her, her toes pointing at an imagined horizon. Then she let herself fall spectacularly on the thick carpet by the bedside, rolling into a ball.

For extra effect, she groaned from time to time. At first the women did not leave their post at either side of the door, but when Lucie did not get up one of them came to investigate.

As the woman leaned over her, Lucie caught her hand and pulled her down, quickly applying pressure on one of the points Anju had taught her. Once the woman sagged into unconsciousness, rather than get up, Lucie continued to groan. The second woman hesitated much longer before coming to investigate. Finding her colleague collapsed on the floor, she rushed to help her. It was then that Lucie went into action. Rolling onto her knees she grabbed the woman's arm and spun her round as she tried to reach a point on her neck. But despite her efforts, the woman managed to break free and ran for the door. Lucie might have caught her, but she tripped over the other woman's prostrate form and tumbled to the floor. As she struggled to her feet she heard the front door slam closed.

Reception committee

The late afternoon air was invigorating as An and Brent winged their way towards Granwich. They had paused an hour in a small wood not far from the town to eat and rest before the final sprint to their destination. The town could now be seen clearly below as they circled down. The town hall stood out as did the canal winding its way through the town. It was a welcoming sight, An thought. She was not used to flying such great distances, and the owl form was not her favourite. She preferred human forms.

As they coasted over the town walls a salve of tiny stones greeted them. A wild screech went up nearby as she swerved to avoid more stones. Out of the corner of her eye she saw Brent plunging to the ground. His fall was broken by a bush that probably saved his life. Continuing to dodge stones that were catapulted in her direction she saw a man heading to fetch Brent still caught in his bird form. She dived directly at the man and at the last moment she transformed into an Amazon. Bringing her full weight crashing down on the man's chest, she crushed his rib cage making a sickening sound. Rolling over she immediately regained her feet and turned to face another man intent on getting hold of Brent.

An leapt forward and struck the man with the flat of her foot in the small of his back spending him sprawling on the ground. She finished him off with a massive blow on his head. No more men dared come close, but a group of them had formed at a safe distance, watching. Placing Brent carefully in the pocket of her jacket, she glanced behind her to make sure no other men were creeping up on her. Then she turned back and launched in pursuit of the men, scattering the group as she laid several of them out before they had time to flee.

Seeing the road free, An wasn't sure which way to go. She urgently needed Ma'gina to heal Brent's wounds but she found the Apotheka guarded by a number of very scruffy men, lounging about in the entrance sharing a bottle of wine. When they saw her heading their way they put down the bottle and started pelting her with stones. One hit her on the shoulder causing a searing pain that shot up her neck and down her arm. When she flexed her fingers, she discovered that the blow had weakened her grip. She was no match for stones. She wouldn't be able to defend herself very long if she couldn't get close to her attackers.

Taking shelter in a deserted house, she made her way through the empty rooms fraying a path between the dust-covered furniture. The back door was broken and hanging off its hinges. She slipped out into the garden that was much bigger than she had expected. It had remained a long time untended; overgrown grasses and flowers gone wild reached up to her waist, scratching her legs as she waded towards the only gate in the high wall that surrounded the garden.

Noise of glass shattering came from behind her. Glancing over her shoulder she saw several men emerging from the house. They were armed with makeshift cudgels. Hastening her pace, she reached the gate only to find it locked. No amount of shaking and shoving would open it. She could transform back into an owl but she had no idea how to transport Brent and her shoulder, which sent a sharp pain down her back each time she moved, might not hold her as a wing. Picking up a thick stick that lay near the gate she tested its strength with her good hand. It would do. Then she turned to face the men.

Rescue and rescued

"What is done is done," Ma'gina said, seating herself opposite Lucie.

"By your acts," Anju commented, "you have declared open rebellion. We need to radically change our strategy and take a more offensive approach," Anju continued, glancing at Dieter who was still apparently sulking after their earlier discussion.

264

"I suggest we make the most of the absence of Horst and some of his men to take back the town. Then we could prepare for a siege." Dieter remained silent.

"What about those Patriciat men that support Horst?" Lucie asked.

Gloria, who had joined then a short while earlier laughed: "Couldn't we give them the potion we'd prepared for Horst's men?" Lucie shook her head. "That's easier said than done."

Dieter came forward from the shadows he'd been lurking in. "I think Anju is right," he said as he shot a glance in her direction. "A radical change of tack is called for. We could probably overthrow those of Horst's men left in Granwich if we take them by surprise. Then you call a meeting of the Patriciat, Lucie. I wouldn't use the poison, though. It's too risky. I suggest we use talk and a little bit of intimidation to win over the majority of the Patriciat men to our cause."

Their discussion was interrupted by the entry of one of the watchers who announced that an unknown woman was cornered by a group of wild men in a nearby garden.

"They are intent on killing her. We need to hurry if we are to save her," he said.

Anju and Dieter sprang into action and ran after the man who led them through a tunnel to the basement of an abandoned house.

"They are in the garden of this house," the watcher whispered.

"How many?"

"Four."

The men were so intent on trying to edge their way closer to the woman that they didn't notice Anju and Dieter arrive. The men had got the woman cornered and were attempting to attack from opposite sides. The woman was strong though. She dealt out several heavy blows forcing the men back, but, judging from the way her other arm hung limp by her side, she was injured. Anju had to get them away from the woman as fast as possible.

Breaking into a run, Anju shouted out. "Four men against one poor woman, how manly of you!"

Two of the men turned to face Anju. They looked confident that they could get the better of a girl as they swaggered towards her. Leaping into the air she broke the first man's neck with a backhand blow as she spun round to tackle the second. Crouching, she turned on one foot, her other outstretched leg knocking the man off his feet.

She followed through with a sharp kick in the small of his back that sent him crumbling to the ground. Out of the corner of her eye, she spied Dieter moving lithely around the other side of the garden trying to approach the two remaining men from behind.

"Who's next?" she taunted the men, doing her best to distract them. "Come and try your luck, gentlemen. Maybe you have a chance with that cudgel," she said, holding their attention.

As she talked she was pleased to see the woman was easing away in the direction of Dieter.

"The one who beats me gets to do what he wants with me."

"Watch out. Behind you," Dieter shouted.

Ducking and swaying to one side, she narrowly avoided a glancing blow from one of a group of newly arrived wild men. In passing, she landed a fist on his nose sending him groaning to the floor, blood spattered all over his face. Several of the men made a rush at her but she somersaulted over their heads, dispatching one of them as she flew passed. The second she hit behind his knees with the club his colleague had dropped. He collapsed like a puppet whose strings had been cut. More and more men were pouring into the garden and moving to surround her. She could hear the grunts from men behind her as Dieter dealt with them. There must be some thirty men surrounding them now.

Instead of venturing any closer, the men formed a tight cordon around them, keeping a safe distance. The woman was crouched near the gate, examining something she'd taken from her pocket. Anju wondered what the men were up to, when she saw several of them carrying forward heavy baskets.

"Stones!" Dieter shouted. "We've gotta get out of here."

As the first stones found their mark, the gate behind them creaked open and one of the watchers called them through. Despite their dodging and ducking neither Dieter nor Anju could avoid getting hit by further stones as they dashed out the door after the woman. The watcher locked the gate hastily behind them and indicated they should follow.

"What'll happen with those men?" Anju asked.

"Don't worry about them. We have a surprise prepared for them."

Delicate operation

The Apotheka was filthy. Lucie wrinkled up her nose: the place stank. The wild men had not only barred access to the building but they had also set out to destroy and defile as much of it as they could. Cupboards had been broken open, their contents strewn across the floor. Chairs had been smashed and one of the tables used to examine people had been cracked in two. Fortunately Ma'gina had been able to move much of her material to safety when she fled to the tunnels. Once the few remaining wild men blocking the entrance to her house had been overpowered and locked away, Ma'gina ordered the watchers and other helpers to clean the reception rooms so they could receive the wounded. In the mean time, Lucie suggested that Ma'gina set up a temporary surgery in her house. A number of people were urgently in need of care and couldn't wait till the place was clean.

Ma'gina and Lucie stood around Lucie's kitchen table examining the owl's wing trying to figure out how best to heal it. They could hear Mia next door dressing the wounds that Anju, An and Dieter as well as a number of watchers had received at the hands of the wild men. The owl lay still, the painkilling sleeping draft that Ma'gina had prepared was having its effect.

Lucie ran her fingers gently along the fine bone structure that supported the wing. "Here," she said. "It's sectioned in two places. I can't find any other serious damage."

Ma'gina stepped back and rubbed her chin. "I can use neither a cast nor a splint," she said. "It might damage its wing."

Lucie lifted the wing slightly and examined the feather structure carefully.

"Could we not sew a splint along the bone? If we were careful, it would not damage the feathers."

Ma'gina moved closer and looked where Lucie was pointing. "You are right, lass. But I can't do that. My eyes are not what they used to be and it would require a very steady hand. Maybe Mia could do it."

"I will do it," Lucie insisted. "I was always very good at sewing, I have a steady hand, good eyesight and an excellent knowledge of bird anatomy."

"Fine," was all Ma'gina replied.

Leaving the bird sleeping on the table they went in search of something light and solid to use as a splint. Lucie also brought her sewing kit. Choosing a sturdy thread, Ma'gina coated it with an unguent to facilitate healing and sterilised the needle. Lucie found a very thin metal rod that was slightly curved like the wing bone.

"Wash your hands," Ma'gina told her. "And rub this substance on your fingers," she added, handing Lucie a small flacon of a clear liquid.

Seating herself opposite the bird, Lucie realised that she couldn't do it alone.

"Can you hold the bird's wing, Ma'gina? Till I get the splint in place."

It took an hour of painstaking work till Lucie was satisfied that the splint would hold and support the broken bone. Laying the bird back on the table, she let out a long sigh. She hadn't realised how tense she'd become with the concentration of the operation.

"Well done, Lass!" Ma'gina said, running her fingers through Lucie's hair. She couldn't prevent the tears welling up in her eyes.

"Oh Sarah," was all she said.

"You should get some rest," Ma'gina suggested.

"I'm all right. I'll stay with the bird," Lucie replied. "I want to be here in case she wakes up."

Ma'gina left the room to help Mia with the many wounded people. After a while studying the owl, Lucie lifted it carefully in her two hands and carried it though into her study where she sat in her favourite chair, cradling the bird.

It had been An who had revealed who the bird really was when the watchers brought her to Ma'gina. Lucie had known a lot of birds and she had been attached to a number of them. But she had never loved a bird like she loved this one. If it had been her daughter she wouldn't have loved it less. The nightmare with Horst had eclipsed the suffering she had felt at Sarah's departure, but now she had the girl once again in her arms her feelings for the girl were as strong as ever. The thought set her wondering about having children of her own as she imagined cuddling them up close or playing games with them, she slipped gently into sleep...

Getting organised

"You must call a meeting of the Patriciat," Gloria said as she gently shook Lucie's shoulder to wake her. "It's urgent!"

Lucie was about to stretch when she remembered the bird in her hands. She looked down at it. The owl lay quiet and warm in her palm, its face snuggled up against her thumb. She gently ruffled its neck feathers causing the bird to stir.

Steady, she said to it in bird language. Your wing has been broken. You must keep still a couple of days. The bird turned its big mournful eyes in her direction and hooted softly.

"It's a splint," she continued in her own tongue, knowing the bird understood. "You mustn't transform. Not yet. The tiny splint might crush your arm."

Ma'gina entered the room at that moment.

"How's your bird?" she enquired.

"Awake," Lucie replied.

"We should give it more of my elixir against pain," Ma'gina said. "When the potion we gave it wears off, it might get agitated."

Lucie continued ruffling gently the owl's neck feathers. "It understands all that you say," she informed Ma'gina.

Mia, who had finished tending the injured, offered to look after the bird while the others went to the Patriciat meeting.

Lucie had messages sent out convening an emergency Patriciat meeting in two hours in the main hall in the Patriciat Council building. Her friends and allies had formed their own council in Lucie's reception room. Lucie sat in a large armchair with her back to the fireplace and in front of her clusters of men and women gathered, some sitting, others squatting, but most standing. Lucie glanced around the room. Such a meeting could never have taken place a few months earlier, Patriciat and commoners sat next to each other talking to people from Mia's world.

As Gloria handed out refreshments she'd prepared herself in the kitchen with the help of a couple of commoners – the servants had fled – Lucie called for quiet and questioned one of the watchers about what had happened in the garden.

"Very unfortunate," he replied. "We blocked the way through the derelict house, planning to keep the band of men prisoners in the garden till we found a better way to handle them. But taken by fury or possibly panic they tried to force their way into the house. It had been abandoned for many years and was none too safe. The men ripped down the wooden buttresses that supported the unsteady walls, planning to use them as battering rams. Predictably, their assault caused the wall on the garden side to collapse. Most of the men were buried alive and those who weren't were seriously injured by falling masonry. Very few survived."

"Were any of you hurt?" Lucy enquired.

"No. When we saw what was happening we kept our distance. We tried to warn them, but they only redoubled their efforts, making things worse."

"Did you try to get any of the wounded out?" Lucie asked.

"We were about to. We'd got shovels and picks to remove the rubble. But a second band of wild men attacked us. Anju and Dieter joined us and we managed to fight them off. A few of them got killed, but we took most of them prisoner. A few escaped."

Lucie nodded. "How many of those men are left in the town?" she asked.

"We searched everywhere but found no more. Judging from the numbers, I'd say almost all of them are either dead or prisoner."

Lucie turned to Anju who was sitting on Dieter's lap in a corner of the room. "Anju. You suggested we prepare for a siege. Granwich has no walls. How would you do it?"

An animated discussion followed about how to protect the town and where to post lookouts. Lucie asked Anju and Dieter to organise the defence of the town along with the watchers and other volunteers.

"We should send out spies," Anju suggested. "To warn us when Horst approaches. Could some of the Patriciat go in bird form?" she asked.

"That won't work with Horst. He can sense people transformed into birds," An said. "But we will at least be able to locate any loose bands of men roaming around. After the Patriciat meeting, I'll organise that," she offered.

The council went on to discuss how they would handle the Patriciat meeting and the council broke up as people were dispatched to prepare things.

The new Council meets

The Patriciat Council chamber was an impressive oak panelled room with seats ranged in five semicircular rows facing the Keeper's chair raised on a dais. Next to the Keeper's chair, but lower down, was a table where scribes sat waiting to note down the proceedings. The room was never completely full as it had been built at a time when the Patriciat had been more numerous. The Patriciat didn't seem able to have as many children as commoners and their numbers continued to dwindle. In addition, several important families had moved away from Granwich, seeking wealth and success elsewhere.

There were five entrances to the room placed equidistantly around the walls with the main one situated on the opposite side of the hall from the Keeper's chair. It was through this door that Lucie walked into the room. At her entrance, all the gathered Patriciat stood and ceased talking to welcome her. She strode along the central passage that divided up the semicircular row of seats into two equal parts. Judging from the numbers, almost all of the Patriciat had responded to her invitation. She had made it clear that both men and women should attend.

Steeping up onto the small dais on which the Keeper's chair stood, she did not sit down but turned to face the Patriciat, remaining standing.

"Be seated fellow members of the Patriciat. You may not know it," she said, raising her voice noticeably, "but Granwich is at war!"

She silenced the buzz of conversation that broke out in the room.

"We have been invaded by a hoard of men under the command of one calling himself Horst."

More noise broke out in one part of the hall. She silenced them again.

"You will all have time to talk if you wish, but now it is I that am speaking. Before we talk about when and what we do about it I need to put a number of things right."

She took a deep breath. This was going to be the hardest thing for them to accept. Change was never easy, especially after years of ingrained habits and entrenched customs.

"First of all we need to talk about the Keeper. The post was created for my ancestor in the belief that it was he that planned and built the canals that brought prosperity to Granwich. That is historically not true. It was his wife that had the idea and drew up the plans and convinced her husband to build the waterways."

Exclamations of astonishment broke out and groups began noisily debating the idea. Lucie was about to call for order when the main door opened and Sarah came walking in. Her arm was in a sling and she was clearly in pain. Despite the fact, she walked head high through the middle of the assembled Patriciat till she reached the Keeper's chair where she turned to face the audience and spoke to a silent room.

"It was a woman that conceived the idea of your canals..." and she briefly told the story of what had happened.

Lucie had never seen a group of people so subjugated by a story. It was as if everybody was living the things described. Sarah concluded: "... so you see, your future Keeper is not that usurper from another world, but the Lucie you know and trust."

Sarah turned back to face Lucie and winked at her and then went to sit in a free seat on the front row, nursing her arm.

As no one objected to Sarah's story, Lucie finally sat down in the Keeper's chair. It was a strange feeling being the first woman ever to sit there. She remembered how many times she'd seen her father and grandfather occupy that seat and how she'd been proud of them. Now it was her turn. A number of people applauded, mostly women.

"The second thing we have to clear up is who rules in Granwich."

The Patriciat looked perplexed. They presumably thought the answer was obvious.

"For many years this town has been ruled over by the Patriciat. That ends today. From now on meetings of the Granwich Council, as it will be called, will include representatives of the commoners alongside members of the Patriciat. The numbers of the Patriciat are diminishing, as are our powers, even if we don't like to admit it..."

Several men that she recognised as being supporters of Horst stood up and complained that she had no right to make such changes. They began pushing their way forward threateningly.

"Open the doors," Lucie ordered in a loud voice. And as the doors opened a good many commoners, many of them from the watchers, entered the room and placed themselves along the back wall. Ma'gina also entered accompanied by An, Anju and Dieter.

"Granwich can only remove the threat it is under if we are all united and fight together," Lucie said. "If any of you men," she said addressing the five supporters of Horst who had shoved a passage to the front of the room, "want to challenge my authority, then I will willingly dual with you. But I don't think you want that, do you?"

An ugly silence ensued. Lucie could see that Anju and Dieter had quietly shifted closer if ever there was any trouble. She unobtrusively signal to them to hold off, even though trouble there was to be because the men made a rush at Lucie. She immediately transformed into an eagle and lashed out at two of the men with her claws. Screams and a strong smell of blood filled the air. Lucie rose slightly off the floor and attacked a further one of the men while the others cowered on the floor their arms over their heads vainly trying to protect themselves.

Lucie transformed back into human form and sat sedately in her seat, wiping her bloody fingers on a cloth that she took from her pocket.

"Does anyone else wish to challenge my authority."

A breath-held silence filled the room. The five men were carried or led out of the room and the blood mopped off the floor. Once the door was closed again, Lucie continued.

"Now we can get down to the business of dealing with the attack of Horst and his men."

In an attempt to convince people that Horst was behind the recent acts of violence, a number of people bore witness to the atrocities carried out by him and his men. Sarah told the tale of Horst's attack on the Littl' people and his treatment of Sally. Ma'gina spoke of the death of Ginger. And several of the watchers described the torture and summary killings of women from Granwich. As the discussion progressed, Lucie sat back in her chair and relaxed as she observed what was happening. She was delighted to see that several of the commoners had shifted to free seats next to the Patriciat and they appeared less and less intimidated as time went by. As the discussion veered to technicalities of how to defend the city, the Patriciat were clearly surprised and even delighted at the depth of the knowledge the watchers had of the city.

Lucie's private council had decided that neither Dieter nor Anju would speak as they were unknown to most of the Patriciat and people might be suspicious. However, Lucie decided the mood was right to present them to everybody.

"I would like you to meet two very good friends who have been secretly training the Patriciat and commoner women in self defence so they can protect themselves if ever they get attacked."

Beckoning to the two of them to come forward, Lucie added: "Meet Anju and Dieter."

Several of the Patriciat men looked astonished and turned to their wives for explanations, but the women just shrugged their shoulders.

"Horst, in his evil schemes, excluded women from the Patriciat Council while he secretly tortured and killed some of them and abused others. Despite that fact and the effective curfew imposed on them, many of the women in this room secretly trained in combat and fed us information about the whereabouts of Horst's men," she added forcefully. "I'd like us to acknowledge their courage. Stand up ladies and take a bow." She stood herself and bowed. Almost all the women in the room stood up.

As they did so, first the commoners then the Patriciat men applauded them. Some of the commoners even cheered. Several of the Patriciat men said they wanted to learn too.

"Anju and Dieter will be in charge of the defence of Granwich. If you have suggestions or want to offer your services, please speak to them."

Looking round the room full of eager people, she was pleased with all that had happened. "We have come a long way tonight. I'd like to thank you all, ladies and gentlemen. We will meet again at the same time tomorrow evening," she said and, with that, she closed the meeting.

Chapter 13 - Calm before the storm

Reinforcements

A large, well-used map of Avan carefully folded to show only the central area around the University was the only object on her desk. Mae liked to keep her office clean and tidy. Clutter got in your hair she was in the habit of saying. For all their considerable knowledge, in her work as secretary to the department she noted that few of the teaching staff had realised how much untidiness got you down. Except Professor Rafter, that is. His room was always impeccable.

"These little pieces of paper that I have stuck to the map indicate the name, the place and the time of an event during our weekend of festivities," she explained to Prof. Dryman. "It's a bit thin," she mused, gently rubbing a spot behind her left ear. "If we don't want to be laughed at, we are going to need something stronger. We need to take the people of Avan by storm, if you see what I mean."

He must have understood because he smiled at the expression. "Couldn't we call back our best students from last year?" Dryman asked as he shifted round the map to look at it from a different angle. "I heard tell that some of them were particularly gifted."

Mae looked up from the map she had been studying, just to be sure that the Professor wasn't joking. He liked to have a laugh, although this was a serious business.

"What we need," Mae told him, "is Sally and her band of friends. Keira is excellent at singing and Brent is a very good storyteller."

Dryman looked a bit dubious, saying: "I have no idea where they are. Abroad somewhere was what I heard."

"I'll ask Professor Rafter. He'll know. He always follows Sally's activities quite closely."

She knocked at the door and entered without waiting to be called in. Professor Rafter was seated in an armchair in the bay window overlooking the river, reading a book. She was surprised to see it was a novel although she didn't catch the title. She liked reading novels. She was always one of the first to take out the latest releases at the town library. Slipping a bookmark between the pages, the Professor placed the book on the floor and rose to greet her.

"How are things going with the Festivities, Mae?"

She grinned. How often did he ask her a question concerning the very subject she'd come to see him about?

"You must be psychic, Professor. How did you know I came to see you about those very same Festivities?"

He ginned back, mischievously. She really liked the man. He made her feel at ease and he had such a way with her that made her sure she was appreciated.

"Do you know where Sally is? We need some help from her and her friends for our Festivities."

She was surprised to see that Rafter looked a little taken aback at her question. He turned his back on her for a moment as he gazed out of the window over the town. His room must have had one of the best views of all the rooms on the campus, she thought.

"From what I know," he finally said, turning to face her, looking very grave, "she and her friends are caught up in an adventure. I'm not at all sure they could get free."

Mae had an uncomfortable feeling that she was witnessing a side of Rafter she shouldn't be seeing. He didn't strike her as a secretive sort of person but then again he rarely confided in her. Of course, she didn't expect him to.

"Are they all right?" she instinctively asked.

"I'm sure they'll be fine in the end," he said evasively.

"Couldn't you go and fetch them?" she asked.

He shot her a shocked look. She was surprised at the extent of the vulnerability she read in that look.

"Is something wrong?" she continued, giving him time to recover.

"No. Everything is fine. I can't go though. I have too much to do here and I am too old for such travels." His answer left her perplexed. He travelled a lot for his work: attending conferences and making presentations all around the world.

"I don't understand, Professor. You often go abroad on trips."

Rafter laughed. "Sally and her friends are not abroad, Mae. They're in another world."

Now it was her turn to be confused. She'd heard of such things. After all, she had been secretary to the Theosophy department for a couple of years. But she hadn't realised it actually happened or that such worlds really existed.

"You could go, though," he continued.

"Me?" she said startled. "I'm just a secretary."

Rafter laughed again. There you go, she thought. That was why he was so likeable. She instantly knew he was not laughing at her. He was a bit like a child laughing because it had discovered something new and surprising.

"Nobody is 'just' a secretary or 'just' a professor," he insisted. "What's more, you have a lot of qualities and competences that many professors would do well to develop," he added, grinning.

Now she really was confused and could feel herself blushing. "I can't do that," she muttered.

"Sure you can," he said. "I can show you how to travel and tell you where to go."

"So you have already been there?" she asked, intrigued.

"Yes," he admitted, "A very long time ago."

"But I can't leave now. There's too much to do with the coming Festivities!" she pleaded, fully aware that she was desperately trying to find an excuse not to go. She realised that she had mixed feelings about travelling to another world. She felt suddenly drawn to the idea now she knew it was possible, it was like being in one of the stories she enjoyed reading. At the same time, the thought of visiting a world quite different from the one she was used to terrified her.

"You were the one who wanted us to fetch them," he pursued. "But I am not going to force you to go, if you do not want to. I have a meeting now. Should you decide to go, come and see me this afternoon and we'll fix things."

Aliens

Mae sat on a bench in the main street of Avan watching the people go by, an uneaten sandwich grasped between her fingers. She normally went to the Mensa at lunchtime because they had good vegetarian food and she knew many of the people who went there, but today she had a sudden urge to be surrounded by the bustle of ordinary life rather than the social whirl of the academic world.

She had never before noticed how odd people looked as they hurried about their activities, oblivious of her. She followed a couple of them with her eyes trying to imagine what they did in life. She suddenly felt like a stranger in her own town. None of these people suspected she was about to travel to another world. They would even be shocked to know that such a place existed.

Rafter had said nothing of the other world. She didn't even know the name of it. Would people there be like this, she wondered? What if they were completely different? She shuddered. And what if she got stuck there and couldn't get back? Was that what had happened to Sally and her friends? Rafter had talked of an adventure. Not all adventures were exciting or pleasurable, that much she knew from her extensive novel reading.

Her thoughts were interrupted by the arrival of Dr. Frick. This was one chance encounter she could have done without.

"Miss Owen," he greeted her, bowing formally.

You couldn't be more alien than him, she thought. Maybe he comes from another world, she grimaced.

"Dr. Frick," she replied, forcing herself to smile.

"Have you got those papers I asked for?"

"They are not ready yet."

"Surely it can't be that difficult to do!"

"You only asked for them an hour ago," she said, hardly concealing her irritation.

"You don't seem to appreciate, Miss Owen, how important this all is. The audit has been ordered by the University Council."

There was no doubt about it: he certainly came from another world, probably one where all the inhabitants were accountants and spoke to each other only in figures. The image was so hilarious she burst out laughing. Fortunately she was able to conceal it by coughing violently. He thumped her on the back with his thin, bony fist several times. As if that would help someone who was coughing. No friendly gesture that, more like a warning blow.

Moving out of reach, she replied: "I will get those papers to you as soon as they are ready, Doctor. Good day."

And she left as fast as politeness would allow. The people in the other world couldn't be worse than him, she guessed. Realising that she had in fact decided to go despite the fear and concern it provoked in her, she took a bite of the sandwich she discovered in her hand and headed back to the campus.

Confidences

She dropped in to see Lyra when she arrived back in the Department. Rafter wouldn't be free for at least an hour. Whenever Mae was in doubt about something to do with the Department she knew she could speak to Prof. Enquist. As a teacher of healing you might have expected her room to smell of medicines but it always smelt of flowers. Lyra had once told her that you couldn't begin healing people if you greeted them with an unpleasant chemical smell. The reek in some hospitals was enough to make anyone ill Lyra had confided, laughing.

This afternoon Mae detected lavender as she opened the door and sure enough several bunches of it were hanging upside down from hooks on the ceiling of her room.

"Hallo Mae. How are preparations going?" Lyra asked her, looking up from a pile of paper she was making notes on.

"That's what I wanted to see you about," Mae began. "Talking to Professor Rafter I suggested that we get Sally and her friends back to help us with the weekend festivities…" And she went on to explain what Rafter had told her. "So he wants me to go and fetch them in the other world," she finished.

"And you can't decide what to do," Lyra completed her sentence for her.

Mae nodded. "I'd really like to go but I am afraid, to be honest. Have you ever travelled like that?" she asked.

"It's not my specialty," Lyra admitted. "Some people are good at it and can travel easily. I never really got the knack," she said.

"So I may not be able to either," Mae said, relieved.

"Well, Professor Rafter is an excellent judge of people," Lyra replied, "so if he suggested you go, then I imagine he thinks you are capable of it." Lyra stood and put away the papers she was working on. "I have to give a course now," she explained.

Instead of leaving, however, she went into her preparation room next door in which she kept all her mixtures and came back with a small glass bottle in her hand.

"Take this with you, if you go. It's a remedy I made myself from special Alpine flowers for when things get too much. A few drops should do the trick." She handed Mae the bottle and showed her out.

An urgent conversation

"Professor!" Mae called out, seeing Rafter making his way hastily down the corridor towards the exit. "Can I have a word with you?"

He stopped a moment, his hand poised on the door handle. "Is it urgent?" he enquired, turning to leave. "I have to be at a meeting in ten minutes on the other side of town." Rafter opened the door and took a step outside.

"When will you be back?" she asked hurrying after him.

"Tomorrow," he said over his shoulder as he headed for the taxi waiting for him across the little bridge that linked the riverbank to the island on which the Department was built.

She couldn't face the prospect of mulling over the idea of travelling to the other world all night. She followed the Professor across the bridge, shaking her head. It couldn't wait, but she didn't want to make Rafter late. Rafter opened the taxi door and turning to her indicated that she should get in.

Rafter told the taxi driver where to take them but she didn't catch the destination because he spoke so quietly. Then turning to her, he asked: "So what is it that is so urgent?"

As she sat back in the seat smartly upholstered in leather she suddenly realised that she'd rushed out without closing her office or bringing her things with her. A cough from the driver reminded her that they were not alone.

"Can I talk openly here in this taxi?" she whispered.

"No problem," he replied. "The driver won't be able to hear us."

His assurance left her perplexed. She couldn't see how the man could not hear them despite the pane of glass that separated them from him but she supposed Rafter had some way of making it happen.

"It's about my trip to see Sally."

"Ah! So you've decided to go?" She took a deep breath.

"Yes."

"You won't regret it," he said enigmatically and looked out of the cab window at the passing streets of Avan.

She waited a while in silence, expecting him to continue, but he said no more. How frustrating. "Professor?" she asked.

"Yes?" he replied turning back to look at her. "What am I to do?"

She had the distinct impression that he was somehow absent, caught up in his own thoughts. It was very uncharacteristic of him.

"How am I to get to this place where Sally is? I don't even know what it is called."

"The Reaches," he told her and lapsed back into silence.

She was beginning to get worried at his behaviour. She had never seen him like that before.

"So how do I travel to the Reaches?" she asked, insisting.

He fumbled in his jacket pocket and pulled out a small ring. Made of gold, it was far too small to be his.

"You use this," he explained. "If you meditate, you do know how to meditate don't you?"

"Yes. Lyra, I mean Prof Enquist showed me how and I've been practicing every morning before I come to work"

"Good. Well, you take this ring in your right hand, close your eyes and meditate thinking of Sally and you will be taken to her. This ring comes from the Reaches. Don't loose it though. I want it back. It's dear to me."

And he placed the ring in her hand, saying: "Wait till you are in a quiet place before you set off."

Cause for concern

The driver knocked on the window that separated them from him indicating that they had arrived. Mae looked outside for the first time. The Royal Avan Hospital. Alarmed, she glanced back at Rafter. Was he ill? That would explain his strange behaviour.

"Are you unwell, Professor?" she asked.

"No. No. Just a regular check up."

He opened the door asking the driver to wait for him. "I'll be about half an hour," he explained to the driver.

"Then I will wait for you Professor," Mae said, "and get a ride back with you to the University."

"As you wish," Rafter said as he hurried off in the direction of the main entrance.

Mae was intrigued and not a little worried. It would be a very bad moment for Rafter to have health problems, what with the audit and the reforms in the University. There were some very good teachers in the Department, but without him it really wouldn't be the same thing. Telling the driver she was going to stretch her legs, she opened the door and got out of the taxi. Mae knew Avan hospital quite well, she'd worked there as a secretary before going to work for the Theosophy Department. She decided to get a drink in the cafeteria and see if any of her former colleagues were there.

Sure enough, she came across a group of interns having a break. They'd become her friends during her time working in the hospital. They called her over.

"Come to accompany your employer on his check-up?" one of the young men asked playfully.

"Not exactly," she replied evasively. "How are things here?" she asked, seeking to change the subject.

They told her the latest gossip full of many names new to her. Things changed quite rapidly amongst the hospital staff. When they stood to go back to the wards, she decided to return to the taxi and wait there. One of the interns took her to one side and, waiting for the others to move off, she said quietly: "Look after your Professor. He's not very well. He'll need all the help and support he can get."

She was about to ask for more information but the intern moved away, clearly not wanting to say any more. Rafter arrived at that moment, walking thoughtfully down the corridor from the radiology unit.

"Ah there you are, Professor," Mae said, hoping she wouldn't appear over jovial. "I was wondering if you'd got lost in all these corridors."

Rafter looked at her for a moment as if he didn't recognise her, then he said: "Of course, you must know this place well, Mae. You used to work here, didn't you?"

"Yes," she replied, guiding him down a short cut to the main entrance. "The place is so big, you need to know your way around if you don't want to waste a lot of time," she told him.

During most of the journey back to the University the Professor remained silent. Mae looked out of the window, fascinated at the sight of people from Avan going about their activities as the afternoon drew to a close.

"Do you still have the ring, OK?" he suddenly asked.

"Yes. I've put it on a little chain around my neck so it doesn't get lost," she told him. "I'll travel to the Reaches this evening."

The car drove into the University grounds and stopped in front of the little bridge to the Department.

"Mae," Rafter said. "I'd like you not to mention to anyone else that I was at the hospital. You know how people worry. There are enough other problems at the moment without having them imagining all sorts of things about my health. It was just a routine visit."

"Sure, Professor," she replied. "I will say nothing about it."

Once inside the Department she was about to go to her office when Rafter stopped her.

"Have a good trip. You should find Sally in a large house in a clearing in a forest. Just tell people you are looking for Sally. They will help you."

"Thanks Professor. See you tomorrow."

Would she see him tomorrow? Nothing was so sure, she thought. Tidying away the few papers on her desk, she took her bag from where she'd left it in the cupboard and was about to go when she remembered Lyra's potion. It was still in her pocket. She wondered if it might be a good idea to take a few drops before she travelled, just in case.

En route

She hadn't felt very hungry when she arrived home, but she'd forced herself to eat a light snack. Who knew when she might next get something to eat? She'd packed a small backpack with a few clothes and some useful objects like an umbrella, a Swiss army knife, a box of matches and a torch. Pulling the straps of her pack over her shoulders she slipped the ring from around her neck where it hung on the thin gold chain she was in the habit of wearing. Placing it in her right hand as Rafter had instructed she tried to calm her mind. It wasn't easy. She was so nervous and excited. After some ten minutes of vain attempts to calm her thoughts she was getting nowhere. She took out Lyra's potion and shook out three drops onto her tongue. The substance had a familiar taste but she could quite place it. She put the little bottle back in her pocket, closed her hand around the ring and shut her eyes, thinking of Sally.

Odd. She must have left a window open, because she could feel a breeze blowing against her face. How irritating. Just when she'd finally managed to relax. She opened her eyes, meaning to go and close the window only to discover she was sitting cross-legged next to a large mound that she could barely make out in the dark. Astonishing. She'd travelled between the worlds without even noticing it. She'd expected some sort of "whoosh" or flash. But she'd just unobtrusively slipped into what she supposed must be the Reaches. Struggling to her feet, she looked around for the house that Rafter had talked about. There were no lights and no sign of a house.

She took off her rucksack and searched for her torch. She was about to switch it on when a branch cracked noisily not so far away. Rafter had told her to ask whomever she met for Sally. But, given the circumstances, she opted for caution and preferred to hide. Drawing closer to the mound she eased her way around it as silently as she could. Luckily the grass under her feet muffled her steps. Several other twigs cracked here and there. Whoever it was, was not alone.

"Yer find anythin'?" a course voice whispered.

"Nope. The boss isn't gonna be pleased, 'specially as we've gotta leave fer the north tomorrow mornin'," and he grunted in pain.

Mae imagined he stubbed his toe on a rock or on a tree stump. She'd managed to make her way along one side of the mound and was now moving away from the voices when her path was blocked by a large rock. Feeling her way in the dark between the obstacle and the mound, she found what must have been an entrance. She wouldn't normally have entered a place she didn't know in the middle of the night, especially not alone, but the voices were getting closer again. They might discover her at any moment.

Stretching out her arms in front of her and gritting her teeth she tentatively made her way into whatever it was under the mound. She hoped it was not one of those burial places, she thought. The idea of finding her way amongst bones in pitch dark made her hair stand on end. Not wishing to venture any further into the place and unsure it would be safe to turn on her torch, she crouched down just beyond the entrance for what seemed like ages. Was it her imagination or was there a faint moaning sound coming from somewhere nearby? It's only the wind, she tried to reassure herself. She couldn't help it, despite Lyra's potion, she was terrified. Unable to stand it any longer, she flipped the switch on the torch and lit up the space around her.

An astonishing sight awaited her. She was in a giant cave that was completely empty except for a stone table or possibly an altar that stood in its middle. The altar was encrusted with many brilliant stones that glittered in her torchlight. The beauty of it moved her profoundly. Pulling herself to her feet with the help of a nearby stone, she set off to examine the cave. Strange hieroglyphs ran around the walls. Had Rafter been there, he might have been able to read them, she thought. There seemed however to be no recent signs of occupation. Making the rounds of the walls, looking for a second way out, she came across a concealed entrance diametrically opposite the one she'd used to enter.

She switched off her torch and ventured outside. It was pitch dark. She wondered if she might not be in another, bigger cavern, but a telltale breeze on her face indicated she was outside again. There was no point in trying to find her way in the dark. She'd only get lost and hurt herself. Back inside the mound she sat down and took out the packet of dried nuts and raisins she bought at the health food shop on her way home from the university and munched quietly in the dark. Washing her frugal meal down with some fresh water from her water bottle, she tried to find a comfortable place to sleep.

Ow! A sharp stone was sticking into the small of her back. She must have rolled on top of it during the night. It was a wonder she'd been able to sleep at all. Rocks and stones really did not make the best of beds. Struggling to her feet, she stretched as best she could. Light was filtering into the cavern through many tiny holes high up in the walls casting a soft warm light over everything. In thinking of her journey to the Reaches, Mae had imagined she'd arrive immediately at her destination, speak briefly to Sally then head back home. So she'd brought very little supplies of food and water. Munching the remaining nuts from her bag she thought over her situation. She could simply return to Avan and tell Rafter she hadn't found Sally but that wouldn't solve their problems with the festivities. And, to be honest, she hadn't really tried looking for Sally yet. She'd explore around the mound in the hope of finding the house Rafter had talked about.

As she eased cautiously out of the entrance to the mound and peered around the rock that concealed it, she was startled to find herself standing only feet away from a makeshift camp. Several men were huddled under blankets, asleep at the edge of the remains of a fire amid the grass glistening with dew. Holding her breath, Mae silently retreated into the cavern and crossed it till she reached the new entrance she'd found during the night. Once outside she was relieved to find no men waiting for her. Instead there was a narrow path close by that wound its way into the forest, the trees of which grew particularly close together. As she couldn't be sure that there weren't men posted further away watching the entrance, she got down on her hands and knees and crawled to the path making as little noise as possible.

Judging she had reached a safe distance from the men, Mae got to her feet and wove her way as fast as she could between the trees along the path. The undergrowth invaded the path in several places almost blocking the way, giving the impression that it was not often used, although the occasional broken branch seemed to indicate that someone or something had gone that way recently. Stopping from time to time to listen if anyone was following her, after an hour she reached a clearing where she was relieved to find a one-storey thatched cottage with a large veranda on all sides.

She took one step in the direction of the house and immediately found herself surrounded by a gang of dwarfs, their arrows pointed at her. Unspeaking they motioned her to walk ahead of them in the direction of the house, brandishing their arrows at her. Unlike the group of men she'd seen earlier, the dwarves seemed clean and orderly.

"I'm looking for Sally," she said halting a moment.

"We don't know no Sally," one of them replied pushing her forward.

Mae's heart sank. This trip had seemed so straight forward when Rafter had proposed she go.

"Surely someone must know Sally," she said out loud, desperate.

"I know someone called Sally," a female voice said behind her. Spinning round she found Sally standing in the porch of the cottage.

"Sally," she called out.

"Greetings, Mae," Sally said. "Put your arms away," Sally told the dwarves. "She's a good friend of mine."

Mae had expected a warmer welcome. Sally seemed so distant. This was an odd place that seemed to make even familiar people unfamiliar. Making up her mind not to be intimidated by these strange circumstances, Mae walked up to Sally and hugged her.

"Am I glad to see you," she said.

Disengaging herself from the hug, Sally turned and went inside saying: "Come in."

Questions

"Why did those dwarves say they didn't know you Sally?" Mae asked as she settled at the kitchen table.

"Because for them my name if Cian'la. Or Nala for short." And she fetched them drinks and a bowl of dried fruit. "And they're not dwarves, but the Littl' People." Seating herself opposite Mae, Sally asked: "So what brings you to the Reaches, Mae?"

Mae was troubled by the tension in the air. Something was seriously wrong and she needed to know what it was. Not answering Sally's question she asked a question herself.

"You seem so tense and wary, Sally. It is so unlike you. Is something the matter?"

A weary look crossed Sally's face making Mae even more concerned. "We are on the verge of war here. And all my friends are in danger."

So that was it. There was little chance she could convince Sally and her group to return for a weekend in these conditions.

"Oh dear! Can I help in any way?"

Sally smiled, for the first time. "You are always so willing to help."

Mae blushed at what she took as a compliment.

"Thanks," Sally pursued. "I think you'd be better off in the safety of Avan." Sipping her drink, Sally continued: "How did you manage to get here? Travelling between the worlds is not that easy."

"That's what Lyra Enquist told me. In fact, Professor Rafter gave me an object and told me to meditate and think of you. So I did. And instead of finding the house the Professor had told me to expect I found some sort of burial mound with wild men camped out nearby."

"Sorry about that. I had to transform the house like that to protect it from those men."

Mae couldn't help her mouth falling open in surprise. This really was like one of those magical worlds in the stories she liked to read, except that she wasn't safely in her armchair reading it.

"When did you arrive?" Sally asked.

"Yesterday evening."

"You've been here so long already. You must be starving," Sally said getting up. "I'll make you some breakfast."

Mae would normally have offered to help but she suddenly felt tired.

"If you don't mind," she said. "I will not help you with the preparations. I feel exhausted."

Sally cast a worried look in her direction then said: "Don't worry. I can manage. How long have you felt so worn out?"

"I just noticed now. It must be because I slept on the floor of that burial mound and I didn't sleep so well."

Sally placed bread and jam and fresh fruit on the table.

"It's more likely you're suffering from the sickness most people get when they travel to another world. It's a shame Jenny is not here. She could cure you."

"Where's Jenny?" Mae asked. She had met Sally's Swiss friends several times on the campus.

"She's in a town called Granwich with Tom. Brent and Keira are also there. That town is at the heart of this trouble." Setting the teapot and mugs down on table she seated herself opposite Mae again.

"You still haven't told my why you came?" Mae wondered where to begin.

"That all seems so futile compared to what is happening here," Mae replied.

"Tell me all the same," Sally said.

"There are some difficulties in the university..." And she went on to explain about the audit and the idea of the weekend of festivities. "So I suggested to Rafter that we should ask you and your friends to come and help us."

Mae really hadn't imagined things this way. When Prof. Dryman had said Sally's group were having an adventure, it never crossed her mind they might be in such danger.

"As you can imagine," Sally began, "that is going to be somewhat difficult in the current circumstances. We just can't up and leave, abandoning all our friends and relatives here, however much we'd like to help."

Mae toyed with the idea of mentioning that Rafter was seriously ill. It might convince Sally to return. That would be selfish of her and she'd promised Rafter not to tell anyone about his visit to the hospital. Oh, to hell with it, she thought. I can't keep this to myself. Sally seemed to be one of the staff who was closest to the Professor; she had to tell her.

"There is another reason."

Sally looked up from her piece of bread, troubled. Mae wondered if she'd guessed.

"Yesterday I discovered that Professor Rafter was seriously ill."

Sally pushed away her food and listened intently.

Mae described the visit to the hospital and the conversation with her intern friend. "I don't know what he's got, but he really wasn't himself yesterday."

Musing out loud, Sally said: "Maybe Jenny or Mia could help him."

"Who's Mia?" Mae asked. "Sorry it's Keira's name here."

The two sat silent for a while, neither eating any more.

"When are these festivities?" Sally asked. "At the weekend in just over a week."

"I can't promise anything. It all depends how things turn out here. The impending hostilities could go on for ages. If I can, I'll speak to the others."

The princess

A racket outside interrupted their conversation. Sally rose and Mae followed her. She must have stood up too quickly because she suddenly felt dizzy. Brushing the feeling aside she went outside to join Sally and the Littl' People. A group of other dwarfs had arrived accompanied by a man and a woman. She recognised Martin, Jenny's brother and the woman must be Fran. Greeting one of the dwarves, Sally beckoned to Mae to join them.

"Meet D'rick. The leader of the Littl' People. D'rick this is Mae, a friend from the other world."

The dwarf bowed and Mae, guessing that was the right thing to do, did likewise.

"You've already met Fran and Martin I believe," Sally said.

Mae nodded and shook hands with them.

"What brings you here?" Sally asked the three.

"Them wild men wot were camped 'round our vall'y 'ave upped and skedaddled north," D'rick told her.

"They're probably heading for Granwich, so we came to warn you," Martin added.

"D'rick thinks we should go north too, to help the people of Granwich in the war that's coming," Fran said. "We figured there was no way the women of Granwich could get through to us in these conditions. They'd immediately get caught."

"How long ago did they leave?" Sally asked.

"Yest'day," D'rick replied.

"We came immediately," Fran added. "We saw no signs of the wild men on our way here. We were accompanied by a large group of archers," Martin told them.

"I sent 'em 'head of us. They'll be waitin' fer us beyond the for'st." D'rick told them.

Turning to Mae, D'rick studied her closely for a moment in silence, much to her embarrassment.

"May I ask wot that is you've got around your neck?" he asked.

Mae had forgotten the ring on her chain.

"It's a ring."

"May I 'ave a look?"

Mae pulled the chain from around her neck and handed it to D'rick saying: "Careful with it. It's my ticket home."

"What do you mean?" Sally asked, clearly intrigued.

"I used it to travel here," Mae explained.

D'rick was examining the ring closely. "I done this ring," he said surprising them all.

"Are you sure?" Mae asked, finding that hard to believe.

"Yeah! I gave it t' a woman 'ere a very long time ago."

"Where did you get it from?" Sally asked.

"Rafter," Mae replied. "He said I must be very careful with it as he wanted to get it back."

"And you travelled with this?" Mae nodded.

"Seems like you've found another princess, D'rick," Sally said.

This was all too much for Mae. What could Sally mean by Princess? Her head ached at the thought of it. The world began to spin around her and the next thing she knew, she was lying on the floor in Sally's arms.

"She's got the sickness that troubles people who come from our world," Mae heard Sally say. "We must get her home as fast as possible."

Opening her eyes she looked into Sally's eyes and saw all the concern written there. To think she'd believed that Sally no longer cared.

"In my pocket," she whispered. "A bottle. Give me a few drops."

Fran came forward and rummaged in Mae's pocket. Finding Lyra's bottle she shook a couple of drops onto Mae's tongue. She immediately felt better.

"Well it's brought some of the colour back in your face," Martin said. Fran offered her a drink of water.

Homeward bound

Some time later, installed in an armchair, surrounded by Sally, Martin, Fran and D'rick, Mae listened to Martin and Fran planning to take her home to Avan.

"We must collect some herbs before we leave," Fran was saying.

"Are you healers?" Mae asked, finally joining the conversation.

They both laughed. "No. We're cooks! Well, not real cooks. We just learnt the art of cooking from the Littl' People."

"Don't listen to 'em," D'rick said. "They're the best!"

An idea sprang into Mae's mind. "Maybe you could prepare a banquet for the festivities we are planning in Avan for next week."

Fran looked at Martin and he looked back. Mae couldn't miss the love and tenderness between the two. It was enough to make any single person jealous.

"I reckon we could do that," Fran spoke for them both.

"And wot d' yer do?" D'rick asked Mae.

"I'm a secretary."

He looked at her clearly not understanding what she said.

"There are no secretaries here," Sally explained.

Mae wondered how she could explain what she did.

"It's someone," she finally said, "whose job is to see that things work out all right, especially in the way things are organised."

"'Ow d' yer do that?" D'rick asked.

"Mostly by writing letters and talking to people."

"Sounds like magic to me!" D'rick retorted.

Everybody laughed. Helping Mae to her feet, they all made their farewells.

"We'll try to come," Sally said. "But I can't promise you anything. Better it be a surprise if we can."

D'rick handed the ring and necklace back to Mae saying: "If ever yer come again, I promise I will make such a ring for yerself," and he bowed.

Mae thanked him. "Do we need to go back to where I arrived?" Mae asked Sally.

"No. Just think of your flat in Avan and you'll get there without any problem. If you hold hands with Fran and Martin they'll be transported with you. Good luck with your preparations." And Sally hugged Mae.

"Take care of yourself," Mae whispered in her ear.

"I will," Sally whispered back.

The others went outside and left the three on their own. Mae had insisted. She needed quiet to concentrate. She looked down at the ring in her hand. If she was holding hands she couldn't keep it in her hand so she hung it around her neck. Strange. She could feel it vibrating. She hadn't noticed that before. She wondered if the Reaches had other effects on her. Taking Fran and Martin's hand, she closed her eyes, telling them to do the same. And she thought of her flat. Just like the first time the change was instantaneous and quite unspectacular. On opening their eyes, all three found themselves standing in Mae's kitchen.

Lunch

"Take a seat," Mae said. "I'll make you something to eat."

"No you won't," Fran insisted. "You sit down and have a rest. You've been on a long journey. Martin and I can cook if we can find the food."

"The larder's over there. You'll find some things in the fridge too. Nothing fancy I'm afraid," Mae said, making her excuses.

"Don't you worry," Martin said.

As they prepared the meal, they questioned Mae about the festivities and what was planned. They made suggestions about what Sally's other friends might do if they were to come. Mae wasn't one to say prayers, but she sent up a silent prayer that Sally and her friends would be able to join them.

The meal was delicious. She would never have been able to make such good food with the ingredients they had available.

"It's a bit like magic, your cooking," she told them. "You manage to make something quite simple into a wonderful dish."

"It's a bit like Sarah's story telling," Martin said by way of explanation. "She carries you away with the words she uses. Well we try to carry people away with the food we make."

Fran laughed. "What a good way of putting it," she said giving him a kiss.

"Who's Sarah?" Mae asked.

Fran and Martin looked at each other mysteriously.

"This is going to take some explaining," Fran said. "Let's get comfortable in your living room. I'll make us a herb'l tea."

292

Martin laughed. "You're beginning to talk like the Littl' People," he said.

The story telling took a long while and despite her fascination for all she heard, she finally had to excuse herself and stagger off to bed. She let them make their own bed on the sofa that opened up forming a double bed. The following morning they all got up rather late. Mae would not be on time for work but then did that really matter she asked herself after all that had happened in the last twenty-four hours. They prepared breakfast together and discussed what to do next. It was decided that Mae would take them to the Department where they could talk of the idea of the banquet with Professor Rafter.

On the campus

Rafter was nowhere to be found on the campus, however. He hadn't been seen all morning, Prof. Dryman told her. If she hadn't known about his ill health she wouldn't have been bothered. Rafter often took off unexpectedly. Some said he went for long walks in countryside, meditating. Others speculated that he liked to read and write in the quiet and solitude of his country house. The comics would have him having a secret affair. The joke never ceased to make people laugh. Mae wondered why. Maybe because it seemed preposterous. In their search for the Professor they met Lyra who had just finished a seminar.

"Can we have a word with you Lyra?" Mae asked.

"Sure," was her answer, "I've got an hour free before my next lecture."

Once they were settled in Lyra's office, Mae presented Martin and Fran.

"These are friends of Sally's," she explained. "They've come back with me from the Reaches."

"So you made it," Lyra said, clearly delighted. "I knew you would."

Mae had the distinct impression that Lyra was proud of her. To be honest, she was proud of herself. What an adventure! Lyra shook hands with Fran and Martin.

"Was my potion any use?" Lyra turned to ask Mae.

"You'd be surprised," Mae said. "It saved my life several times!"

"Surely you're exaggerating," Professor Enquist countered.

Martin shook his head. "She's not. People from our world get seriously sick when they go to the Reaches..." and he briefly explained why. "My sister Jenny can put it right, but she was not available to help."

"Mae collapsed," Fran went on. "Your potion revived her and made it possible for her to stay in the Reaches a little longer."

Lyra looked a little confused. "To think that I gave you that mixture on a whim. What a coincidence!"

Nobody made a comment, but Mae was sure they were all thinking like her: there is no such thing as coincidences.

"We were looking for Prof. Rafter. You haven't seen him, have you?" Mae asked.

"No. I had an appointment with him but he phoned to say he had something urgent to do and couldn't come."

Mae wished she didn't know he was ill. Her concern transformed every piece of news about him, however insignificant, into a sinister omen.

"Fran and Martin have suggested they organise and cook a banquet for our festivities," Mae said. "They're wonderful cooks. I can tell you, I've eaten some of their food."

Fran explained that they were not really cooks but had learn the art of cooking from the Littl' People in the Reaches.

"This is excellent news," Lyra said. "I really like the idea. Although I'm not so sure about the banquet, a buffet might be a better idea. If we organised a banquet people would have to sign up and we'd have to organise a suitable place for it. With a buffet, we would be more flexible."

"Mmm," Fran said smiling. "We could do a buffet, Martin. We'd be able to give people a much wider selection. And we have a chance to go looking for more local wild plants to use."

Mae could see that Lyra was excited at the idea.

"Would you mind if I come and help you. And I'd like to bring some of my students along. I suspect they'd learn a lot."

"No problem," Martin said.

"We always went collecting with a whole group of Littl' People, then we cooked together. Maybe your students would like to help us cook."

"I'm sure they'd be delighted," Lyra said.

"When would we have the buffet?" Fran asked.

"I suggest we end up with the meal on Sunday at one o'clock in the afternoon to close the festivities," Mae said, knowing that she knew the tentative programme of the weekend better than anybody. "During the morning, you could possibly give a demonstration with the help of Lyra's students for people interested in cooking."

"Could your students be free early Monday morning?" Martin asked. "We need to begin looking for material."

"I'll tell them now. I have a course with them in a few minutes. No, even better, why don't you come with me and explain your plans to them."

Fran and Martin looked delighted at the idea.

"Just one suggestion," Lyra added as they rose to leave. "You'd better not tell them you've been to the Reaches. It might cause complications later. We are in a rather tense situation with the University at the moment and we don't want to invite trouble. People probably wouldn't understand that side of our work."

The two agreed and went off to meet Lyra's students, leaving Mae alone to finally go to her office.

Altercation

When she arrived she found Dr. Frick waiting outside for her. He was furious.

"I've been here for nearly an hour. You are not very punctual. And you certainly aren't very efficient. I still haven't received those papers I asked you for several days ago. I must talk to Professor Rafter about him getting a better secretary. This won't do."

Bother. Mae had completely forgotten the nasty little man and his "papers". She felt a surge of guilt. She prided herself on her efficiency. Her trip to the Reaches had thrown everything out of its usual order. All the same, she wasn't going to let herself be treated so badly by this skinny monster.

"May I remind you, Dr. Frick," she said, stressing his name that Fran had told her meant money in German, "that politeness is one of the key foundations of collaboration. You seem to have forgotten that. Now, please let me get on with my work and you will have your papers later today."

The man went bright red in the face. She wondered if he was going to explode or have a heart attack. Instead, saying: "You'll regret this", he turned his back on her and slammed the door causing the windows to shake dangerously.

Mae had been preparing the papers that Frick had ordered for about half an hour when the phone rang.

"Department of Theosophy, Mae Owen speaking," she replied. "Good morning Miss Owen. John Martin here, secretary to the university Administrator."

The university Administrator was one of the few people who had a male secretary. Mae had only met him briefly once.

"He has asked me to convene you for an audience in his office in half an hour."

"John, may I know the reason for this convocation?" Mae asked, sensing that it was no ordinary meeting.

"I'm afraid I don't know Miss Owen. Good day." And the man hung up.

Convened

The Administrator's office was situated on the second floor of the administration building at the heart of the campus. Mae knocked on the secretary's door. One didn't knock on the Administrator's door.

"Good Morning, Miss Owen," the man said. "Take a seat outside. I'll call you when the Administrator is ready to see you."

The bench was hard and uncomfortable and the corridor surprisingly busy. A number of people stared at her as they went by. She tried to ignore them. On her walk all the way across the campus Mae had wondered why the Administrator wanted to see her. Could it have been because of Rafter's illness? Whatever the reason, she felt increasingly apprehensive. Plunging her hands in her pockets to stop them fidgeting she discovered the remains of Lyra's potion. Now would be a good time to take some she thought. The moment the tiny drops splashed on her tongue she felt better.

John half opened the door and said: "He's ready to see you now."

Entering the Administrator's room she was surprised to find Frick there. Suddenly everything fell into place. How could she not have thought of that possibility? She was pleased she had taken some of Lyra's potion. If it had managed to save her life in the Reaches, maybe it would be able to save her now too.

"Take a seat, Miss Owen," the Administrator said. "Dr. Frick has filed a formal complaint about your behaviour and your failure to do your work."

Mae took a deep breath trying to calm the fury welling up in her. "Not only were you extremely impolite to him but you have repeatedly failed to provide him with essential documents he asked for."

Mae wondered if these men would ever give her a chance to tell her side of the story and even if they did, would they believe her.

"Normally I would fire you immediately," the Administrator continued, "but you have a record for good work up to now, so I have decided to organise a disciplinary hearing. In the meantime you are suspended."

Mae was surprised at the calm she felt at this decision. It was presumably the effect of Lyra's potion.

"Do you have anything to say for yourself?" he enquired.

"I am glad you have given me an opportunity to defend myself. I look forward to throwing new light on this affair," she said. "As for the suspension, I believe you will find that I must be presumed innocent until proven otherwise. I will talk to Professor Rafter and if he wishes I will continue to do my work as usual."

She could have sworn that a brief smile flickered across the Administrator's lips only to be rapidly replaced by a stern look.

"Fine. I will notify you of the date of the hearing," he said.

"Could you provide me with a copy of Dr. Frick's accusation, please," she asked.

"Ask my secretary to send it to you. Good day Miss Owen."

"Good day, Sir. Good day, Dr. Frick."

The latter didn't bother to reply.

"The injustice of it riles me," Mae said to Lyra as they sat drinking herbal tea in the latter's office. "But what upsets me most is that it is an additional concern for Professor Rafter. He's got enough on his mind at the moment."

"Yes, this audit is extremely troublesome," Lyra said.

Mae was glad Lyra had understood her allusion to Rafter's troubles as she did.

"I wonder if Dr. Frick has been looking for an excuse to undermine the Professor?" Mae mused.

"Sounds unlikely to me," Lyra responded.

"It wouldn't surprise me. He's a really nasty piece of work," Mae retorted. "Sounds like I'm going to have to find a new job," she added.

She would really regret having to leave. It was not just because she liked the people so much, but more that she had the feeling that she was in the right place at the right time.

"I've really enjoyed my time here," she said.

"Don't give up, Mae. We'll find a way." Mae stood up and handed Lyra her cup.

"I must get back to my work. Who knows, maybe Dr. Frick has spies to see if I am working or not."

An urgent mission

She had not been back in her office more than a few minutes when the phone rang. What trouble could it be this time?

"Mae Owen," she announced, picking up the receiver.

"Rafter here," came the answer.

"Professor," Mae said, relieved to hear his voice. "Where are you?"

Having asked, she knew immediately it wasn't the right question, but she'd have to let it go.

"I'm at my country house. I need your help. I urgently need some medicine from the hospital but I can't fetch it myself. It's something special that you can't get from a chemist's. Could you go for me? Take a taxi if you need to. I'll pay for it when you get here."

"Of course I'll go, Professor. I'll leave immediately. Will they know what to give me?"

"I'll ring them. Please hurry, it's urgent."

She dialled the taxi company and ordered a taxi, sent off Frick's papers by internal mail, packed a few papers in her bag that she would work on later that evening and hurried towards the exit. Rafter's illness sounded really serious. It was strange, she thought, that a man so well liked as Rafter should suddenly find himself alone in adversity because he didn't want anyone to know he had a serious problem.

She was brutally awoken from her thoughts as she bumped into someone just outside the main door.

"Going home already," a familiar voice said. Frick.

What rotten luck. She glanced up at him only to find a cruel smile on his bony face. She sidestepped, aiming to continue on her way, but he stepped in front of her and firmly took hold of her arm.

"You are hurting me, Dr. Frick. Please let go of my arm," she pleaded.

He ignored her request.

"Where are my papers?"

"Sent by internal post this afternoon," Mae replied.

Instead of letting go, he squeezed her arm even further till the pain was unbearable.

Gritting her teeth she said: "If you continue to hurt me, I warn you, I will have to defend myself."

Instead of ceasing, he made a move to grab her around the neck with his other hand. Ducking under the arm that held her tight, she twisted it behind his back, releasing his hold on her. Then she kicked his feet from under him and stuck her heel in the small of his back causing him to sprawl facedown on the ground, groaning. Rubbing her arm, she walked away across the bridge to the waiting taxi.

"You all right, Miss?" the driver asked.

"I'll have a bruise on my arm probably, but otherwise I'm fine," she replied.

"Nasty fellow that. And to think that such things could happen even on the University campus. You should report him to the police," the taxi driver said.

"I'm sure he'd find a way to prove that I attacked him," Mae replied.

She told the driver to take her to the hospital and wait for her there. She had to see the head of the oncology unit. Cancer. How terrible. She knew that lots of people survived cancer, but the thought of the Professor being so ill worried her immensely.

On her way out from the specialist's office she met one of her nurse friends in the corridor.

"Have you got anything for a bruise, Tina?" she asked.

"Let me look," Tina asked.

Ugly red weals had formed where Frick's fingers had gripped her arm.

"This is really terrible, Mae," Tina said. "I'll give you a cream that will help, but you should go to the police."

Mae thanked her and hurried back to the taxi. Once inside, they headed for Rafter's country house. She had already been there several times for informal gatherings of the Department. Those had been joyful occasions, not like now. Rafter himself answered the door. He was dressed in a dressing gown. He handed her some money for the taxi.

"Have you brought the medicine?" he asked, his voice a bit breathless.

By way of answer she handed him the small packet the specialist had given her. "Shall I fetch you some water to take it with?" she asked.

When he nodded she headed for the kitchen and brought back a glass of tap water. He swallowed the pills and then collapsed in a nearby armchair.

"Wouldn't you be better off in bed, Professor?" she asked.

"To be honest, I don't think I can make it up the stairs," was his reply. "All of a sudden it's got much worse."

He sounded quite helpless.

"You stay there," she said, "and I will see if I can't make you a bed down here."

There was a large sofa in the living room that would do as a bed. She checked the first floor and found fresh sheets and an eiderdown in the linen cupboard. She made up the improvised bed and helped Rafter shuffle to the sofa. Once he was properly installed she asked him if he was hungry.

"I have eaten nothing for over a day," he admitted, "but I don't think I could eat anything all the same."

He lay back on the sofa but seemed to have some difficulty getting comfortable. After a while he settled, presumably the medicine was having its effect. Once she was sure he was asleep she wandered from room to room not knowing what to do or where to go. Finding the Professor's library open she went in and scoured the books wondering if Rafter had anything about the Reaches. Finding nothing she made her way back to the living room to check on Rafter. He was still asleep. Night had fallen in the mean time and with it the room had become quite cold. Mae lit a fire in the fireplace and settled down in an armchair next to the sofa watching the flickering of the fire. After a while she closed her eyes and drifted off to sleep.

Chapter 14 - The Trial

Defence works

The sun was close to the horizon, a gigantic red fiery ball that scorched all that got in its way. It had been a very hot day, far too hot. The men and women of Granwich had sweated building defence works and several had succumbed to the unyielding heat, adding to Ma'gina and Mia's concerns. And now dark storm clouds were gathering along the mountain range to the south. It was difficult to tell if they augured relief from the heat or the advent of something much worse. A strong wind was rising and, as it gusted through the parched streets of the town, it brought with it the smell of cut grass from the wide area around the town cleared by its inhabitants.

"We want to be able to see them when they come," Anju explained to Lucie.

A small group of people followed their new Keeper as she made her rounds of the defences. Lucie was pleased to see how readily the people of Granwich had accepted the leadership of Anju and Dieter in preparing the defences. They might easily have rejected these visitors from another world, especially as Horst came from the same world as them. That many of the women knew and trusted the pair probably helped a lot.

"What's that?" Lucie asked, pointing to a narrow channel of water that flanked one side of the town. The surface was aflame with the scarlet rays of the setting sun.

"There's a fold in the ground on that side of the town. It must be a geological fault. We diverted some of the water from the canal into that fold making a natural lake that will help protect us," Anju explained.

"We need to limit the places where they can get access to the town. The fewer the ways in, the easier it will be for us to defend ourselves," Dieter added.

A mixed group of commoners and Patriciat passed nearby carrying hammers and spades, laughing and joking together. Lucie greeted them, asking for news of their work.

"We planted a prickly forest," one of the commoners said, laughing.

Lucie looked questioningly at Anju.

"They've been driving many stakes into the ground, each topped with a razor sharp metal blade. The stakes are quite short and most of them are concealed by a covering of hay. Anyone trying to navigate their way through that 'forest' will have to watch their step and go slowly. No one could storm us from that side," the girl explained. "It was Dieter's idea."

As they were about to return to her mansion where they were to discuss strategies in private, Lucie caught sight of Greg's wife Frieda trying to pass unnoticed on the other side of the road. Greg had been one of the ardent supporters of Horst from amongst the Patriciat.

"Frieda!" Lucie called out. The woman, who was in her early twenties, looked terrified. "You don't need to be frightened," Lucie said, knowing full well that the woman's fear was understandable. After all, had not Lucie attacked her husband during the Patriciat Council when Horst's supporters had tired to overpower her?

"How is your husband?" Lucie asked as the young woman approached cautiously.

"He's still in bad shape," Frieda replied bitterly.

"Do you have a healer to look after him," Lucie enquired.

"Yes," the woman mumbled and hurried off not bothering to take her leave. Once they had walked a way down the street, one of the watchers spoke: "We should keep a closer eye on her."

"Why do you say that?" Lucie asked.

"We've been seeing strange movements of people related to those Patriciat that tried to attack you."

"You should do that," Dieter agreed. "The last thing we need is people on the inside working for Horst. Our defences will trap us if someone lets Horst's men in."

Seeing the delicious cold buffet that Gloria and some of her friends had prepared for her and her advisers, Lucie suddenly realised how hungry she was. They had taken over two hours to walk to the various defence systems that Anju and Dieter had set up around the town.

"You have done well, Gloria. I'm ravenous."

The others agreed with her. People milled around helping themselves and then moved away with their food and drink. Forming small groups they pursued their talk about strategy as they went through into Lucie's study. Lucie was about to call the meeting to order when a watcher came running in.

"There's a large force coming along the main road," he told them.

Lucie could feel the tension mount in the room. They had all been waiting for and dreading this moment.

"Is Horst with them?" Lucie asked.

"Not unless he is disguised as one of the wild men," the watcher replied.

"How many are they?" Dieter asked.

"About a fifty."

"Must be a diversion," Anju commented. "They'll be coming from another direction."

"That doesn't stop us having to handle them," the watcher pointed out.

Anju and Dieter had divided those of the town's people who could fight into a number of groups of various sizes. They now gave orders for the smallest of those groups to prepare.

"Wait till the very last minute before you use the traps," Dieter ordered.

The people present in Lucie's study had crowded round to hear the news and provide suggestions. The increased tension seemed to have made people more talkative. Lucie had abandoned the idea of holding a formal meeting. Things seemed to be taking their own course. As the discussions continued, two more watchers arrived to announce similar groups of wild men marching towards the town down other roads. But reports indicated that each of these groups halted just out firing range, none of them engaging the forces in Granwich.

"Sounds more like the beginning of a siege than a diversion," Dieter remarked.

The major concern, Lucie realised, was that they were unable to predict Horst's strategy and that was making everyone increasingly nervous. Despite all their preparations, they couldn't respond till Horst made a move and he seemed to be taking his time.

Distractions

Horst sat by the unlit fireside, his mud-spattered boots resting on a delicately embroidered poof. He swilled the schnapps around his glass and, sniffing it appreciatively, swallowed a large mouthful. All the while he'd taken the potion to make him look young, Schnapps had been forbidden. The two didn't mix well. But now that he had reverted to his real face, he could drink as much as he liked. It was strong stuff, stronger than he was used to in Germany. It made his eyes water.

"Good stuff, Greg," he said looking at Greg and his wife who stood nearby.

"It's our best vintage," Greg explained. "I had Frieda fetch it especially for you."

"I hope no-one saw her bringing the bottle here," Horst added, not bothering to address the woman.

They were the typical subservient sort you often found amongst followers, always snivelling for attention, constantly afraid of making even the slightest of mistakes, terrified of being punished and quite incapable of acting on their own. Not that he wanted them to take any initiatives now they'd smuggled him into their house in Granwich.

"When are the others coming?" he asked, taking a final swig of the schnapps before he handed the glass to Greg's wife to pour him more.

"They should be here any moment, Master," Greg replied.

Horst preferred them to call him "Master" rather than use his name. No need to keep it a secret now that hostilities were declared. And it reminded people of their correct place in the world. You didn't want to let followers get on too familiar terms with you.

"We have to be cautious. Our houses are being watched," Greg said nervously.

A quiet knock at a back door had Greg scuttling off to see who had arrived.

"Where's my drink, woman?" Horst asked.

The young woman was clearly terrified. Her hand was trembling as she passed him the glass.

"Give my your hand!" he ordered.

She obeyed reluctantly. Pushing up the sleeve of her dress that covered her wrist and part of her hand, he pulled her closer and bit the fleshy part of her hand at the base of the thumb. She squealed and tried to pull away but he bit even harder till he could taste blood. As he released her hand he licked his lips.

"We'll continue later," he informed her as she stood next to him shaking but not daring to move away. "I wouldn't mention it to your husband though. He might get upset and that wouldn't do, would it?"

"The others have arrived, Master," Greg said enthusiastically as he entered.

Seeing his wife standing next to Horst, he halted abruptly. After a few suspended seconds, he continued almost mechanically into the room followed by several Patriciat men. Not really the ones he'd have chosen, but then you couldn't always choose your followers. Standing some distance away, they shifted nervously from one foot to another like a gaggle of lost hens.

"Gentlemen," Horst began, his voice full of irony. "Have you done what I asked you to do?"

Several nodded, a couple muttered "Yes."

"Good. I have one more thing I need you to do. I have to get into Lucie's house so I can surprise her when she returns. You are to create a diversion."

Once he'd explained what they were to do, he made sure that Greg went with them. He had planned his own distraction with Greg's young wife. Greg found several pretexts to delay their departure but finally they left. Finding himself alone in the room, Horst went to look for her. Having searched the downstairs rooms, he found her upstairs, curled up in ball on the bed whimpering.

"Now. Now," he said. "Is that how you greet your Master?"

He closed the door behind him and padded softly towards her. He flexed his fingers, cracking his knucklebones.

"Don't you want to please me?"

The woman was shaking so much that the bed began to creak. He placed his hand firmly on her shoulder, digging his nails into her skin through her flimsy blouse. She froze instantly, her rigid body hard and brittle under his fingertips. A slight movement on his part would have been enough to shatter her in tiny pieces.

He shifted closer and was about to roll her over on her back to get better access to her when a racket broke out in a nearby street. A resounding crash was quickly followed by shouts and the sound of running feet. The idiots. They had started too early, far too early.

He should have known he couldn't count on them. Greg must have set things off early deliberately in an attempt to spare his wife. Reluctantly letting hold of his grip on the woman, he grunted and gave her a forceful shove causing her to roll across the bed and crash onto the floor with a sickening thud. Turning his back on her screams, he made for the door.

The diversion had worked perfectly. Horst walked straight into Lucie's house without meeting the slightest opposition. It was as if he were dropping in on an old friend after a late-afternoon stroll. The whole crowd, along with their precious new Keeper, had run off to see what the noise was about. How naïve! They were so set on keeping him and his men out of the town that they couldn't imagine he had been with them for several days already. Settling to wait in an armchair in Lucie's bedroom, he went over his plans. So far, despite the incompetence of Greg and his gang, everything was going as he'd wanted it to. The people of Granwich would soon welcome his men into town without the slightest opposition and he would be the town's new Master.

Schoolgirls

A noise of feet from below caught his attention. Someone had entered the house. Lucie, no doubt. He was looking forward to seeing her face when she saw him waiting there for her. Few things really gave him pleasure in life, but he reckoned that might.

"Lucie?" a child's voice called out. "Where are you?"

How unfortunate, he thought. Some little brat on an impromptu visit. The steps were getting closer. The child must have climbed the stairs. He'd have to deal with it quickly. He didn't want anyone getting in the way of his plans to capture Lucie. He turned his chair slightly so that he couldn't be seen from the door if ever the child came in. Maybe the kid would just go away.

It didn't. It walked straight into Lucie's bedroom as if it had all the rights. It was only when the child reached the bed that Horst saw who it was: that meddling little girl that was always with Lucie. What a shame she hadn't drowned when he pushed her in the canal. Her arm was in a sling, he noticed. Nobody would be surprised if she had

306

another accident. Only this time it would be fatal. The girl stopped in mid-flight, presumably sensing someone else in the room and turned to face him. Rather than trying to run, as he'd expected her to do, she stood there looking at him with a mixture of disgust and fear. It took him only three paces to reach her and a moment to twist her wounded arm till she screamed out for him to stop.

"Aren't you going to welcome me home, Sarah? That is your name isn't it?" Horst said, twisting her arm a little more.

Tears were gushing from the girl's eyes but the screaming had stopped. Strong stuff, he had to admit. She'd take some breaking this one.

"That's better. I might be forced to break your arm if you shout again."

He made her sit on a chair and tied both hands behind her back with one of Lucie's sashes, ignoring the girl's appeals to let her broken arm go. Then something strange happened, the girl began quietly telling a story:

"Once upon a time, there was a fat little goblin sitting on a tree stump counting his money ..." At first he thought she might be delirious, but as she continued he felt that he was slowly loosing control of himself and slipping away, as it were, into the story ... Staggering to his feet he slapped her across the face, bringing her story to an abrupt end. Then he tied a scarf around the lower part of her face blocking her mouth, making it impossible for her to talk distinctly. She offered no resistance as his blow had rendered her senseless.

He had to admit that the storytelling trick could be very useful. Shame it was wasted on a mere girl. He wondered if he could read about it somewhere or force the girl to teach him how to do it. He imagined the influence he would get if he developed such a gift. Yes. He would force the secret out of her somehow. Then he'd get rid of her. Wouldn't do to have a rival.

Footstep on the stairs brought him back to the present. This must be Lucie, surely. To his great surprise it was another young girl, who was a couple of years older that Sarah. She didn't spot him immediately such was her surprise at finding Sarah tied up and gagged. She was about to free the girl's mouth when he hit her hard across the back of her head causing her to crumble in a heap on one of Lucie's thick carpets.

What was this? Did Lucie have a harem of young girls at her disposal? Other men might be excited at the prospect but the idea left him cold. The only thing that interested him in the situation was that it might reveal a weakness in Lucie that he could exploit. He yanked the girl to her feet causing her to groan, dumped her on a chair and tied her up next to Sarah. He took the precaution of gagging her just in case she tried to bewitch him too.

As he sat back down in his armchair, he examined the two girls. Both remained slumped on their chairs, unconscious. There was something strange about both of them but he couldn't put his finger on it. Instinct told him to be wary of them. They were more than they seemed. For the third time he heard footsteps on the stairs. If he hadn't been impatient to get Lucie under his control, he might have enjoyed the sport of seeing how many schoolgirls he could collect in one evening.

This time, however, it was Lucie. He recognised her voice immediately when she called out Sarah's name. Unlike the second girl, however she was cautious and didn't rush into the room, but stayed in the doorway.

"I wouldn't rush away or shout out if I were you," Horst said, still concealed from her by his armchair. "I might have to hurt your two little friends here."

Now that she knew he was there, staying concealed only had disadvantages so he rose and turned to face her.

"Are you not going to greet your future husband?" he asked, not bothering to keep the disdain from his voice. "Come in Lucie and make yourself at home. Why don't you take a seat?"

It wasn't a question but an order, however she still hesitated in the doorway no doubt calculating if escape were possible. A look of horror and disgust was set on her face.

"Ah yes. This is how I really look," he explained, realising that this was the first time she'd seen him without his potion to make him young. "I told you to come in!" he snapped. And to prove he meant business he strode over to Sarah and gave a sharp pull on her wounded arm, causing the girl to momentarily regain consciousness and scream.

"What do you want?" she asked, all meekness, the defiance seemingly drained out of her.

He was not one to underestimate an opponent, however. He was particularly cautious with her. He prided himself on his ability to judge people, although he had at first expected her to be an easier conquest. Reseating himself in his armchair, he ordered her to stand in front of him. Eyes downcast, hands by her sides, she did as he bid.

"That's better. Now you are going to convene your group of supporters, but not a word about me being here. We wouldn't want anything unpleasant to happen to your little friends here, would we?"

"What guarantee do I have that you won't hurt them anyway?" she asked.

"None at all," was his curt reply.

Shrugging her shoulders she turned and left. Horst followed her out of the room and went down to let Greg and his men in by the back door. Some fifteen of his men had been progressively smuggled into the town and hidden by his Patriciat supporters. Having the men hide nearby in Lucie's house, he settled in Lucie's study to wait for the meeting that was likely to be very interesting.

Biting back

The pain in her head was excruciating. An's thoughts were all blurred. She wanted to rub her head but she was unable to move her hands. Taking a deep breath she tried to recall what had happened. She remembered seeing Sarah tied up on a chair then everything went black. Someone must have hit her over the head. She cautiously opened her eyes. For a while her eyesight was as blurred as her thoughts, but little by little things came into focus. She was in Lucie's bedroom and Sarah was slumped in a chair next to her. Both of them were tied up.

"Sarah!" she whispered. No answer. "Sarah can you hear me?"

The girl remained motionless. Her state was worrying. She had to get both of them out of there before who ever it was had trapped them came back.

The obvious solution was to transform, but it was risky. If she got the wrong form, the material binding her might well rip her limbs apart. None of her human forms would do. They were all too big. And becoming a bird might damage her wings. She cursed herself for not being more versatile in the forms she could adopt. Until she'd become an owl to accompany Brent to Granwich she'd never changed into anything other than human forms. They had always sufficed. She needed something that didn't have arms and legs for it was with those that she was attached. A snake. Ugh! She wasn't very fond of snakes. She tried to recall seeing a snake. There were a number of them around her parents' house but she generally avoided them.

Her thoughts were interrupted by the arrival of a man. She smelt him before she heard him. He stank. She quickly closed her eyes till they were only slits and pretended to be unconscious. The man, who was filthy, sidled up to Sarah and began running his hand up along the girl's thighs and up under her dress. Sarah groaned clearly aware that something terrible was happening but unable to shake off her unconsciousness. The man yanked apart her legs and got down on his hands and knees in front of the girl.

Enough, An thought. She slipped into the form an adder and slithered silently off the chair and across the floor till she reached the man who was busy pulling his dirty trousers down. She sank her fangs in his bare buttocks letting the venom flow freely into his body. Not waiting to see what happened, she transformed into her Amazon form and throttled him before he had a chance to scream in pain. Cutting the bonds that held Sarah with the knife she always carried in her Amazon form, she picked the girl up in her arms and tiptoed to the door. Downstairs people where arriving in small groups. An watched, concealed by the banisters. When Lucie arrived, An tried whistling softly to attract her attention, but the woman seemed so preoccupied she didn't notice and walked straight on into the study closing the door after her.

Once the door was shut she intended to go down to the basement and escape into the tunnels, but her plans were thwarted when several large men stepped out into the hall from neighbouring rooms and stood in front of the study door keeping guard. To make things more complicated, Sarah was stirring as if she were about to regain consciousness. An couldn't afford having the girl attract the men's attention so she retreated to Lucie's bedroom and lay Sarah on the bed. When Sarah opened her eyes, An put a hand over her mouth and indicated that she shouldn't speak. She helped Sarah to her feet and they made their way to Lucie's dressing room. Once the door was closed they would be able to talk.

"It's Horst," Sarah said nursing her arm. "He's back and here in this house. Although he seems to be much older."

"He must have forced Lucie to call the council together because I saw them all arriving," An informed her.

"I bet he's using us as a lever to force her to do what he wants," Sarah said. "All he would have to do is to threaten to hurt me. She'd give in immediately."

"There's nothing we can do for her at the moment. She's in the study downstairs and it is heavily guarded," An said. "We need to get away and warn the others. Is there no other way down than the main staircase?"

"Sure. There's the servants stairs. But it is on the other side of the house."

"Do you think you can walk?" An asked.

"I reckon, if we can find something as a makeshift sling for my arm."

The landing on the first floor served as a balcony overlooking the wide stairwell on all four sides. Sarah and An had to reach the far side in full sight of the two guards posted below if they wanted to escape down the corridor to the servant's staircase. As they tiptoed around the landing keeping as close to the wall as they could, two more men appeared below, exchanged a few whispered words with their colleagues gesturing to the first floor and then headed for the stairs.

They'll find that dead man, Sarah spoke in her head, and come looking for us.

An had forgotten that Sarah could do that. The men wouldn't have to look far, An thought. She and Sarah had some ten more feet to go to the door and they wouldn't make it before the men reached their level. There was nowhere to hide.

"Keep absolutely still," An whispered and she transformed into the adder again and slithered in the shadows towards the head of the staircase. She waited till the men reached the landing and the first had entered the room before she planted her fangs in the calf muscle of the second man who staggered forward into the room, tripped over some shoes and fell flat on his face. Dogging out of the way of his clumsy feet she sped towards the other man who had kneeled to examine the one she'd killed earlier.

She was lucky that neither of the men called out. Presumably they had orders to keep quiet. She was about to bite the second man when he sensed her coming and dodged out of the way, raising his club and bringing it down where she had been only seconds before. She slithered under the bed to gain time and exiting on the opposite side from him she transformed into her Amazon form. The man was still looking for the snake under the bed as she drew her knife and ran around the bed to catch him. Once again he saw her coming and sidestepped her attack. She had to duck as he dealt a massive blow with his club that barely missed her head. He was a strong adversary and knew how to fight. Her knife was no match for his club in such circumstances.

Despite the handicap of forced silence, he had managed to corner her on the far side of the bed. As she swayed to avid his blows, she wondered if she should transform back into a snake. It was then that man's onslaught abruptly halted. His eyes glazed over, his hands sank to his sides and the club fell noiselessly on Lucie's carpet. Seeing a chance to get beyond his defence, An pushed forward with her knife and slit his throat with a swift movement of her hand. Wiping her knife clean on the man's shirt, she turned to see Sarah standing in the doorway, leaning against the wall, her eyes closed. Stories, of course.

Leaving the three dead or dying men in Lucie's bedroom, An took Sarah's good arm and led her around the landing until they finally reached the door opposite.

I hope it's not locked, Sarah spoke in her head. Lucie often keeps it locked.

For once it wasn't and the pair slipped into the corridor beyond, closing the door silently behind them. There was no light in the corridor and outside night had fallen.

If we change into owls, Sarah suggested in her head, we'll be able to see better.

She was right. And lucky they did, for there in the dark some twenty feet away sat a wild man cradling his club in his arms.

My wing hurts too much Sarah told her silently, otherwise we could fly by. Let me tell him a story instead.

An had no idea what Sarah told the poor man, but he started giggling and rolled over in a bundle and began snoring loudly. The two tiptoed by and made their way down the narrow winding staircase. Not stopping at the ground floor they continued down to the basement where they discovered the wild men had set up camp. Lumps of food littered the floor and makeshift beds of blankets and bits of clothing added to the confusion and the stink. Fortunately none of the men were present. Presumably they were all on duty above making sure nobody escaped Horst's grip. The way was free into the tunnels.

They found Mia and Ma'gina in deep discussion with Tom and Jenny in Ma'gina's underground laboratory.

"... Yes, but the watchers warned us that something was afoot," Tom was saying, apparently disagreeing with Ma'gina.

"And they were quite right," Sarah butted in, surprising all four who hadn't noticed their arrival. "Horst is back in Granwich. He's got Lucie hostage and possibly all her advisers too. We managed to escape," she added nodding in the direction of An, "thanks to An's courage and strength."

An was glad to see that the four of them were safe at least. She felt responsible for Tom and Jenny because she had been partly responsible for sending them off to Granwich in the first place. She felt a great affinity for these people from the other world that she found hard to explain. Maybe it was having a half-sister from that world. An told them that she'd seen Lucie's Council arrive and that the place was heavily guarded by Horst's men. Apparently they had been smuggled into town by some of Horst's supporters.

The question that was uppermost in her mind and surely in that of all the others was what to do now. They were caught in their own trap. Horst's blockade on the roads coupled with the defence system they had built rather than protecting them had them at the mercy of Horst now that he was inside the town. In seeking to defend themselves they had cut themselves off from escape.

"We are trapped here by our own defence works," An said.

"There is one way out," Mia put it. "But it won't be easy to use."

Ma'gina seemed to know what she was talking of because she said: "It might work if Horst believes that we are stuck in the town."

"Are you two going to tell us what you mean?" Sarah said.

"We had been planning a massive exodus of the women and children but we abandoned the idea when we realised we would never get through Horst's men spread, as they were, around the neighbouring countryside. Now, however, they are all concentrated in a few places and we might manage to get by them without them noticing," Ma'gina explained.

She sent Mia to fetch the watchers some of whom were always posted nearby in case Ma'gina needed them. When they arrived they brought news that a meeting of Patriciat Council had been called for that evening with only the men invited. They'd heard rumours that Horst was back and that he planned to put Lucie up for trial along with Anju and Dieter as her major accomplices.

"Here's what we plan to do," Mia explained.

Half an hour later when all the details were fixed the meeting broke up and people went their separate ways, each with tasks to do.

A dream

Mae had had a most strange dream. She kept her eyes closed and went back over the dream trying to remember as much as possible. Sally was calling for help. She was stuck on the crest of a hill amongst a number of large rocks. All around a hoard of savages were trying to get at her with their pointed sticks and clumsy clubs. She had the impression that there was more to the dream. But, try as she would, it eluded her. Opening her eyes she saw that the Professor was awake and looking at her.

"How do you feel?" she asked him.

"Better. Did you sleep well?" he asked.

"Fine, apart from the dream."

"Tell me about it," he said.

She didn't want to bother him with that, not with him being so ill. There were other worries.

"It's not important, Professor."

"Tell me all the same," he said making an effort to sit up causing the covers to fall to the floor.

As she made him comfortable and wrapped the covers around him she told him what she remembered of the dream.

"Sally is trying to send you a dream message," he explained. "I thought I felt something," he added. "You should go immediately," Rafter told her. "Do you still have my ring?"

"Yes. But I can't leave you here alone Professor."

"You must go. Sally needs you urgently!"

He insisted so much that it worried her. Maybe there really was something seriously wrong with Sally.

"Ok. I will go, Professor. But I would like to call my friends Fran and Martin to come and look after you. They are friends of Sally. I brought them back from the Reaches with me. They are the most excellent cooks."

Rafter looked a little concerned but agreed. "As long as they tell nobody else about my illness."

She made sure the Professor was settled comfortably and she phoned Fran and Martin who were staying in her flat to give them instructions how to reach the Professor's country house. Then she

314

went into the Professor's library and found a quiet place to sit and meditate. Taking a small swig of Lyra's potion for help, she thought of Sally and felt the tell-tale pulsing of the ring hanging on the chain around her neck. The next thing she knew she was cramped in a small space between two rocks next to Sally.

"Mae! You came! We need to get out of here fast!"

Mae ducked as a shower of small stones rained on them.

"You know Keira, don't you? My friend from the library. Can you transport us to her?"

Mae tried to recollect Keira. She didn't know her as well as Sally but she had met her quite often and had even been to several of her concerts. Taking hold of Sally's hand she thought of Keira and imagined her voice. It was difficult to concentrate, as they were being shot at with all manner of projectiles.

Suddenly the onslaught stopped, and silence fell before a great cry went up as the men decided to make the final assault. In was in that short moment of silence that Mae managed to catch the thread, as it were, and this time felt the shift as they were transported elsewhere.

"Mia," Sally said as she opened her eyes, clearly not at all perturbed by this form of transport.

Mae herself felt a little giddy. Was she getting sick already? Last time it had taken longer. She gripped hold of the doorpost to stop herself from falling.

"This is Mae from the university I used to go to," Sally told them.

The older woman who introduced herself as Ma'gina invited Mae to sit down and one of Sally's friends that she'd already met asked her: "Do you feel tired and nauseous?"

Mae nodded by way of reply.

"She was ill last time she came," Sally informed them.

"Close your eyes, Mae and relax. I will anchor you here. That will cure you," Sally's friend Jenny told her.

Mae wondered what she would feel. She had expected a massage or some sort of laying-on-of-hands, but Jenny didn't touch her. The first thing to happen was the swirling stopped. Then she became more solid somehow. She hadn't noticed before that she felt insubstantial, but now that she no longer felt like that she realised it was how she had been: a mere shadow of herself.

"You can open your eyes, Mae," Jenny said.

"She's strong," Jenny told the others, "Once I opened the paths for the energy it seemed to flow into and out of her like a river."

Mae wasn't exactly sure what Jenny meant, but she gathered it was a good sign and she felt a little embarrassed.

"How did you do that, Jenny?" Mae asked to cover her bashfulness.

Jenny explained briefly.

"Maybe you could help Professor Rafter. He's ill."

She saw a look of concern settle on Sally's face but the young woman said nothing.

"So you can travel between the worlds?" Ma'gina asked her.

"Yes," was Mae's reply.

"Good. Then you will be able to take Tom back to your home with you."

Mae turned to look for Tom and found him seated in a sort of wheel chair that she hadn't noticed before. What had happened to him, she wondered. He hadn't been hurt or handicapped before he came to the Reaches. It was decidedly a dangerous place.

"We were wondering how to transport him out of here. It's not easy overland with a wheel chair," Ma'gina added.

"I'll go with him for a short while," Jenny said. "I won't be needed here and I want to see if I can help the Professor."

Mae was delighted. "Thank you," she said, surprised to find tears welling up in her eyes. She really wasn't the tearful type, but this place seemed to work unexpected changes on her.

"Mae," Sally said, pulling her to one side. "I want to thank you for coming and saving my life."

"You should not thank me," Mae replied as they stepped out into the corridor and walked a few paces away from the others. "You should thank the Professor. He insisted I come. He said you needed me. I didn't want to leave him, what with him being so poorly and everything. But at least Martin and Fran are looking after him while I'm away."

Sally looked alarmed. "Doesn't he have expert medical care?"

"Sure. But he's at home for a while and he doesn't want anyone at the University to know he's ill."

Mia joined then and, taking them both by the arm, she led them further down the underground passageway.

"Listen." Mia said. "I'm going to ask you to do something, Mae. It will be very dangerous and I will understand if you refuse."

316

Mae wondered what was coming next. It all sounded so dramatic.

"You remember Anju and possibly the German Inspector called Dieter. They are both here. And they are in a very sticky situation along with the leader of this town, a young woman called Lucie. They are to be put on trial for treason. They could well be executed very soon if we can't get them out of here."

Sally let out a gasp of shock. She was clearly unaware of what was happening in the town.

"My request," Mia continued, "is that you return to us and take all of us back to Avan."

"I would do it myself," Sally explained, "but the guy who's responsible for all this mess has stolen the necklace that I use to travel between the worlds."

"What makes all this more difficult," Mia continued, "is that we don't yet know how we are going to reach them. That's why it is so risky."

The whole thing seemed somehow unreal, Mae thought. If she had been more aware of the dangers she might not have accepted, but she couldn't let these people she knew be hurt. She had devoted her working life to helping others and this was part of it.

"I will come back," Mae assured Mia and Sally, "as soon as I have settled Jenny and Tom in Rafter's country house."

Both women gave her a hug and then drew back.

"Promise me one thing," Sally said, "whatever they say, you do not bring Jenny or Martin or Fran back with you when you come to fetch me!"

Mae agreed.

Having said goodbye to those who remained, Mae went with Jenny and Tom into a neighbouring room. She'd said she needed a quiet place to leave from. Holding hands with Jenny and Tom she thought of Rafter's country house and immediately felt the shift as they were transported to the Professor's study. I'm getting good at that, she congratulated herself.

She asked Jenny and Tom to wait there while she checked how the Professor was. He was in deep discussion with Martin and Fran and seemed much better. Judging by the smell they must have made him one of their delicious meals.

"Professor," she said, interrupting their conversation.

"Ah you're back. How is Sally?" he asked.

She didn't wish to worry him so she replied: "She's fine now. I just had to get her away from the Indians."

Rafter looked surprised. "I didn't know there were any Indians in the Reaches," he said.

Mae laughed. "I didn't actually see them. They were throwing things at us. So I took Sally to a safer place."

If only he knew. Luckily he didn't.

"I have brought two more people with me from the Reaches, two good friends of Sally's. Do you mind if they stay here for a few days?"

"Can they cook too?" Rafter joked.

How good to see him so much better.

"No," Mae told him and calling the two in from the study she explained that Jenny did some wonderful healing and might be able to help him.

"Greetings Professor. We met once before," Jenny said. "Mae is very kind, but I am no miracle worker. I use the earth's energies. I will see if I can be of any use to you, but I can't promise anything."

"Excuse me Professor, but I have to leave again," Mae said. "I promised Sally I would go back."

"I'll come with you," Martin insisted.

"No, Martin," Mae said, as firmly as she could. "I also promised Sally and Keira not to bring any of you back. Not now at least."

She thought he was going to insist but Fran put her hand on his arm and he remained quiet.

"Mae," the Professor said. "I would be very happy if you brought Sally back with you. I would like to be able to talk to her again. Who knows what will happen in the future."

She knew exactly what he meant, and didn't want to think about it. There were those tears again. Running her hand across her face to conceal her emotion, she added: "That's exactly what I intend to do, Professor, although it might take me a day to do it. Don't worry, we'll all be back in time for the Festivities."

She nodded to the others and left for the study. She didn't even bother to sit down but shifted to the Reaches as she walked into the next room.

Mockery

Lucie could not move. Her legs had been lashed together around her ankles and her arms were tied up around her wrists. She couldn't

318

speak either. Horst had seen to it that she was efficiently gagged. She could however see and hear what was happening now that they'd removed her blindfold. She watched the male members of the Patriciat file silently into the Council Chamber. Few of them dared look at her. Many of them seemed scared. One or two had smug grins on their faces. Turning her head slightly she could see Anju and Dieter similarly trussed up next to her. Somewhere behind her she could hear Horst talking quietly to one of his men, too quietly for her to distinguish what he was saying.

Since Horst had forced her to convene her group of advisers in her home under the threat of harming Sarah and An, one nightmare had followed another. Anju and Dieter had been overpowered by a band of Horst's men and tied up when they attempted to defend her. Gloria, for all her gentleness, had been dragged off brutally at Horst's orders. All the other women were tied up and carried off. One or two of the commoners in her group were killed outright when they attempted to free her. Others were carted away to an unknown destination.

Thank heavens Ma'gina, Jenny and Tom had not attended the meeting. Maybe they knew something was amiss. Her group had been rapidly dispatched under the guard of Horst's men and she had been kept for long hours forced to stand in a dark room without food or water till finally Horst had sent men to fetch her. They had blindfolded her and led her under escort to what she discovered was the Patriciat Council Chamber when they'd removed the blindfold.

Once the Patriciat men were assembled, the doors were closed by Horst's men who lounged on either side of each of the entrances eying the Patriciat suspiciously. It seemed quite incoherent that he should be so resolutely opposed to the commoners when he didn't hesitate to work such filthy specimens. She heard the scraping of the Keepers' chair behind her as Horst stood to address the gathering.

"Gentlemen," Horst began. "We have been betrayed by this woman," he said, his voice loaded with disgust as he pointed at Lucie. "She has conspired with agents from another world," and he pointed menacingly at Anju and Dieter, "to undermine the Patriciat. She has insisted that a woman head the Patriciat when the Keeper has always been a man. She has also sought to weaken the Patriciat influence by inviting commoners to be a part of the Council."

He walked forward till he was standing between Lucie and the Council. "But she has done far worse things that you are not yet aware of. If any of you still harbour doubts about her guilt, the witnesses I will bring before you will set you right." Lucie imagined he would call his staunch supporters as witnesses, not that that would convince those members of the Council who were faithful to her. Horst had other ideas, apparently. He had his men drag in Abigail, one of her servants. The girl was badly bruised and could hardly stand alone.

"Tell me what you said earlier this evening," he ordered. Abigail cast a terrified glance in Lucie's direction. Lucie nodded back, hoping that the girl would grasp what she meant by doing so. Horst forced Abigail to look at him as he ran his fingers across her face. It was almost a caress, but the girl did not mistake his intention. She staggered as if she'd been hit and would have fallen if one of Horst's men hadn't yanked her to her feet.

"Speak girl when I tell you to!" Abigail still resisted and Horst took her chin between his thumb and forefinger and lifted her head till she was staring into his eyes. Through her tears, Abigail blurted out what he wanted to hear.

"My mistress has been having secret meetings with the watchers."

Lucie was sure that Abigail couldn't possibly have known about her meetings. None of her staff were aware of her dealings with the watchers. Horst must have forced her to say it. He continued to interrogate her for some ten minutes, punctuating his questions with further accusations about Lucie.

"So you see, gentlemen, this woman," and he pointed at Lucie, "who pretends to be your Keeper, as if a woman could be the Keeper, has actually being dealing with the enemy. And her servant here has clearly been an accomplice."

He let go of the servant that he'd been holding by her shoulder, causing her to fall heavily to the floor. One of Horst's men pulled her up by the hair at which she screamed.

"Let us not waste time with such petty traitors," Horst said and he nodded to his man who drew his knife, pulled the woman's head back by her hair exposing her throat and made as if he were going to slit it, causing a number of people to gasp in shock, many others looked away. Lucie would have screamed if she hadn't been gagged.

"No, we will not execute this girl," Horst continued. "I abhor unnecessary violence." The velvet tones of his voice left the assembled Patriciat with no doubts about Horst's real attitude to violence. "She is not to blame for what her mistress did." And he signalled to his man to lead the girl away, trembling violently.

The next witness was Gloria. Lucie hardly recognised her. Her face was all puffy and her eyes bloodshot. They must have tortured her too. Her friend's eyes were fixed on the ground and at no time did she look at Lucie.

"This woman, despite being a member of the Patriciat," Horst pursued, "conspired with the Keeper's Daughter to turn the women of Granwich against their men with the help of these two foreigners," he said, nodding in the direction of Dieter and Anju, "and to have women usurp the role of men as the rulers of Granwich."

… and so it went on as Horst brought one tortured witness after another, many of them women, all of them battered and worn down, to testify to Lucie's treason.

Lucie's legs ached from standing so long with her ankles tied together and her hands lashed behind her back. At times she thought she would fall, but pride kept her upright. Her mouth was parched and the filthy cloth they'd used as a gag made her nauseous. As the witness came and went, tiredness gave way to lassitude and resignation. The whole "trial" was a mockery. Nobody questioned the treatment the witnesses had clearly received, Lucie thought in her distraction. No counter voice was to be heard. No witnesses for the defence were called. She wanted to scream with frustration at not being able to act.

At that moment the main door to the Council Chamber opened wide and in marched Sally, flanked on one side by An and the other Sarah and a young woman Lucie did not know. They were closely followed by a band of Horst's men carrying clubs and knives.

"This man is a brutal coward!" Sally proclaimed as she reached the front of the room. "How can you sit here silently listening as he parades supposed witnesses before you who have clearly been tortured? Is this the kind of man you want to be your new Keeper? Is this the kind of person you want to trust your future to?"

"Silence woman!" Horst exclaimed, clearly furious at being interrupted. "You have no right to speak here!" his voice loaded with hatred.

"I have every right to be here. Far more than you," Sally replied. "My mother is a member of the Patriciat."

Lucie was surprised that Horst had remained silent so long. He was hardly a man to be at a loss for words. He must have been stunned by the sudden arrival of Sally and the three other women. Lucie herself wondered how they had managed to get through the guards posted outside. During this time, Sarah had cut the bonds holding Lucie and removed the hateful gag. Now she was in the process of freeing the others.

"You see how she encourages women to meddle in things that don't concern them," Horst said addressing the Patriciat men. He had clearly recovered from the shock and once again considered himself master of the situation.

Having freed Anju and Dieter, Sarah stepped forward and made to speak but before she could open her mouth, Horst flew at her, grabbing her by the throat. His face was twisted in rage, his teeth bared in a snarl. He seemed to have gone stark raving mad. His behaviour was totally incomprehensible, Lucie thought as she rushed to defend Sarah. She didn't need to worry because Anju was there before her sending Horst sprawling on the floor.

Horst got up immediately and unhurriedly brushing the dust from his jacket, he called his men to his side. They formed a tight pack around him that followed him as he advanced menacingly towards Lucie and her friends, forcing them backwards against the wall beside the Speaker's chair. Lucie was surprised when An grabbed hold of her hand on one side and Sarah on the other. Standing side-by-side, all now holding hands, they stood facing Horst.

"Well gentlemen," he addressed the Patriciat Council.

In the heat of the action Lucie had completely forgotten them. They sat unmoving, watching the confrontation between Sally and Horst without daring to say the slightest word.

"Now we have captured all the main conspirators … except for that meddling old woman that masquerades as an apothecary."

Despite the disgust she had for him, she marvelled at his ability to regain the initiative and act as if he were really the master of them all. Horst turned to look at Sally.

"We will be able to root out this ill and finally free Granwich of these accursed women. They will all be executed tomorrow at dawn in the square in front of this building. In the mean time, my men will scour the town for any of their supporters and they will also be executed."

Things were certainly not going well, Lucie thought. She was less worried about herself than about what would happen to the people of Granwich, in particular the women and children. She had never disliked anyone so much in all her life. A great shout of protest rose up in her. She wanted to step forward and take arms against Horst, but An and Sarah kept a firm grip on her hands, refusing to let her go. Struggling to break their grip, she warned him: "You will pay dearly for every person you harm in Granwich."

Horst didn't bother to respond with words. Instead he stepped forward raising his hand to hit her. She would have stood firm against him but instinct made her duck.

"Now," shouted Sally.

Lucie felt a strange wrenching feeling not unlike when she transformed. What had he done to her? To her surprise, instead of being hit by Horst, she suddenly found herself in a large room lined with books and no Horst in sight.

"Where are we?" she asked of the small group standing next to her still holding hands.

"In our world," Sally told her. "In Professor Rafter's country house, to be precise."

"This will not do," Lucie protested, shaking her head desperately and breaking free of the grip of the others. "I have to get back. I cannot abandon the people of Granwich at such a time!"

That she had been saved from certain death only strengthened her feeling of responsibility for her compatriots in their own hour of need.

"Don't worry," An told her, a grin on her face. "Ma'gina is looking after them. They will come to no harm. Everything is planned."

Lucie was furious at not knowing what was happening to her people. It left her feeling powerless to act.

"And we will return in a few days," Sally added.

"As soon as the festivities are over," the new woman said.

"I insist you tell me what is going on, immediately," Lucie said.

"I could say the same thing," a deep mail voice said behind her.

She spun round to find an elderly man dressed in what seemed like a multicoloured coat under which he was wearing long loose trousers.

"Meet Professor Rafter," Sally said. "Professor, meet Lucie, the Keeper's Daughter, or rather I should say the new Keeper of Granwich."

"Oh Professor. You look so much better!" a young woman exclaimed. It was the same one Lucie had seen in Granwich when Sarah and the other women had burst in on Horst's mock trial.

"And this is Mae," Sally explained. "She is the one who saved your life."

"Thank you, Mae," she managed to say, despite her preoccupation.

Glancing around the room she realised that Sarah was no longer with them. "Where's Sarah?" she asked, addressing no one in particular.

It would be terrible if Sarah had been left behind in the grips of that hateful man. She shuddered at the thought of what he might do to her. A tall slim man with a shock of light brown hair stepped forward.

"She is still here," he said, looking her straight in her eyes. "But not in the form you expect."

So this was the man Sarah had once been, she realised.

"My name is Brent," he told her. It was all just too much for Lucie who, despite her efforts to control herself, burst into tears. Feeling the man take her tentatively in his arms and console her, stroking her hair, only made things worst. Her whole body was wracked with sobs.

Chapter 15 - The Exodus

Flight

Ma'gina took the tiny vial that Mia held out to her and cautiously added its contents drop by drop to the ruddy brown mixture that began to bubble ominously. The gas given off smelt unpleasant but was not noxious. One drop too many at this stage could cause the pot to boil over wasting irreplaceable ingredients and poisoning the two of them at the same time. She finally breathed freely when the vial was empty and the colour of the mixture cleared until it progressively became transparent.

Ma'gina had refused to contaminate the town's water. It was against her principles, she had insisted, as you never knew how the underground water sources were connected. You could poison the whole region without realising it. Given the extreme circumstances, however, she had accepted only because she modified the poison so that it rapidly lost its effect, although she kept the fact to herself. The batch they had just completed was destined for the town's wells. The first batch had already been added to bottles of wine and beer for Horst, his men and supporters as well as any unfortunate Patriciat men who weren't aware of the plan.

"The carts have just arrived on the far side of Stone Circle Hill. They are concealed in a small wood not far away," a watcher informed Ma'gina as he arrived in her underground laboratory. "The people of Smeth'ick have managed to provide us with twelve to transport the elderly and the ill as well as some food and drink for the journey," he continued.

Another watcher arrived and announced that all the women and children and many of the commoners were gathered in the tunnels waiting for instructions.

"What is happening in the Council Chamber?" Mia asked.

Several watchers were at work there. It was they that would stay on in the town, forsaking the safety of flight so as to keep Ma'gina and the others informed of what was happening.

Ma'gina was glad that Mia had not wanted to leave with her friends and An. She needed the girl's strength and know-how for such a complicated and dangerous operation. Hundreds of lives were at stake. She was getting too old for this sort of adventure.

"They are still shut in the Council Chamber and the women are about to enter," one of the Watchers replied.

"Then it is time to go," Ma'gina announced.

She divided up the potion into three separate glass bottles and handed them to three of the Watchers giving them precise instructions what to do with them and, above all, what not to do with them.

"If ever you get caught," she added, "smash the bottles on the ground. None of this substance must get into the hands of Horst."

One of the watchers grinned. "Don't worry, Ma'gina. It'll find its way into his stomach not his hands."

She was not as confident of the outcome as the watchers. Horst was a wily opponent who wouldn't get caught so easily. The three watchers left immediately each carrying their precious bottle, and hurried off down the tunnels in different directions.

With Mia's help, Ma'gina had already hidden as much of her material as she could, not wanting Horst's men to find it. That which couldn't be hidden or taken with them had been reluctantly destroyed. Now the two of them set off down one of the tunnels with the remaining watchers to lead the people of Granwich out of their town and hopefully to safety. They found the people silent but expectant when they saw her arrive. She nodded to one or two people but spoke to no one. She made no speech to the assembled people. It was not necessary. She had already had the watchers and some of the women who had trained with Anju and Dieter pass amongst the people explaining something of what was about to happen as they ushered them down into the tunnels.

It was Mia that led the way to the Stone Circle tunnel with Ma'gina close in her wake and a mass of people shuffling after them, lit only by a few torches. The tunnel had a troubling way of hiding from anyone else that tried to find it. Only Mia knew the way and only she could open the door with her voice as a member of the Sisterhood of the Stones. Once the door was closed no one else would be able to follow them.

She and Mia stood on either side of the door as the inhabitants of Granwich filed between them. Ma'gina was pleased to see that the elderly and handicapped all had someone to help them and the young children were carefully watched over by their parents. It would be so easy to get separated from the others and loose your way in the tunnels. As the last people were stepping through the door, Ma'gina thought she could hear distant shouts down the tunnels. Could someone have got lost? She didn't want anyone to be left behind, but she couldn't take the risk of waiting to see. It might be Horst's men. She hastily followed the others over the threshold and up the slope to the hill beyond while Mia closed the door, singing softly to it.

Cavalcade

"OK," Mae said, linking her fingers together behind her head and leaning backwards in her armchair. She had to admit that she admired the determination with which Lucie sought to return to her people. "I will take you back to Ma'gina," she promised.

What Mae didn't tell Lucie was that she hoped to bring Keira, or Mia as the people in the Reaches called her, back for the Festivities in Avan. What would their festivities be without Keira's voice? She was well known in town and half the people would come just to hear her sing. The two young women sat alone on the veranda of Rafter's house, lit only by a couple of candles placed on the table.

"Thank you. You can't imagine how much it means to me to get back to my people," Lucie replied.

The young woman was wrapped in a shawl that Mae had found for her because evenings in Avan were much colder than in Granwich. Earlier, over an excellent meal prepared by Martin and Fran, the company had explained the situation to the Professor and filled Lucie in with the details she was unaware of. Lucie had refused to wait till the Festivities were over and return with the others to the Reaches.

It was Lucie that broke the silence. "I know so little about this place," she mused, speaking more to herself than to Mae. "Before Sarah entered my life I was engrossed in my birds and the aviary. That was my world. I couldn't imagine my future without them. Now I hardly ever think of them. Of course I knew I was the Keeper's Daughter, but it didn't seem important. Now, all my attention is given to Granwich and its people. I am the Keeper whether I like it or not. Things change so rapidly."

Both of them remained silent for a long moment then Lucie asked: "What do you do, Mae?"

"I look after a large group of people in what we call a university. It's a place where clever people come together to share their knowledge with others. But for all their intelligence, they are not always so wise and have some difficulties organising their activities. So I try to make sure that everything works smoothly."

Mae thought back over the last few weeks. They could hardly be called smooth. She wasn't even sure she had a job to go back to.

"I don't always manage though. And now it seems my life is going to change radically too."

Lucie nodded as if she understood, but she seemed so preoccupied that Mae stood and offering her hand to help Lucie stand up she said: "Let's return to the Reaches." The moment their hands touched, Mae transported them to Keira's side in the Reaches. It was easier for her to home in on Keira, as she didn't know Ma'gina so well.

The sound of hundreds of feet marching hastily along a stony lane contrasted singularly with the silence of Professor Rafter's house. It was like a whole army on the march, she imagined, not that she had ever heard an army on the march. Mae's eyes adjusted rapidly to the dark of the moonless night, revealing a swaying procession of people and carts spreading as far as the eye could see. In the distance ahead of them she thought she could see lights.

Next to her, Lucie had wasted no time in greeting Ma'gina and Mia, who were delighted to have her back safe and sound, and was talking in hushed tones to the old woman and the people they called the "watchers".

Pulling Mia to one side, Mae greeted her and asked in a whisper what was happening.

"We left Granwich an hour ago. We're heading for a southwards track that runs not far from Smeth'ick. It will lead us to the mountains and finally to a place called the Lost Meadows where we should be safe for a while. With a little luck, we have two of three days before Horst's men get after us."

Perfect, thought Mae. Just the time she needed for Keira to return to Avan for the festivities.

"Now that Lucie is back to help Ma'gina, will you return with me to Avan to sing at the festivities?"

Keira shot a questioning glance at her before replying. "My place is here. I can't abandon these people."

Mae had expected as much. "Your roots are in Avan. Many people miss you there. Your voice is famous. Without you, the festivities will not be such a success. The survival of the Department depends on it." Mae paused for a moment. "All your friends have returned for the festivities and they will come back here in three days time. Surely it is the least you can do for those who made your trip here possible."

Keira remained silent for a long moment, thoughtful, walking forward slightly to one side of the procession. "We will stop in an hour's time for a rest. I will ask Ma'gina then if she agrees," Keira finally said.

Well it was better than nothing.

A league after the turning south, Lucie called the procession to a halt in a small valley surrounded by trees. Food and drink were handed out sparingly and people made themselves comfortable for a short sleep while a watch was posted in case anybody tried to approach them. Mae went with Keira to look for Ma'gina. They found her deep in conversation with Lucie and several of the watchers.

"… we aren't going fast enough," one of the watchers was saying. "Even if we have three days head start on him and his men, they'll catch up with us easily if we continue at this rate. And our tracks are easy to follow."

For all their haste, Mae had to admit that the procession was not moving forward very quickly. She thought of several solutions all involving things from her own world, none of which would work here in the Reaches. She wondered if everybody held hands could she transport them all to Avan. Even if it were possible, they could hardly hide so many people from the local police and authorities. What they needed, she realised, was some way of transporting all these people, not to Avan but elsewhere in the Reaches.

"Where are these Lost Meadows?" she asked, interrupting the discussion.

Several people looked at her strangely, possibly wondering who she was.

"About four days journey to the south," Keira replied.

"And who lives there?"

"The Littl' People," Keira said.

"I'm sorry," one of the watchers said, clearly a bit irritated by her interruption. "But we have more urgent matters to discuss."

Mae paid no attention, continuing her train of thoughts. "Is not D'rick the head of the Littl' People?"

"Yes, lass," Ma'gina said. "How do you know his name?"

"I met him once."

"I still don't see where this is getting us," the watcher pursued.

"Simple," Mae said. "If I know him and he is near the Lost Meadows, I can transport people from here to there."

"But there are nearly two thousand people here," Lucie objected.

"I will begin with ten people. That should work. And then each time I will try to take ten more."

"It might work," Keira said, enthusiastic.

"You will have to stay till the last Keira, I mean Mia, so I can find my way back to you."

"I will stay with Mia," Ma'gina said. "I suspect the transfer may drain your energy after a while and you will need the help of my potions."

The moment had come for her to ask her question, Mae thought. "If I transfer everyone to the Lost Meadows, will you allow Mia to accompany me to Avan for three days to join the others?"

Keira burst out laughing, startling the others, who were all making an effort not to make too much noise. "Meet Mae," she said. "The Magician of Organisation. She gets things done where nobody else could succeed."

Ma'gina chuckled. "If you mange to transport us all to the Lost Meadows, lass, you'll merit more than just taking Mia away for three days ..."

Journeys

Several watchers were to go with Mae on the first trip so as to warn D'rick what was about to happen and to have him move to the Lost Meadows so that the other people would arrive there directly.

330

Mae didn't really need the help of the watchers but she knew better than to discourage people who wanted to help. Holding hands with her fellow travellers, she thought of D'rick and immediately felt the tell tale wrenching that hailed the shift from one place to another.

They found D'rick standing alone outside a large wooden building. Her arrival startled him but the moment he saw her, he bowed deeply, saying: "Greetin's, Princess."

As he led them inside and offered them some delicious soup, she told him what was happening and what she planned to do. He listened in silence to her explanation and to those of the watchers then he stood, saying: "I 'ave somethin' fer yer." And he left them sitting alone around their empty plates. Not wanting to waste time she rose and piled the plates up, looking for somewhere to wash them.

"Don't troubl' yer self with that," D'rick said when he returned, followed by a large group of Littl' People.

One of the women took the plates from her as the others gathered around.

"I said I'd give yer a ring of yer own, well 'ere it is." And he produced a thin gold chain large enough to hang round her neck with a delicately sculptured pendant suspended from the end of it. To her surprise all the Littl' People burst into song. She didn't understand the words, but the music was extraordinarily moving causing tears to spring to her eyes. When they had finished, D'rick stepped forward and hung the chain around her neck.

"That'll 'elp yer bring the peopl' 'ere."

The pendant was delicately engraved with an image of a young girl like herself and a wild bird circling above her. As she examined it, she could feel the same vibration she'd felt with Rafter's ring, only the pendant was much stronger.

She thanked him and taking her leave of the Littl' People she followed D'rick into a series of tunnels as he explained the Lost Meadows they were heading for. She asked a lot of questions as she mulled over how such a place could support so many people. The climate was clement at this time of the year, so people could live outside. And there was ample drinking water. However, he explained that the animals in the meadows were sacred so hunting was out of the question.

"Are there fruit or nut trees?" she asked.

There were some, but not many. The Littl' People fetched much of what they need to eat from valleys beyond theirs.

"The people of Granwich will be very vulnerable if they can't produce their own food," Mae told him.

He agreed. "I will talk to Ma'gina about it," Mae said as they emerged into the Meadows. The Lost Meadows were well protected by the range of mountains that surrounded them and the tunnel they had used was one of the few ways in.

"I'll be off," Mae said, taking leave of D'rick and the watchers. She found Keira and the others further along their path.

"We decided to continue and not await for your return. See it as a precaution," Keira said.

Mae gathered the first group of people together. She would try twenty in one go to see if it were possible and next time she'd add ten more.

"Can you prepare the next group for me?" she asked Keira. "I'll be back immediately."

Making sure everyone was holding hands she moved to the middle of the line and was about to step in between two people when it crossed her mind that having them spread out might lead to unfortunate landings at the other end depending where D'rick was.

"Have the next group bunch together," she said to Keira as she huddled all the people in a tight bundle around her. Then she mentally reached for the energy of the pendant and slipped across space to D'rick's side.

The transfer went smoothly until almost all the people were transported to the Lost Meadows. She discovered that if she took more than fifty at a time it became a strain so she limited herself to that number. Now with only a few groups left to go she began to feel seriously tired. It was more difficult to concentrate on the pendant and use its energy. She paused longer between the trips, sitting wearily on a large stone trying to get her strength back. When only one group of not more than ten people remained, Ma'gina examined her closely.

"You need to rest a while longer, Lass. Maybe food might help. Are you hungry?"

Mae's eyes had a habit of closing as she felt herself slipping off to sleep. A sudden alarming thought crossed her mind: what if, in one of those moments between waking and sleep, she were to transfer inadvertently to some place where there was someone she knew? She might end up almost anywhere.

"I must stay awake," she groaned. And she explained to Keira and Ma'gina her fear.

"Take off the pendant," Keira ordered. "And don't you have a ring Rafter gave you as well?"

Mae begrudgingly did what she was told. She found it difficult to part with the pendant. It was as if it had become a part of her. But once she had handed them over she felt much less tired.

"It's a shame Sally is not here," Keira said thoughtfully. "She could transfer the rest of us and let you have a rest."

If only she had the strength, Mae thought, she could fetch Sally. She dug her hands deep in her pockets and let her head hang as she closed her eyes. It was then she discovered the little bottle with Lyra's potion in it deep in one of her pockets. Opening her eyes painfully she pulled out the bottle and took two swigs. The effect was immediate. She felt much better. Standing she turned to Keira and Ma'gina.

"I'm going to fetch Sally and I will send her back to you. I will not return this time. I need to rest. Tell D'rick I'll come and see him soon. Good luck, Ma'gina."

And before they could stop her she grasped Keira's hand and slipped between the worlds, homing in on Sally.

"That was really sneaky," Keira said, clearly not as annoyed as she pretended to be.

"I had to make sure you came back," Mae replied, finding herself uncomfortably stubborn but too tired to do anything about it for the moment. Sally spun round at the sound of their voices and embraced them both. Mae collapsed in a chair and swigged the last drops of Lyra's potion. Then she explained the situation to Sally.

"Ten people!" Sally said, surprised. "I'm not sure I can manage so many," she added.

"You could do it in two goes," Keira suggested.

Mae had decided not to part with her pendant, instead she handed Sally Rafter's ring, instructing her to take good care of it.

"Tell the others where I have gone," Sally said as she slipped away.

Lost

"We've doubled the guard and nobody has tried to slip through the blockade," the man reported as he shifted from one foot to another, not daring to look Horst in the eye. "In fact the town is surprisingly quiet. The streets are deserted. It's as if everybody has gone to ground."

Horst waved his hand, dismissing the man without as much as a word. Despite their cringing servility, there was no doubt about it, the Patriciat men were more sophisticated than the rabble they called "his" men. And they didn't stink. The sudden disappearance of Sally and her accomplices from the Council Chamber had won over several new members of the Patriciat to his cause. He'd tried to turn their pretty conjuring trick to his advantage, explaining that the woman had stolen the talisman from him that was needed to travel between the worlds, and that without it, she had no powers at all. She was nothing but a simple woman like any other.

She must have found another talisman, he concluded, pursuing his thoughts. So there were several of such objects. The one he'd confiscated was firmly shut in a safe in his house in Granwich. He'd spent several evenings reading up on such things trying to figure out how they worked. It galled him to think that a mere woman had managed to use it where he had not succeeded.

A sharp knock resounded at the door.

"Come in," he called out.

A group of four Patriciat men entered boldly, one of them challenging him angrily.

"What have you done with our women and children?"

"They've disappeared without leaving a trace and some of our family heirlooms have disappeared with them," another added.

So much for their servility, he thought.

"I have no idea what you are talking about," he replied. "Tell me exactly what happened," he added, taking control of the situation.

Each dutifully described the empty home that had awaited them when they returned from the Council Meeting and the complete absence of any sign of struggle or panic. Curse those women, Horst thought, always causing trouble.

"Have any other people disappeared?" he asked.

They didn't know. They'd come immediately to see him. They couldn't have fled, Horst thought, remembering the tight guard he'd put on all exits from the town and the barriers the people of Granwich had set up themselves, hoping to stop him getting in.

"Call a Council Meeting ... immediately," he ordered. "We'll soon find out."

A wild clamouring greeted Horst as he opened the door of the Council building. Horst's first impression when he crossed the threshold of the Council Chamber was that the Patriciat had gone raving mad. Men were standing on benches shouting incoherently, others were fighting each other, but most of them just sat sobbing, their heads in their hands. Tables had been overthrown, chairs broken and glasses smashed. Papers and files were scattered across the floor and were being trampled under foot. Horst stepped back out into the foyer and ordered his men to fetch buckets of ice-cold water. When they returned, he had them douse the crazed Patriciat.

"Gentlemen!" Horst said, breaking the startled silence. "I hear you call the men who work for me "wild" in private, but what are you? Savages? You should be ashamed of yourselves. Has the Patriciat really sunk so low?"

Nobody dared reply. He stepped forward, grabbed one of the stunned men by his collar and, pulling him to his feet, ordered: "Explain what this is all about!"

Shuddering noticeably, the man replied: "All of our women and children have disappeared. There's not one left in town."

A wail went up from one of the men. "My wife was pregnant. The baby was due any day," he called out.

"My grandparents have gone too," another added.

Horst realised that if he let them all talk, there'd be pandemonium again.

"What about the commoners?" Horst asked, trying to keep control of the situation and divert attention.

"They seem to have disappeared too," a man next to him, replied.

How could they possibly have escaped the town despite the constant vigil of his men, Horst wondered.

"Sit down gentlemen," he said. "Either they are hiding somewhere in the town or else there must be some secret way out. We need to organise a thorough search of the town first..."

Seeing that several people were shivering he ordered that wine be brought for everybody. Not that he was concerned about their health, but it struck him that he'd be able to get his way more easily by seeming to be more concerned about them and a little drink would make them even more malleable. His men carried in a crate of bottles they'd found in the kitchen's of the Council building and opening them, handed the bottles out to waiting groups of men. Horst too took a bottle but he didn't drink from it. He wanted to keep his head clear. It was for the same reason that he also stopped his men drinking the wine.

Setting the untouched bottle down on a table, he turned to address the assembly.

"Have any of you any idea where they might be hiding?" he asked.

To his surprise, by way of an answer, several of the men suddenly rose and ran for the door. Suspecting they had something to hide he ordered his men to stop them. The Patriciat men became frantic, insisting they needed to go to the toilet. More and more of the Patriciat men rose and made a rush for the door. Till the sheer numbers of them and their apparent desperation gave them the strength to force their way out into the foyer and beyond. Some clearly hadn't made it in time as a tell tale stink rapidly filled the Chamber. Horst cursed. The wine of course! This was a well-laid plan indeed. He picked up the bottle he'd abandoned on the table and cautiously sniffed at the neck of the bottle, but could smell nothing untoward. He immediately thought of Ma'gina. It could only be that old woman. He swore out loud this time.

Calling his men to his side, he hastily quit the Patriciat building, hoping to leave the stench behind him. Unfortunately several of his men were taken ill too. They swore they hadn't touched the wine. He could only concluded that the water must have been poisoned too.

"Don't drink water or wine from here!" he ordered his men.

And he sent a party out of town to fetch fresh water from the inn he'd stayed in during his first visit to the Reaches. With any luck water there would be drinkable. Leading the search himself they systematically scoured the houses of the town, beginning with those in Patriciat quarter. He didn't expect to find people hiding there but it was a good pretext to pry into people's homes. The only possibility he could imagine for hiding or escaping was underground tunnels, but they had already searched the basements of several houses without finding the slightest indication of hidden passages.

The house they were currently searching apparently hadn't been lived in for a while. The furniture was grimy with dust and the air smelt dank. In the basement, mould had formed on the walls leaving ominous dark streaks. Once again they found nothing. Horst turned to leave when he heard a distant muffled shout. Signalling to his men to stay quiet he listened carefully. Silence.

After several minutes waiting, breath held, he decided he must have imagined things. Then the shout came again, weaker though. This time he'd pinpointed where it came from: behind a large wardrobe. Nothing special was to be found inside it, so he got his men to shift it, revealing a door behind. It was locked but the lock was rusty and gave way rapidly when they used a crowbar. As the door swung open he immediately knew he'd found what they were looking for: the secret passages. Suspecting traps, he sent a band of his men in to explore with torches and lanterns while he returned to his house.

Caught

"We found these two hiding in the tunnels," one of his men told him, pushing a couple into the room.

Commoners. A man and a woman. Both filthy and frightened. Both badly bruised too.

"You are lucky we found you," Horst said, not bothering to get up from where he was seated. "Abandoned like that in the dark without food or drink, you could have come to a terrible end."

The two stood silent, their heads bowed.

"Bring them some of that good wine we opened earlier this evening," Horst told one of his men. "These two must be very thirsty."

His men gave him a querying look to which Horst replied with a nod. Glasses were found and wine was poured but before they could drink it, Horst suggested they all go outside in the fresh air.

"It must have been suffocating in those tunnels. I'm sure you'll appreciate the clear night air."

The two were wary of drinking the wine, but with encouragement each took a swig.

"Now tell me," Horst pursued, "what were you doing in those tunnels?"

"We got lost," the man said laconically, swallowing another mouthful of the wine.

"Where you all alone?" Horst continued as the man finished off the glass.

"Yes," the woman put in, finishing her glass too.

"Good wine," she added.

Neither said any more, but stood there looking at their empty glasses, presumably hoping they'd be offered more. How naïve. Surely the wine should have had an effect by now. The men from the Patriciat had been running for the toilets after less time. He could see his men smirking in the background as they watched the couple drink, expecting them to burst into a sweat at any moment. For some unknown reason the wine didn't seem to have the same effect on them. An antidote, Horst speculated.

"Bring them back inside," he snapped at his men and turned to make his way indoors.

Enough of this charade, he thought. "Where have they all gone?" he asked, twisting the man's ear till tears sprang from his eyes with the pain.

Half an hour later the two had no further secrets from him. When he'd finished, he ordered his men to carry them away, whimpering, to be disposed of. So Ma'gina had planned a vast exodus of the women and children of Granwich. Unfortunately neither of his two informants had any idea where the rabble was heading. They had got lost in the tunnels, as they said they had, and had been unable to find the exit used by the others. They hadn't even been able to say in which direction to look, such was their confusion in the labyrinth of the underground passageways. Further searching underground, he reckoned, would be a waste of time. They must have surfaced somewhere and such a crowd of people couldn't travel unnoticed. He called off the search and sent his men to circle the outskirts of the town to seek traces of the mass exodus.

A battle of wits

There were about ten horses left unattended in the stables. He ordered some of his men to feed and water them and then prepare them to travel. Judging from the state of the stables, Ma'gina had not used horses or carts, unless she'd enlisted help elsewhere. They couldn't have got far trailing so many children and old people.

The moment news came that tracks had been found he was mounted and ready to leave. The fugitives had emerged from a tightly planted wood on a low hill, where carts had been waiting for them. Judging from the tracks, most people had walked. Progress must have been slow, he thought, as he spurred his horse into a gallop.

They followed the tracks northwards till some miles from Smeth'ick where the procession had abruptly turned south. They rapidly came to the place where the cavalcade had stopped for a while. Poorly hidden remains of a doused fire indicated that the fugitives were not so far away. It was there that something strange began to happen: the further they followed the tracks the less people they seemed to be following. He slowed his pace, wondering at first if it was a trap. Not that women and children could do much against him and his men. But there were the commoners too. He had his men search at some distance parallel to the track but there were no signs that people had fled away from the main group.

It was almost dark when they caught sight of what remained of the exodus: a small group of not more that ten people huddled around a partly concealed fire. The fading light didn't make it easy to see exactly who was there, although the faint flickers of the fire revealed that it was mostly men. Still suspecting a trap, he moved forward cautiously. He had his men tether their horses out of sight amongst the trees and advanced slowly on the grass verge of the track.

The group had camped not far from the place where he'd had all the trouble with Sally earlier. A sudden shiver ran down his back causing him to stop in mid stride. It was no time to get superstitious. That was for old women and children. He forced himself to continue resolutely. Hiding behind a large rock, he now had a good view over the camp. There were nine men and one woman. He recognised her immediately. It was the hated Ma'gina.

Weighing up the possibilities he figured that if they tried to rush the group there was a good chance the woman could escape if the men stayed to protect her. No. He'd have to wait till they slept. Then they could creep up and overpower all in one go. He didn't care if the men got killed, but he wanted the woman alive. She would be his prize and he was set on taking her back to Granwich to humiliate before she was executed.

He could already imagine the scene. The old woman was dressed in rags, her hair filthy, hanging like rats' tails. She bore a heavy wooden weight attached around her neck that forced her back to bend even further as she was pushed forward through the streets of the town. People jeered as she passed by and threw rotten fruit and vegetables at her. Her hands and feet were bound with chains. At every other step she stumbled and fell. Despite her condition, pride drove her to struggle to her feet, or was it the whiplashes of his men that drove her to get up. She wouldn't be able to withstand such treatment very long and effectively there came a time when she could no longer push herself up on her feet. Instead she went forward on her hands and knees, causing blood to flow as the rough cobblestones took their toll...

A sudden movement in the camp below caught his attention, wrenching him from his thoughts. A second woman had joined the group. It was none other than Sally. He could make out her face quite clearly. He could have sworn that she glanced in his direction and nodded at him. Thank heavens he'd confiscated her pendant. He immediately discarded that idea when he remembered the way the women had escaped from the Council Chamber.

He rose and rushed down the hill towards the camp with his men, startled, running after him. The ground was uneven and running was difficult. He had to be careful where he put his feet. As he approached the fugitives, he could see them coming together in a tight group around Ma'gina and Sally. As if that would protect them. Jumping over a wide trench he caught his foot in a root and plunged to the ground headfirst. Luckily the thick grass cushioned his fall. He rolled over and sprang to his feet immediately only to find that there was no longer anyone there. They'd disappeared in the short time he was down.

"I'll get you," he shouted, shaking with fury and frustration. He didn't care if they couldn't hear. He didn't give a damn if his men heard either. Blast her. No woman had ever dared make such a fool of him. "And I'll make you pay for this!" he growled, clenching his teeth as he kicked clods of earth over the remains of their fire.

"Boss," a voice hissed in his ear as a hand shook him gently by the shoulder.

Opening his eyes he saw one of his men leaning over him. He must have fallen asleep.

"All's quiet. We can go when you want..."

Relief flooded over him. It had been a dream. Stretching, he got to his feet and surveyed the scene below. All members of the group were asleep apart from a couple on watch. He decided to act quickly, just in case his dream was a premonition. Horst signalled to his men to circle round the camp and close in. Capturing the group was surprisingly easy, despite the fact that the watchers had seen him coming and given the warning. It was already too late. Remembering his dream, he had them tied up at a safe distance from each other.

Then he went to take care of the old woman. He wasn't sure exactly what to do with her, now that he'd got his hands on her. His fantasies of torture suddenly seemed rather puerile and ill thought out. He wasn't oblivious to the fact that the women knew things that might be useful to him. And knowledge was power. But she wouldn't easily let herself be bent to his will. He'd have to take his time and wear her down. His men had tied her to a tree at the foot of which she now sat, her eyes closed.

"Greetings, old woman," he said, crouching down in front of her.

It was the best he could do. She opened her eyes and stared at him, unspeaking, unyielding. For all his self-assurance, he felt uncomfortable. He caught himself wondering if it was not her that would bend him to her will. He shrugged off the idea and broke off their staring match, saying: "I'll speak to you later."

He wanted to threaten her, but somehow he suspected that threats of violence would not work. He needed a way under her defence. She might give in if he had got hold of her young assistant, but she seemed to have fled with the others. Where had they all gone, he wondered as he stood and walked away. Several thousands of people could not just disappear and he doubted they could transport so many people to another world. Not knowing made him feel vulnerable, a feeling he didn't relish.

"Keep a close eye on her," he told those of his men detailed to guard duties. "Call me if anything out of the ordinary happens." And he slipped away into the night to get some rest.

Desperate

That there were a number of people around was clear from the faint sound of breathing and the occasional groan or grunt, although Sally could see no one till her eyes adjusted to the dark. She remained quiet and unmoving. A faint smell of burning wood hinted at a fire but it was mingled with an unpleasant, putrid smell that she couldn't place. An intuition warned her that danger was very close. Luckily she had learnt how to go unseen. She remembered teaching Keira how to do it. She kept her thoughts quiet and unobtrusive as little by little the scene unfurled in front of her. She was standing quite close to Ma'gina who seemed to be attached to a tree. There were two hunks keeping watch over her not more than ten feet away. Conversation would be impossible. Mae had told her that Ma'gina was with a group of watchers but she could see no signs of them. She saw no signs of Horst either, although she imagined he was nearby.

Shall I go and have a look? Vee asked in her head.

Be careful, she thought, Horst may be able to sense your presence.

While Vee was gone, she shifted as close to Ma'gina as she could without attracting attention.

Horst is asleep higher up the hill, Vee informed her. The rest of his men are scattered around the camp. Most of them are asleep. The watchers are tied up behind us, not far away but they are too far from each other to be able to hold hands.

Can you tell Ma'gina we're here? She asked him. Tell her I'll take her away first and then come back for the others.

He didn't bother to answer but slipped away again.

She doesn't agree, he told her. If she goes they'll see it and kill the others.

Can you talk to the others and free them? Sally asked. They seem to be less well guarded. And tell Ma'gina what you are going to do.

"Well, well, well. Look who we have here," Horst's voice startled her.

She spun round to face him just as he grabbed hold of her shoulder.

"Search her. Remove any jewellery she might have and give it to me," he ordered.

Give me the ring, Vee whispered urgently.

Sally hesitated a fraction of a second. After all, it was her only way of escape. Then she decided, holding it in her free hand behind her back. She felt the faint touch as Vee took it from her. Seconds later the men were on her, roughly rummaging through her clothes, ripping pockets and sleeves in their haste.

"Nothin', Master," one of the men said.

"Tie her up some way away from the old woman." Horst came and placed himself squarely in front of her. "So how did you get here?" he asked. "Have you learnt how to travel without your little trinkets now?"

Sally didn't want him to know the truth. "It must have fallen out of my pocket," Sally said, pretending to be upset and annoyed.

"When daylight comes, we'll help you look for it," Horst offered.

Sure, she thought, so you can confiscate it like you did the other one.

"Finding it won't do you much good!" she retorted.

But he ignored her outburst. "Keep a very close eye on both of them. And don't let them talk to each other," Horst ordered as he retreated into the shadows.

A few minutes later, a shout went up behind her followed by the sound of scuffling in the bushes. What she heard alarmed her. Could they have caught Vee? It seemed unlikely, but the idea continued to scare her.

"They've gone!" she heard one of Horst's men call out. When questioned who had gone, the man replied "Them men wot we tied up back there."

Vee must have managed to free them, she thought. She heard Horst tell them to keep quiet and a long silence followed. She could make out the faint sound of his boots on the ground as he searched the area.

"She must've untied 'em," a voice whispered.

"Impossible!" another added, "they was still 'ere when we caught 'er."

As she listened to their attempts to understand, she felt Vee return.

I took them to D'rick, he informed her. You have many talents, my friend.

Remember, I am mainly you. So it's not so surprising if I can do things you can do.

Their mental conversation was interrupted by the arrival of Horst. She just had time to think: Tell Ma'gina what has happened. If you get an opportunity, get her out.

"So there are two of you," he said.

A deep-seated panic took hold of her as she imagined he'd discovered her secret.

He can't possibly know, Vee reassured her as he returned. Don't worry. He thinks you've got an accomplice.

"It's difficult to keep a secret from you," she said trying to play along. She was normally good at that sort of thing, she remembered her talk with the German detective inspector at the funeral, but for once she felt uncomfortable not knowing exactly what to say.

"Bring me a cup of water," he told one of his men. When it was brought, he pulled a small bottle out of his pocket and let a few drops fall into the water.

"I think our guest is thirsty," he said with a chuckle.

She struggled, trying to keep her mouth closed, but Horst prized her jaws apart and poured the liquid down her throat. She coughed and spat part of it at him but he persisted till he managed to make her swallow some. Very quickly she felt her vision cloud over and her mind go numb. Was this the end? She wondered as she collapsed at the foot of the tree she was tied to.

Undoing knots

He felt himself slipping lightly away just like when Sally slept. Vee rarely stayed awake when she was asleep. But now he had to fight the strength of the drug to stay present. If he succumbed he might loose the ring and their chances of escape would be gone. He paced the few feet between Ma'gina and Sally, both fast asleep and both tied to trees. What could he do? He could not take both together, but if he took only one it would mean even more trouble for the other. He played out in his mind what might happen if he took Ma'gina first as Sally had suggested but the many horrors that occurred to him brought an end to his imaginings.

He didn't even attempt to think through the idea of taking Sally first. At least he could free them, so he spent some time struggling with the knots that held their sleeping forms to the trees. When both were finally freed he realised that the first light of dawn had appeared in the east. He still had no solution and Horst would be back at any moment. He ceased his pacing and looked around for signs of Horst's men. They all slept, even the guards. Maybe if he were quick he could get Ma'gina out and come back for Sally.

It was at that moment that Horst stood up and stretched, making his way towards Sally. The young woman had collapsed in such a position that her legs and arms were sprawled, offering an open invitation to lasciviousness. Horst towered over her, looking down at her unconscious body. Then the inevitable happened. He bent forward and began running his hand along her thigh. Vee had to do something. With the effort needed for an insubstantial person to move substantial objects he picked up a stone and threw it at Horst's head. It hit its mark causing the man to grunt with pain and stand up abruptly, looking for his assailant.

In that split second Vee knew what he had to do. It was neither Ma'gina nor Sally he had to transport elsewhere, but Horst. He stepped in his direction, caught hold of the tail of his coat and transported them both to the ruined city in the Dream Realm that

Sally had visited with Brent so long ago. Horst clearly knew what was happening to him. He'd already travelled between the worlds. He thrashed about trying to grab Vee, but there was nobody there for him to get hold of. The moment they arrived, Vee took several steps away and merged into the surrounding granite blocks on the windswept esplanade. He'd never been there himself, but Sally had told him all about it. Enough. He had no time to waste. He headed back to Sally.

When Vee returned, Horst's men were still asleep, unaware that their leader had been spirited away. Vee slipped into Sally's mind but she was still firmly under the effects of the drug. Ma'gina however was awake. I'll take you first, Vee said, as he clasped her hand and transported her to D'rick in the Lost Meadows.

When he returned to Sally, several of Horst's men were awake. Two had hold of Sally and were shaking her.

"Wot 'ave you done wi' our Master?" they shouted.

Sally's limp form made no response. If he was to transport her back to Avan he had to get them to let go of her. It wouldn't do to have those two brutes suddenly appear in the Professor's house. So he whispered in their ears. It was a message from their master. They were not to harm the girl, but to watch over her from a distance. She was dangerous. They hesitated, clinging on to her arms.

"You 'ear that?" one of them asked.

"Yup. Maybe we should do as he says."

"But it in't 'is voice," the first protested.

How can you know what my voice sounds like when I talk into your head, you daft idiot? Vee added.

They finally gave in and let go of Sally who sagged to the ground in a heap. Now was the moment. They might change their minds. Vee took hold of Sally's hand and immediately transported her to Rafter's place where he left her unconscious on the sofa as he went to look for Keira to help.

When Sally came to, she found herself lying on the Professor's sofa with her head warmly nestled on Keira's lap. Her friend was gently stroking her hair and singing softly to her. Vee must have managed to get me out, Sally thought, remembering the predicament she'd been in.

Don't worry about Ma'gina, Vee replied to her unspoken question. She's OK.

In front of Sally stood Professor Rafter in his dressing gown, his hair a wild jungle, a look of concern on his pale, unshaven face. He seemed much thinner. The illness had done him no good. Around him gathered all her friends. Brent had resumed his male form and was looking somewhat stern and ill at ease. She wondered if he missed being Sarah. She wondered if he missed Lucie. An, in her young girl form, winked at her and flashed an impish grin, while Mae stood next to the Professor holding his arm and discreetly offering support. Calm and collected as ever, she had a thick file of papers held under her free arm. Jenny had taken up her place behind Tom in his wheelchair, the unfortunate victim of Horst's cruel machinations. Dieter, for once relaxed and content, stood with his arm around Anjou's shoulder, beaming. That was an unexpected couple, Sally thought, noticing that Anju had laid her head on the former Inspector's shoulder. And finally there was Fran and Martin holding hands, their faces slightly powdery, no doubt from some culinary creation they'd just made.

"Pleased to have you back, Sally," Rafter said and the others all nodded their agreement.

"Pleased to be back," Sally replied, propping herself up on one elbow on Keira's knee. "I'm starving. Anybody got any food?" she asked, causing everybody to burst out laughing.

About the author

Not wishing to pursue the route traced out for him by grammar school and university as a mathematician, Alan McCluskey turned to English, which he taught to foreign language students in France and Switzerland on a part-time basis for many years. His favourite teaching method was role-playing often with quite unexpected and not so catastrophic results. One pupil once confessed, with typical candour and ambiguity, that he had taught her the creative value of madness.

He attended fine arts school for a while as he continued to teach, studying cinema and video. He went on to make a number of works of video art shown in different festivals around Europe and directed some ten short television programmes about artists. He was one of the three organisers of an international video festival in Geneva, he founded a video art association and created a short-lived European bilingual magazine about electronic arts.

He enjoyed the challenge of organising large-scale networks, coordinating a worldwide network of companies selling Internet domain names, for example. In a quite different sphere, he created "The Hundred Venues" with friends: a network of a hundred screening venues for electronic arts across Europe.

For a year he played at being the CEO of an Internet start up. Apart from drafting business plans and convincing investors to give them five million, it was one of those rare times in his life that he systematically wore a suit and a tie in a vain attempt to appear different from the geeks who went about the office barefoot.

Almost all of his activities have involved writing. Although professionally he mostly had to write reports and studies, he tried to create occasions to adopt what he called the Martian perspective, which entailed questioning the self-evident. He has brought that questioning perspective, along with a passion for images and what they can reveal, to novel writing and artwork together with a long-standing fascination for the dream world and the magic of fantasy.

More information

For more information about Alan McCluskey's writings, including his photo-blog, see the Secret Paths website: http://secret-paths.com or the Secret-Paths Facebook page: http://www.facebook.com/Secret.Paths or you can follow Alan McCluskey on Twitter: http://www.twitter.com/Almacme.